The Sacred Skulls Series

BOOK 1

Kito

The Chosen One

Gregory JL Thomas

A catalogue record for this book is available from the National Library of Australia

ISBN-13: 978-1-7638741-3-8

gjlthomas@outlook.com

Contents

N
FOREST
JUNGLE
MOUNTAINS
OCEAN
RIVER
TUSSOCK
SAND
THE RIFT
MAGNAR WALL
NORINKO'S VILLAGE
DOME
THE PALACE
GREAT DIVIDING RANGES
GREAT EASTERN RANGES
MIDDLE KINGDOM
TURTLE POOL
HASUCA'S HAVEN
CITY OF SAMOS
TARIM CAVES
COLONIAL DIG
YELLOW RIVER
RIVER SOLLYA
PORT OF SAMOS
KADRA VILLAGE
DEVIL'S ISLAND
BALZAC'S PLACE
ROCKY REEF
ROCKY REEF
DEVIL'S PASS

Character List

MIDDLE KINGDOM

The Palace

Emperor Hannu Koe

Prince Hannu Hasuca, brother to Koe

Sha'Doe, mistress of Hannu Koe

Desora, son of Hannu Koe

Sen Ya San, Head Matron

Wa Maki, Head Messenger, eunuch

Tammirie, daughter of Maki

Assets - Chun, Norinko

Hao, Emperor's Guard

Bolli, Emperor's Guard

Grand Master Xiang, Master of the Guard

City of Samos

Silk Factory

Tark Fly, owner

Kain, Tark's father

Staff - Ringcha, Janing

Vessel Yard

Patch, owner

Alexa, partner to Patch

Admasin, Manager

Yuna, wife of Admasin

Kalgan, Admasin's son

Kadra Village

Sankun, sage

Kale, village elder, brother to Ringcha

Luhou, daughter of Kale

Tarim Caves

Wa Maki

Sen Ya San

Tammirie

Jeng, daughter of Tammirie

Yaan, raised by Maki & San

Hao,

Bolli

Colonial Dig

Zekec, Dig boss

Workers - Jong, husband of Quinn

Orton, grandchild of Jong

Manchu, elder, father to Kai & Mikka

Narpa, friend of Kai

ZIMBALI

King Mabutu

Mensa, Port of Begonia, wharf boss

Trina, former Queen to Zimbali

ORION

Pharoah Ezra

Queen Sofira

Princess Rani,

Prince Aitan

THE VESSEL SHIRAZ

Captain Tarrant

Slaves – Baako, Cho,

Matken, Lendud

Ayton, cook

1 Sha'Doe

Sha'Doe's lungs burned. Sweat trickled down her neck as she pulled back the jet-black, sweat-sodden hair from her big green eyes. Though her chest heaved, she breathed silently through an open mouth, not wanting to alert her pursuers to her position and yet be able to hear them. High in the mountains of a foreign land, this young woman ran for her life.

Distracted by the excitement from the crowd beyond, she looked at the huge structure that was the Palace of Middle Kingdom. The solid base was sculpted from stone, with the top floors constructed from huge timbers. Only a little of it could be seen from the Arena, as it wrapped around the hilltop in a large arc.

At least two hundred royals, nobles and serving peasants sheltered under the balconies, bracing themselves for her arrival. Apparently, she was being hunted for their entertainment.

A noise close by brought her mind back to the task at hand. She looked across to her right, to a small rocky outcrop. The trees were sparse in the arena itself as they blocked the view, but behind the rocky outcrop towered an enormous oak tree. Dry autumn leaves of orange and red littered the ground. How many victims of this barbaric game had the red giant tree witnessed under its massive overhang?

She let her senses take a moment, but something wasn't right. Someone had already set the ambush. How could she evade it and not get caught in it? There was no way to snare the ambushers without being heard. If she turned back, she would run into trackers, but ahead was the trap.

***

With the pride of Middle Kingdom resting on their shoulders, the two trackers, Settenya and his young colleague Kiebuttoe, worked slowly and carefully. Their prey had taken down three very experienced comrades already. None should have been taken so easily. The game was slowing down, and the Emperor would become impatient. He always said a fast game was best, a crowd pleaser. Reluctantly, they pressed on.

They came over the ridge onto the final slope. To their right was their ambush location that would hold three of the Emperor's Guard, and ahead was the Palace. She could only be down to the left. Settenya glanced at Kiebuttoe, who had understood the situation and was looking down from the crest of the final ridge. They were close to their prize, and what a prize she was. A special import for the Emperor's harem, Sha'Doe had defied the Head Matron, Kamutto. Reluctantly, the Emperor had agreed that this kind of behaviour could not be condoned, and so he had thrown her as bait to his guards. It would lift their morale.

Settenya looked at his greedy-eyed companion. He couldn't trust Kiebuttoe to flush out the bait. Even though it would mean he would have her second, it would be better than having to answer to the Emperor for a bungled attack and not having her at all. He tapped his comrade on the shoulder to signal his intention and backtracked past his crouching comrade, then slowly headed over the ridge to close in below her. He must take the time to get this right.

Settenya moved down by the Palace's perimeter wall. He could hear the enthusiasm of the crowd just above him. He had to go far enough to push Sha'Doe up into the clearing. She must either pass into the ambush or towards his greedy comrade. Best not get to her too late, though, or she would not be worth having. She was by far the nicest piece they had been given for a long time, and the Emperor must be praised for his generosity. She was cunning, though. Settenya hadn't heard or seen a sign of her.

He headed back up towards the clearing. She must be out by now. He broke out around the bottom end of the bushes to see

Kiebuttoe already had her. He was on his knees, bent over Sha'Doe, who was crouched down with her back to him, trembling. Kiebuttoe had his face in her neck and was holding her hands down across her stomach. Settenya smiled to himself. *Not like Kiebuttoe to wait for his senior officer, maybe he is learning.*

He walked up boldly and took Sha'Doe by a handful of hair so he could stare down into her terrified eyes, but he didn't see fear. He saw hatred and the glimmer of a smirk.

With a flash of steel, she lunged up to stab him under his right arm with one dagger and in the windpipe with another. His sword dropped to the ground as he grabbed his throat with his left hand, his useless right arm hanging limp. Staggering back, he saw Kiebuttoe, now slumped to one side, his body held up only by the sapling protruding from his chest. Its leaves and bark ripped off, hot blood and sinew dripped off it.

Kiebuttoe was already dead, and it was Sha'Doe who held the daggers.

As Sha'Doe ran back over the ridge, Settenya's eyesight faded but he could just make out her silhouette crawling up the old oak tree. She had a cat's grace and stealth, a true predator, holding a short sword in each hand. Dizzy, he tried to call out, but his lungs were filling up with blood. Most of his men had served him for many years. He had even campaigned with some of their fathers, but now this foreign woman was to end it all and not even in a real battle. On both knees now, he gargled, foretelling his demise as she leapt at the last of his dedicated Guard. Settenya's body slumped forward. His vision gone, he could only hear the sound of his final guard's death knell.

Up on the balconies, the Emperor drew the attention back to himself. "Well now, that's what I call a real game. Do you not think so, people? Inventive! I think she has given us a real treat today." He patted the top of his left hand with his right as he watched Sha'Doe in the arena making her way to the exit.

On her way, Sha'Doe noticed a stump, cut off waist high, with four shackles on it.

The Emperor turned to his Grand Master of the Guard. "Master Xiang, bring her to me. Oh, and see that she doesn't have her feathers ruffled. I know our fledgling has somehow soared with the eagles today, at the expense of some of my best guards. Go!"

Master Xiang bowed deeply and motioned at two of his guards to follow him. The Emperor's smile broadened as he thought, *How long is it since a woman has come out of the Arena alive, much less untouched?* All imported women were put into the Arena for sport. It was not expected that any came out but if they did, maybe they were good enough to improve the Royal stock. This one certainly was.

Sha'Doe approached with her chin held high. Once she had dispatched Kiebuttoe and Settenya, she could have slipped back over the ridge using the huge oak as cover but she could never leave without her homelands' sacred gold.

"Ah, the star of the day." Everyone politely clapped hands to acknowledge the Emperor's statement. The Emperor noticed Senior Matron, Kamutto, break through the crowd. *This could be fun,* he mused.

He rose from his chair. "Well, that was exciting. It has been quite some time since we have had a champion triumphing in the Arena. I am tempted to give you the opportunity to go another round."

Sha'Doe's face was unreadable. She knew this game and she also saw the Matron standing to her left though Sha'Doe didn't make eye contact. Calmly, she responded. "If it is the Emperor's wish then it is what I will do."

He strode slowly around her, leaning in so close she could feel his breath on her neck. "Really, Sha'Doe? You think you could go another round and win again?"

She focused directly ahead. "I have no idea. It is not my call, Emperor, but yours."

Sha'Doe was unlike the other women. Her cheeks were full and soft. She was tall, her breasts were large and high and the men doted on her. She was wearing a simple, soft leather tunic and trousers. Her breathing was now even, though she was far from out of trouble yet. Standing just a pace away from the Emperor, he was one of the few who could look at her at her own level, being taller than most from Middle Kingdom. Her skin crawled as he looked her up and down, not that he was hard on the eye, it was her lack of choice in the matter. These people were barbarians to her.

The Emperor clasped his hands behind his back. "You know my Guard has never lost a war and yet, I *do* think you could just about win another game." The smirk on the Matron's face was hard to miss. He continued. "Are you willing to apologise for abusing my Matron, Sha'Doe?"

"To you, the Emperor of these lands, I do apologise. I am afraid I cannot apologise to your Matron."

The Emperor raised one eyebrow. "Oh. And why is that, Sha'Doe?"

"Because where I come from, it would be an insult to the Emperor himself that she slapped me, the gift, to you."

The Matron's face dropped its smirk and began to turn as white as the impending snow. The Emperor had to look away to avoid laughing out loud. "Really? Though you must have provoked her somehow?"

"I asked for my bracelets and armband to be returned, that's all."

The Emperor looked to the Matron as he rounded Sha'Doe again. "Bracelets and armband? I haven't been informed of this matter. Matron, what is this she speaks of?"

The Matron opened her mouth but remained speechless.

Sha'Doe spoke calmly to explain. "When I arrived, I had jewellery. The Matron relieved me of it all for my bath but afterwards she said she knew nothing of it. It is not about the gold, Emperor, they were a keepsake from my mother."

Eyeing the Matron as he spoke, "Gold, Sha'Doe?"

"The purest, solid gold, Emperor."

The Emperor signalled to Master Xiang and the two moved away and leant on the balcony rails. He spoke in a low voice. "What do you think, Xiang? Did the Matron steal?"

The Master shrugged. "Well, I couldn't say, Emperor, as I wasn't there."

"Could you ask around? There must have been others there. What do you think of Sha'Doe; could she do another round?"

"I couldn't be sure. We may be lacking daylight for another full round, Sire."

"We could just try her with five men, Xiang."

"She moves with grace and speed."

"Yes, yes, I am not asking for a foretelling, Xiang, I'm asking for your gut feeling." The Emperor shook a fist. "Damn, she is something we have not had here before."

"Yes, I think you could lose more good men to her, only to lose her also. Any man would be pleased to have her in his harem. Correct me if I am wrong but did she not just play the Matron at her own game."

The Emperor tapped his fingers on the rails in contemplation. He looked over to the Matron, now seated, eyes as wide open as her mouth, panic-stricken. She was being comforted by another matron who had served in his Palace for as long as he could remember. She was older but not unattractive, buxom and still in good shape. She had been one of the first concubines to serve him as he broke into manhood.

The Emperor beckoned for her to approach. "It's nice to see you have been keeping yourself so well for these years … Matron Sen Ya San, isn't it?"

Matron Sen Ya San bowed deeply then stood before the Emperor. "It has been my pleasure of course. How may I be of assistance to you this afternoon, your Excellency?"

"You will take Sha'Doe to my quarters and see she is bathed, fed and given something more suitable to wear. Perhaps a single purple garment, yes silk I think, nothing more of course. You understand, Matron."

"I believe I do, your Excellency."

"Also, see that Kamutto is cleaned up. I believe she may have served her last for the throne."

With an unpleasant tingle up her spine, Sen Ya San recognised the Emperor had not used her title. "Once Kamutto is cleaned, have her sent down to the caves, the Guard may need a little moral boost after today's events."

Matron Sen Ya San bowed deeply again then turned to walk away casting a knowing, sideways look at Master Xiang. They had been friends for many years, growing up together in the Palace. The Emperor was keen on a second game but after talking with Xiang, he opted not to. It would probably be safe to say Sha'Doe now owed her life to the Grand Master.

Someone called out Matron San's name. She turned to see who'd beckoned her. It was a bitter looking Kamutto still seated in her chair. She snapped at Matron San. "What is it you think you're doing?"

"I was summoned by the Emperor and now adhere to his every command. You, however, are to be sent down for a well-deserved, perfume bath."

Kamutto faltered before replying. "Well, yes alright then. A perfume bath you say?"

Matron San dipped her head ever so slightly and motioned to two maids. "If you could escort the Matron down for a bath, someone will be in later to fetch her."

Kamutto lifted her arms and the two maids helped her to her feet. Matron San had to turn away. Lost in her thoughts, everyone else had left except Sha'Doe who was trying to talk to her.

"Head Matron, I believe I am to go with you." Sha'Doe's voice was soft and unthreatening.

Not intimidated by this tall, beautiful woman, Sen Ya San looked her in the eye, albeit craning her neck to do so. "Quite an achievement today, Sha'Doe."

"Quite an achievement yourself, Head Matron."

"Only I didn't ask for this."

"I didn't ask for my keepsakes to be stolen."

"I would know nothing about that, Sha'Doe. Now, I have much to do, please try to keep up."

2 *Rani*

In a distant land, the three pyramids, with their white casing stones, shone brightly in the morning sun. The meandering river glittered as it flowed gently past. On the banks, under the Great Pyramid of Orion, were limestone gardens. River waters fed the fish sheltering under the giant water lilies and bridges. Overhead, pergolas laden with grapes and passionfruit vines shaded the walkways from the growing heat of the day.

Pharoah Ezra walked arm in arm with his daughter, Rani. Thoughts of the impending departure of his beloved daughter lay heavy on his mind. He reached up and plucked a bunch of green grapes and handed them to her.

"As a child you would eat these until you were nearly sick, my love."

Rani gave her father a gentle nudge as she took the bunch. "Yes, and I still love them today, as I still love you, Father."

"Yet you won't stay in this land, my Princess."

"Father, we have been over this many times. You know no one could ever replace you, and I will still be a Princess to this land, but I will also be a queen to another. Since I was a little girl, I have watched King Mabutu come to barter with you. One could say he is as popular here in Orion as he is in his own province. This is a good joining for both nations."

"Yes, of course, my child, but I did not raise a beautiful daughter to be a bargaining tool with one of our neighbours."

She reached up to hold a finger to his mouth. "Ah, no buts, Father. I am not a bargaining tool, I'm simply a woman in love."

A call came from a higher level in the gardens. Queen Sofira looked down at them, her eyes sparkling like the mother river itself. She laughed, shaking her head. "My dear husband, as smart as you are in your leadership of this great nation, you still haven't learnt that you will not live to win an argument with your own daughter." She clapped her hands. "Come, the both of you, fresh food has been arranged for us to enjoy."

Rani motioned towards the river. "I was going to wait for Mabutu, Mother."

"Patience, child, I have a messenger waiting at the wharf. Mabutu will be brought to join us as soon as he arrives."

As they sat around the table, their light talk of the season's harvest and cropping on the river banks was broken with the sound of heavy footsteps.

Rani leapt from her chair. "Mabutu, you're here!" She dashed over and flung her arms around him before he could even reach the top step.

Gathering her up in his powerful arms, he hugged her warmly. "Rani, my love, you are as radiant as ever." He placed her down and stepped forward with an extended hand to greet her father. "Ezra, as always, I thank you for your hospitality in receiving me here. I see you have kept my wife well." He gave Rani a wink. Ezra merely dipped his head in reply as they shook hands.

Sofira studied her husband as he stood before the dark man. Though they were of the same height and her husband was broad for their society, Mabutu was a hulking man. In fact, he was the biggest man she had ever seen. It was not uncommon for Sofira to go to the markets with the maids; she felt it kept her in touch with her people. She had seen more than her fair share of dark men come and go at the port, sadly, many entrapped in slavery.

Mabutu's father had died on a hunting trip, so he had become King of his large land, Zimbali, at an early age. He'd been coming to Orion since Rani was just a girl. Sofira had never felt anything but comfortable in his presence. Mabutu approached and bent over to kiss Sofira on either cheek.

"Mabutu. Welcome once more to our table. Please, join us."

Mabutu pulled a chair out for Rani and she shuffled it beside him as he sat. Sofira motioned to Ezra to make an effort with conversation. He held out a hand as if to ask, *'What?'* She bobbed her head towards Mabutu who had begun to feast on the fresh fruit and old cheese.

Ezra coughed quietly into his hand. "Ah, yes, Mabutu. I take it you had a pleasant trip up the coast?"

Sofira rolled her eyes. Mabutu didn't look up, though a small smirk did cross his face. He stopped eating. "No, Ezra, I did not. Did you not hear talk of the cyclone that came up? We almost smashed onto White Island but managed to get to Audun Cove where we found sanctuary. The weather was too bad on the ocean, so not wanting to be late and inconvenience you, I decided to buy a camel and make my way across the desert instead. When I reached the river just a little way downstream, I swam out to a passing vessel for the journey up to your port."

Ezra's eyes widened. "Really?"

"Yes, though I do believe I am on time, Ezra?"

Ezra glanced across to Sofira, who was shaking her head with a grin. He turned back to Mabutu. "Mabutu, that's an extraordinary tale. Yes, you are indeed on time, but just for future reference, you need not risk your life simply to be on time. You have always been quite meticulous, and if you were late, we would assume there would be a very good reason. I believe running into a cyclone of all things would suffice."

The three laughed as Ezra finished his concerns. He beckoned a servant. "Would you fetch a cup, some water and a little wine for our guest? Mabutu, you must be parched. How many others escorted you over the desert?"

Mabutu finished his mouthful, pondering the question. "Well, none. There were plenty of offers, some quite insistent, but I felt I was as qualified to navigate the journey as any and saw no point in risking other lives over my own, Ezra."

Ezra frowned. "So, you saw risk but went anyway?" Sofira shot him a cold glance.

"Ezra, getting out of bed in the morning is a risk." Mabutu leaned back in his chair. "That risk increases as we step outside and increases further as we set out anywhere away from our homes. If we go out into the desert or on a hunting trip, we take on more risk but …"

Before he could finish Ezra spoke over him. "I would have thought you had learnt that from personal experience, Mabutu."

Sofira cut in with alarm. "Ezra, no!"

"Father, how could you?" Rani's chair scraped the floor as she abruptly jumped from her seat.

Mabutu put his hand on Rani's shoulder and spoke quietly. "Rani, please sit down." She glared at her father. "Rani, take a seat," Mabutu prompted. Without taking her eyes off her father, she sat with a small thud. "Rani, you will now apologise to your father." Mabutu's deep voice was smooth and even. He had led a large nation for many years, though diplomatic and fair, he was also known for his authority. Rani looked to her mother for support but Sophira was looking down at the table. Nothing. Mabutu spoke again. "Rani, we are guests at your father's table, and I will have no disrespect under any circumstances."

Rani relented. "Father, I am sorry for my outburst."

Mabutu couldn't help but smile at his new wife's diplomacy. He restored his attention on Ezra who was looking as stubborn as ever. "Ezra, if you do not approve of me, then why did you give your own daughter's hand to me?"

The tension at the table slipped away at the candid question and all eyes were again on Ezra. He was silent for a moment. "It was not my choice to give my daughter to you, Mabutu. It is not a question of whether I like you or not. It is the fact that you are not of this land and tomorrow you will be taking her away from all this." He waved his hand, conscious of Sofira glaring at him. He didn't dare meet her stare.

"Ezra, you need to understand, my nation does not need this joining. Some of my people do not want it either. There were plenty of parents ready to give their daughters in marriage, but my heart didn't listen to them. My heart didn't even listen to my own head. But when my head listened to my heart, there was only one resounding answer. Love. Love is the reason that a man will buy a camel and cross a desert in a storm. Love is the reason that a man will risk swimming the mother river knowing there are crocodiles in it. And love is ample reason for this joining, Ezra. If my love for your daughter is not enough for you, then it is I who is sorry. Sorry for you, Ezra, because it is all I bring to your table for your daughter."

Ezra's facial expression remained unchanged. "When you set off from Audun by camel, Mabutu, was this not a reckless decision sent to you by your own love-sick heart?"

Mabutu almost scoffed. "Ezra, you know yourself, I have crossed those sands between our nations many times. As I said, I felt I was as qualified to navigate as any."

"You also said you saw no point in anyone else risking their lives. So you do admit it was a risk?"

"I also said it was a risk getting up in a morning, but I don't intend spending the rest of my life in bed. It's how we manage the risks. For example, there are many crocodiles in the mother river, yet I swam out to a passing vessel. When I swam, I did a gentle breaststroke instead of the more powerful overarm, so as not to draw attention to myself."

Ezra couldn't let it go. "But you admit there was still a risk there?"

Just then a fish jumped in the waterways of the lower garden. Mabutu thumbed over his shoulder. "There is risk in going to the lower level of your water garden with the fish coming and going and the crocodiles hunting them, but you still go there."

Ezra expected someone to comment about how safe the water garden was. No one did.

Mabutu continued. "I have even seen you dip your feet on a hot day, and I have enjoyed sitting with you, Ezra, but it had risk."

Ezra lowered his voice. "Do you still hunt, Mabutu?"

"Yes."

"Even after your father died?

"I saw the giant tiger lilies in flower as I came in earlier. I know they take years, generations even, to get to that size and they only flower every few years. If your father was taken by a crocodile there last year, would you still be going there today, or would you send down the hired help to do all the garden work as you would consider it too dangerous for yourself to tend?"

Conscious that the servants had heard the question and now waited for his answer, Ezra chose his words carefully. "You are right, Mabutu. The water garden has been there for many generations to enjoy and mostly, with pride, we have always tended it ourselves. My grandfather always told of the time he had to chase out a sunbathing crocodile from a garden footpath. That was why he built up the front wall from the river, though he never stopped using the garden."

Mabutu leant back in his chair. "He managed the risk then?"

"I believe so. You are right to say your nation does not need this joining. With that tongue of yours, you could sell sand to our neighbours."

The tension eased, and the mood around the table lightened as they returned to the enjoyment of the food at hand.

Ezra spoke softly. "I am sorry I brought your father into our discussion, Mabutu. Everyone held your father in the highest regard, and none more than us." He reached out and held Sofira's hand.

A tinge of regret shadowed Mabutu's face. "It was like any other trip. A few of us had tracked zebra from inside the jungle and out to the elephant grass. We were really close, but the grass was so high that we couldn't know that a full-grown lion had also picked up its scent and was tracking upwind on our right flank. When the zebra stopped for a moment, two men saw their opportunity and threw their spears. Father was first to rush forward to finish the kill. It was an accident that the lion also rushed in at the same time. In the thick elephant grass, neither saw the other coming. It really was just unfortunate. Two more spears were thrown, killing the lion in an instant, but sadly, Father never stood a chance. I cradled his head as he suffered his last few moments on earth, and like the hero he was, he got to send his love to his wife and children, then all his people. Not that any of us needed to be told."

Sofira almost whispered. "Oh, Mabutu, that is truly too much to bear."

"It is life, as it is death, Sofira. It is how we live our lives that matters, and what people remember of us when we leave them behind. I feel Father left the best of memories."

Everyone listened to Mabutu and his understanding of life. They finished their midday meal and the four enjoyed light banter together for some time afterwards. Finally, Ezra stood.

"I am sorry, my friends, I do have business to attend to at the port before the day is out. Mabutu, I trust you will be our guest for at least one night?"

Mabutu stood immediately and reached out to shake hands. "Of course, Ezra. I have a problem I wish to discuss with you later, if you have time."

Ezra frowned. "Well, of course, my friend, I will make time right now, Mabutu. What is it that troubles you?"

Sofira hinted at Rani to join her side of the table; this was men's talk.

"Ezra, I am searching for your opinion on the sudden death of our friend in common, the Emperor Gauxi of the Middle Kingdom."

Ezra sipped his Hanqet, the favoured, locally brewed, beer. "Yes. It troubles you then?"

"He seemed so fit and well last time I saw him, just the autumn before."

Ezra gazed into his beer. "I have spoken to others who had seen him just a few days earlier, too. They're also unwilling to accept his untimely passing." Mabutu remained silent as Ezra continued. "It also troubles me that Hasuca has not taken the throne. It seems that Hannu Koe has it. What is it you know of this?"

"Hasuca has been trained in every way for the position. I have to say, I have rarely met Koe. Have you had the pleasure yourself?"

Ezra licked the foam from his top lip as he put down the golden goblet. "Yes, Hasuca was becoming a young man, but Koe was just a boy when they and their father came upriver. They had been told, and rightly so, that we made the best cotton. They wished to exchange livestock and rice for as much as they could get."

Mabutu raised his eyebrows a little. "How did they seem to you then?"

"I liked Hasuca. He listened to every word and never once did he interrupt."

"And Koe did?"

"Yes, several times. Emperor Gauxi seemed, at times, almost embarrassed."

"What did the boy want?"

"More."

"What, lunch?"

"No. He wanted more cotton. When I explained I could not promise cotton I hadn't grown, he wanted to give less livestock. That was when I began to see embarrassment on his father's face. I tried to explain that it was not how much one could get from the exchange but how much one was prepared to offer." The enthusiasm grew in Ezra as he remembered the scene.

"What happened then?"

Ezra sat back. "We talked briefly on the subject, then suddenly the boy stood so abruptly his chair slid back and fell over. He threw his cloth down on the table and stormed off to the vessel, ranting. I think the only word I understood was *imbecile*."

Mabutu thumped the table. "No!"

Ezra slapped the table right back. "Yes, I tell you. Imbecile!"

Looking even more concerned, Mabutu shook his head in disbelief. "The thing is, Ezra, that hot-headed boy is suddenly the new Emperor. At least for now."

"I agree. Hasuca is still living in the Palace, though. He and his father were very close, anyone could see that. Maybe when he is over his father's sudden death, he will take up the reins."

"You think Koe is just in temporary leadership?"

"One can only hope."

"And their father's sudden death?"

"I wouldn't like to speculate, Mabutu."

They threw back their drinks, and once the golden goblets were back on the table, Ezra held up a hand for a refill. The two women had hardly spoken to each other on the other side of the table, the men's conversation was far more interesting, and the implications were huge for all the surrounding nations.

"I am pleased you have come, Mabutu. I feel now, more than ever, that we need good relations." He considered his next words. "I know you are also a man of the spirit world, so I will confide this to you and you alone." Mabutu listened intently. "My spiritual advisor has said he can see trouble for us all. Not yet, but soon."

Mabutu didn't flinch at the information. "My shaman has indicated problems ahead, too, Ezra. It concerns me that you have also had a poor future told, though our open discussion reassures my faith in our relationship."

Ezra eyed Mabutu closely. "My advisor spoke of deception and war of nations. These are big issues."

"Did he say where?"

"He couldn't see."

"I was told of 'sands of blood' between us, Ezra."

The women gasped, and Ezra's face paled. He spoke in almost a whisper. "Under the Great Ranges, there is a cabin in an oasis. There, a woman called Bandji dwells. The first sign of trouble and you get a message to her. She will forward it to me."

"I know the woman. You will do likewise?"

"Yes, Mabutu. Our nations are tighter than ever. It must stay that way."

***

The next morning, the Mother River again glittered in the sun as Mabutu and Rani boarded their vessel. They climbed onto the raised, rear deck to bid their farewells to Ezra and Sofira.

Mabutu spoke first. "May the Gods keep you well and your land be prosperous."

The captain gave a call, and the oars pushed off the wharf.

"May you look after my daughter like you keep your lands, Mabutu."

Sofira slapped Ezra on the chest. "What he means is, we love you both and wish you a safe and enjoyable journey."

Mabutu's deep voice carried as the crew rowed from the wharf. "My people and I will treat our Queen with the respect and dignity she deserves."

The four waved to one another as the vessel moved downstream. Sofira leaned into Ezra. "Well done, Ezra."

He frowned. "For what?"

Still waving, Sofira smiled. "You did well yesterday not to mention his deceased Queen Trina, or their missing eldest son, prince to the throne."

3 The Emperor

In Middle Kingdom, the Emperor stood in his favourite bay window. He looked down over the valley below, admiring the beauty of the forest. Evergreens, like the lettok trees, pines and monkey pods were easily seen towering over the broader oaks and maples, now turning from light orange to a deep red. As far as the horizon, the hills rolled, green and red, red and green, as if some of the forest was on fire. The afternoon sunlight seemingly ignited the colours richer. Snow clouds made a patchwork of the otherwise deep blue sky.

The Emperor closed his eyes, soaking up the warmth of the winter sun. Hands clasped behind his back, his long, wavy hair was pulled together over his left shoulder and down his chest, his purple silk garment absorbing the sun's rays. He opened his eyes and looked down the palace's many storeys to the forest floor below. Small patches of snow had settled. Soon it would be eight feet deep or more.

The palace had been built on a system of caves terminating into one majestic cavern. The caves provided winter stables for the horses. The first levels of the palace were made of rock and only had high windows for light and ventilation. These areas were for food storage, cooking and servants' accommodation. The top six floors were framed using great timber beams, some of the rooms spanning a hundred feet. The centre of the palace was open courtyard, some hundred and twenty feet below the roof. There was an abundance of light for the great variety of trees, shrubs and herbs that grew in large garden beds raised in stone. Some trees reached to the roof, providing a pleasant outlook from balconies that circled the courtyard. Whilst snow may have settled on the roof, the courtyard was a tropical oasis.

The Emperor was brought back from contemplating the valley by the sound of laughter outside his office. As his two guards pushed open the solid oak doors, the Emperor stepped forward to greet a man, neither as tall nor as broad as he, though lean and very athletic.

The visitor wore leather trousers and a knee-length leather coat with silk garments underneath. His long blond hair hung down his back. His most striking feature, loved by women, was his eyes, one yellow, one green. His name was Prince Hasuca. The difference between the half-brothers was startling.

The late Emperor had many concubines during his reign, but only two had produced heirs. Hannu Hasuca, being first born and then Hannu Koe. Hasuca's mother was crowned Queen, and Koe's mother was never at ease with the lack of title for herself or her son. There was always tension between the two women when they were alive.

Emperor Koe waved his arms with enthusiasm as his brother descended the stairs. "Ah, Hasuca, did you see the game today? Wasn't she just outstanding?"

Like strangers on the road, they clasped forearm to forearm, left hands on right shoulders. Hasuca feigned a smile. "Outstanding, you say? Indeed, my brother, it was quite a spectacle. What have you done with the foreign woman, Sha'Doe?"

Hasuca had not seen his brother so excited about any woman before, much less a foreign one. He observed his brother carefully as the Emperor prepared to answer.

"Why, I have had her cleaned up and taken to my room. What would you care? You're not smitten with this foreign girl are you, my little brother?"

Hasuca didn't miss the threatening tone in Koe's voice. Despite him being the older brother, Hannu Koe had assumed the throne. When their father had unexpectedly died, the younger brother had threatened to start a civil war for the throne. Distraught by the sudden loss of his father, Hasuca just let it be. Koe always had a dark side. Hasuca could have fought and won, as he was by far the people's favourite, but, distraught by his beloved father's death and shocked at the threat from his own brother, he couldn't even consider sending his own people into a bloody conflict.

Their father had set a standard difficult to match. Koe had, however, exceeded everyone's expectations. It seemed he really cared, at least on the surface, for all his people.

It had taken a long time for Koe to trust Hasuca. He might have expected a challenge, but as long as the duties of the Emperor were being fulfilled, Hasuca accepted the status quo. To be fair, to date, Koe had done this with reasonable grace, but Hasuca would never have thought to invent the 'game' or the 'pit.' It certainly was not the sort of culture his father would've wanted to be introduced in his land.

Hasuca walked to the tall bay window, leaving ample room for his brother to move beside him. He must now show tact. The Emperor was a master of game play, one of the qualities in his leadership of the nation. "No, no, Koe, you know full well I have more women than I can deal with."

The Emperor filled two silver goblets with a heavy red wine from the decanter. Just before the late Emperor had passed, a gypsy called Bandji came from a far land and had dropped off the two silver goblets for each of the princes, stating that they were a gift. Dropping the crystal stopper in place, Koe picked up the goblets and returned to the window. "Why is it you will not be my Master of the Guard, Hasuca?"

Hasuca took the goblet. "I have told you why." He sniffed it and then took a sip.

"Well, tell me again. Explain it to me like it's for the first time, my brother."

A warm feeling welled in Hasuca. Was it the red wine? Or the poison he always checked for if his brother poured the wine? No. There was that reference, '*my* brother' again. Were they becoming family again? It was strange for Hasuca. Despite all the people in the palace, he still felt alone. Could his only brother really become his best friend? It reminded him just how much he missed his father.

"Xiang is the Master of the Guard and has been for longer than we have lived. He taught us both how to defend what is important to us with any number of weapons or none at all. Did he not?"

"Yes indeed, he did. I, too, have fond childhood memories of Xiang, but he has had his day. Now it must surely be your turn. Come, work with me. Together, we will get rid of those beastly Barbarians of the North. Work with me, my brother." The Emperor shook his fist to emphasise his wish.

Hasuca took another sip of wine. Looking down the valley, he could see the ancient ginkgo trees turning purple with the first of winter's touch. He chuckled, remembering that, as a small child, he had asked his father: 'Who has set all the trees on fire?' His father's full laugh was missed echoing in the hallways and rooms of the palace. Hasuca's smile died away as he remembered his sudden death. He looked at Koe. "How is Magnar Wall coming along? Has it failed somewhere?"

Koe noticed his brother's changed mood, though Hasuca was difficult to read. Most could not read him at all. "No, the Wall is fine, but that does not mean we can't go forth and show them who is mightier. As the strongest nation on earth, we have the right and duty to flex our muscle of domination. Do we not, brother?" He walked to the table, removed the crystal stopper and returned with the decanter. He topped up Hasuca's goblet before his own, which he placed on the broad windowsill. With a foot up on a low stool and his elbow on his knee, he pointed an emphatic finger. "The thing is, Hasuca, we must develop as a Nation. As an Empire, we must grow and to achieve this, we must expand our borders."

"Then what is the Wall about?"

Koe flicked a dismissive hand. "Aagh, it's just something for the peasants to do when they are not working the fields – idle hands and all that, Hasuca. You know the rules."

Hasuca shuffled uncomfortably. He had known this day would come, but had hoped for more time to prepare. Prepare for what, he didn't actually know, except that it was contrary to everything their father had taught him. It was against the Gods and tradition. All the legends told of the cycles of life, and all earth's children had the right to shelter, food and peace. Whether you were the Emperor himself or a Barbarian, you had that right because you were born of the Gods. It was the right of birth.

Hasuca checked his tone of voice. "Those are big plans, brother. I can see why you need fresh blood to help lead your men, but Xiang is a genius of war. No one has ever outmanoeuvred him. For a time, they may have held him at bay, but he has never been outwitted. Would we not be wise to keep him close at hand, Hannu Koe?"

Koe looked at him through narrowed eyes. He raised his chin and a frown crossed his brow. Hasuca continued before his brother could object. "Well, Koe, I know you have a plan; you might as well come out with it."

Koe smiled broadly. "Ha, so you *are* in then?" Annoyingly, he prodded Hasuca's chest with his index finger.

Hasuca pushed his brother's prodding hand aside. "So, I take it you will be heading north to sort out those unruly Barbarians?" It was the best comment to make right now. At best, a refusal would result in being evicted from the palace and into the cold snow. He took a large swig of wine. Getting Koe to go north would buy some time, and the Barbarians were a pesky lot with their insistent attacks on the Wall. It should help Koe to blow off some steam, flex his muscle of leadership and ego, then allow time for the snow to thicken and hold off his plans. Hasuca drank some more, looking out over the vista before him. He had almost forgotten his brother was still there until Koe leant over and refilled his goblet yet again.

Koe motioned towards the table against the wall. "Come, my brother. Let me show you what I have prepared."

Hasuca hadn't noticed the new planning table. Its top sloped, and a ledge across the bottom held pencils. Across the top was a flat strip. Hasuca couldn't see a need for it until Koe placed his goblet on it. Koe tapped the map three times and began.

"This is the gateway to the future, brother. The City of Samos. It is the busiest port in the world. They put through silk, cotton, wool, grain, even livestock." He retrieved his goblet. "Can you believe it? Shipping livestock? Amazing. If a man were to take control of this town, he would be …" He paused. "… when *I* take control of this town, it will be the first important step to my destiny." He drank deeply and headed back to the decanter still in the bay window.

***

Hasuca thought about what his brother had just put to him. He had to give it to Koe, he was always ahead of everyone. Way ahead.

The map was a well-detailed representation of their homeland, the Middle Kingdom. To the left was the Western Dividing Range and to the right, the Eastern Dividing Range. The Barbarians were to the north, separated by Magnar Wall and to the south was the City of Samos. From there, the river Sollya ran out into the inland sea, with Devil's Pass well below. It was the only way for any vessel to enter or leave Middle Kingdom. A treacherous reef with rocky outcrops made the inland sea what it was, the defence of a fortress.

Koe returned with the decanter, topping Hasuca's goblet without pausing. "When you get a new horse, you put it on a short lead and whip it so it knows who the boss is. It is just the same with peasants. I will – *we* will take control of the Port of Samos then we will have control of imports and exports. We can ration all nations from this one stand. I can't believe it's so easy! Within a few seasons, they will be throwing their Crystal Skulls at me."

He slapped his forehead, laughing towards the ceiling. "How is it that no one has seen this before?"

Hasuca felt faint as he barely uttered his one word. "What?"

Koe scarcely noticed. "Yes. I will be the *Chosen One*."

Hasuca was on dangerous ground but could not, in all conscience, walk away from this. "Koe, it is not for you to choose. Legend has it the Skulls choose."

Koe lunged forward, standing over Hasuca! With flame-red eyes, he spat his words. "They have already chosen, fool brother! *I* am the ruler already with the two Skulls I have."

"Really? I have never seen them?"

Koe poked Hasuca in the chest again, his low voice shaking with passion. "When Father and his troops returned from Norinko's village after the Barbarians had set upon them, I saw the Skulls. I saw them both!"

Hasuca looked at Koe with astonishment. "Both, Koe? Two Crystal Skulls are here, in this palace?"

Koe turned back to the window, the veins in his neck pumped up. He waved his right fist at the sky. "I will look into their eyes and absorb all knowledge and attain immortality! I will be God-King of the world!"

Hasuca was now desperate. "Brother, if you are not the Chosen …"

Koe spun on his heel. "Do not even say it! Do not! I *am* the Chosen One. It is set in the stones of this very palace!"

"May I see them? The Skulls. Never have I seen them, Koe."

Koe was as silent as he was still. Hasuca didn't doubt he had seen them as a child, but he suspected Koe did not actually know where they were now. He had to keep Koe on side. He also had to get to the Skulls first. "When do you wish to start this endeavour of yours, brother?"

Koe grabbed him by his shoulders and shook him. "*Our* endeavour, brother. *Ours*."

Hasuca broke out of Koe's grip and walked over behind a silk screen. He didn't really need to urinate, but he wasn't going to stay in his brother's hold either. Things were worse than he could have ever imagined. Hasuca could see no winning here. If Koe was not the Chosen One by the Sacred Skulls, he would be turned into sand and blown away on the winds of dissolution. Even worse, if he was chosen, society would be destroyed to its core. Koe would not stop until it was done, and he was the only power. This was not going to be an easy fix. Koe was the Master of the game, and yet it was he, Hasuca, who would have to save his nation from certain disaster.

Legend had it that any people that went to war without the blessing of the Gods, for no reason other than to protect their own borders and themselves, were breaking the laws of the world and in doing so, invoked battle with the Gods themselves. Surely that was not a war man could truly manage. But, there was always an opposing power to keep the balance in the universe and as such, the Gods also had opposing power. This was the power of the seven Sacred Skulls. To keep the peace, the Gods had sent the Seven Skulls to seven nations and told them they were the guardians of each of the Skulls.

Only if the Chosen One got them all together in the Valley of the Sacred Crystal, could they grow to be as strong as the Gods. But only the Sacred Skulls could choose. If one stared into the Crystal Skull, he, or she, would find out if they were worthy. Either way, there would be no coming back.

Hasuca returned to the map and swiped up his goblet. He didn't usually drink this much. "Well, come on then, Koe. When?"

"It is warmer in the south, so I thought early spring. We will take winter to prepare the plans. Only the closest to us will know anything is even in the wind. Secrecy is essential; Samos must have no idea. In my mind, Samos already has a new leader, in me. They will get a leader to take the people to the next level, a leader who will get things moving and stimulate unimagined growth." He shook his fists again, spitting saliva in his excitement, transported by the passion of his dream and lust for power. "If I wish to take control of the City of Samos then I can and I will! Can you not see this, Hasuca?"

"Yes, of course, I simply don't see the point in disrupting the entire city's cogs of commerce when, at the end of the day, the only thing you want is the port. I am merely suggesting, only take the port." Hasuca took a deep breath. His brother had been edgy these past few months, and he couldn't let himself get too exasperated. One of them had to remain level-headed. "Koe, if the port has that much influence over nations, surely it will have power over its own city."

"Indeed, my brother, less to take, less to control, but with the same result. Agreed, but know this, Hasuca ..." His eyes narrowed. "If we only take the port and the city turns on us, we will be surrounded and outnumbered. That is not what I call a sound plan, brother."

Hasuca, careful not to falter, replied in a low voice. "If we have the port, we have them. They will know this. We will affirm it to them if they challenge us." He leaned forward and in the most menacing voice, surprising even Koe, "By all the Gods, we will burn the lot, stock and all!"

"Ha! By the tail of Samos City, brother, I think you have it! That's it! I knew I could count on you. If we go in on the back of summer, they will need all their supplies to feed the peasants. Their own stores will be low as they'll be at the port, *our* port."

The Emperor grabbed Hasuca and shook him vigorously by the shoulders. "By the Gods, Hasuca, I am going to be the King of the world! Yes, Hannu Koe, God-King!"

Koe stormed to the window. "Gods, do you hear me?" With his arms outstretched, he shook an angry fist at the winter's sky. "Yes, that's it! I, Hannu Koe, future God-King of the world." He raised his face to the heavens. "Stop me if you dare. Gods hear me. Show me your faces if you dare!" A roll of thunder rumbled in the distance. "Ha. Your feeble rumblings speak volumes of your cowardice and nothing of your courage! Watch and weep as I devour your world in my own time!" He wiped the spit from his chin. "Hasuca, we must have a party. Yes, tonight we celebrate, though, brother, no one needs to know why."

Hasuca closed his eyes in silent prayer, asking for forgiveness for his part in this charade. In truth, he hoped that the people of Samos City would indeed have the courage to surround the port and burn it down with everyone in it, himself included.

Just then, there was a knock at the door. "Come," commanded Koe.

The two huge doors were pushed open, and Matron San entered.

"Ah, Matron San, your timing is perfect. I was just about to send for you. We will be having a feast tonight. See that everything is prepared in the Den." Matron San bowed deeply and held it. Koe was about to move away, but noticed she had not stood to leave. "Matron? Was there something in my instructions you didn't understand?"

The Matron stood up straight. "I have actually come to seek your wise counsel, Emperor."

Emperor Koe pursed his lips. "This wouldn't have anything to do with Kamutto, would it?"

Intrigued, Hasuca stepped up beside his brother and gave the Matron a curt dip of the head. She bowed again in return, then spoke to the Emperor. "I see the Emperor is as perceptive as ever. Yes, it is in the matter of the Matron Kamutto that I seek your counsel, your Excellency."

A childlike smirk came to his face. "Do you think I should have put her through the game, Matron San?"

The Matron knew better than to comment directly on this. "May I speak to you from the heart, Your Excellency?"

Hasuca respected the insight and strength with which the Matron approached the unpredictable Emperor.

Emperor Koe was slightly intrigued. "Yes, Matron, just this once. What troubles you?"

She faced him square on. "I would like to put in a plea for her fate, Your Excellency."

The Emperor almost choked on his wine. "And why would I let her go, Matron? No, she insulted the gift bearers and this nation and *me!*" As he finished, he leaned forward.

Matron San was on very shaky ground, but she remained firm. "She has served this palace for two generations of Royal family. She has served to the very best of her ability every step of the way. I am not asking you to let her go, just not send her out this way, Emperor."

The impending fate of the Matron began to dawn on Hasuca. "Just what have you done with Matron Kamutto, brother?"

Koe smirked. "She is, as we speak, downstairs getting a bath. Is she not, Matron?"

"This is true, Emperor." San looked to the floor.

Hasuca steered his rising temper. "And then what is to happen to her, Hannu Koe?"

"Well, it has been a hard day for the Guard, losing some of their own. They could do with a treat, so I improvised." He waved a dismissive hand. "Nothing to get in a flap about." He turned away to fetch his decanter and top up his goblet.

Hasuca fought for composure. "Am I to understand she is to be used as entertainment, in the *basement?*"

The Emperor snorted without opening his mouth and shrugged.

"Are you to tell me she is to be sent to the stump in the Guards' Den? Koe, she has served here all her life! She even served Father when he came into manhood."

"Yes, and from what he said, she wasn't very good at that either." Realising his decanter was almost empty, he looked about for another.

Hasuca implored, "For the love of the Gods, Koe!"

The Emperor spun on his heels and angrily pointed a finger. "NO! The damned Gods have nothing to do with it! *I* am the one in control here, and do not forget it! The Gods are nothing but feeble figments of your superstitious little minds."

Hasuca trembled with the rage he battled internally. The Emperor swayed a little. "Yes, I am the mightiest! Your Gods do nothing but rumble about in the clouds while you lot come to *me* for counsel. *I* am your God. You want a more apt ending for Kamutto? So be it!"

"Koe! Have you no mercy?"

The Emperor scoffed as he ascended the stairs, swiping another decanter on his way. They made their way through the labyrinth of corridors down to the bathing rooms. The Royal Guard were caught by surprise to see the Emperor there and scurried forward to open the doors. Inside, Kamutto was just getting out of the water to maids waiting with towels. Neither covered by water nor cloth, she was unsure whether to bow or cover.

The Emperor waved his hands as the Matron began to bow. "Aagh, please, Kamutto, at least spare us the unfortunate loss of your figure." As she snatched the towels, he looked to the ceiling. "Gravity can be so unkind," he groaned.

Hasuca remained in the hallway. He heard a door to his right open, and out stepped a eunuch by the name of Wan Maki. His story was a curious one. One day, he just walked into the palace and asked to serve as a eunuch. Most who served the palace this way had either been injured in the most unfortunate manner in battle, or were born with the curse of nature herself. One could only wonder what sort of problem or problems a family man must have to make such a request.

Just then, the doors from the bath house next door opened, and the tall figure of a woman stepped into the hall. She had her back to Hasuca. The long, silk garment hung down from her broad shoulders. A rope belt was threaded through eyelets and the bow to the back hung down over her firm buttocks. She moved with the grace of a dancer as she turned towards him. Her belt lay flat across her belly and her upturned breasts caressed the cool air. Hasuca saw none of this, lost in her big green eyes. Their eyes locked, and momentarily, time stopped for them both.

Koe hollered out. "Hasuca, do come in and close the doors, some privacy for Kamutto if you would."

Hasuca drew himself away and stepped inside. Xiang nodded to Hasuca as he took hold of the doors to close them.

"Master Xiang, in, not out, thank you," said the Emperor casually. He took another swig of his goblet as the Master closed the doors and turned to face the room. His face impassive, he was secretly pleased to not truly face Koe in combat. Koe had the family talent for both speed and power, but moreover, his unpredictability meant Xiang simply never knew what Koe was to do next.

The Emperor feigned a sigh as he topped his goblet for the umpteenth time. "It was brought to my attention this afternoon that I may have been a little hasty today. Firstly, Master Xiang, would you explain what is to happen to Kamutto?"

Kamutto looked at Sen Ya San with confusion. The Emperor was always quite particular about titles. Where was hers? Sen Ya San was quite careful not to meet her stare, though she could feel the burn of it.

Master Xiang gave a polite cough into a fist. "Of course, Emperor."

The Emperor delighted in watching the colour drain from Kamutto's face.

Master Xiang coughed again, sounding more artificial than the first. "It is my duty, Kamutto, to bring you here for a cleansing bath," another cough into a tighter fist, "Then deliver you to the basement for the entertainment of the Guard."

Kamutto's mouth gaped open. Her knees trembled before giving way, pulling her towels off as she slumped to the floor. Clumsily, she gathered them as she looked up to the smirking Emperor. "But I have served you and before you, your father, my entire life. Your father was my first …"

The Emperor screwed up his face. "Aww, spare us the details. Grief woman, have you lost all decorum? However, you will never guess what just transpired." He stepped in behind Matron San. "This woman comes into my office and asks me for my counsel with a problem *she* has. Can you believe that? She comes to me and asks for *your* mercy." He swept his arms out wide as if to emphasise his graciousness.

Kamutto looked at Matron San again; this time, it was full of confusion and hope. Still, the Matron ignored her. She pleaded to the Emperor. "Yes, yes, spare my life so I can continue to serve you and your palace, Your Excellency. I will serve like I have never served before."

The Emperor looked down at the aging woman. "Really? Would you say that you would serve with your life, Kamutto?" His voice trailed off at the end, but no one in the room missed the question. Some closed their eyes so not to bear witness to the games he so loved. The room was deathly quiet. Kamutto opened her mouth, but nothing came out.

The Emperor turned to the Master. "Xiang."

Master Xiang looked down into the pleading eyes of the old Matron. She looked quite pathetic, short, fat and naked on her towels. He wanted to pull his sword right there and save her the embarrassment, and everyone else the pain of watching, though he would not dare move a muscle unless asked to.

"Xiang. Your short sword, if you will."

Xiang drew it out steadily as Kamutto's eyes followed every inch. Her jaw trembled, and a quiver broke from her lips. The Emperor rolled his eyes and took another swig, handing the Master the decanter. He inspected the short sword as he held out his goblet for a refill. "Meticulously maintained as always, Master."

The Master tried to refill the goblet without spilling any as it swayed about.

"Hasuca is right to speak as well of you as he does, but will it pass a simple silk test? It is said that it is all that can separate war heroes from the dead and forgotten. Would you not agree, Master?"

"Yes, Your Excellency."

The Emperor didn't look at the Master. "Kamutto, below you in the caves is another stump. Have you seen it?"

The Matron shook her head, spite swelling in her now. "No, it is strictly forbidden. I have always followed edict to the last letter, only to find myself here, like this."

"Yes, that would be your fate today. You know how the game is finished most of the time, but today is different. Today I will offer you a second option, as I am a man of great character." He paused as if pondering his own greatness. "As I have had a request made to me of my now Head Matron Sen Ya San and, with respect for her, I, your Emperor, will offer you this meticulously sharpened sword to simply end it here, with your dignity intact."

In a half-drunken stupor, the Emperor couldn't hide his glee.

Kamutto's hands shook as she reached up to take the short sword. The Emperor stepped back to observe. She thought back to how many women she had seen lose the game. How many times she had thought so little for the foreign women and their ghastly demise. Not once had she ever thought to speak for any of them. Now she was to be treated just the same as they were, by her own Emperor.

Tentatively, she placed the tip of the sword just under her sternum. In one violent movement, she drew the sword up until the hilt slapped her belly. She slumped forward and her head cracked with a sickly sound on the stone floor. Her body slumped to the side.

The Emperor took back his decanter. "Well, if that isn't the darndest thing."

No one moved.

Finally, Matron San approached and knelt beside Kamutto's body. She rolled Kamutto onto her back. She took hold of the sword but she couldn't pull it out. It was as if she was to mortally hurt Kamutto. Then a hand covered over hers; it was Hasuca. He nodded as they drew out the sword. Master Xiang was there to relieve it from them, wiping it on his own silk gown.

The Emperor burped. "What a ghastly mess. See, this is cleaned up, would you, Matron San, the bath also." Without another thought, he ascended the stairs as the guards swung open the doors. At the top, he paused. "Let this be a lesson for you, Matron San."

Through glassy eyes, she looked up at him as he swayed, pointing his decanter directly at her. "Be careful what you ask for, I just may give it to you." With a final sweep of his garments, he was gone.

The Matron clenched her eyes shut, trying to compose herself as Hasuca grabbed her by the arm. "You didn't do this to her, Matron, you did this *for* her. She would have died on the stumps tonight, or tomorrow, but she died here, quickly and with as much dignity as she could possibly have after her own actions today."

The Matron tried to smile at him. *Gods, he is like his father. How did Koe become Emperor?* Lost in her own grief for a moment, she hadn't noticed the Master acquiring more help from the corridor.

Hasuca shook her gently. "You have had a trying day, why not wash yourself and lie your head down?"

"No, I have my duties to do before morning." She stood up straight, wiping her hands on her gown. The room was filling up with the smell of body fluids, but there were many ready to help. "Master Xiang, could you deal with the body please."

He dipped his head. "We will take good care of her."

The Matron addressed the maids. "We will need clean water and soap. No one is to leave until it looks, and smells, like new."

Hasuca left them to their work. He stopped in the corridor and held his head in his hands as he had so often these recent months. The pain could be so intense. The visions he was getting were not like any he had ever had and were strangely confusing. Unsteadily, he walked towards his quarters, relieved to be free of his brother's ranting and the unfortunate passing of the Matron, but he had yet to foil his brother's unhinged plan.

***

Over the next few months, Hasuca meditated over his concerns, but there was no obvious way forward without civil war. All he got were his visions of a little brown boy.

4 Hasuca

The smell of thick smoke wafted up Hasuca's nostrils. His head ached, in fact, his entire body ached, rendering it almost numb with pain. He could hear the muffled sound of two men cursing and talking. Through blurred eyes, he tried to make out the figures leaning over him. One man was huge and dark skinned. His trousers were in tatters, and his tunic was just as badly battered and covered in blood. As hard as he tried, he couldn't make out any features at all. The other man was a little clearer, also quite tall but lightly built, and had long, wavy blond hair, like his own.

Hasuca felt a shift to his core, now free of all his pain, he could see clearly. The smoke was from a burning cabin. It was just a humble thing, built into a rocky cliff. In front of it was a small grass meadow and surrounding that were some of the tallest trees he had seen. Water bubbled out of a small spring into a pond to one side of the cabin and meandered across the meadow then down the hillside. It was quite beautiful.

Hasuca had the sensation of floating up above his own body as the two young men leaned over him. Looking down over the setting, he could see himself lying on the meadow as he drifted further away; a dying man, badly beaten and bleeding out.

The cabin was fully ablaze now, lighting up the night for all to see. He could see into the tree line, and amazingly, it was full of spectators. Animals of all kinds, sparrows, eagles and crows landed on the backs of the bigger beasts like the elephant and rhino. Tigers, leopards and the jaguar stood shoulder to shoulder. Reindeer, the common milking cow and wild boar all stood as witnesses as he did himself to his own death.

He couldn't hear what the men were saying, but then a woman spoke to him. "Do you recognise these men, Hasuca?" Her voice was deep and resonant.

He was floating higher and higher. "No, I do not."

"Are you sure?" she questioned.

Hasuca watched some more, then the big, dark man leaned back. The other man was not upset by his passing, but strangely, Hasuca knew who the blond man was. He was unmistakably his own, unborn son.

To him, the scene made no sense at all.

Laying the older man's hand over his chest, the dark man stood and roared but one word. Hasuca couldn't quite make it out as he'd drifted too far off.

The woman spoke to him again. "Do you know these men, Hasuca?"

Hasuca was playing the word over in his mind, trying to make out what the young, dark man had said.

"No, I told you. I do not."

***

Hasuca blinked and focused on the ceiling. He was back in the palace. Feeling a little groggy but with the headache gone, he tried to sit up. A woman's hand helped him, propping him up with pillows. He had done this several times in the last few months; it was becoming very concerning.

"Here, have some water. It will help clear your head." He took the goblet and drank. She spoke again, almost like a friend, concern in her whisper. "Hey, easy with that, Hasuca. You keep doing this. We need to find out why."

Looking up, he was pleased to see Sha'Doe standing over him. She had her back to the rest of the room. He looked around at them all and back to Sha'Doe. She slipped him a cheeky wink. He took another drink to hide his own small grin. The woman's voice was one and the same. She was not a part of his vision, but what had brought him back.

"Alright, I'm feeling pretty good now. Who are those two men?"

There was a shuffle of feet as Sha'Doe moved aside. "Sorry to be of bother, Prince Hasuca, but these two men were found with you in the hall. They say that you were already unconscious and they were trying to help, but we have kept them hostage, waiting for your return to identify them, if you would."

Hasuca looked at them both. They were wearing clothing that suggested they had just walked in from the snowstorm that was still blustering outside. They had their hands pulled up their backs with loops of rope around their necks. Neither one was breathing easily.

"Who do you work under, men? Who is your leader?" Hasuca asked.

The men glanced at each other. It was difficult to tell them apart. The one on the left spoke first. "We are freelance fighters. We work for money, Your Excellency." They did their best to bow at the waist.

"I am not the Emperor. You will not call me by that title again." The edge to his voice suggested he was getting back to his normal self. He sat up and turned to get out of bed as Sha'Doe coughed. He looked at her questioningly, and she shook her head, motioning downwards. Following her lead, he lifted the covers. He was naked. He glanced back to the two men who were politely looking away, though his own guards were not.

"Guards, when you have closed your traps, you can cut these men free. Then you will wait outside."

One opened his mouth to protest.

"Even with me in this state, you would not like to argue with me. Would you, guard?"

The guard stood to attention as his comrade hurried forward to cut the two prisoners free. Both guards then made a hasty retreat, closing the doors as they backed out.

The two freed men had trouble getting their arms around in front of themselves, though neither made a sound of protest. Hasuca shot Sha'Doe a, 'Well, where are my trousers,' look. With a smirk, she turned to retrieve his clothing. He gave her another look. She rolled her eyes and turned her back, also blocking the view from the two men as they went through a few moves to stretch out their arms.

Feeling dignified again, Hasuca stood beside Sha'Doe, doing up his waist sash. He didn't turn away from the two men though spoke to her. "The clothes were cleaned and folded. How long have I been asleep?"

"I don't believe you were asleep, Prince Hasuca, but in answer, three days."

"What? Well, that would explain why I'm famished."

"Prince, this is the fourth time since Matron Kamutto died. This could kill you, Hasuca. You need to see your medicine doctor." Her voice trailed off with emotion.

Hasuca considered his dream. "No, Sha'Doe, this will not kill me." He pondered the two men who were now standing before him. "Men, were you tied up all this time?"

They gave a curt bow. "I believe we were, Your Excellency," they responded with another bow.

Hasuca frowned. This was getting silly now. "As I said, I am not the Emperor. Never have been," he thought about his dream, "And apparently, I never will be. So, you never call me that again. Are we clear on this?"

"Many say you should be …"

"ENOUGH!"

The strength of his temper flare caught even Sha'Doe off guard, causing him to flinch. Both men dropped to their knees. Hasuca calmed himself. "Get up now." The men scrambled back to their feet and bowed again. This time, it was Hasuca's turn to roll his eyes. "I need food, I'm going to the kitchen," and he left.

The two men looked at Sha'Doe. One said in a low voice, "We can take you from here back to where you belong, Princess

Sha'Doe. Your family miss you and need you." There was a long pause before the men urged, "Even the Snake King stated …"

Sha'Doe silenced them with a raised hand. "My place is here and now, I can feel it. This Palace has a purpose for me somehow. Besides, there is no point in me leaving without the gold bracelets for the Sacred Skull. I have befriended Koe to get them back, but it will take time. We have already spoken on this, and you will do as I have instructed." She took a breath. "Is there no sign of Izan?"

The two men dipped their heads. "Because we have seen nothing to indicate where he is, we can only surmise he was taken in by a caring family. We are sorry, Princess, we have failed you."

"I know you have been thorough." She indicated for them to leave. "Return to Samos and find Izan, then take him back with you. Send both my apologies and my love to my King and Queen. You have far to go; be safe."

As the men scurried out, Sha'Doe turned back to the empty bed and smiled, rubbing her stomach as she did.

5 Royal Blood

There was a rap at the door. "Enter," said Sha'Doe as she faced it. She quickly bowed as the Emperor moved towards her. "Your Excellency, I was not expecting you. Why do you knock in your own palace?" As she spoke, her confidence returned.

"My dear Sha'Doe, should an Emperor not show his Lady respect?"

She took her time to answer. "I was not aware I was your Lady, as so many other women would wish to be, sire."

"Ah, that's my girl, ever modest."

He watched her closely and, clasping his hands behind his back, walked to the window. The palace's horseshoe shape meant that her window had quite a different outlook to his own, though this room was rather small, almost insufferable.

"How is your brother, sire? I heard he has been sick again. I did send a message to inform you."

"Yes, I had my own physician sent to him. I have so much planning to do and without him to help with the remedial work, well, I don't have anyone else I can trust for it."

She watched him getting lost in thought. "What planning was that, sire?" Aware of her apprehension, she forced her tone to be smooth and low.

The Emperor moved slowly from the window. *Have I trusted her with my preoccupation? Surely not pillow talk?* "You had two messages sent to me this week, Sha'Doe. One was for my brother, and the other?"

"Ah, yes, of course, sire. In all the concern over your broth ... Prince Hasuca, I do believe I rather forgot myself." She knelt at his feet and took a big breath. He was unpredictable at the best of times.

The Emperor groaned, and before she could say a word, he grabbed a handful of her hair and pulled her head back firmly. "Well, out with it then, woman. As I said, I'm a busy man."

"Your Excellency, I am pregnant."

"You're what?"

"I hope Your Excellency is not upset, but I do believe you have made me pregnant, sire."

Sha'Doe had crossed oceans, walked foreign cities, been captured by the Emperor's own Guard, put in 'the game', but only now was she truly afraid. He was as likely to celebrate as he was to say she was unworthy of carrying his seed in her foreign body, then throw her from her window to certain death.

"What? WHAT?"

She flinched. She had been lost in her own thoughts. He pulled her hair down backwards, his left knee in her back. Steel flashed before her, and she felt a knife pressing into her throat. She was paralysed.

"Your Excellency, everyone here says you're incapable of producing children."

His face turned red with rage, spitting foam through gritted teeth as he moved the knife in front of her as if to get ready to slash her throat. "You stupid woman, you just insulted this palace for the last time!"

She didn't take her eyes off the tip of his knife, which gleamed as it caught the light. "Emperor, now I will prove them wrong. You *did* make me pregnant. If you wish it, I can tell everyone it is not you at all." The blade seemed to ease a little. She tried to steady her voice. "I can show them it is *they* who have the problem, if I am to have *your* child." She was sure that her scalp was bleeding from the knot of hair he'd pulled.

The knife lowered to his side momentarily, then suddenly he pulled her hair again, and the blade gleamed in front of her once more. "The child is of mixed blood!" he shouted. "And to have a bastard child is worse than none at all."

"It is of full Imperial blood." The steadiness of her voice surprised even her.

"It's what?" He held the knife steady. "What did you just say? You lie and I will kill you and your unborn child."

"I am a Princess of my homelands. If I bear you a son, *he* will be next in line to the throne of my homelands as well as here, sire."

He lost his rage as quickly as it had risen. Still with a handful of hair, he stepped back and pulled her to her feet, then reintroduced her to his knife. "And just where would that be?"

"When I came here by vessel, we travelled into the morning sun for many full moons until we came to Devil's Pass."

The Emperor's mind reeled. "There is no land over there."

"There *is* land, lots of it over there. You have not been there yet but our people have been coming here occasionally for a long time."

"And how am I to believe *you* are any sort of Imperial, hmm?"

"Think on it. I have come from afar, yet I know your language as well as anyone and a little better than some I have heard here." He shot her a look almost as cutting as his knife. She quickly continued. "I know your etiquette and customs and have the fighting skills to take your own Guard on their own ground. Only a trained princess would be capable of all this. What's more, I know it for all the mainlands of this world. I could go anywhere and do as well."

"Well, we will see about that." He had switched to the language of the desert people of Audun, who lived over the Western Dividing Range.

"A simple test. Can you perform another, Your Excellency?" she replied in the same language and dialect.

Slowly, he released her hair and sheathed his knife. She stood, straight and defiant, struggling internally to control the adrenaline coursing through her veins. She would show him no weakness.

"You say if it is a son, he would be next to the throne in your own lands?"

"Yes, that would be correct, sire."

"Very well, you may live until the birth. If it is well, you may nurse it. If it is a boy, you may also have some say in his training. If he is to go back and claim what is naturally his, he will need to know how to conduct himself in your lands. Wouldn't you agree, Sha'Doe?"

"Indeed, I would, sire. We are very strong in etiquette and training, and only I can give him our language, in the right tone. He must be groomed to the highest level to be accepted into his rightful place, Your Excellency." She was holding her abdomen, the protective stance of a pregnant woman.

A fleeting smile passed over his face. "Very well then, I will have my physician come and give you a full check-over to see that you are fit to carry the Imperial seed and, in fact, to confirm that you are carrying anything at all. People make the strangest of claims just to be in my favour, to get and keep my attention. Still, not really surprising, is it, Sha'Doe?"

He headed for the doors, then spun to face her in an exaggerated grandiose manner. Her chin rose just a little in anticipation of his next demand. "I will tell the Guard that you are not to leave this room, and no one is to enter unless I have given them clearance to do so. If you are carrying my child, I will see to it that you come to no harm. That is my duty to you now, Sha'Doe." He moved through the doors, not waiting to hear any response before it clicked to a close behind him.

Sha'Doe listened carefully; she couldn't hear what was said but his instruction seemed thorough, if not lengthy.

She spent some time gazing out of the window, wondering how she'd ended up here, only to find herself pregnant to Royalty of another land. She rubbed her slightly swelling front. How could he doubt it? She had thought she'd left it a little late to be telling anyone. Most of the maids had passed more than a knowing look and, as they say, a woman can tell.

There was a rap on the door.

"Enter."

A small, frail man descended the stairs and, stopping at the bottom, bowed. "The Emperor has sent me to attend to your every need, my Lady." He bowed again.

"I see. I will be honest, I'm surprised to be getting a male to tend to me. And your name?"

"Maki, my Lady. I believe I have been sent in my capacity of Messenger of the Palace. If you have any problem, it is my duty to get the right person for the job. I can be as fast as any. Also, my, shall we say, slight frame, is misleading as a measure of my strength. A male I was, a eunuch now I am, my Lady." He stood before her with a cheeky grin. Regardless of his high-pitched voice, she liked him already.

"Ah, so your job is to fetch the right person for any particular problem. Well, I suppose that's better than having an entourage at my door. Also, my name is Sha'Doe, please, at least in this confinement, call me by my name, Maki. Let's not make this room any more stifling than necessary."

He moved towards the window, eyeing her belly as he passed. "As you wish, Sha'Doe," he said, moving his attention to the view. "It does look to have set in for a long winter, although you are well on your way." He slid his hands up opposing sleeves, holding his elbows.

Watching him closely she decided there was nothing to hide. "Yes, Maki, you are quite right, I am well on the way."

"Indeed, Sha'Doe. It must seem strange to spend all your adult life showing your feminine figure only now to hide it with those baggy clothes."

She chuckled. "Ah, you are an observant one, aren't you? I don't know if there is going to be much I can keep from you."

"I hope you have no need to keep anything from me, at least not while pregnant, Sha'Doe. So, if there's anything you need or that I can get, now would be the time to tell me. I have no idea what customs you have in your own lands."

"Thank you for being sensitive to my customs. Yes, there are a few things that would help. Shall we share a cup of Imperial tea with our discussions, Maki?"

"Ah, a custom we *can* share. An excellent idea, Sha'Doe."

6 New Life

For months, the snow settled on the heavy wooden windowsills around the palace. In the Den, the fire burned in the centre hearth. Over the flames, a huge brass dome danced in the firelight, hanging from a chimney that passed up through the solid wooden beams straining over the broad room. Beneath the timber work, among wisps of narcotic pipe smoke, concubines talked in low voices. The mood shifted with a tap on the door.

"Come."

The doors were made of black beech timber. The five brass hinges on each door strained to hold their weight as two guards heaved them open. A eunuch stepped in and bowed deeply.

The Emperor waved his goblet about. "Yes, yes. Well, do you have a message or not? Speak, you impotent fool."

"The midwife sends her congratulations, sire. It is a boy." He bowed deeply again, awaiting further instructions.

The Emperor shot to his feet. "Yes! *That* is how you serve your Emperor, you bunch of empty hags. Excellent! Impotent fool, have more opium and some red wine brought in. I have the need to celebrate further." He pushed aside the two young concubines.

The Emperor started his concubines young, as he believed they needed preparation to carry the Imperial seed; however, until this day, none had produced offspring for him.

"Oh, and eunuch, bring me a virgin. Yes. One that is still pure, so she can be trained as an example of today's Imperial success."

The eunuch gave a quick look at one of the concubines pushed aside. When she was chosen for His Excellency, Maki had volunteered to serve the Emperor also. Now, looking at her, his heart ached. Not because of the appalling way the Emperor treated his concubines, or even because she was so young – after all, worse things could happen to young girls outside the palace. Here, she was kept warm and fed well, her clothes were the best, and she had little chores outside of entertaining the Emperor.

What hurt was the fact that she was so intoxicated that she didn't even recognise him as her father.

"Be gone, cockless one, you have perved quite long enough."

Realising his mistake, Maki bowed and backed out before the Emperor took it in his mind to have him tossed into the pit or worse. He headed down the hall, hands up his sleeves and clamped on elbows, attempting to stay focused on his instructions without being consumed by the very slow demise of his own daughter.

"Ah, there you are, Maki."

Forced from his sorrow, Maki looked up to see Matron Sen Ya San. The very proper Matron had served the Imperial family for two generations. Her family had been concerned when the Emperor had shown interest in her, but were also delighted with the honour and had given it their blessings. She had not borne fruit of any sons and so was retired to the kitchen, a momentous change. Now she dwelt in the palace basements. No heating, no silk clothes, but uniforms that she washed and mended herself. Above all, she was not permitted ever to have sex again. If a former concubine bore a male child to anyone but the Emperor, death would be immediate. However, as Head Matron, she now occupied a small room with a window. Life could be worse, much worse.

"Yes, Matron, I was in the process of searching you out."

"Really, Maki, you look like a man who has just seen his own lost daughter."

"Nothing much gets past you, does it, Matron?" He bowed to give her the respect he felt she deserved. She returned it for the same reason.

Putting an arm through his, she said, "I have not walked these halls since I was just a girl to not have learnt a lot about my people, my dear friend."

A smile warmed his ragged face, a face ravaged from leaving his loving wife to be close to their daughter. Ragged from the sacrifice of becoming a eunuch, only to be called a cockless fool by the very one he served. He patted her on the hand. "Sen Ya San, you are the youngest to ever make Matron, aren't you?" He didn't wait for an answer. When he'd left to become a eunuch, he'd told his wife not to wait for him, though it still stung how fast she had coupled with a friend well known to them both. As a eunuch, he saw little purpose in the companionship of women, but he always felt a warmth he didn't quite understand in the company of the Matron. "So how many years have you served the family in these halls now, Matron?"

"Oh, come along now, Maki. Did you think that little ploy was going to get you to discover my age? A lady does not divulge such a thing."

"I'm sorry, my dear Matron. It was foolish of me to think I could extract such delicate information with such a clumsy ruse. I do believe your mind is as sharp and proud as my manhood once was." They laughed together.

He rubbed her hand vigorously. "Now, the lesser reason I wanted to see you, Matron, was that the Emperor has ordered more poppy and some red wine. I do believe he has sired a boy."

The Matron was silent for a moment. Maki didn't interrupt. His patience would be rewarded. She stopped walking and faced him. "I hope his eyes are of the same colour – brown, or green, for that matter."

Maki scrunched his forehead, but before he could question her comment further, she continued, "I will make up the order, and I may include some delicacy. Yes, monkey brains still in their skulls, I feel. He always goes a little crazy for them, though the Gods only know why. Half my staff struggle just to prepare them. Be assured, Maki, it will be done at once." With that, she bowed and left him in her wake.

He decided that since everything was taken care of, he would go and check on mother and child, and so continued his way along the corridors to the birthing chamber. Once it had been announced that at last one of the concubines was to give birth, there was an instant air of excitement. The birthing chamber for this generation had been, until now, unused.

After hundreds of generations, it was unimaginable that this one was not to produce a son, breaking the Imperial line. More than once, Maki had considered that there was altogether too much pressure for one of the courtesans to conceive a child, and all that opium could not but mar the quest. His slightly improved mood after meeting the Matron disappeared, as the image of his drugged daughter returned.

Arriving at the door to the birthing chamber, instead of womenfolk cooing over a newborn, there were the sounds of much commotion and the unmistakable screaming of a woman who had already given birth – giving birth. He burst open the door to see for himself.

Sha'Doe was indeed giving birth for a second time. Bodily fluids and blood dripped from the stone birthing table, Sha'Doe herself, was delirious.

Maki shuffled down the stairs and grabbed one of the nursemaids, who seemed to be in shock. She didn't respond but just stared at Sha'Doe on the table. He gave her a vigorous shake. "Nursemaid, for the sake of the Gods, do your job!"

Panic flashed across her face. "She is going to die."

Maki let her go and grabbed another attendant.

"Yes, Maki, look, we are busy. What is it you want?"

"Where is the doctor, nursemaid?"

"We were not given a doctor. With the early winter, they are all trapped with the Emperor's Guard up north. All we have are the few tools over there."

Maki saw the soft leather pouch rolled up on a corner table. "So be it. Do you at least have a messenger?"

"I thought I was talking to him, Maki."

"I am no longer the messenger here. Send for Matron Sen Ya San and speak to no one of this, do you understand?"

"Yes."

"Now go. Be fast."

***

A monkey's head sat on a wooden block, eyes open with a plum in its mouth. Matron Sen Ya San was shaving a ring around its head, ready to make an incision to remove the top of its skull. She would then carefully pull it back as a makeshift lid. Monkey brain was served warm, fresh and raw. Some of the staff made such a fuss for so little reason. How hard was it to prepare the monkeys for the Emperor? Yet she inevitably ended up doing it herself.

A panicked, breathless nursemaid burst into the kitchen. The other servants gasped at the blood on her front. No one dared come into the Matron's kitchen in such a state.

"Who sent you?" Matron asked coldly.

"Please, Matron," she gasped, "Maki has asked for you to come immediately."

The Matron wiped her hands on a cloth. She pointed to one of the maids and in a low voice instructed, "Finish this and see it is served to the highest standard. Now move." She turned to another maid standing open-mouthed. "Maid, take this nursemaid and fetch her water to wash, then get her a new kitchen uniform. Burn these." The Matron looked into the young nursemaid's eyes. "Now, my dear, I take it Maki is in the birthing chamber?"

The woman nodded as tears welled up.

"I take it this blood is not yours?" The nursemaid shook her head. "Then pull yourself together, woman." She addressed the kitchen staff, her stern voice barely audible. "This did not happen. Am I quite clear? Nursemaid, you work for me now, and from this moment, you will conduct yourself according to the rules down here, or you will answer to me. Understood?"

"Yes, Matron. Thank you, Matron."

50

"Very well. Now get on with it, maids, or do you wish for further instruction?"

The kitchen hustle resumed. Beside herself with concern, the Matron mumbled, "Gods in the heavens above, please take me before this spoilt little excrement of an Emperor gets to breed further." That brought her train of thought back to the very problem before her, the birthing chamber.

***

Through the pandemonium, Maki's eyes set on the tools, his mind on what must be done if this child of Imperial blood was to be saved.

He rolled out the leather cloth. Each tool, meticulously cleaned, had its own place. Below the table were two containers, one painted white, the other red. He placed them on the table, then pulled the red stopper and tentatively leant forward to smell it. Chloroform. He poured some on a clean cloth then looked at the second bottle, pulling the cork. It smelt good. Tipping a little on the table, he shrugged, then drank from the decanter. "Ah, white wine."

He wiped his mouth on his sleeve, then held the chloroform-soaked cloth over Sha'Doe's mouth and nose. Her muffled screams subsided. He placed the leather pouch at the table's end and moved around between two stirrups.

Sha'Doe's breath was ragged and irregular as she drifted in and out of consciousness. She had lost so much blood and couldn't last much longer. Repeatedly, her body heaved. There were unexpected sounds and more clear fluids rushed out onto Maki's clothing and over the floor. The second baby moved and made its chaotic entry.

"For the love of the Gods, Sha'Doe, you were indeed the fertile one." He looked at the two babies. "Put them on the blessed nipples to suckle. The first drink contains some of the mother's spirit. It is their one chance." The women moved quickly to comply.

Best efforts were made to comfort Sha'Doe but her body contorted and more contractions came. Again, she pushed then cried out a huge contraction. As another baby's head popped out, her body lay still.

Maki quickly moved around the table and whispered in her ear. "Sweet dreams, our golden child. We have all come to love you on your too short a stay. Gods' speed."

He rolled the leather pouch out over her stomach. One of the nursemaids stepped over and grabbed him by the arm. "What do you think you are going to do to this poor woman now, messenger boy?"

With his spare hand, he gently removed the nursemaid's grip. Over just a few seasons, this foreign woman had won the hearts of so many in the palace. "Yes, I am a messenger boy, and I have been Sha'Doe's personal *messenger boy* for these last few months. Few in this land know this wonderful woman as well as I. She is already dead, and only the Gods can change that, but I may be able to save the child that is still half in her. What do you think she would want, nursemaid?"

She looked at the baby. There was movement, not unlike that of a butterfly emerging from its cocoon but, without intervention, this butterfly would perish. On more than one occasion, the nursemaid had been summoned into Sha'Doe's quarters. Maki had always been there to serve Sha'Doe. Often, they had been laughing like teenagers. Now, like all of them, Maki was suffering the loss. She patted his arm. "Of course, Maki, you must do what you think is right."

***

Matron Sen Ya San scurried to the birthing chamber. It was a journey she had made numerous times these last few weeks in preparation for this auspicious day. She turned the last corner and was relieved not to hear screaming. Just as she thought, a mountain made of a mole hill. She shook her head. *This generation ...*

She opened the door to the chaos of the birthing chamber. Pale-faced, Sha'Doe's head was lying to the side, her unblinking eyes staring at the Matron. There was more blood and fluid than she would have thought possible from one human being, mixed about the floor with bloody, saturated towels. Sha'Doe's legs had relaxed to an unnatural spread, and, there in the middle was Maki.

He didn't even look up when she walked in, though he did speak. "Please, Head Matron, do come in and close the door. We have much to discuss." He continued to make cuts, the sound of slicing was all that broke the otherwise silent room. Concentrating, Maki took care not to hurt the baby. The two newborns suckled on the dead woman. They did appear to be getting something as they fed quietly.

Matron Sen Ya San watched Maki make cut after careful cut. He'd always spoken well of Sha'Doe and he was doing what had to be done. In a low but firm voice, she instructed one of the nursemaids. "Ish Wone, we will need a surrogate mother immediately."

Wone looked blankly at the Matron.

"Nursemaid Wone! The babies will only get so much from this. They will need something more, and well before the Emperor is to see his son. It needs to happen now! Do you understand me, nursemaid?"

"Yes, of course. You are right, Head Matron." She looked about the room, not quite knowing how this was specifically her problem or how to resolve it.

Matron had an uncanny knack of knowing what was going on in the heads of others. "You will need to go downstairs and organise some ..." she looked at the two babies and a third on the way, "... quite a lot of goat's milk and feeding bottles."

Ish Wone nodded and made her way to the door.

"Wone."

"Yes, Matron."

"You cannot go like that. Do you have something here to change into?"

"Yes, I think I have something in the next room, Matron."

"Good, go change now … and Wone …?"

"Yes, Matron?"

"Not one word of this. Nothing is wrong here. Do you understand me, Ish Wone?"

Wone scanned the room. "Of course, Matron, I will be discreet and tend to this duty with the utmost decorum."

"I know you will, that is why I chose you, but be prompt."

Ish Wone's cheeks flushed with pride as she exited the room via the side door. Matron turned her attention back to the room. She clapped twice. The women snapped out of their grief. "Very well, ladies, I know this is hard for you, but we must be professional and we don't have much time. Those of you who do not have a baby in your hands will go and fetch more towels and begin the clean-up. No one is to leave these rooms. If you need something more, you will address me. Is this clear?"

They muttered an acknowledgement. One nursemaid came forward. "Head Matron, we will need buckets …" Her eyes teary, she shook her head. "A lot more buckets."

"I will see to it."

Sen Ya San was about to leave the room when she heard a whimper of a cry. She turned back to see Maki lift the third and last baby clear of its mother's deceased body.

***

The Emperor paced about the Den, well spent. "A son no less. You have been shown up by an immigrant, an Imperial immigrant at that. Yes, you heard me, our son is not just heir to my throne, he's also heir to the throne of the south-east lands of Palusa. He will follow my lead, my legacy, to be the second God-King of this miserable earth. That's it, my serving whores: Emperor today, God-King tomorrow!"

He raised his hands above his head, inciting the Gods to respond. "Is there anyone mighty enough to stop me? Of course not. Who? Who could possibly stand in my way? I, the most

54

powerful man in the world, can stretch my wings of power and soar to new heights, taking with me the future of the world. A boy born from *my* destiny will rise to lead *your* destiny!"

A knock on the door.

"Come."

The maid carried a gold tray with three monkeys' heads on it. They were set looking outward with fruit cuttings displayed around them.

"Oh my, what a treat. This is truly the day of all days. I simply must indulge."

The maid placed the tray so carefully as to not have any roll off, then quickly excused herself, feeling nauseous.

***

Maki looked at the Matron. "Three babies and two breasts. What is the third one to do?"

The Matron tilted her head. "What would you have me do with it?"

A maid holding one of the nursing babies spoke quietly. "Here, this one has gone to sleep, put that one on here, the milk still flows, I think." Another nursemaid took the third baby and put it on the nipple. It suckled.

Matron Sen Ya San took the sleeping baby. She walked in front of Sha'Doe's still-open eyes. She gently rubbed her index finger from the baby's nose up between its eyes to its forehead. The eyes opened and focused on her. Big, round eyes, one green, one yellow. The Matron moved her finger down to the little nose and the boy closed his eyes again. She whispered to Sha'Doe. "He is as perfect as his father, whom you loved so."

She touched the forehead of the baby to Sha'Doe's own forehead before placing the now sleeping baby on the deflated belly of the woman. He squirmed a little, then with a big sigh, settled.

The Matron locked eyes with Maki for a moment. Maki motioned to the other two babies. She moved up close so no one else could see what she was doing. With her index finger, she gently rubbed the second baby's nose up between its eyebrows. It blinked and looked right at her. Its eyes were big and green, like her mother. The baby girl had finished feeding so the Matron placed her with her brother, on their mother.

She walked around the table to examine the last-born baby. Another boy. "Good, there is hope yet." When she ran her finger on its nose, the eyes flew open. She shuddered and took a step back. The boy carried on suckling but its eyes remained staring at the Matron. She ran her finger back down between his eyes to the end of his nose. His eyes closed then sprang open again.

Maki motioned to one of the side doors and Matron followed his lead. She glanced back at the baby and saw it was looking at her as she moved around the table and headed for the door. She was compelled to break its stare, but she knew it was still watching her.

7 Deceived

In the Den, the Emperor paced around the central fire, still ranting about his power and control. He stopped by the throne to select another fresh monkey brain. Carefully, he removed the lid and greedily slurped the contents.

"Ah, a day to mark in your feeble brains my empty sluts. This is one of the greatest days in the illustrious history of Middle Kingdom. The next generation has begun. Sha'Doe has borne me a son, and she will bear me more. This import has risen to be your Queen, and why? Because her stature is of a high enough standard to accept the Royal seed. Look at you all. You have become a doped-up bunch of hags that will now answer to her in my absence."

He grabbed a silver spoon and scooped out some more brains. He closed his eyes, savouring the taste as he placed it on his tongue. A dribble of red saliva ran down his chin and he wiped it up with his finger and sucked it clean. The concubine at his feet looked on with great interest. He bent down, watching her eagerness at the prospect of sharing with him.

"You would like some? Would you like to share with your Emperor?" he drooled. Her eyes swelled at the sight of the blood and brain as he took another spoonful. Her mouth opened with anticipation. He chewed slowly. "You want to feast, hmm? Come to me, come feast with me."

Eagerly, she licked her lips. The Emperor let a little crimson dribble down his cheek and whispered, "Come, share with your Emperor. Come to me."

She leant up and slowly licked up his saliva, up his neck and chin, missing nothing. The Emperor took another spoonful and slowly chewed it. Dropping the spoon, he took her by the chin and squeezed it, forcing her mouth open as he leaned over her like the starling feeding its young.

"Yes, my fledgling, you will do anything to serve, won't you?"

She swallowed the last of her feast and nodded eagerly. He picked up the spoon once more and scooped out one of the eyeballs and offered it to her. "Here, my dedicated servant, I will let you have the greatest treasure of all. But tell no one, will you?" The eyeball wobbled on the spoon. He held a finger on his lips. "Shhh, just you and me, alright?" She looked about suspiciously and nodded, opening her mouth to accept the treat for her alone.

The Emperor laughed as the eyeball slid in.

She rolled it around in her mouth, then gagged. The Emperor wagged his finger. "Ah ah, no wasting now, chew it, my dear, chew hard," he whispered. She rolled it around, trying to get a hold of it in her teeth. "That's it, my dear, bite it hard, bite down on it now."

It popped in her mouth. She gagged some more and a little spurted out. The Emperor quickly moved aside, a laugh breaking his lips. She finally managed to swallow some, gagging twice more as she finished.

"Tell me, my fledgling, who is the eunuch to you, hmm? Who is he?" The Concubine tilted her head in confusion as the Emperor continued. "Is he your Pappy? No, he is a eunuch, though I didn't see lust in his eyes when he looked at you. Is he maybe your uncle then?" The concubine tilted her head to the other side, like a dog trying to understand its master.

"Are you my Pappy?" she asked.

"Ha. I would not have you for my daughter, silly slag. No, no," he snorted, giving her the second eyeball as he stood.

The Emperor ascended the steps to the main doors as two maids scuttled forward with slippers and clothing. Whilst he was being dressed, he turned to the concubines. "Well, my empty slags, I am going to see my son and your Queen." With a flourish of self-adulation, he headed for the door.

The last thing he heard was the popping of the eyeball.

***

In the room next to the birthing chamber, Maki closed the door behind the Matron. He laid the leather pouch on the table and faced the Matron, who had backed up to the wall, leaning on it. "What was that about?" He waved an arm to emphasise the question.

The Matron was ghastly pale. "I do not know what that last thing is, but I think we should do the people of this world a favour and kill it now."

"Kill it? Like bolts of lightning you will! I have just spent, I don't know how long, saving it. What's more, I will have nothing to do with the slaughter of an innocent infant."

"Maki, I'm telling you here and now, there is nothing about that child that is innocent. It is evil. Pure evil."

"Oh, nonsense, woman. We've had a confusing, trying day we would all like to forget. The thing I don't get is the Emperor has not been blessed with a child in all this time, yet now he's given three." He picked up a towel and proceeded to clean the tools. He looked back at the Matron. "What sex was the second born?"

Lightning flashed through the valley announcing the coming of another mean, winter's storm. She stared across to the window, taking a moment to quantify her thoughts.

"Matron, what *is* the matter with you? What sex is the second born?" Maki stood perplexed in his blood-soaked clothing.

"Maki, the firstborn is a boy. He has the eyes of his father. You know as well as I that for that he will die. The second is a girl. She has her mother's eyes and may be allowed to live. The third is the Emperor's son through and through. He will get everything. The first is the rightful one. Maki, we must save him."

"In the name of the Mighty Gods, woman! Are you suggesting we hide him? That would be suicide."

The Matron eased herself away from the wall. "If the Emperor finds out there is a third child, he will hunt it down and when he finds it, he will kill it. I have looked into the soul of this one. He must not fall into the Emperor's clutches. He must not." Her voice trailed off.

"And what did you have in mind?"

"We must leave the palace. Immediately." Her voice was just a whisper.

Maki's eyes opened wide. "What?"

Matron rushed forward to hush the now-shaking man.

"Have you gone completely mad, woman? That's preposterous. There's already over eight feet of snow, and it's still snowing. It is well below freezing. You have spent your time in the kitchen. Have you ever thrown a ladleful of boiling water out the door only to watch it freeze before it hits the ground? That ..." He marched to the window and thrust a pointed finger at the falling snow, "... that is what is out there today! It will be even colder tonight. No, this is not going to happen, not now." He marched past her, back to cleaning the tools.

She grabbed him by the arm, but he spun away from her. "No, I am going to die an old man. If that baby is to live, it will live. If it is in its fate to die, then it will die. Who am I to interfere with the workings of the Gods?" He choked as he finished his protest.

***

Feeling happier than he'd ever been, the Emperor walked through the halls on his way to see Sha'Doe and his son. The Emperor of Middle Kingdom had a son! Not just a son to continue his line of Royal blood, but one for him to teach, grow and guide to be the next God-King. Yes, life was good. *Why do people waste their time looking up to the Gods? The Gods did not give me a son. The Gods have no control over anything,* he pondered.

"Emperor, Emperor. May I have a moment of your time, please, Emperor?" A messenger hurried to catch up.

"Yes, you can have exactly the length of time it takes for me to walk to the birthing chamber. So, I suggest you keep it short and interesting. And if you say my name one more time, I may throttle you just for the joy of it. Now what is it?"

"Your Excellency, I have been worried about your brother. He has been very ill again, slipping in and out of consciousness."

***

Matron San knew Maki well enough to see when it was no use pushing him any further. She returned next door to oversee the cleaning process. The floors were being finished, Sha'Doe's body had been removed, and the Matron looked around for the babies.

Seeing her confusion, one of the nursemaids stepped forward. "Head Matron Sen Ya San, they have been taken into the nursing room. This way please."

"Well, of course they have. And our dear Sha'Doe, who has taken her?"

"I do hope you're not upset with me, Head Matron, but no one wanted to interfere with your discussions with Maki, so I asked one of the guards to fetch Master Xiang. He took care of everything. I also asked him to be respectful of our loss, and that it was to be discussed with no one at this point. He said it was his duty to inform the Emperor. I asked if he could return and speak with you first."

"You did well, nursemaid ...?"

"Oh ... nursemaid Tam Bora, please."

"Very well, nursemaid Bora, carry on."

Matron San moved through the working maids to the door on the far side of the room. She thought about what she and Maki had discussed. Heavens forbid they had been overheard. She took a breath and entered the next room. Three nursemaids, no less, were nursing the three babies. Only two had the customary purple silk wrap, the third had a plain, clean towel wrapped around it. It was customary to have two wraps on hand per birth, but no one had ever conceived three babies before, at least not in the palace.

The Matron walked to the nursemaid with the plain wrap. "Which of our treasures do we have here, nursemaid?"

"This is the one with the eyes, bright eyes like ..."

The Matron quickly cut in. "You will never again mention that in this palace!" She looked left and right, then addressed them all. "No one, do you all understand me? No one will ever talk of the eyes of this child. For that matter, no one will mention this child. There are but two babies here, one boy, one girl. Are we all quite clear on this?"

No one dared to argue with the Head Matron. Without truly understanding the magnitude of it, they all mumbled their oath.

The Matron pointed to the nursemaid with the baby wrapped in a plain towel. "You will come with me." The nursemaid followed Matron San back to the birthing chamber. Cleaning was almost finished.

Just as the maids prepared to leave with their buckets, the Matron addressed them. "Nursemaids, again, not one word of this child. Sha'Doe died giving birth to her second child. Understood?"

Too tired to do anything other than agree, the nursemaids nodded their pact.

***

The Emperor rubbed his hands together with excitement. "And what would you have me do about Hasuca? Do I look even remotely like his physician? I think not."

"I thought it my duty to inform you that your brother made good progress the last few days, but his illness has been quite abnormal. Each time it is worse, and it seems he could fall sick again at any moment."

The Emperor marched on as if he hadn't been spoken to. "Yes, but he has taken us all up this path more than once before. So, when you have some news, true to the concept of the word, give me notice." They turned another corner. "Ah, here we are, and so you are out of time. Hasuca managed to recover quite well, so that is all that needs to be said on the matter. Now, are you aware that

I have a son?" With that, he entered the birthing chamber as the doors swung closed behind him.

Unprepared, Matron San gasped to see the Emperor stride in. She was holding the sleeping boy with two different eyes, dressed in plain clothing.

The Emperor's face lit up at the sight of him. "Ah, there he is. The future of this most powerful nation." He took the boy from the Matron without a second look at her. "Yes, here is my boy, the future God-King of the entire world. This is a moment in time to be treasured for all of time."

At that moment, Maki walked in, frozen still at the sight of the Emperor holding a baby. He looked at Matron San, whose wide eyes said everything.

Maki wished he'd taken the baby and fled the palace as the Matron had wanted. If the infant opened his eyes it would be certain death – for more than just the boy. He watched in silent horror as the Emperor held the baby out on his forearm to admire his face and hummed a tune – badly. The baby still had its eyes closed and Maki prayed the baby would sleep long enough.

The doors from the adjoining room burst open and in came nursemaid Bora, holding another one of the newborns. The Emperor's face darkened like the winter's sky outside.

"What is the meaning of this? Matron Sen Ya San, *now* if you would!"

"Pardon me, Your Excellency. I was about to explain, but it did not seem appropriate as you were intent on your son. If Your Excellency would be seated, I do have some grave news."

The Emperor looked at the extra child and back to the one he had in his arms. Maki's mind was in a whirl, trying to work out how to get this explained without losing a child or his own head. He moved a chair forward for the Emperor to sit.

The Matron stood before him. If nothing else, she may be able to catch the baby before he smashed it through the sealed window.

"Excellency, I am sincerely sorry to bring this news at such a special time for you. It is my duty to inform you that our Queen-to-be, Sha'Doe, died giving birth to your second baby. I ask for your forgiveness in this matter, though I have not had time to take care of all the details as yet."

"I would have thought, Matron, keeping *me* informed would have been your highest priority."

The Matron didn't blink. "Indeed, Your Excellency, but the immediate pressing matter is feeding the two babies. I have done my best to cover this matter already."

"And what exactly have you done about this most unfortunate matter, Matron?"

Maki interjected. "Excellency, if I may. I have had one of the nursemaids go and fetch goat's milk for the, er, the twins, sire"

"Oh, you did, did you? Goat's milk for the ROYAL family! *What* were you thinking?"

Maki lowered his head, wishing the floor would swallow him whole. "Indeed, sire, goat's milk is very close to mother's milk. We did manage to get both the babies fed in Sha'Doe's dying moments but I'm afraid we need to have a strategy for their next feeding time before it happens, sire. After all, you are the only one to sire a baby in the palace at the moment, and so we did not, do not, have a surrogate at this juncture, Your Excellency."

The Emperor shook with rage. He stood up to glare at both the Matron and Maki. He now had the boy's head in his large hand and was not holding him with his free hand at all. The Matron watched the boy's sleeping face. In a low voice, the Emperor spoke. "You mean to say your contingency plan is to feed the twins with animal's milk, Maki?"

"Until we have a surrogate mother to feed the boys, sire" The Matron looked at Maki's face. He ignored her, looking instead at the new baby in the room.

"I have two sons? This *is* a day to remember. Two sons. One to play off against the other to get the best from both. We will see which one is the stronger to lead this most powerful nation on to its destiny. Yes, perfect." He put out his other hand to take the baby from the nursemaid. Unsure, the maid looked at the Matron.

A chill ran up Matron's spine. It was the girl. She hurried forward. "Emperor, may I help?" Before he could answer, she took the first baby and turned him around so the Emperor was not looking into his face. She then motioned to the nursemaid to hand the second baby over to the Emperor.

He smiled broadly, holding the two babies. He moved to the window, looking at the reflection of himself holding his children. He spoke so low that even the Matron and Maki could barely hear. "So here we are, Father. You are gone, and I have the sons you said I could never have. Look who has not one but *two* boys. Your Gods have no power, and I have everything I desired. What can you say to that, you feeble old fool?"

A lightning bolt struck a tree directly in front of the palace. The thunder was instant, shaking the palace to its core.

The baby dressed in silk startled just for a second and began to scream. The other, wrapped in a plain towel, just opened his eyes and looked directly at the Emperor in the impromptu mirror. The Emperor stared at the reflection, then blanched.

It was as if evil itself took over the Emperor's soul when the lightning struck the tree. He kicked the chair out of his way, and it hit the wall on the far side of the room and splintered. As he walked forward, he held out the baby in silk. The Matron took it and handed it to the nursemaid, nodding for her to bolt. There was no saving the boy with different coloured eyes. This was for the Gods to sort out now.

Maki grabbed one of the brass buckets full of unused towels and held it out. The Emperor dropped the baby into the bucket as Maki shoved more towels on top. Snatching it by the handle, the Emperor swung it around over his head. On its first turn, it hit the Matron across her forehead. Maki barely ducked in time. The Emperor was oblivious and continued to build momentum with every turn ... three ... four ... five turns. With a scream of hatred and raw anger, he released the bucket.

The bucket's bottom hit the window dead centre and, as if in slow motion, the window flexed. Just for a moment, it seemed it would hold but in truth, there was no hope of stopping the baby in his intended brass coffin.

With a loud shatter, the window gave way and the brass bucket disappeared into the freezing air outside with but a trail of towels.

For a moment, it was deathly quiet.

The freezing air and snow flurries poured into the room. The Emperor turned toward the doors. "Well, that is the bastard child taken care of, now to remove his bastard father! GUARDS!"

Two guards had already burst through the doors at the commotion. Through gritted teeth, the Emperor commanded, "You will fetch Master Xiang and tell him that he is to bring Hasuca with him immediately! There will be blood spilt for this! I can assure you of that! Now, GO!"

Like death itself in motion, the Emperor's black garments wafted in the freezing air as he ascended the stairs.

Maki hurried to the aid of the disoriented Matron. He attempted to hold her down but she slapped his hand away. "Would you get off me. I have many matters to attend."

"I will be attending your funeral if you don't give yourself a moment, woman."

Defiantly, Matron stood then collapsed. Maki caught her and eased her to the floor, propping up her back. He turned to see one of the nursemaids entering the room. "Maid, there is a towel over there and fetch some water, quickly now."

The Matron murmured. "What a fuss. Would you stop holding me down and unhand me at once!"

"I'm holding you up, not down, you old fool, and stop your demanding. We have much to work out."

The Matron brought her knees up and held her ankles for balance. "So, what would you do with this situation now, Maki?"

Being careful not to let her go, he moved in front of her. "Here, cup your hands like this." He coupled his hands as if he was getting a drink from a stream. "Hold them over your nose and mouth. Go on then."

Indignantly, she did.

"Good. Now try to slow and deepen your breaths." She tried to take her hands away to speak but he grabbed them so she had no choice. "Slow and deep." He smirked at her angry frown over her hands. "Slow and deep," he repeated. Her frown deepened.

Nursemaid Tam Bora returned with a clean towel and fresh water. Maki spoke sternly. "Listen very carefully. Take the girl downstairs. She must not be known to the Emperor. Do you understand me? Never!"

She repeated the instruction. "You think it is better for her not to be known to the Emperor."

The Matron lowered her hands slowly. "You did it on purpose, didn't you, Maki? When you let it slip about the two boys, you were already protecting the girl."

Maki ignored her as he pushed her hands back over her face. "She will be fine on goat's milk until she can eat solids. Let her be known only to those who need to. You have goat's milk in the kitchen on a regular basis. It will not be hard, just think before you act. She will have a life as the daughter of a serving maid. She will be educated, clothed and fed right here in the palace. Understand, Tam Bora?"

Bora lowered her voice. "Why have you kept this one the secret? I don't understand, Maki."

The Matron cut in. Maki tried to put her hands back but she slapped his hand away. "Maki is right! You will work it out in time but we don't have time right now. Go down and find Shu Memottu. Give her my apologies and tell her what has happened. Tell her that I am asking her to take you into her employment and to see to it that this child has a chance in life. Memottu will see that no harm will come to either of you."

Bora took the towel, dipped a corner in the fresh water and began to mop the Matron's forehead. Maki grabbed the towel. "No, Bora, you must go and go quietly. Now!"

Gracefully, the nursemaid got to her feet, bowed deeply and left the room.

The Matron took a breath. "Are we doing the right thing, Maki?"

"If the Emperor knew he had a daughter she would never have a chance in life against her brother. We have done what we have done. Now, if you'll excuse me, I have some important business to attend to."

He stood, but before he moved away, she grabbed him by the hand. "Where, Maki? Where will you go?"

An understanding passed between them. "Far from here." He helped her to her feet. "There are nursemaids in there who can help. They will need direction."

He stepped back and bowed to her. The Matron watched him go, then walked wearily to the window where the freezing wind blew flurries of snow into the palace. She peered down to the snow-covered ground below, turning over the recent events in her mind. What was it? What had she witnessed? *Think, woman, think.*

8 Misdirection

Maki made his way through the warren of halls, wondering how he was to survive this day. One thing was for sure, the Emperor was in his own world of hurt and over the next few days, he would bring a world of hurt to those around him. Maki would be in line for a slow and painful death. He would rather freeze. It would, at the very least, be more dignified.

He opened the doors and found himself in the hall of lust, the Den. He looked about for his daughter. The fire in the large, central hearth had burned down to a huge mass of coals. It gave enough light for him to see some concubines sitting about drinking wine and smoking opium while others slept.

He searched feverishly as he heard a sound not of the Den, but that of a dog snarling. In the corner, three concubines were tormenting the cornered dog. Curious, Maki made his way over to the laughter and tormenting. He stepped over some bodies, wondering if they had overdosed and were, in fact, dead. The serving of opium and wine had now gone on for a full day, and maybe was for some, just too long.

Maki was close to the snarling dog. "Alright, girls, you have had your fun now, leave the animal alone."

Surprised, they spun to see Maki. "Hey look, it's the cockless fool again."

Another pointed. "Hey, yeah, it's the perv from earlier. Want to have another perv, cockless one?" They stepped aside, revealing his daughter backed up in the corner with the monkey skull in her hand. Her top lip curled up as she snarled, blood dribbling down both sides of her mouth.

Maki froze. "Dear Gods, I am too late."

He eased forward, trying to be gentle. "Hey, Tammirie, what do you have there?" She was unmoving. "Hey, my girl, it's me, Maki. I have come to see you."

She pulled back and snarled again.

Maki crouched down, slowly edging closer. "It's okay, you know me. Everything will be alright now."

She backed into the corner, her legs pulled up to the side, impassively staring at him. He reached out and stroked her arm. "I am your …"

A foot kicked him fair in the middle of the back. Crouched down, he was pushed forward, slamming his head into hers. His head spun. Behind him, the laughter and taunting continued.

"There they are in the corner kissing, K.I.S.S.I.N.G!"

Maki rolled up onto his hands and knees, his head swimming in pain. All he could hear over the ringing in his ears was their taunting. "K.I.S.S.I.N.G!" The monkey head lolled back and forth on the floor. On shaking legs, he stood up with it in his hand. His eyes focused briefly on the three concubines who mocked him. He didn't care which one he hit. He threw the monkey head with all his might. Two women immediately fell to the floor and the monkey's skull hit the rafters overhead. For a moment, it rattled about then crashed down in the middle of the hearth. Red-hot coals flew everywhere and took hold with a whoosh. The flames took hold immediately. Eons-old cushions and scatter-pillows were instantly ablaze.

Maki returned to Tammirie, now unconscious with blood trickling down her forehead. His own head throbbed in sympathy. He scooped her up over his shoulder and staggered for the door. He stepped over the two concubines and smiled grimly. *Two with one shot. Could only be the Gods' will.* He started to grab some robes off the Emperor's clothes rack when a guard burst in to confront him.

"I know what you're thinking, Maki, but you can't just take the Emperor's clothes like this!"

Maki studied the guard for a moment. He grabbed a richly embroidered silk gown and stuffed it in the guard's uniform. "Get one of the mats, set it on fire and burn what is left. Take this home and give it to your wife and tell her five good reasons why she makes you happy in your life." The guard offered little resistance as Maki took what he needed and left.

The guard was dumbfounded at the chaotic scene of panicked concubines as the fire grew stronger. Through the growing haze, one circle of concubines handed around the smoking pipe. Fire from the hanging drapes caressed the back of one of them and her hair singed as the fire took hold. They were oblivious to the growing pandemonium.

Maki blended with those fleeing the Den for the hall. The guard grabbed another garment, stuffed it down the other side of his uniform and heaved a burning mat at the rack before merging into the crowd himself.

Maki's shoulder ached, but he didn't let up his pace. He could hear the screams of the women upstairs. A perfect distraction. He descended the lower echelons of the palace until the smell of the fire gave way to that of the underground stables.

"Not far now, my love. Hold on now, Tammirie, you hear me? Father's got you now."

He collided with two guards as he turned a corner. They frowned to see him with his parcel over his shoulder. Maki didn't hesitate. "Quick men, a fire has broken out upstairs, quickly! They need help or the palace will be lost!" He'd only gone around one more corner when two more guards appeared. He shouted. "Fire! Fire!"

Maki laboured under his precious load. His feet left trails as he dragged them through the sawdust that now spread over the basement. He finally came to a corridor that led to the outside of the palace. In the dim light, he could make out the figures of two men. They hugged one another and shook arms, speaking in low voices too quiet for Maki to hear. One of them opened the door, a blast of frigid air blew in, and the other was gone.

The remaining man watched for a moment then closed the door, latching it firmly. He was caught by surprise when he saw Maki. "Who are you to be down here at this time? Ah, Maki isn't it? What's this you have on your shoulder? Put it down this instant." It was Grand Master Xiang.

With the care of a loving father, Maki lowered his package to the ground. Slowly, he pulled the garment away from the girl's face. The bump to her head had formed to a swollen lump that had split and blood stains had dribbled down to her mouth.

Master Xiang stepped back. "By the Gods, what happened to this poor child, Maki?"

"It is a long story, Master Xiang. This is my daughter. If the Emperor finds us, we will die in a fashion to his liking."

Master Xiang looked at Maki and the large lump on his head. He wondered how the frail man had been able to carry her all this way on his own. "Where are you headed, Maki?"

"Out of here to the ... out of here ... away."

Master Xiang nodded. He'd seen men and women do amazing things for the love of a child. "Very well, Maki. Wait here and rest. I will not be long."

Maki looked down at his shivering daughter. Exhausted, he lay down beside her in an attempt to keep her warm.

***

"Maki, have a drink, just a little at a time, easy, just a little. That's the way."

Maki opened his eyes. In the dim light, Matron Sen was kneeling over him. He sighed deeply.

"That was a big sigh, Maki. Did I disturb your slumber?"

Maki smiled weakly. She gave him another drink. "And don't bother with your attitude either, Maki, just drink a little more. I have some food for us before we depart on this foolhardy trek."

Maki looked up to see Master Xiang grinning. "I wouldn't bother arguing, she has you pegged." He gave a cheeky wink then knelt beside the Matron. "I don't know about this damned trip of yours but all hell has broken out upstairs. You might as well try whatever it is you have planned.”

Maki scoffed, hitching himself up against the wall. “You old fool, I don’t have a plan.” His smile slid away. “How much food do we have for two people?”

The Matron answered solemnly. “We have enough for two, for a week,” she motioned at Tammirie, “But with her also, it will last maybe four or five days.”

Master Xiang eased himself up. “The snow is nine or ten feet deep out there. You can’t travel carrying her. I have one of my men making an adjustment to your supplies. I hope you will be pleased with it, but I have no way of knowing how you can withstand the nights. Last week, we found a man frozen to his horse. They were both dead, still standing, just ten minutes from here.”

Maki ignored the negativity. “Matron, can you fetch me ten servings of goat’s milk on a belt with a feeding bottle. Master Xiang, can I have some snowshoes, please? I do have one task to complete before we leave.”

Before either could answer, Maki pulled on the furs Master Xiang had brought over. The Matron went to question him on the goat’s milk but his mind was already elsewhere. She considered the unconscious Tammirie. *Maybe it will work.*

Maki went outside as Master Xiang shut the door and stood guard. The Matron felt the strain on her old legs. She’d not really thought of herself as old, but this hectic pace was taking its toll on her. After this day, the Emperor would seek to have her slaughtered. Staying was not an option.

Back in the lower kitchen, she searched around where she had spent most of her working life, until this morning, *Or was it yesterday morning?* She thought she would serve the palace her entire life, but now ... *Ah and a feeding bottle. As if the girl needs a feeding bottle. She may be young but I would have thought she was off the titty a long time ago.*

With everything together, the Matron made her way back into the tunnels and paused briefly when she smelt a cooking fire. She smiled at the thought of a hot meal before leaving.

As she came around the last corner, she heard Maki cooing, then the gentle squawk of a baby. She stood stock-still at the sight of Maki squatting by the fire with a baby on his lap.

He realised she was back. "At last. I was getting a little worried about you. You can only keep these little screamers quiet for so long you know. Would you?"

The Matron saw the tongs and hot stones. She'd heated milk a thousand times but now found herself unable to move.

"Matron, we are waiting. Now, quietly."

Still, she didn't move. Her wrinkled old face was a blank canvas. Maki motioned to the baby with his chin. "Ah, you're wondering which one this is, aren't you?" He grabbed a big, brass bucket from behind his back. "Ha, worked well, don't you think?" He chuckled at his proud achievement. "Matron, the hot stones, if you would."

San fell to her knees, staring at the baby and moved aside the blanket to reveal its face. "Oh, bless the Gods! Bright Eyes … is alive!"

9 The Boy

The canopy of the jungle barred most of the midday's hot rays whilst the understory sent the rest of the light fragments dancing over the jungle floor. Soundlessly, the panther slinked to the river's edge, a chunk of blood-dripping meat suspended from its teeth. A low growl, and puffing in the day's heat, he had eaten his fill and was thirsty. Another low growl as he saw a canoe coming downriver.

One man paddled; another dangled a small boy in the water. As the boy was pulled up by one leg, he gasped a desperate breath, and with a splash was gone again, then back up, a breath, and down again. The laughter of the two men was deep and menacing. The panther crouched; survival first. The panther saw the boy, and the boy saw the panther.

For a fleeting moment, the boy thought he saw someone on the riverbank just before being dunked again. As they pulled him up, his jaw trembled. *Try to stay calm,* he thought. *They must be looking for me.*

Tyab was sitting at the rear of the canoe, watching Maha tormenting the boy. The boy was not black like the rest of them, but not white either. Tyab knew who his father was. The boy had better never return, or they would all be killed by jungle tradition, as was the way.

***

The white sandy beach was backed by rainforest. At the coast of the jungle lands of Zimbali, the trees were not as tall as the inner jungle, though the canopy still soared up hundreds of feet. Its flora and fauna were the Earth's most diverse.

The biggest watercourse to emerge from the jungle's labyrinth of mountains and valleys was the Begonia River. Its port was the largest and a safe distance inside the breakwater. Tides were benign there, so the wharf wasn't high but extended a very long way out. It was the only port that could support the big galleons that frequented this part of the coast. Port Begonia was the nation's trading stronghold.

The wide, wooden walkway was lined with numerous shops and storage sheds. The proud, dark people wore colourful clothing as they carried heavy loads on their heads. Mighty galleons and countless small boats and canoes were crowded with people bartering and trading.

The darkest of men making his way along the wharf measured head and shoulders above any other. He abruptly pushed aside anyone in his way. He was Mensa, and, as second son to the King and Queen, was the wharf supervisor. He and his bullies ruled, literally, with a mean fist.

Mensa was heading for the *Shiraz*, a galleon from the land of endless dunes, Audun. This galleon was far longer and towered over anything else that frequented Mensa's wharf. Inside the high bow was the galley with a low chimney puffing smoke. Behind that was an extensive deck where the cargo was tied down. The captain's room was next, with a pole that flew the flags of the next ports it was going to.

The captain's door opened onto the rear deck before the steps up onto the rudder deck. Here was where Captain Tarrant would spend his time at sea, looking over his cabin to the horizon. Below the top decks were the oar shutters that ran almost the entire length of the vessel. Once the drums rolled, the oars would be put through the shutters to push the mighty galleon away from the wharf to begin the next intrepid journey to another port, another land.

Mensa and Captain Tarrant had a longstanding business relationship. Mensa smirked as he heard the captain hurling abuse at his deckhands. He walked smoothly down the plank onto the *Shiraz*, stopping a short distance from the captain.

Tarrant spoke over his shoulder. "Well, it's greetings to you, my friend. You got the merchandise you mentioned?"

"I never could get close to you on that old piece of junk you captained before. I expected it would be easier on this new vessel, you old sea buzzard."

Captain Tarrant turned to stand face to face with the bulking wharf boss. A good deal shorter, he did the best he could, gawking up. He thumbed over his shoulder. "You mind your mouth, you piece of monkey shit, or I will toss your ass to these hungry sharks lurking about today." Tarrant looked up at Mensa's head. "What happened to ya bloody hair – you in disguise or something?" They clasped forearm to forearm and shook firmly.

Mensa rubbed his smooth head. "It would take more than a haircut, I feel." He swung the sack down from his shoulder. "This is it, the boy." He backhanded the captain on the chest. "Get this. I send two bums upriver to get him, but they get drunk and fall asleep in the canoe on the way back. The boy paddles them back here, right into my hands. Doesn't that beat all?"

The captain adjusted his crumpled leather cap, which looked like it had been mauled by a lion or similar. He noticed Mensa didn't call the boy by name. "You really do have the luck of the Devil, boy." He took on a more serious look. "How many more before yous get what you're after, Mensa?"

Mensa considered the question. "Two. But once I get the Queen, he will be easy pickings."

Captain Tarrant pulled the pipe from his mouth and spat to one side. He prodded Mensa's chest with it. "I never took on such a task, but if anyone can pull this off, you can. Had it worked out all this time, didn't you?"

Mensa pushed aside the pipe. "It has been a long time in the making, but yes, I'm getting closer. I would have it now if the Pharaoh had not come along and ruined a perfectly good plan."

"Losing his daughter is a high price he's going to pay for that. Mind you don't suffer a backlash."

"On the contrary, my friend, it will make him my ally."

"Yous be careful doing the Devil's work for him. You might get burned."

Mensa held up his black hands. "Ha, who would know? It looks to me like I'm already burned."

The two men laughed. The sack Mensa had carried onto the deck moved. Mensa eyed it coolly. "I don't care what you do with this one. Just be sure he never sets foot on this land, or everyone involved will die. Do we have an understanding, Tarrant?"

The captain met Mensa's stare. "Well then, best I play it safe and do a little shark fishing along the way."

"Shall I put this one in the hold for you then?" Not waiting for an answer, he kicked the sack, sending it flying over the first five steps. It bounced twice before hitting the bottom and rolling along the floor. The string tying the top unravelled, and a boy half rolled out of the sack. He was bleeding from his nose and his left earlobe was hanging by a thread of flesh. The boy didn't move.

Down below, a black man even bigger than Mensa looked at the boy sprawled out on the floor. Suddenly something caught his attention. The big man peered up into a dark recess of the rafters. Through the shadows emerged a vision of three beautiful spirit women staring back down at him. One was clearly of his kind; one of the other two looked at him with the most intense, green eyes. They stared at one another for a time, then the vision faded into the abyss. The big man pulled his attention back to the boy. *To have three beautiful guides watching over him, he must be someone special.*

Above deck, Tarrant scoffed at Mensa. "The sharks will make a quick meal of him. You've done half my job for me, boy. What did you do with the two drunks? I know they would've paid a price."

Mensa grinned at Tarrant. "Ha, you know me well, my friend.

Yes, I stripped and pegged them out over a red-tailed ant's nest. As we speak, they will be sobering up to find that they are getting their privates sunburnt. But it won't be so bad. The ants will be getting their fill on the little honey I basted on them. It's when that runs out that the ants will get nasty. It takes three days to get rid of one ant bite. I would sooner be stung by bees." Their raucous laughter carried on the breeze.

"I suppose you'll still charge me extra for the boy?"

Captain Tarrant took a puff on his pipe. He hadn't yet bought a boy for this voyage, and it was to be a long trip. He kept his thoughts to himself. He would not like to be on the wrong side of the cold, calculating Mensa. "It's an extra that much is true." He spat again. Tapping the pipe on the back of his hand, he chose his words carefully. "No, Mensa, I'll not charge ya one ounce more because I know you'll stand by your word. I get control of these waters and all cargo to pass over them. That's what we agreed, right?"

"I need an ally on these waters. One I can trust. If you think you can be that man, business for both of us will thrive. A win for me and a win for you, old man."

Captain Tarrant lifted his chin and used his gnarled fingers to scratch his grey beard. "Win-win, you say, boy, sounds good to me." They shook hands once more and, without another thought of the boy, Mensa left along the plank.

Tarrant wiped a bead of sweat from his temple, took off his old leather cap and mopped his head. He thought of the two drunks lying on the ant nest in the unrelenting sun and winced.

His oarsmen sweated profusely as they loaded supplies. He checked their work to be sure the load would not shift in rough weather. "Be sure to tie off those ropes properly, or I promise you, I'll be making shark bait of ya."

The men didn't so much as lift a head, toiling under the burning sun. Tarrant scratched his chin once more, then remembered his little treat. The boy. He walked down the stairs into the oars room.

The sack and the boy were gone.

He adjusted his eyes to the gloom and was about to move deeper into the oars room when a man appeared before him. "You looking for this, Cap?"

Tarrant looked at the huge, black man indicating at the seat to his right. There, still out cold, lay the boy, covered with the sack. Tarrant reached out but the black man stood firmly in his way.

The roof was six foot six, but this man needed to hunch. "No, Cap, not this one, not this time, not this trip."

"You black piece of shit. Who the Devil do ya think yous talking to? I'll make a sea anchor of you. Don't think I won't, Blacky."

Baako didn't shift. "Then this life will be gone to me."

There was a loud thump on the roof and a man called out in pain. Tarrant spun about and headed for the stairs, mumbling. "Damn fool boys. If me cargo is damaged there'll be a whipping and pays docked."

Baako looked at the boy and spoke to the man at the porthole. "Yuasa, hand me the salty rag. I need to fix the boy's ear."

Yuasa looked at Baako. "No, wait until we get out of the harbour, tonight I will get it. Harbour water not the best you knows, Baako."

"Yes, but I want to put on the ants before he wakes. It would draw less attention."

Yuasa cautiously looked at the two drummers throwing dice at the back of the boat. He reached up and pulled a rag from a slot over one of the joists. Carefully, he tore off a small strip and put the rag back. He reached under his seat and pulled out a length of rope, tying the rag to it. Checking the drummers again, he popped it out of the porthole, left it there for a while then pulled it up soaked in salt water. He passed the rag to Baako.

Gently, Baako cleaned the earlobe. Yuasa's attention was on one of the men further back, who showed his teeth and waved two fingers at him. Yuasa waved three fingers, and the man turned to another further back, repeating the gesture. Baako looked at Yuasa and shook his head. The man, Cho, was from Middle Kingdom.

Baako had tended his wounds when Cho had come aboard. Everyone said he would die, but Baako stayed with him and he lived. But three ants were a lot to use on a small boy. Valuable because they were for wounds that may be sustained on a rough voyage, they couldn't all be used on a boy. However, Baako was insistent, so Cho gave up the container without further hesitation. He looked at Yuasa, who checked the two drummers again. They were absorbed in their wagering game. Yuasa gave the signal, and Cho lifted the bench seat ever so quietly.

The bench seats, for the rows of three oarsmen, covered an on-board latrine. Twice a day an oarsman had the duty of carrying buckets of water down to flush the waste.

Cho lowered the seat. A few maggots crawled over a small rusty tin. He opened the lid and inserted the maggots, then tossed the tin to Yuasa. Carefully removing one ant from the group that was fighting over the maggots, he held the ant whilst Baako held the cleaned earlobe together. Yuasa pressed the insect onto the cut flesh. It locked on with its large jaws, sealing the wound. Yuasa twisted the body off, leaving the ant's head and jaw locked tight. He repeated the process twice more, ending up with a clean wound.

The boy groaned and slowly moved. Rolling onto his back, he opened his eyes. He looked up to a familiar, smiling face. "Father, what has happened? Where are we?"

Baako spoke softly. "You will be all right, boy. We are going on a big trip together."

The boy drifted off to sleep. Baako looked up at a surprised Yuasa. "You're the boy's pappy?" asked Yuasa.

Baako chuckled. "No, I never saw this boy before."

"You only need to have known his mother for a night to be his pappy," Yuasa said with a sly grin.

Baako smirked at the humour. "Sadly, I have not had the chance to have loved a woman for much longer than this boy is old." His mind searched back for a distant memory of a time gone by.

For a long time, Baako had been down in the lower deck with a steel collar chained to the floor. Mensa had handed him to Tarrant for free as slave labour on the condition that Baako and his mother never returned to Zimbali. It had been far too long since he'd seen his mother. There was just one port where Baako was allowed up deck to see her, the City of Samos and this was meant to be one of those trips. He had accepted that this was now his life, but only if he knew his mother was safe and well.

Captain Tarrant's door slammed, and the abuse began. The gangplanks were thrown onto the wharf and a whip cracked twice as two men called out in pain. The stairwell darkened as a flood of stark-faced men descended into the oars room.

"Watch your every move. He has a scorpion up his ass today."

Still the boy slept. This was going to be a trip to remember. A trip of great change.

With a flurry of abuse, the drummers started the beat, and all the oars were in the water. They were on their way.

Baako tried not to think about his mother. It had been so long, but for all the captain's faults, Baako had never caught him out in a lie. Tarrant had assured him that his mother was fine; they just hadn't been given the right cargo for that port.

He reminisced about growing up in the jungle. How privileged he had been to be the son of a great man, the King. It was still a good life for those who knew the jungle. He looked down at the boy, wondering what the boy's story was.

After some time, Captain Tarrant came down the steps. "Are ya to let that dead weight sleep the trip away?"

"No, just as soon as I feel he is right enough, I will have him flush the benches and fetch drinking water and bread for the men. He will earn his keep like everyone else on this voyage, Captain."

Tarrant grunted. "You see that he does". He turned to leave the way he came when Baako's deep voice answered. "Do not forget, Tarrant, the boy didn't choose this voyage, he's just here now."

The captain faced Baako, his spit just missing the sleeping boy. "Don't you forget your place in this, Blacky." He fingered the whip on his belt as they locked eyes for a long moment, then left.

Yuasa looked past Manjee to Baako at the end of their oar. "You had better not think that just because you been on this boat longer than the rest of us, he won't throw you overboard as a sea anchor."

Manjee was shorter than Baako but taller than Yuasa, which was why he rowed in the middle. He was from the land of the Pyramids, Orion and was put into slavery for crimes against the land, but in fact was an innocent victim. His teeth were black from a bad diet, but he spoke a little better than Yuasa. "He does have a point, Baako. What is the boy to you anyway?"

"When he rolled out of the bag, he looked up at me and I felt a connection. I don't know why, I just did."

Manjee started to mock. "Oh, isn't that just the sweetest thing. Hey, Yuasa, the big fella's got a heart."

Yuasa took the lead. "Oh yes, that's our Baako. A little boy spills two drops of blood, and who is there to mop up after him? Baako, guardian angel of the Mighty Spirit." The two sniggered.

Baako pushed his oar a little further forward.

Yuasa looked at his hand. "Hey, Manjee, look, I got a splinter in me little finger. What should I do?"

Baako took a longer stroke forward but maintained a dignified silence.

Manjee held up his dirty right hand, calluses in the palm and salt sores on the back. "Oh no, I have a broken nail. What should *I* do, Yuasa?" They laughed again. They only had one hand each on their oar as they slapped each other on the back.

Baako swung back the oar and slammed the men on the temples. Both dropped like stones with Manjee falling over the still sleeping boy. Baako's oar creaked as he resumed rowing, his powerful arms now doing the task of three.

The boy stirred and emerged from under his unwanted covering. He sat for some time, looking about and getting his bearings.

Without pausing his rowing, Baako spoke just to the boy. "You all good?"

"Yes, thank you. My head hurts, but I am good." He looked up at Baako, surely the biggest man he'd ever seen. Sweat dripped from his efforts as his back and shoulders bent the massive oar with every stroke.

Hands on hip, the boy asked, "And what may I ask is your name, kind sir?"

Baako smiled. *Courage and good manners.* "My name is Baako. I have been a slave to this captain for longer than you have been walking this earth. So, what is your name, my young companion?"

The boy opened his mouth, then shut it again. He frowned, then lowered his head for a long moment. Baako waited patiently. The boy's eyes unfocused as he searched the recesses of his mind. Eventually, he looked up, a little bewildered.

Baako spoke quietly. "You've had a nasty bang to the head. It will come back to you when it's ready, lad." He gave the boy a wink and a small smile.

"You say you have seen this before? I will be fine soon, you say?" A glimmer of hope lit his young face.

"Sure, boy. See the man three rows back behind me?"

The boy had not yet noticed just how many men were on this vessel. He struggled to identify which man Baako meant. "Yes, sir, I see him."

Baako knew this was untrue, but it didn't matter. "When he came aboard this vessel, he was bleeding from both ears. Everyone said he would surely die, but he lived, though he didn't remember anything for a long time. Then, in a bad storm, he got another bump on the head and just like that, it all came back."

The boy's eyes finally came to rest on an individual with a shaven head with many scars over it. He continued observing the room they were in. The floor was curved so any water that seeped in ran to the sides. The ceiling was the same. To the front was a ladder into the galley; to the rear, steps led up to the rear deck. He also saw that behind each of the oars with men rowing, was a bench seat. "Three men to an oar, twenty oars per side, plus two drummers, that makes one hundred and twenty-two men." The two on the floor were still unconscious. "Mostly doing something. Please, Baako, what can I do?"

Baako had watched the boy processing this in his head – most on the vessel couldn't have counted the men at all. The boy wasn't as black as those in Baako's tribal lands, although his skin was not white either. His steel-blue eyes had a depth to them that they, along with his height, belied his young age. He was well-mannered and well-spoken. Baako liked that. He explained where to get a bucket and a scraper, then waited for his return.

"Very good, see that little hatch just in front of my oar?"

The hatch in the vessel's side was almost at floor height and big enough to fit the bucket through. The boy studied it carefully so Baako chose to say nothing. The boy opened the hatch and squatted to get the water.

"See the rope on the handle? Put the loop on the hook beside the hatch, just in case."

The boy nodded as he did so, then bent down to put the bucket out. In a flash, he was gone.

Baako lurched forward, but his steel collar stopped him short. He turned and grabbed Manjee, flinging him towards the porthole. Having just woken, Manjee screamed at the water rushing past.

Baako shook Manjee's legs, yelling, "You will grab that boy or I will let you go!"

Manjee leant out as far as he could with Baako holding onto him. The water surged over him as his hands searched. Finally, he let out a yell, and Baako pulled them in, the boy still holding the bucket. With a deep belly laugh, Baako lifted the boy up, the bucket sloshing salt water everywhere.

Abruptly, the drums changed their rhythm. The room instantly fell quiet. Baako lowered the boy, staring at the two drummers. They were grim-faced, looking directly ahead. Baako's smile dropped. He would let them be, for now. He heard footsteps as Tarrant stopped behind him. Ignoring him, Baako lifted the bench seat and a scurry of cockroaches rustled off. Wide-eyed and pale, the boy stepped forward toward the latrine. The cockroaches dropped to the bottom as maggots writhed along the sides.

"Well, boy, it will be your job, twice a day, every day, to flush this out. You think you can do that?"

The boy moved to go to the end of the seat, but in his eagerness, he forgot that the rope was still on the hook. It snapped tight over his left shoulder, whipping him around and pulling him down at the same time. He fell to his knees and dropped the bucket, spilling its contents over the floor. The two drummers laughed aloud.

The captain glared at Baako. "A waste of me cargo space, dragging the boat down and making the men work harder than they need. What is that slacker doing sleeping?" Yuasa was still out cold. Tarrant began to pull his whip from his hip.

Baako stepped in front of him. "I'm sorry, Captain Tarrant. It was my fault for not putting the oar in the water properly, so when we put on the weight, it jumped back and smacked him in the head. He will be up soon enough. I can go on without him till he's better."

The captain marched to a drummer. "Is this true? If he lies, by the hot coals of hell, I'll make a sea anchor of him right now!"

The drummer avoided looking at anyone and took his time to respond. Baako reached down to grab his chain and gently put some weight on it. Without a sound, it pulled tight on the bolt in the floor. He waited for the answer.

"I didn't see what happened, Cap."

The captain studied him for a moment, then eyeballed the other drummer. "And what of you, did ya see what happened?"

The second drummer had his answer ready. "I did hear a scuffle, Cap, but didn't see anything in time to say how it happened. It may be as Baako says, maybe."

Baako stood up straight with his right leg in front of the chain, hiding it from the captain's view. He put more tension on it, and the boards groaned under the strain.

One row back, Acrom saw the chain. He knew how wrong it was that Baako was wearing it. He looked at the big man's massive back. His muscles were poised and knees slightly bent, putting immense weight on the chain which was wrapped around his wrist. The floor creaked.

Acrom pondered the situation of the crew. Some of the oarsmen were chained criminals, others were free, paid workers. They'd come from various provinces, Zimbali, Orion, Audun and even Samos in Middle Kingdom. Like Baako, most had loved ones in various ports. He weighed it up, over one hundred and twenty men from five different ports, on one boat. He sighed. *Those are bad odds. Very bad.*

Just when it looked like Captain Tarrant had reached a decision, the boy stepped out from behind Baako and spoke. "I'm sorry, Captain. I will get my sea legs soon enough, and I promise to work as hard as any man on your very fine vessel, sir."

The captain stroked his beard. "Oh, you do, do you? Well, boy, if you want to be one of the men, you have to be treated like one of the men." His whip cracked.

Baako instinctively dropped the chain and bent over the boy to protect him. The whip lashed over the two of them. Finally, Tarrant dropped the whip to the floor. He was breathing hard. The men looked at Baako's back. New welts formed and sweat mixed with beads of blood. Neither he nor the boy had cried out. Slowly, Baako stood to his full height. He stood defiant before Tarrant.

Equally defiant, Tarrant stood in front of the hulking frame and coiled his whip. He put his fists on his hips. "Just one more thing, and he will not make it to the next port. You 'ears me, Blacky?"

Baako spoke softly. "I 'ears you, Captain." Some of the men snickered at Baako's mimicking.

Captain Tarrant looked around the hold for the culprits, but the oarsmen remained straight-faced. "Right," he snapped as he headed for the top deck.

Baako stepped forward towards the drummers, and the chain on his neck snapped tight just short of them. They flinched, averting Baako's glare.

***

That night, the men spread out. The unchained men were free to move to the top deck to sleep in fresh air. Those in chains, like Baako, had to sleep where they were. The boy rolled up his sack and gave it to Baako for a pillow.

Baako watched him sleep, wondering about the three beautiful spirits.

10 The Shiraz

Most mornings, the boy was the first to rise to get everyone their rice drink. He always served the fat drummers last; this gave the oarsmen extra time. He had worked out a routine. First, he went back to open the hatch, being careful to latch it so that it would remain open. Baako had warned him, 'If you don't latch it open, Enki the Sea God will rock the boat, slamming the hatch closed. I have seen boys lose their whole hand this way.'

The boy left the jug on the hook. Bracing himself in the hatch opening, he dipped it in the water. He had become adept at his chores and was able to fill it to the brim every time. The only thing he hadn't worked out was why the drummers were so fat.

The boy did one side, then crossed over to the other side and removed the plug from the end seat.

Matken, a weedy little man with malice in his eyes, watched him. "Why you wastin' ya time with that, ya dumb bastard. Just a waste of time likes ya self, that's what I say, boooy …"

"You should know why I'm doing this, Maaaatken."

Matken's head snapped around as several of the men snickered behind him. He spun back to the boy. "Cheeky little shit, who does ya think ya speaking to?" The boy ignored him, continuing with his chores. "Where is ya from, hey, boy? Looks at ya. Ya eyes too big, ya skin too light and too dark. Yous belong no wheres."

The knot in the boy's stomach tightened. He closed the seat and moved back to the next one.

"So, tell us, where's ya from, boooy?"

The boy now choked back tears. For the life of him, he couldn't answer. He looked up to Lendud, who pulled hard on the oar beside Matken. Lendud seemed to be focused on nothing in particular in front of him. Next to him, the sweat trickled down over Cho's bald head and ran down over well-defined muscles as he observed the boy.

The knot in the boy's stomach tightened a little more.

"Come on, booooy, everyone's listening. Where's ya from?" Matken hissed. "Tell us, boooy. What's ya pappy's name?"

The boy knew he was different, with his skin and steel-blue eyes. He looked to Matken, whose eyes danced with laughter and malice.

"Yous don't know, does ya, boooy? You really is a bastard, boooy."

The boy knew he was of good blood, but he just couldn't remember. The knot in his belly tightened too much, and he snapped. Without considering what he was about to do, and without thinking of the mean captain, he acted in the blink of an eye.

In three quick paces, he ran forward. Keeping his eyes on Matken, he leapt up and grabbed the oar Matken was on and swung under it. Feet together, he smashed them into Matken's face. Matken's head snapped back with a crack, still with the boy swinging through. They tumbled over the seat. The boy was now on Matken's still body. With all his rage, he rained punches down on the malicious man.

His rage so strong, he didn't notice the big hands come down and lift him clear of his victim. Lendud wrapped the boy in powerful arms and whispered in his ear. "Shhh, it's over now. Stop now, shhh."

The boy came around to find himself sobbing out his shame.

There was a call from the drummer. "There he is, Cap. He started the whole thing!"

The boy looked down at Matken, he was going to get his just deserves. A hand reached in, grabbed the boy by his hair and pulled him up. The security of Lendud's arms fell away. "Captain, what are you doing? Stop! Let me go!"

The captain didn't let him go, nor did he stop dragging him. "You come onto my vessel and starts trouble again. I will let you go alright, boy."

The captain dragged the boy past Baako and up the stairs, but was careful to keep well out of reach of the big, dark man.

Outside, the light was blinding. The boy clenched his teeth. If he were to be whipped, he would give Tarrant no joy for it. Tarrant slammed the boy onto the deck and instantly blood spilled from the back of his head. The sun exploded behind his eyes. He could now see the stars as the sun turned to fog.

***

As the fog began to clear, he opened his eyes to the rustling of leaves from the trees high above him. He peered up at the lower canopy of the jungle. He felt at peace with himself. All his pain and grief immediately dissipated. The men and boys who were running about were dark. Dark like Baako, one even looked like Baako. Some had bows, others were putting darts into long tubes as they looked upwards.

Chimpanzees jumped though the canopy as the arrows and darts flew. The boy saw one chimp hit as it ran along the branches. It screamed as it changed its direction. The boy glanced to the people but they seemed not to notice. He quickly made chase on his own.

He ran through the humid jungle. Watching above, he could see the chimp slowing down. It came lower in the canopy then stopped and pulled out the dart. Just for a moment, it turned the dart around in its fingers as if making study of it then swayed and fell from the branch.

The boy ran forward to find a small gully just ahead. He slid down the bank and searched. He was on his own. He checked his right hand and saw he was holding a spear. He pulled the knife from his left hip and walked towards the end of the gully. There, staring back at him, was the chimp lying on its back where it had slid to the bottom of the embankment.

The boy instinctively knew what he must do.

He rolled the knife in his left hand, getting close to the chimp. He saw a hint of recognition in the chimp's eyes. It understood.

Now stood over the chimp, the boy hesitated. The chimp pursed its lips and made low cooing sounds. The boy felt akin to it somehow. Suddenly, the chimp's eyes swelled in fear, but it wasn't looking at the boy; it was baring its teeth as it glared past him.

The boy spun on his heel to see the tiger before him. The boy had his weapons, but the tiger had its own formidable defences. The only advantage was in the planning and surprise of an attack, but this was lost to the boy. He was on his own and the tiger stood in the way of his only escape.

He watched as, in slow motion, the tiger began to pace forward. Powerful. Confident. The drying leaves puffing out from under its huge paws, its shoulders flexed as it paced, ever closing the distance between them. On the jungle floor, tree roots poked up from the ground. The boy dropped his knife to the leafy floor.

Two hands on the spear, the boy stepped forward, glaring into the dark, menacing eyes of this natural-born killer.

***

Cold, salt water snapped the boy back to reality. He opened his eyes and stared down into the abyss. He was weightless and just for a moment, it seemed surreal. The boy held his breath. Without warning, his legs snapped out tight. He screamed in pain through his gritted teeth as he was suddenly dragged through the water by his ankles.

This was Tarrant's sea anchor.

There was only one way to freedom, back up the line. Instinctively, he curled himself forward and pulled himself up the rope until he could push with his feet to stand up along his bindings. The hull of the vessel carved a line through the water. Still submerged, he could see the paddles crashing in, moving along the hull then disappearing again. He looked up to the rudder, and as he did, he began to move higher. Suddenly, he broke the waves and snatched a quick breath before sliding back under.

Tarrant looked over the side as the hemp rope snapped tight. "'Tis a shame, boy. You hads something about you." He pulled the tobacco tin from his pocket and a knife from his belt, gawking at the horizon. "Storm's a brewin. Best I warn the cook to lock down the fire." Licking off the tobacco, he slipped the knife away and headed down the stairs. He heard a deep, husky voice.

"Captain."

"Not now, Baako; I got duties."

The voice didn't falter. "Yes now. Right now, Captain Tarrant."

The captain slowed to a standstill. The drummers stopped the beat and the oars stopped rowing. A hush came over the crew. Over one hundred and twenty men on board and not a sound.

The captain slowly turned back to face the big man. "I have the key to your mother's life, remember. I could have her head delivered to you if you don't mind your tongue, Blacky." Tarrant only called Baako 'Blacky' when he was angry. Tobacco-black spit broke through his teeth. "You is chained to my vessel. That means I owns you."

Baako stepped back over his chain. The entire crew watched as he bent his knees and wrapped the chain around his arm several times. Without a word, he began to pull. His huge thighs swelled as the boards began to groan. Baako stared at Tarrant as the timbers pulled up further. The muscles in his back and shoulders strained. Fuelled by anger of the boy drowned, he continued to pull. Finally, he roared out, and with a huge crack, the timbers splintered.

Baako stepped forward with his untethered chain in his hand. "I hold my own chain, Captain. So, who owns me now?"

The captain appeared even smaller and whiter, with Baako towering over him, though he didn't turn a hair. Neither a tremble nor a bead of sweat formed on his brow.

"Where is the boy, Captain?" Baako's voice was low and controlled, as was Tarrant's answer.

"I wont's tolerate trouble on my vessel, you knows this. I deal with the boy as I deal with anyone. He won'ts be coming back. Go see for yourself, if you dares with that chain around ya neck." A smile almost cracked his old, leathered face.

Baako brushed past the captain and, for the first time outside of Samos, went to the top deck. As he got there, he heard the captain bellowing. "A strip of leather on me hip says you lot had better get the oars going again."

Baako went onto the rudder deck to where the hemp rope was tied off. A deep furrow crossed his brow. The rope went directly down under the front of the rudder, not pulled out to the rear as he would have thought. The weight of his steel collar was more evident as he leaned over the side, and he pulled the rope; it was tight, unmoving. He had worn the collar for longer than he wished to think on, but right now it was really cutting his wick. He looked back to Tarrant's room. Baako was already in a world of hurt, he might as well go all the way now.

He turned the handle on Tarrant's door but couldn't bring himself to go in. It was an invisible line that blocked his entry.

"Just thought you could go right in, did ya, Blacky?"

"No, Captain, just see no point in this anymore," pulling on his iron collar. "I know where my mother is. I know my place and my job. There was never a need for this."

Tarrant sniffed. "Don't come much clearer than that, but then I did always like talking to ya." He went inside and rattled about for some time before returning. "Well, get on ya knees." Baako knelt. Tarrant stepped behind him, suddenly grabbing a handful of hair and kneeing Baako in the back. He snarled in his ear. "If I don't get to Samos port, Tark will kill ya mamma. You gots it, Blacky?"

"I know, Cap, I know."

Tarrant unlocked the collar and let it drop. It fell onto the back of Baako's legs, and he groaned through a closed mouth as he stood to face the captain. "I couldn't pull it up."

Tarrant looked confused.

"The rope, Captain. I couldn't pull it back up. It's stuck under the vessel."

"What does that matter now?" Tarrant gruffed.

Tarrant moved onto the rudder deck and peered over the side. "In the name of the Creator and sea critters, how did it get under there?" He pulled off his leather cap and wiped his brow.

Baako could feel the sun on his back and the sea breeze on his face, but he knew not to overindulge. Sometimes life could hand out the hardest slap of reality. He picked up the chain and carried it over to the large box outside Tarrant's cabin and dumped it in.

Tarrant watched Baako head downstairs. "Well, I'll be danged." He turned back to the rope and tugged it just to check. It was a futile effort. He removed the rudder rope so he could move it side to side. The rudder seemed loose enough. He slipped the rope back on and walked down to the box outside his cabin. Baako's chain was on the top. Custom-made, it was easily the biggest he had in there. *And now I let the black bastard walk free! I must've surely lost it.* He slammed the lid shut.

The kitchen door opened and the cook, Ayton, stepped out. "Cccaptain, I sssays there a sstorm a brewin'. Bbbest eat nnnow."

The captain licked a finger and held it to the sky then stomped down the stairs to address the men, mumbling to himself as he went.

Downstairs, he walked to a side hatch and spat. "Alright you scumbags, cut-throats and pick-a-pockets, there's a mean storm brewin' and it's already drawing us in. Best you have your last food and a little rest. It will be on us by nightfall. Be a long night and by sunup, expect to have a few bruises and a story to tell ya families. I see a few younger lads here. By the time it's over, there will be only men and a few of you won't make it at all. Enjoy ya meals." He spat through the hatch again and left.

The men ate in relative silence, and before long, they were back on the oars.

The day turned to night and the thunder rumbled overhead. Tarrant had locked the doors to downstairs and to his cabin to keep the water out. At the rudder, Tarrant gripped on tightly as he navigated his precious *Shiraz* against the turbulence. Lightning slashed through menacing black clouds almost constantly now. This was going to be a test of his vessel *and* his men. He pulled his leather cap down tightly around his head and sat on the side, letting his muscles rest as much as he could.

The torrential rain started abruptly. Tarrant couldn't see the bow or the towering swells as it lashed his face, though he didn't need to. He could rudder a storm with his eyes closed.

Under the heavy cloud, the lightning was almost blinding, but it gave him a glimpse of the next massive swell being hurled at his prized vessel. Each time it crested a wave, he reaffirmed his grip on the rudder, feeling the swell pass under and ensuring he pointed the vessel straight down the back of it. Even if he was just a little off, the swell would try to massage his vessel into a death roll. The runs down the back were longer and steeper than ever; sometimes, the vessel would gain so much speed that he wondered if it would just plough right into the next swell.

As time wore on, the struggle began to take its toll on the old seaman. His body ached and his shoulders burned. Even his teeth hurt from clenching. The storm was relentless.

A wet slap on his back almost knocked him from his post.

Below deck, the oarsmen had hung up every second oar and turned around so to double the number of men on each oar. Six men to an oar gave better holding to the floor as the swell passed.

When the vessel crested, it cut through, letting the waves wash high along the side. Sometimes they were high enough to slap the oars so hard that three men couldn't hold them, with a gruesome result. But it was better to die instantly than to live a cripple. For the slaves, instant death was common. A man chained to the floor by his neck couldn't be thrown far.

The galleon was sinking ever so slowly, and the storm was finding its way into the hull. There was nothing anyone could do.

Baako looked at Zuvich on the oar next to him. An experienced seaman, he had a look of dread on his face as the bucket the boy had used to clean the seats floated by.

Each time the vessel was in a trough, they heaved with all their might. No one could let up until the vessel was near its crest, then they would put the oars to the floor so that the passing swell couldn't throw them.

Over the howling wind, the older seamen called encouragement to the younger ones to steel themselves and to have faith in their team, but as the night grew, their inexperience began to show.

As the swells outside pushed on the oars inside, the young ones became more concerned about who was sliding into whom.

"Hey, shove over!"

"Stop banging into me!"

The older men yelled for them to stay on their oars, but the young ones were more focused on pushing away the men sliding into them, disregarding their oars with ghastly consequences. The neglected oars, now unrestrained, threw the men still trying to anchor them to the floor. Some were flung into the sides of the vessel as their chains snapped tight. The blood-red water sloshed back and forth over the bodies.

Baako's attention returned to his first concern. After the boy had given Matken his bashing and been dragged away, Tarrant gave the cleaning job to Matken to finish. But Matken was lazy. He never put away the bucket, nor closed the hatch and now water poured in and, with every rise of the bow, impaired the buoyancy of the vessel.

Outside, Captain Tarrant fought the rudder long and hard in the unrelenting storm. The swells continued and the wind roared on. From the rudder and the nature of movement of his vessel, Tarrant knew that she was sinking. Little by little, she was taking in water. He began to consider defeat.

He squinted ahead. A dark shadow moved on the deck right before him. A bolt of lightning coursed through the sky overhead. The dark form was no longer there but his cabin door was open, swinging wildly in the wind. He clutched the rudder as the vessel slid into another trough. Lightning flashed, and his ears rang from the immediate thunder that followed.

The door appeared shut again. Tarrant could even see the timber latch across it.

Below deck, water seeped through the ceiling above. Baako wondered how much water was now in the cargo hold down below. A dark shadow passed him. He shivered, surprising himself. Fear was rare for Baako. Had this storm unnerved him?

The vessel crested another swell and he got down on the floor to hold the oar with all his might, waiting for the water from the hatch to wash over him again, but it didn't. He could see the hatch was shut and tied off properly. The bow of the vessel began to rise again and he rowed on with tremendous effort. *Was that a chain rattling?* With the howling wind, rain and thunder, it was hard to tell. He found himself asking for more lightning so he could see about and settle his nerves.

The night seemed endless until, finally, the lightning lessened and the thunder appeared to be behind them, but they were sinking.

Outside, Captain Tarrant could also feel the change in his vessel. It was carrying too much water. The vessel still crested each wave, but it sat lower and took on even more water. If this continued, the men would be worn out, and eventually they wouldn't escape the storm. It would swallow them whole.

Lightning flashed across the sky as they pushed through.

"We're too low, too low in the water," mumbled Tarrant. He thought he could see the cargo covers flapping in the wind. "Great. Now it's me cargo getting wet!"

The rudder demanded his entire exertion. He would soon have to accept that his aging arms were beyond finished. His heart leapt when he saw boxes of cargo spill over the side. The rain was still too heavy to see beyond his vessel, but it moved a little faster now with the load lessened. The swells became longer and flatter, but they were not out of danger, and, at the crest of every swell, his eyes searched carefully.

Downstairs, less water now slopped about. The swells were less severe and the oars were in little danger of getting struck now. The men still held them to the floor but they now rested on them, instead of bracing themselves in fear.

Baako looked at the sweat-sodden men, beaten by fear and exhaustion. The drummers shuffled nervously as Baako, now unchained, approached. He didn't stand over them but kept a small distance. "Would you do me a favour?"

"And what favour would that be, Baako?"

Baako's white teeth flashed in the dull light as he answered. "Set a steadier pace as we dig into each swell. The men are spent, and we have passed the worst of it. We just need to keep going now, that's all."

The crew were indeed spent, but they needed to keep going. One of the drummers looked back at Baako's proud smile with hatred. "Yes, I know this. I will ease up the pace and you will also return to your post now."

"As you say."

As he took up his place on the oar, Baako began to sing. It was an old song of slaves and seamen conquering the mighty ocean. At first he sang alone, but soon the older men joined Baako's deep, confident voice. As they sang, they forgot their fear, aching backs and tired muscles. Even the younger ones memorised the words and joined in as the vessel washed over the swollen seas. As one song rolled into another, they never noticed that they were now rowing full-time at one steady pace until Tarrant came to undo the hatches. They were clear of the storm. A mighty cheer went up as the oars were dropped to the floor.

Baako walked over to Tarrant. "I'm sure you had the worst time up there, Captain, as did we all. How about letting the men come top deck for a breath of fresh air?" There was no sound beyond the creaking of the woodwork and the roll of thunder far behind.

Tarrant cleared his throat. "Listen up, boys. It has been the worst of storms this time, so I will give you all permission to come top deck." The men clapped. Tarrant raised his hand and the room went quiet. He counted the gaps between the oars. Some of the lost men had cost him a lot of money. "We will remember those who sacrificed their lives to the storm to save your miserable hides, but when I's say it's time to resume your duties, I'll have no arguments. Is this clear?"

The men broke into cheeky banter as they headed to the stairs.

Lighting a candle, Baako descended into the hull of the vessel where the supplies were stored. Boxes bobbed on the water and others lay beneath it. All their food and drinking water could be lost.

Tarrant frowned from behind him. "How did we get so much water on board?"

"The last man to use the water hatch didn't close it properly. It came open halfway through the storm, but none of us could let go of an oar to do anything about it."

Helplessly, they watched as a half-submerged box let out a small burp of bubbles and then disappeared beneath the water.

"I lose me cargo, many an expensive oarsman and now me food stock. This is not a good trip." He ascended the stairs. "Not good at all."

Baako eased himself through the water, being careful not to get his candle wet. Everything had shifted, and it was impossible to move without bumping into submerged boxes. He saw the flicker of a candle from the other end. It was Ayton.

"Ayton, how did you fare with the storm?"

Ayton didn't look up but continued with his inspection. "I-I-it, it will n-n-not be g-good, to be far from l-l-land I think."

Baako surveyed the mess. "How can you save some of this, Ayton?"

"I c-can't save an-any of this but, I al-always p-p-put some up-upstairs and tie down." Ayton bumped into something. "Ah, he-here we are, hey b-black m-m-man, help me with this wou-would you."

Baako waded towards Ayton, trying not to make too many waves. "What are you hoping to find here, Ayton?" He didn't wait for an answer from the stuttering little man. For all the talking Ayton was known to do on his own, it was nevertheless hard to get into conversation with him. He reached down and found the end of a wooden case.

The two men raised the chest to the surface and Ayton pulled over one of the floating barrels and rolled it into an upright position in the water. They lifted the chest onto it, pushing the barrel to the floor. The chest was not completely out of the water but it was high enough to open. When Ayton cracked the lid, water flowed out along with sodden loaves of bread.

"I would hazard a guess that we won't be using those," offered Baako.

Shouting came from the top deck. Baako headed as quickly as he could towards the stairs.

Low, black clouds hung heavy overhead. It seemed they would collapse at any given moment, instantly crushing them into insignificance.

Tarrant yelled up at the sky and lashed and cracked his whip at his own flagpole. As his eyes adjusted to the light, Baako saw the boy standing out of Tarrant's reach, up on the flagpole's crossbar. Baako pushed through the gathering crowd. "Captain Tarrant, if it would please you, I may be able to help." He walked forward, being careful to stand on the whip as he did so. "Captain, sir, we have a bigger problem."

The tired and parched captain looked at Baako. His eyes narrowed. "What do ya mean exactly, Blacky?"

Baako motioned to the stern. "If I could speak on the quiet, Captain."

Tarrant pulled hard at his whip, glaring into Baako's dark eyes. Baako took a sidestep and headed to the stern, resisting the temptation to check the hemp rope again. "Captain, I have been downstairs with Ayton, and it's not good. We have lost all our bread and have only a little gruel and fruit that Ayton put up in his quarters as the storm hit. If it were not for him, we would have nothing at all."

Tarrant stood well away from Baako. "You means because of that little shit …" He clenched his teeth but spit still somehow sprayed from his mouth. "… we have next to no food! Is that what you is saying, Blacky?"

"Captain, Matken was the one who left the porthole open, not the boy."

Tarrant's hand went to his hip as he stepped back. Venting his frustration, the whip lashed as Baako instinctively held his arms over his head. He had once seen a man's eye explode from Tarrant's whip.

Then the whipping stopped. Baako lowered his guard to see Tarrant still looking at him, empty-handed. Their eyes followed the whip back to the boy. There he was, with the last two feet in one hand and the handle in the other. He stood in front of everyone, calm, proud and defiant. He pointed with the whip handle at Tarrant. "Enough! Enough whipping. Enough brutality and enough violence from you, Tarrant. You are the captain of your own vessel. It is yours but you will own the men no more. We will do as you say as the captain of your vessel, but you will beat us no more!"

Tarrant's weather-beaten face reddened with rage. "Who, on this vessel of mine, do yous think you are, b-o-o-o-y?"

"I am a boy with my own free will, and I will serve you until port, sir."

A mumble went through the men as they folded their arms at Tarrant, raising their chins as they did. Tarrant had heard of mutiny before, but no one had ever dared challenge him on his own vessel. He made eye contact with Matken, who nodded slowly as he made his way through the angry group. No one noticed the man slipping between them.

"Very well, boy," said Tarrant. "Everyone on this vessel knows it's ya job ta clean the seats then when ya finish, what's it ya meant to do, hmm?"

"Well … I put the scraper and bucket away, you know I always do, Captain."

Tarrant's confidence returned as Matken slipped out of the crowd, right behind the boy. "Hmm, and what of the hatch, boy? See ya didn't close the hatch properly and now me vessel's full of water. Guess where all that water went? Into the hull. And where do we keep the food, hey, boy? In the hull! So now it's ya fault that we have no food ta feed the men. Your fault!"

A murmur went through the men. At the same time, Matken lurched forward and grabbed the boy in a chokehold. The boy was about to point out that he wasn't there before the storm broke, but Matken held him so tight he could barely breathe. Tarrant laughed as he walked closer.

The boy's mind raced. As Tarrant got close enough to take his whip back, the boy kicked out at his chest and flipped himself over the back of Matken. As he did so, he slipped the loop end of the whip over Matken's head and pulled tight, choking him. Still holding the whip at the back of Matken's neck, the boy began to drag him to the side of the vessel. Matken choked as he grabbed at the noose about his neck, stumbling backwards.

Tarrant landed with a thump onto the deck from the impact of the boy's kick and clutched his chest as he broke out in a coughing fit.

Still dragging Matken backwards, the boy lobbed the handle of the whip. It hit its target and dropped down inside the vessel's planks. The boy ducked down, sending Matken tumbling backwards over the side with a splash. The handle snapped up against a plank, jamming hard.

The boy stood defiant before the rest of the crew. "You all know I was put out to the sharks long before the storm hit. It was not me that lost your food but the man on the end of this whip. Is there a man amongst you who wishes to save dear Matken?" He stepped aside as if offering an invitation.

Matken was being dragged along the side of the vessel by his neck, his arms above his head, holding the whip. It was hopeless.

The boy stared at his onlookers. He saw Lendud. "There is still time to save him." He saw Cho. "Weren't you friends with him, Cho?"

Cho, his anonymity suddenly lost, walked to the vessel's side. He moved around the boy towards the stern. Matken had badgered so many men on these voyages and set up more than one man to end up as a sea anchor. Now Cho looked down at Matken's dilemma and marvelled at the poetic justice. From a parched throat, Cho drew phlegm and spat, hitting Matken's forehead. A cheer went up and Cho raised his fist with the pride of a winning fighter.

Baako helped Tarrant up and sat him on the rudder deck. It had been a good blow to the chest. The old man still looked broken.

Baako cleared his throat. "Very well, men, listen up. The captain has handed out his orders and it's my job to see them through." No one objected. "Like you, the *Shiraz* has taken a beating and needs our help to be able to finish the voyage. Ayton." Ayton stepped forward and Baako lowered his voice. "Ayton, take five strong men and sort out what food can be saved from the flooded galley."

Ayton was a little nervous, but more than enough men stepped forward to help. He walked off to his task, happy to have those who wished to help follow on.

"Zuvich."

Zuvich stepped forward, appearing worse for wear. "Zuvich, you and some of the older crew can clean up the top deck and secure the leftover cargo. Somebody could break a leg up here."

Zuvich made his way back through the crowd with some of the older men moving in behind him.

The next chore was one that required a strong stomach and some tact. Baako looked about. The answer was in front of him. "Cho and Lendud, we have suffered our losses, as you do in a storm like this one. Can you take care of the deceased and mop out the – oh, I don't think we will need to do the mopping." He finished with a broad smile, which quickly slid away as it dawned on him.

"Boys, where are your chains?" He felt Tarrant stiffen up in front of him. He quickly kneed the old man in the back, knocking the wind out of him again. Someone had to keep the men together, and Baako felt qualified for the job. His past life had made him so.

Cho was the first to speak. "It was the boy, Baako. He came to me and released my collar. It made the difference. I don't think I could have survived much longer with it. You know how it is."

The rest spoke up, telling him how the boy came to them in the dark, released their chains and gave them water. Baako discretely put his foot on the tails of Tarrant's shirt just to be sure he didn't lunge at the boy who was staring at Tarrant, unafraid.

Baako moved the conversation on. "Manjee, take the rest of the men and start to get all that seawater back to the outside of the hull where it belongs." It was a big task and everyone went to help. With just the three of them now remaining, Baako stepped down from the rudder deck. "Boy, I thought you were ..." He nodded to the hemp rope still pulled tightly over the side.

"I know. I made it back onto the bottom rudder brace."

"If it was such a safe place, what brought you top deck again?"

"I was going to stay there until we made land, but I could feel the vessel getting slower and lower in the water. I couldn't just stay there and see how it all ended".

With some difficulty, Tarrant got to his feet. "I never left the rudder. How did ya get past me?"

"Well, I didn't. I was going to jump over you, but the boat lurched and I bounced right off your back. It was dumb luck I landed on the vessel at all."

"Oh yes, I's remember that. And that's when I saw that me door was open."

"Yes, I'm sorry, Captain Tarrant. I stole your keys to free the men of their chains and that was when I saw that someone had left the hatch open and water was pouring in."

Tarrant scoffed, then stepped forward and offered his hand. The boy took it at first with uncertainty, then clasped the captain wrist to wrist.

"Well, Captain," Baako said, "if you wish to change into something dry, I will go down and help the boys with putting the ocean out."

Tarrant released the boy. "Yes, but first ya can get me whip back. Just don't feel right without it on me hip."

Baako glanced at the boy, who moved quietly away.

"Baako, I knows what ya just did then."

"What do you mean, Captain?"

A wry smile came over Tarrant's salt-smacked face. "You and that blessed by the Mother and Father boy have saved me vessel, Baako. I's not forgets this." It was a rare show of appreciation from the old sea captain.

"Captain, were you good friends with Matken?"

Tarrant frowned at the big man leaning over the side and stepped forward to see for himself. The vessel had almost stopped completely now, allowing the whip to loosen. The water around Matken swirled a deep red. He was on his back, holding the whip above his head but from the hips down, his legs were missing, bitten off by a shark. Matken's blood was discolouring the ocean.

Tarrant leant over the side and tugged the whip. Matken's hands were still locked onto it. "Aag, he wasn't too bright when he worked with us, he's still not too bright, dead." He took a deep breath and shouted. "Let go of me dammed whip, ya dumb corpse!"

Matken's eyes rolled open to look directly up at Tarrant. "Please, Cap, just pull me back up. It's a coming back, I know it is. I promise I'll be good for ya."

Tarrant spat. "Ha! Ya promise me nothing. You leant on the oars all ya life, ya useless pick-a-pocket. Look at ya arms, no muscle tone at all. yous a useless thief and a useless waste of space on me vessel. Now let go of me dammed whip before I ... just let it go, ya thicket!" Tarrant looked at Baako's stunned face. "What? Well, he is a thicket, ain't he?" And with that, Tarrant headed for his cabin, returning a moment later carrying a long pole with a hook on the end.

"Captain, you're not going to gaff the poor bastard?"

Tarrant stopped sharp, pointing the gaff at Baako's face. "Ya watch ya mouth, black fella, that's still a white man down there." He leaned over the side and began to smack the top of Matken's head. It was hard to understand how half a man could put up a fight, yet he did.

Tarrant was ferocious in his attack, poking and prodding until finally, Matken's hands slipped. Tarrant gave the whip a vigorous flick, and it was free. He let out a "Ha!" as if he had won some kind of fair fight.

Matken whimpered as he tried to stop the bleeding. "I never gives you any grief, even when ya comes down and takes me to ya cabin in ya drunken stupor."

With a face to rival the dark clouds above, Tarrant changed the hold on the gaff. It was now a spear. He drew his arm right back to take aim, then froze. Directly under Matken loomed a huge shadow. Its teeth bared as it opened its massive jaw, showing the bits of torn cloth and flesh within it. The shark's mouth easily engulfed Matken. It closed its jaws and sank beneath the surface, leaving Matken's last words hanging in the air.

"Ya man lover."

Tarrant lowered his arm. "Wasn't worth me gaff anyways." He turned and walked away.

Baako gazed down at the water and what was left of the blood floating about. It diluted before him, wiping Matken from existence with the pop of a final bubble.

Once the men got everything as it should be, they rowed back into the edge of the storm, just enough to collect fresh rainwater. They used anything that would catch water and reloaded the barrels. It was with relief that they finally rowed well clear and were able to rest.

The light was fading and Baako headed back to his spot. He looked at the sleeping boy and considered what the child had done these past few days. He eased himself down beside the boy with no name.

The boy backed up against him, not seeking warmth but security. A boy, all alone, not knowing where he had come from, and with no idea where he was going.

11 Behind Closed Doors

Hay rustled, and a horse stamped its hoof. The hay rustled again. A rat darted out and ran along the stone wall, scurrying from room to room. When the rat came across some steps, its whiskers twitched as its nose tested the scents. Detecting no danger and the promise of food, it proceeded up the steps into the lower palace, stopping only as human footsteps came and went.

A glow came from under a door. The rat squeezed under the thick, oaken frame, its long tail dragging behind. This stone, basement room was large with no windows. It would be pitch black if not for the candles on the floor in each of the four corners.

The door opened and the rat scurried to one of the side walls. The hall light showed an outline of a small girl facing the wall, wearing a blindfold. A well-built, manly figure dressed in full combat costume stepped in and closed the door behind him.

Neither spoke.

The man drew his sword. In a flash of candlelight, the girl spun, wielding her own sword. Faster than the eye, the two blades struck, blocked, clashed and yielded. The two figures danced around each other, switching from aggressor to defender, to aggressor again.

The man was assertive and experienced. A revered war hero. The girl was small, light and nimble, with a grace born of instinct from her mother with the natural skill and ability of her father. A formidable opponent.

The two toiled relentlessly, looking to find a flaw, a mistake born of fatigue or frustration in one another but neither relented. One by one, the candle wicks were cut off but the combat with razor-sharp blades went on until a sudden knock at the door. The girl cartwheeled to the corner behind the door, motionless, her sword raised.

The man calmly answered. "Yes?"

The door eased open with a small squeak. "Master Xiang, the Emperor is asking after you," said the guard in a low voice.

Master Xiang nodded, not looking to the darkest corner, he asked his blindfolded apprentice, "Why did you put out the candles?"

"I decided if I must work in the dark, Master, then maybe you should also."

"What about the rat?"

"He was on his way to our food stalls and there he is not welcome. I will remove his headless body."

"You did not remove his head when he entered. Why?"

"Because I was using his eyes until you beheaded him, Master."

"Some would call that cheating. Do not do it again." The Master didn't wait for an answer but left with his guard, sheathing his sword.

As they headed up the hallway, one of the men coughed politely into his hand. "Master, if I may, why do you risk your own life to train this little girl?"

The Master slowed his walk to a stop and faced the questioner. He could see all three guards wanted to hear the answer. With a quiver of a smile, the Master asked, "You all stood outside to guard my back, so you heard the match being played. Would any of you like to take my place in there?" With no response to take up his offer, he continued. "Am I safe to carry on serving my palace as I see fit?"

The questioner, followed by his comrades, dropped into a full bow. "Master, you must know there is not a soul in this palace that would see harm come to you. It was merely a question."

Just then, the small girl came out of the room, her blindfold now a makeshift rat coffin. She closed the door and saw him. In the dimly lit corridor, he saw her form the words. 'Thank you, Master.'

He smiled as her large, green eyes shone back at him, remembering her remarkable mother, Sha'Doe.

12 No Credit

On the *Shiraz*, the loud bang of the food hatch opening marked the beginning of the new day. The men mumbled in protest as they tried to stretch tired muscles. It was barely daybreak.

Tarrant coughed. "Listen up, men. I know it was a bad storm but we're not on land yet. Food is short, so get what we have into you. We have a long day. Tomorrow I want to be at Devil's Pass. Enjoy your breakfast, it may be the last."

Silence hung over the room. They knew the food had been lost in the storm. Land tomorrow seemed good, but they could barely raise themselves off the floor, let alone row. The older ones pushed forward, fetching the food trays. Sitting there wasn't going to get the vessel to shore.

Zuvich handed one to Baako. "Where is our youngest man, Baako?"

Just waking, Baako shook his head. "I can't say, Zuvich. I hope you've slept well, my good man." He reached up and took his rations.

"I was asleep long before our new rudder man came to bed. How about you?"

"I got what I got. Good to have plenty of water on board, though."

"Indeed. We can go an extra day or so without food, but water, no."

Baako chewed his first spoonful of gruel and grimaced. It didn't taste right and it didn't look right either. He finished his mouthful and looked up at Zuvich with a sparkle in his eyes. "Good thing that kid cleaned the seats, hey."

"That's what I like about you, my friend. You can always see the brightness in any day regardless how dark it may seem."

"But of course. It's still a day, Zuvich."

Zuvich laughed as he turned to fetch his own gruel. Baako wondered how far they were from land. Zuvich had calculated that they had food for two days yet the cook was already thinning out the gruel with maggots. He scrunched his face at the thought.

Soon enough, the drums started to roll and the men took up their oars. The rhythm of the drumming started gently, the men had aching muscles to warm up. Baako started to sing in his deep, earthy voice and the older men were quick to join in, prompting the rest to follow. It helped to forget about sore hands and feet, and bad gruel.

The day passed without incident.

***

That evening, for the first time, Baako had the choice of going top deck. He felt the calluses around his neck from years of wearing the slave's necklace. He saw no point in being free to move and being frozen to the spot; it was mind over matter. He eased himself up quietly onto the deck, the last thing he wanted was to startle Tarrant. "I say, Captain, how is our progress coming along?"

"I was a wonderin' how long it'd take you to come top deck, Baako." Tarrant hesitated. "We should see land tomorrow."

"Captain," Baako gently re-enquired, "how far are we *really*, sir?"

The very first stars of the evening were already out. Tarrant lifted his cap and scratched his head. "Two days ago, I seen stars I never seen before. I only knew which way to go when the sun came up. It's too early to say Baako but I think everything will be well. It will just be gruel until Devil's Pass then we can reload for Samos. We'll be fine."

***

The following morning, Tarrant came down and stood before the drummers. "Keep a good pace on you, boys, we'll be seeing Devil's Pass soon enough," with a slither of a smile on his face, "And good morning Baako, would you like to take the rudder today?"

"Well thank you Sir, but I fear the Gods have already made me black enough."

Tarrant could be heard chuckling all the way to the rudder.

"Psst, Baako." It was Zuvich behind him. "Is you afraid?"

"Yes, I am afraid. Afraid the men are strung out. I mean, *right* out. If someone cracks, I want to be here. Up there I am of no use to anyone. Tarrant himself looks like he is about to snap. We just need to get to Devil's Pass so the men can have a wash and sleep on the beach."

Zuvich knew Baako spoke with wisdom and truth. It was to be a solemn day on the oars for everyone.

***

It was near midday the following day when Tarrant called the boy. The boy dropped what he was doing and scrambled up the stairs.

Tarrant was waiting for him at his rudder. "Your eyes are better than mine, boy. Hop up on my cabin; tells me what you can see."

The boy quickly scaled the ladder. He could hardly believe his eyes when he saw the faint peak of a mountain.

Baako heard the commotion upstairs. Concerned, he dropped his oar and marched up the stairs, but when he stepped into the light, Tarrant was on his own, laughing, and his whip was still on his hip. There was a noise from somewhere above. Baako peered up and sighed in relief. The boy was up the flagpole, standing on the cross brace, pointing almost dead ahead. There it was: Devil's Pass.

He called out to the boy swinging out so precariously. "Hey, who do you think you are, a nesting crow or something? Come down off there, now! You have jobs to finish, and you left the hatch open. Now, get down, boy."

The boy nimbly jumped down, and they headed downstairs. Shaking his head with a smile, Baako took his place on the oar once more. As he took a breath to sing again, he chose the song of how the Gods had formed the homelands and instantly everyone understood what he had seen and was quick to join in.

It wasn't long before Devil's Pass was visible through the portholes.

Baako listened to the younger men's stories. Those on a wage talked of what awaited them in the town. The women, the drinking and the tall stories. He smiled at their high hopes and big talk. Most would have a hot meal, pay for a good bath and sleep for three days in a bed of straw until it was time to board a vessel again. Only some might get close enough to smell the sweet scent of a woman, although that wouldn't stop the yarns and boasting when they came back on board.

Soon they were docking in Devil's Pass and hanging up oars. Baako and Zuvich clasped wrist to wrist. Baako looked at the big smile on the boy as he joined them. He scooped him up in a bear hug.

"Put me down, you big oaf. I'm not a sack of potatoes. Put me down."

Baako gave the boy one more squeeze and put him down. The boy faced Zuvich, who had his hand out. A little surprised, he clasped the older man's wrist and, like men, they shook.

"I find myself in your debt," said Zuvich.

The boy raised his chin. "I don't think any man on this vessel owes another a thing. After the one who went over the side, the rest of us are as we belong. So, I must be in your debt also."

The boy found himself surrounded by well-wishers, and he revelled in the attention.

Baako looked on. There had been something about the boy from the onset, *But what?* He went top deck in search of Tarrant but found he'd already left the vessel.

Halfway along the wharf, Baako could see the man known as Balzac. His family had been accused of sorcery and banished from the mainland. It was said that his great-grandmother had a dream and that they discovered the magic iron ball, which helped them become one of the most powerful and wealthy families. With the iron ball, they ruled the coming and going of all vessels from the inland sea. Ships going through Devil's Pass had to stop and pay a tax for the privilege, although the Pass was used long before the family arrived. Legend had it that the first vessel that had refused to pay a tax was sunk before it reached open water. Since then, everyone had paid. No one knew how they flew the iron balls but, from time to time, if someone forgot to pay the tax, they quickly remembered when the mighty, magic iron ball came whistling over their bow.

Captain Tarrant stood opposite Balzac, his shoulders tense. Until now, Baako never set foot on land unless they were at Samos, but Tarrant was on his own, facing Balzac with his two bodyguards standing behind him. Balzac himself was tall and heavy-set, though he still seemed to carry a chubby, baby look.

"Captain Tarrant, I'll let your vessel pass through, but you'll pay twice on your return."

Tarrant was exhausted and exasperated. "Come on, Balzac. The men are spent. They needs a day's grace to rest up and load a few supplies to get us up to Samos."

Balzac's reply was simple. "No credit."

Baako coughed, and a panicked Tarrant spun around. "I know you're there, Blacky, you walk like a baby hippo. No need to cough on me back, ya big oaf." He pointed at Balzac. "You know I'm good for me credit. Just one night."

Balzac frowned, but a fleeting look of recognition crossed his face when he looked at Baako. "You. You're Mabutu's eldest son, aren't you?"

Tarrant paled like his entire world was imploding. It was a secret that couldn't be lost now.

Baako thought of his mother. "No, no, no, sir. I could only wish to have a family tree as big as that one, but I, er, I's tink it's good of yous tat yous tink I is but ..." Baako tried his best to keep a silly grin on his face. "Sir, ta mens are abouts ta set the vessel on fires. Sir, it woulds be okays if I set the men outs to have a swim? It's a been a bad ride dis time."

Balzac squinted at him, unconvinced. "Very well, then. And your name is?"

"Ah, his name would be Tybor," intervened Tarrant.

Balzac looked the huge black man up and down. "Well, Tybor, would you join me and Captain Tarrant for dinner? I believe it to be pheasant. We trapped it some days ago, and it has been hanging to mature."

Baako's mouth watered as Tarrant answered again. "No, you have made your position quite well known, thank you, Balzac. I's will not forget your hospitality." He turned to leave, but Baako stood in his way. "Come on, Ba – Blacky. Get your ass back where it belongs."

Baako snapped out of his pheasant-inspired trance. "Oh, yes'm, sir."

Balzac watched the muscled form of the man called Tybor leave. Without question, he was Mabutu's double.

One of the bodyguards leant forward. "Well, that worked well, sir. First, the captain argued to stay, then he couldn't leave quick enough."

"It would have been more fun to have them at my table for an evening, though."

"Why is that, sir?"

"Because, unless I am very mistaken, that *is* Mabutu's missing son."

"Really, sir? Should I get a message to Mabutu in Zimbali?"

"What flags does the *Shiraz* fly? Where have they come from?"

"Well, I do believe they have just come from Begonia, sir, but they're going to Samos. Your flag is up there too, sir."

Balzac sighed. "Well, I would hope my flag is up there. No one can get to Samos from Begonia without going through my port, can they? Is Mensa still running the port of Begonia?"

"Yes, he is. Would you like me to send him a note of advice about his brother's whereabouts, sir?"

"No, you will not mention this again," he said, addressing both of his bodyguards. "I have made myself perfectly clear, haven't I, men." He cast one more glance as the *Shiraz* pushed off, then cut between the two guards and began the march along his wharf, stopping once more at the sound of a whip cracking. He thought of how long Baako had been missing. Baako's callused neck was well scarred, and though he no longer wore the collar, he was still submissive to the shrivelled, old seaman. The whip cracked again and he closed his eyes as his gut began to knot at the thought of King Mabutu's son being treated this way.

13 Flying Fish

Tarrant walked back and forth in front of the rudder deck, chewing tobacco and mumbling blasphemies. Balzac *had* recognised Baako. His effort in keeping him a secret was almost lost. Balzac may try to send a message but Mensa wouldn't let it through, he reassured himself.

They took the remainder of the day to cross the inland sea. The men hadn't been happy to be on the vessel another night, the beach was so inviting. At dusk, jungle appeared on the horizon. The captain told Ayton to serve dinner, and dropped anchor.

Ayton nervously addressed Tarrant. "Um, sir, um, we … we only have f-f-food for tonight, um sort of, um."

Tarrant cut in angrily, "Oh, for the love of the Creators, I got the picture, man! I swear, one day I will cut your tongue out and teach you to write. Now, feed the men what you have and shut it. You hear me? Tell no one!" and waved his bunched-up whip in the cook's face. Ayton didn't stay one moment longer.

Turning, Tarrant was startled by the boy standing behind him. "How much did you hear, boy, huh?"

The boy pondered the question. "I heard, but I see little point in alarming the men, sir."

Tarrant patted the boy on the head as he barged past. "Yes, though I may have to feed you to them before tomorrow's out." He licked his lips as he headed for his cabin. "Just one drink," he told himself.

He paused to adjust his vision to his dark cabin then moved to the bedside and knelt to retrieve his precious crate. It had moved quite a bit in the storm. Licking his lips, he slid it out from under the bed, his mouth watering as he pulled out one of the bottles given to him by Mensa. His dealings with the man were bound to unravel if Balzac said anything, and Mensa was not a forgiving man.

He took his bottle of red wine and mug to the bow and closed his eyes, trying to forget the look on Balzac's face, but most of all, he was trying to forget the cold, unforgiving eyes of Mensa.

Sipping his red, he watched the sun set over the inlet and jungle. The clouds over the Great Eastern Range turned from snow-white to pink and then to fire-red. Rolling over, the clouds' appearance changed effortlessly as the sun slipped away for another night.

He took another swig. *The boy must be dealt with. Baako back in a collar too.* Firm and decisive was the only way. He drank some more. He'd just dropped his third empty bottle when he heard a thump then a moment later, another. He staggered back around the kitchen towards mid-deck, hand on whip.

More thumping.

Ayton nipped out of the kitchen behind him, and Tarrant was relieved he wasn't the only one who had heard something. From out of the dark, something crashed into him, knocking him over. His mug flew from his hand and rattled across the deck. Then more thumping.

Ayton bent down to help him up. "It's a g-gift, Captain. It is a g-g-gift from the s-sea, s-sir."

Angrily, Tarrant shook his arm away from the clumsy cook. "What on the Gods' earth is you on about, fool?"

Baako appeared from the rear of the vessel. "Captain, look! Look at all the fish!"

Tarrant finished righting himself on the railing then, in the dim light, he saw scores of flying fish flopping about on his deck. He pulled his hat from his head. "Glory be. I've heard of the odd one flying onto a vessel, but this? I never seen the likes." He slumped back against the side of the *Shiraz*. "Never I seen the likes of it."

Ayton's eyes were affixed on something and Baako followed his gaze. On top of the captain's cabin, the boy was sat with his legs crossed, hands on knees, and his head slumped. Baako slowly climbed onto the cabin roof. The boy was not awake. Gently, Baako bent down and scooped him up.

Ayton called up. "I-is he a-a-all right, the b-b-boy?"

Baako whispered. "Yes, I think he's fine. And now we are all going to be fine. Is there enough food now, Ayton?"

Tarrant shot Ayton a questioning look.

"I never w-whispered a w-word to no one b-b-but you."

Tarrant grumbled profanities. "Well, be sure this deck is cleaned off and there's a good meal for the men by morning!" He staggered off to fetch another bottle.

Downstairs, the boy slept on. The trip had taken its toll on the young boy, though he'd coped better than some of the men. The sound of Tarrant fumbling about up on the deck didn't bode well. He was talking to himself again. Soon it would get louder and more incoherent. Baako moved in beside the boy. He heard a bottle drop and roll away to the side of the vessel as Tarrant stumbled into his cabin. He came back out again, arguing, quarrelling with a woman. Always the same woman. Baako listened for Tarrant's steps coming down the stairs. Gently, he scooped up the boy and slid him over to Zuvich. Tarrant reached the bottom step, looked about and stepped forward.

Baako sat up. "Well, Captain, how are you this evening?"

"Where is the boy, Blacky?"

Baako got up on one knee. "What do you want with the boy, Captain?" He stood to his full height and spoke in a lower voice. "Hmm, Captain? You don't want the boy tonight. You don't want the boy any night, do you, Captain." There was a chance the captain would be too drunk to remember tomorrow, but it was a gamble.

Tarrant swayed a little with a crooked smirk.

Baako stepped in front of him. "Captain, we have had a journey that should have sent us into the arms of the ocean Goddess. But it didn't." With his head, he motioned to the empty seats of men lost in the storm. "Well, not for most of us anyway. The men are tired, dead-tired. And so are you, my captain. Sleep, my captain, sleep."

He waved his giant hand in a dance, and in the dim light, Tarrant followed the black fingers, swaying side to side with their motion. "Sleep. You need it. I need it. Sleep, my captain, sleep."

Tarrant, heavy-eyed and much the worse for wear, simply turned and left, tripping up the stairs as he went. Baako returned to his spot and settled, as best he could.

***

The next morning, the whip cracked and the bone-tired crew jumped into life. With a bang, the food hatch dropped and, in the poor light of daybreak, they retrieved their food bowls. Baako looked at Tarrant's worn face as he whirled his whip to crack over their heads. Tired and hungover, it was not going to be a good day.

There was little talk as the men got food and water into them for the impending up-river row. Spirits were low after yesterday's failure to dock, but the flying fish were a welcome meal.

Soon enough, the vessel was cutting through the water with a grace and beauty born of the ocean herself. Other than a small bow wave, it silently entered the mouth of the tidal River Sollya.

Huge crocodiles claimed the attention of Tarrant as they basked on the banks of the river. They could strike like lightning when they had the need to. Each of the fruit trees had its own collection of reptiles beneath, waiting for a young primate to fall.

Downstairs, through the porthole, the boy looked in awe at the colour of the flamingos. His open hatch was not much above the waterline and, mesmerised, he watched the sinister shadows of crocodiles gliding through the water.

He resumed his duties with a bounce in his step. He knew all the men on board, though some would still not speak with him. They would speak about him in their own language. He saw no reason to tell them that he understood their language, though he couldn't fathom how. The boy found Ayton an odd character, but called him a friend just the same. He always let the boy eat out of the bowls after the crew had finished. Ayton had shown him how to prepare the food and given him tips on food storage. As he said, 'It was good life skills.'

Finishing his duties, he returned to his porthole. "Baako, how far up this river do we need to go?"

"A little way yet, boy." Still working his oar, Baako studied the boy for a moment. "You have not asked once this trip – now we are nearly there, you start questioning. What's on your mind?"

The boy searched for his answer. "Well, I see Ayton is cleaning his kitchen for the first time. So, I wondered if we are nearly there. You have been up this route before, Baako?"

"Oh yes, boy. I have been up this river many times. It's called the River Sollya, and it will take us to the City of Samos in Middle Kingdom. Have you been to a city before?"

"I can't remember my own name, so no," he answered lamely.

This was a well-educated boy. He was used to asking questions yet he couldn't recall his own name. *Yes, maybe mother could help?*

"Baako, what are you thinking?"

Baako smirked. The boy was indeed intuitive. "I know a woman who may be able to help you find where you came from ... I mean, your homeland, boy."

The boy's face lit up. "You mean she ... she might know my village?"

"Easy, boy; she may be of no help at all, but there was a time when all Zimbali looked up to her with the respect of a Queen. When we meet with her, I know you will show her the same respect."

The boy carefully, respectfully, asked, "When, Baako? When will I get to meet with this woman? Will it be a voyage we are to make soon?"

Baako nodded at the boy's eagerness. "Well, I'm to meet with her tomorrow, maybe today. It will depend on the captain and what cargo we must move. The trip isn't done until the cargo is released. You will see the men that are free paid, as that is the end of their trip. The men that start to load the cargo again will be our next oarsmen." Baako changed the topic. "So, I think I have called you 'boy' for too long; how about I call you 'Brother' from now on?"

The boy stepped back, looking up at the big man. He could think of nothing better. "If that would be alright with you, it would be mighty fine with me, 'Brother.'"

Baako chuckled. "If Ayton is cleaning, then Tarrant isn't going to feed us again. How about you get another round of water, keep our bellies full."

***

Before long, they were docked in the port of Samos. The men were quick to hang up the oars and move the remaining cargo. The boy stood in the galley, giving a ladle of water to the men as they went back down. Baako received two ladles since he was twice the size of everyone else *and* he carried twice as much cargo.

The boy grinned as his Brother went by, down out of sight for his next load. Suddenly, the room darkened, and the boy's smile faded when he saw what was blocking the light. Standing there was the ugliest man he had ever seen, and he *stank*.

"My name is Tark. You will call me 'sir' or Mr Fly."

The room was indeed abuzz with flies. Before the boy could reply, the man reached in with long, bony fingers and grabbed him by the neck, almost strangling him. Dropping the bucket, his legs kicking, the boy screwed his face up at the stench of the man.

Tark's short, cropped hair emphasised his tall forehead. His long, ugly face was darkened by heavy brows and dark eyes, and over his shoulder hung a long, shiny chain. The clothes were badly worn; in fact, the only thing about this man that was worth something was his boots.

The boy loosened Tark's hold and ran for the stern. Just as he turned the corner, he saw Tarrant. The boy ran to him, but, with a tight fist, Tarrant punched the boy on the forehead. The boy slammed down on his back, forcing the air from his lungs with a whoosh.

"Ha! Well he didn't get far. Good work, Captain Tarrant."

Splayed on the floor, the boy searched for help. Where was Brother? He tried to call out, but he couldn't draw breath. Dizzy now, his vision fading, his head bumped back down on the deck. He could just make out the whip cracking and the chain dropping to the deck.

The sun exploded behind his eyes, and the last thing he heard was Tark and Tarrant laughing.

***

The chimp, with its dying breaths, reached up and stroked the boy's head, its lips pursed again. It tilted its head back to the other side, still stroking the boy's head, trying to pacify him, and a connection was made in life and death.

Then the chimp peered over the boy's shoulder; with widening eyes, it bared its teeth. The boy could see fear in its eyes. Rising to his feet, he turned in one smooth motion.

Behind him was a massive tiger. A fully grown, seasoned killer. The tiger trotted towards the boy with confident, eager paces.

Dry summer leaves puffed out from under huge, powerful paws. Its summer coat didn't hide the muscles in its massive chest, shoulders bulging with every step. Its fur stood up as if it needed to look even bigger than it was. Ears and whiskers back, it was hard to miss the fury in its snarling face. The boy could see no fear in the dark, menacing eyes of this natural-born killer.

The boy looked down at a tree root and he knew what he had to do. Stepping forward and pointing the tip of his spear at his avenger, he let out his most intimidating warrior call.

The tiger leapt, and his world went black.

14 Chain Man

Something was being dragged. It sounded like metal on stone. The boy was hurting. He opened his eyes to see that people were looking down on him as he slid past their feet. They weren't like people he'd seen before. They had narrow eyes, were well-tanned, and were short. As he was dragged along, men grabbed their children as if to protect them; women gasped and covered their mouths. He tried to move but his arms were locked tight at his side. He looked down to see his whole torso was immobilised, wrapped in chain.

The boy looked up the chain to see a swarm of flies buzzing around a raggedly dressed man. It was Tark Fly, with a tight grip on the chain over his shoulder. He was laughing as he paced along, dragging the boy. Ahead, a dog growled at the din of the rattling chain on the cobbled street. Tark spat his well-chewed coffee leaf, hitting the dog between its eyes. It yelped, bared its teeth and backed away.

Darkness ensued as the boy was dragged into a building. Tark yanked the chain and sent him spinning into some chairs. His body slammed on the cold, stone floor. As he tried to scan the large room, everything was whirling. He saw faces of despair, concern, pity and hate. He repeatedly tried to stand but staggered sideways, crashing into more chairs.

Finally, he stood.

Tark walked around, picking up a chair from behind him. With all his might, he flung the chair into the back of the boy's knees. The force of it took the legs from under him, yet only through gritted teeth did the boy cry out as he fell to the stone floor. Tears fell silently from the crowd that watched this strange-looking boy.

Tark tossed his head back and laughed. He turned and began to walk away, then, hearing the laboured movement of chairs, he stopped in his step. In slow, painful movements, the boy pushed aside the shattered chair to get unsteadily to his feet. Tark slowly turned in disbelief as the boy stood, defiant. The boy spat a wad of blood to the floor and smiled at Tark.

Anger prickled Tark's skin as he marched swiftly forward, the dragging chain rattling over the stone floor. The boy limped towards Tark. He could see nothing but his objective. Down beside his legs he held two broken chair legs.

In the crowd, some old men pushed through to the front to protect the women.

Tark was known throughout Middle Kingdom. No one ever dared to defy him. A murmur of wonder went through the crowd as the boy limped towards the large man.

Tark leaned back, dragging the chain and loading his shoulder to strike. He strode forward as the boy limped towards him. The boy could see the menace and hatred in Tark's face – he wanted to cut him down. He was focused, almost smiling, as Tark swung the chain. He raised up the two sticks and leaned in as the chain bore down on him. The chain slammed into the boy's chest, tearing his shirt. As the boy flew backwards, the ferocity of the chain slashed at his chest. Wood splinters flew everywhere as he hit the ground. His body rolled several times and went limp.

The men held the women back as Tark raised his hand to flog the child again. Then suddenly, with his temper gone, he lowered his arm and looked at the boy's back. The boy's torn shirt had landed up over his head. From his left shoulder to his right buttock were four long scars. The unmistakable mark of a big cat.

Tark shook his head and casually began to roll up his chain. He muttered in a low voice, "Be sure he doesn't die on you. I can get good money for a boy with this much pluck." As he left, the men lowered their arms, and the women moved through.

Janing quietly manoeuvred her way through the crowd. Some

of the women ran their fingers over the boy's scars, while others just looked, pointed, and talked. She knelt beside the boy. He was still breathing. She looked at his scars, then rolled him over to see his face. Contrary to his size, he was very young. His wounds were not as bad as they might have been, the wooden legs having taken most of the chain's impact.

She turned to one of the men. "Ain, do you have a knife?"

"You know we can't have knives, Janing."

Frustrated, she sighed. "Well, when you take the silken rolls from the weaves, you have to cut them. What do you use?"

"Oh, you want clippers. Why did you not ask for clippers then?" He headed away.

Janing spoke to the gathering. "I need your help to get this boy up to our living rooms."

The gossiping stopped. They looked from one to the other, no one making eye contact with Janing. She held her hands out. "Well?"

A soft voice spoke. "Hear me, people. You all know who I am, as not one of you has been here longer than me." They listened. Huang never spoke but went quietly about her work and kept to herself. She cast her eyes upon the crowd. "I have seen many people stand before the chain man. I have seen some die of their bruising days later, and I have seen men die on the spot, their necks cracked like summer twigs. I have seen men beaten and dropped into the salty well …" Huang pointed through the open door at the well. " … only to slowly tire still begging for their lives as they drowned."

She stood before the crowd. "These men have been your fathers, your sons, brothers and lovers. They have died in vain. You are still here, and they are all gone. This place has changed you. It has changed all of us. Once, we were hardworking people tending to our crops, going about our chores, and looking after friends and loved ones. Now look at us. I see bitter gossipers who do not care enough or are too afraid to help a boy, *this* boy, who would not stay down to Tark."

One of the women spoke. "Who are you to talk of our crops, our chores, loving our lovers?" She looked up into Huang's old face. "You never had a lover. You are just a bitter old maid who's never been betrothed."

"That is true, Lang. I was taken before I was betrothed, but I worked the crops, I tended my chores, and I loved my family. I lost my maidenhood to Tark's father, Kain, when he carried the chain." Huang looked at the crowd like a hawk searching the field for mice. Eyes dropped back to the floor.

"This room, this silk spinning factory, has been for the most part, the entirety of my life. I did lose my maidenhood in that room ..." She pointed to Tark's office then pointed up to the living rooms. "And that is where I slipped a weaving needle in my womanhood so I would never give Kain or Tark their next chain man. I did it well enough so that I could never have a child of my own. I may seem a little *bitter* to you, Lang, as this is not the life I would have chosen for my worst enemy, but it has been *my* life." She stood eyeing them all.

A few of the women moved forward to stand next to Huang. Janing turned back to the boy and began to undo her apron. Ain arrived back with clippers and she took them from him and cut along the waistband of her apron. Kneeling, she folded her apron in half and placed it on the boy's wounds. The apron changed colour to the stains of blood beneath it.

A hand rested gently on Janing's shoulder and she looked up. It was Que. She smiled at him. "Yes, Que?"

He gave a small dip of the head. "Me and some of the men are now ready to move him to our living rooms."

Janing stood as they gently loaded the boy onto a stretcher. Under the light of pole lanterns, they carried him through the silk factory. As Janing reached the top of the stairs, she saw that the bed was already made. There was a bucket of water and, sitting to one side, was Janing's aunt, Ringcha, mashing a balm in a wooden bowl.

"Ah, Ringcha. I could have used your help downstairs."

Ringcha didn't stop mashing as she slowly looked up.

Janing continued. "But I see you have things ready up here, and I thank you."

The men arrived with the boy and placed him softly onto the bed.

Janing was grateful for the intrusion. Ringcha had a way of putting people in their place whilst smiling as she did it. They began to remove the impromptu bandage and clean the wounds. Extra lanterns were placed around the bed. Others would go without light, but tonight, no one would complain.

"Janing, my eyes aren't what they used to be. Could you see if there are some wood splinters in this wound?"

"Yes, Ringcha. I have some in this one also. It explains why he is bleeding so."

"You remove the splinters. I will begin to pack up the smaller lacerations with some balm."

Once finished, they let him rest.

Lang stepped forward to the foot of the small bed. "Interesting. When he stood up to Tark, he seemed so big, but when you look at his face, he is just a child. He never had a chance against that monster, not one chance."

Ringcha wiped her hands. "Yet, when you compare him to our children, *he* is a monster."

Lang shook her head. "He is no monster, just big for his age. Look at that face. He is just a baby, and the skin colour … where could he be from?"

Huang stepped into the light. Her wrinkles showed her years of hardship. She made a curt bow which the other women reciprocated then returned their attention to the child.

Huang studied the boy for some time. "When I was a child, my grandfather used to tell me and my brothers a legend. It was said that when things were at their worst, when the Devil's friends walk among us, a saviour would come. He would be a man like no other.

He would bear the tag of the animal Kingdom to tell all that the Kingdom had challenged him, yet he stands among us. He would be the man of many Spirits." She pointed a skinny, withered finger. "This boy here carries many spirits and bears the tag of the animal Kingdom."

In silence, they absorbed the legend.

Ringcha was the first to speak. "If Tark sends him to the Emperor for a good price, your spirit boy will be sent to the pit. No one escapes from a fight with dogs and wolves. What are we to do to save him, Huang?"

Lang attempted to change the subject. "It is a story told by a grandparent too many years ago to count. It was never meant to be taken as fact. Huang, I didn't know you had brothers. What happened to them?"

Huang continued to stare at the boy. "The first year, my eldest brother died of the bruising from the chain. The second year, my next brother died in the salt well. In the third year, three of my nieces were brought in, but before Kain sold them, I got to talk to one of them. She said Kain had led a raid on our village as a warning not to come to this silk factory anymore. This message was sent out to all villages by one young man. Kain castrated him with a hot knife. There were no other survivors, save the three young women. Maybe it was just a story told to children by a campfire, but this boy … this boy of mixed blood … *has* the scar of the animal Kingdom. This boy stood up to Tark and *still* he breathes." With that, she turned and walked into the night.

***

For two days, the boy slept. All the women offered to keep watch in turns, and even some of the men came to see how he was faring. Finally, the boy woke up.

He tried to open his eyes but felt too light-headed to move much at all. It was dark. He could hear groaning and tried to move to see who was hurt, but couldn't.

A hand came down on his shoulder. "Sshhh, stay still."

Water touched his mouth. Instinctively, he turned away, holding his breath.

"Easy, boy, easy. We are trying to help you."

It was another voice the boy didn't know. She lifted his head gently. He felt a cup to his lips, and his tongue came out to test. *Water. Fresh water.* He began to drink then, realising how thirsty he was, gulped it down.

"Easy, easy. It has been some days since you last drank."

His body shook as he reached up to hold the cup, and he held the hands that helped him. They seemed no bigger than his, though soft.

She spoke. "That's it, boy, easy. Rest up and you will be all right."

But there are no women on the Shiraz? He struggled to sit up, spilling water over himself and the bed. He moved his feet over the side as his body shook with pain. He had to find his way back to his vessel, to Baako and the men. It was his place now.

The woman gathered him up as he collapsed at the edge of the bed.

***

He felt himself struggling to breathe, unable to move. It was dark and getting hot. A heavy weight was pressing down on him. Trapped, he began to panic, trying to get room to move, to draw a breath. Then he saw an older man with narrow eyes and long, greying hair. His long, moustache joined his beard which ran down his chest. The man had kind eyes. He came walking towards the boy, holding up his hands, calming him. The man stood in front of him.

The boy tried to ask his name but his voice produced no sound.

The man spoke. "All in good time, my friend, all in good time. We have time when we learn to stop rushing and pushing."

"So, I am dead?"

"Goodness no, I hope not, my young friend," the man laughed.

"We have met somewhere before, then?"

"No. When the time is right, we shall." The man moved away. "They are here for you now."

"When? Where do I need to go to find you? How will I know?"

"Now there you go again, rushing ahead. When the time is right. They are here to help you now." The man was now walking away.

In panic, the boy called out. "How can I know? How will I know?"

A distant voice came back. "I will find you. I will get you ..."

The immense weight moved away and light shone bright again. A powerful arm scooped him up. The air was cool and fresh. His body was limp but the strong arms held him securely. The boy knew it was his father. He looked at the way the light scattered through the canopy, dancing over the drying leaves of green and gold. The jungle looked spectacular.

Ever more tribesmen came to see his kill. They were pointing and laughing, shaking his father's hand. The boy wanted to see his father, but he couldn't turn his head. He peered down to see the tiger his father had rolled aside, freeing him. Its huge jaws were wide open. Its body was stretched, as if still in a leap but through its chest was his spear. It had gone into the chest and up through its spine at its hindquarters. Instant death. The men pointed and cheered at the tree root which had the butt of his spear lodged under it. The spear had broken, but not before it had killed the tiger.

The boy looked at the chimp, slumped on the bank. It was dead, though smiling.

Men and boys came to shake his hand as they spoke his name. The boy listened, but all he could hear was the ringing in his ears. The more he tried to read their lips, the more they seemed to fade. Bouncing on one foot and then the other, holding their spears and blow pipes at their side, they started to chant his name.

With an effort, he tried to read their lips ...

***

"Hello, so you are back with us again?"

He felt that small, soft hand come under his head again. He drank steadily before she lay him back down. He blinked his swollen eyelids and through small slits he could see a roof. Though he couldn't focus, he knew he was in a house somewhere. He closed his eyes. "So tired."

"Rest, boy, you are strong and will be all right, son."

Son? The boy put out his hand and the woman took it. "Momma? Momma, is that you?"

Her hand squeezed his. "No, son, I'm not your mother, but we will all care for you as best we can. I must go to work now. You rest, someone will return to give you water soon. Rest now."

Sleep came easily.

***

It took some days, though soon enough, the boy was up and eating with the rest of them. Outside of asking how he'd gotten there, he hadn't said much. It was assumed the boat that he spoke of, the *Shiraz*, had left dock two or three days after he arrived. Vessels never stayed longer. The boy's pained expression was evident as this was explained to him. He told them that if none of them could go to the docks and check, no one could be sure. No one was allowed to leave to see for themselves, so if it kept the boy's hope alive, it was all well with them.

There was one thing he was able to do. He listened and, before long, he was stringing words together in their tongue. He seemed to understand what they'd said, then repeat what he'd heard. His ability to learn was as strong in him as his ability to heal.

One evening, the boy sat in the food hall for the first time. Everyone sat in a large circle, and bowls with a sticky kind of rice were handed out. Then, some of the younger women came around with trays of sauce and vegetables, plus a little meat, and each of them would serve themselves.

The man called Que spoke. "Boy, we have all called you 'boy'. It is like a name, but not. Anyone who can make a stand against

Tark deserves a name. What is your name – Boy?" A chuckle went about the room. Que always had a way with words to make them laugh.

The boy opened his mouth – and closed it again. He looked at all the expectant faces, then down at his food bowl, tears welling up. He remembered the elderly man of his dreams. The chimp, the tiger, his people dancing around chanting his name, but it was not a word he could hear. He remembered Baako's dark face with shiny, white teeth telling him, *Don't worry, boy. When the time is right, you will remember.*

He wiped his eyes and took a deep breath. "When I was put on the vessel *Shiraz*, I got a bump to the head. I don't remember a thing before that."

There was an awkward silence, then Que spoke again. "Well, that is no matter, son. What did they call you on this *Shiraz* vessel?" Que's soft manner made it easier for the boy to keep his composure.

"On the *Shiraz* they just called me – boy." Then his eyes lit up and he smiled a little. "Except for Baako. He was one of the big slaves; he looked out for me and he called me Brother." He swallowed back his tears. "But I guess he has left with his vessel. I should have left with his vessel, with him, with my vessel." His tears glistened in the lantern light as they trickled down his golden cheeks.

***

When the boy was strong enough, he began to help around the silk factory. The dreaded Tark stayed away, but they all knew that, when the boy was healthy again, Tark would look to profit from his existence. The wealthy few always sought to profit from the existence of the rest.

Then the morning arrived. Huang was instructed to deliver the boy to Tark's office, where she told him to sit on the floor and eat his breakfast. Alone, in the middle of the floor, he heard a commotion outside. Through the window, he could see old man

Que from the factory.

The old man pointed in Tark's face, insisting, "He is just a boy. You don't have the right!"

Instantly, and without warning, Tark swung his chain over his shoulder, smashing Que to the ground. He swiped the little man up and dangled him over the salt well. A faint smile passed over the old man's face. He took aim, and his bloodied spit hit Tark in the face. It was the last thing the old man would do as Tark immediately dropped him to his death.

Tark stiffened. He turned to the factory, and there, looking out of the window, was the boy standing on a chair. For a time they stood, locked eye to eye. Tark shivered slightly and backed away from the window. The boy didn't blink his steel-blue eyes.

Lang walked into the courtyard seeking Que. Pleased to move his attention, Tark approached. "You. Come here." Lang quickly obliged and knelt at his feet. "Fix some provisions for two and tell Bing to advise my father I need him immediately. Fetch my horse and a spare. Go!"

"Yes, Tark."

Tark headed back to his office, swung the door open and strode in. The boy was back sitting on the floor eating breakfast. He didn't look up.

Tark looked at Huang who stood beside him. "What are you doing in my office, old hag?"

"Please, Tark, if you wish to get a full price for this boy, he must be in good shape. The Emperor will only pay the most for the best."

"Yes, that is so. That is also why I can't sell all of you and go into retirement."

The west wall of his office was covered in chains and padlocks. He selected a short chain with small links and moved along to the padlocks. Selecting one, he went over to the boy who was handing Huang the empty food bowl. Tark grabbed him by the hair and lifted him to his feet. The boy didn't let out a squeak as Tark began to lash his wrists.

Huang spoke again. "Tark, sir, if the boy's wrists are bruised, you will get less for him. Is he riding a horse or a mule?"

"For someone that says nothing for two full seasons, you have a lot to say this morning." He bent at the waist, eyeballing the old woman. "And why would that matter to the price of the boy?"

"If you put the boy on a mule, then he could surely be of no trouble to a man like yourself, Tark."

Tark's grubby face was just a few inches from hers now. "Would there be anything else this morning?"

"Yes, Tark. The boy's name is Kito … Chan Kito."

"If I do not care what *your* name is, old hag, what would I care for the boy's name?"

Still Huang didn't lift her head. "Years ago, the Emperor's father led a small group to meet with the Northern King, Tzu Hsi. It was intended to be a meeting of peace, but upon their arrival at one of the Emperor's own villages, they were set upon. In the attack, the Emperor saw his best friend, Ta Tuku, being cut down by two men. Both men were of the Chan family."

Tark stood up straight, growing bored. "Yes, yes, and so?"

"All the Chan families were driven north to breed with the barbarians. All are now of mixed blood." She tilted her head towards the boy.

"Ah, so you think I should lie to our Emperor, do you, nag?"

Huang didn't flinch. "Tark, can you say this boy is not of mixed blood?"

"Well, of course, he is of mixed blood, woman!"

She continued quickly. "Well then, we can't be so sure he is not a Chan, sir. His size, his skin colour, I think he may be a Barbarian Chan."

Tark's father, Kain, entered the office, dressed in his favourite leather pants with his purple overcoat. As always, he wore his two belts, one red and one black.

"Kain, I would like you to meet the reason I've called you here today. This is Chan Kito, I will …"

Kain broke in. "You're not telling me he is one of those mixed blood Chans, are you?"

Stunned, Tark attempted to give an air of control. "Yes, Kain. As I was saying, I have a Chan that I wish to sell to the Emperor, so I need you to look after the factory whilst I'm away."

Kain fixed his eyes on the boy and hooked his thumbs into his black belt. "Yes, yes, of course, Tark." Lowering his voice, "Tark, there is a rumour about changes, changes from the throne for the city. I feel you should offer this boy Chan to the Emperor, as a gift, perhaps."

"Kain, what are these changes you speak of? I haven't heard anything around the city."

"Think on it, Tark, you must stay on top of your game. The Emperor's son has had much training. The Emperor hasn't done much since the loss of Hasuca many years ago, but when his son comes of age, if there is not a plan on the Emperor's table, I will eat a sea captain's hat."

The truth was, a man wearing an eye patch and calling himself Cusaha had come to Kain's door just last night and told him the story. As bearer of the black belt, Cusaha had said it was important for Kain to know.

"Really?" asked Tark. "What would the Emperor want with the city of Samos? It is his already."

"Yes, the city is in his lands, but it's controlled by a whole lot of business people, including myself. He will be looking to assert his power to show and teach his son about the business of the throne. If we can offer him a goodwill gift, we may become a part of his future plan. We may even get a bigger piece of the pie."

Tark walked to the window to see if there was any sign of his horses. He had never understood politics. He opened the window. "Bing, I said to get my horse and a *mule*. Swap out that horse before I come out and put you down the well with your friend." Tark slammed the window closed. "But why Samos, Kain?"

Kain slapped his sides with an exasperated moan. "Is it not obvious to you? Whoever has Samos has the Great Southern trade, and *that*, my son, is *real* power."

Tark scowled at the boy and Huang. He'd forgotten the old hag was still there, not that she would understand anyway. "My ride is here. Kain. I must deliver Chan Kito as a very important gift."

With a broad smile, Kain slapped him on the back. "Indeed, you must, Tark. This is a great day. I don't care where you got the boy, but he will certainly buy us favour, a lot of favour, with the Emperor of Middle Kingdom no less." He waved one finger in the air,."This gift has come at a critical time indeed. Tark, I feel this is truly a great day!"

***

The horses' hooves clattered on the cobbles as they trotted through the crowded city streets. Tark carried the chain and lock, and had indicated that at the first sign of trouble, Kito would wear them. Once at the outer reaches of the city, Tark had Kito take his own reins and move to the front. By early afternoon, they had reached the edge of the jungle. It felt good to move out of the sun but the humidity in the jungle was oppressive.

From time to time, Tark would whistle a little, though not a word was exchanged between them.

As it grew dark, finally, Tark spoke. "There is a cove up ahead, but we won't be stopping there tonight."

Kito looked at him blankly. It was a strange comment to make. When they reached the cove, Kito pondered it as they passed. It seemed like a good place to camp.

"They call it the Cove of Lost Souls," Tark said in an unaccustomedly quiet voice. They continued on until it was pitch black. "This will do now."

They dismounted, and Kito released the mule of its load. He began to gather sticks to start a fire when Tark grabbed him by the arm.

"No fires! No point in drawing attention to ourselves."

Kito dropped the firewood. It was unusual to be camping and not have a fire, so their meal for the night consisted only of dried meat and bread. The chain rattled as Tark unceremoniously chained Kito to his saddle, then settled down to sleep.

The travelling pattern continued like this for a few more days. The jungle changed as they climbed. The canopy of trees became lower and less dense, eventually opening out onto several grassy areas. There was a rustle as a pheasant flew up from the long grass. Swiftly, Tark loaded his crossbow and took aim. It landed on the other side of a small field, and Tark headed over with his horse. A rabbit scarpered in front of Kito's mule. Tark spun about in his saddle, arm outstretched, seemingly not taking aim. It tumbled to a halt. Dead.

This was not going to be a man Kito could easily run from. *Least of all on this mount,* he thought. There had to be a way to his freedom, to his way home, wherever that was.

That night, Kito was asked to make a fire to cook the game Tark had prepared. It was a veritable feast after the dried meat and bread. After their meal, they rested. Kito looked at the big man. He was clearly happier and more comfortable out here than in the city.

The jungle turned to forest, and the grassy fields became larger and more regular. They ate fresh meat every night now, and the fire had another purpose; the nights were getting cooler.

They journeyed on.

"There is a campsite just a little further up. We will stop there for the night."

Kito didn't respond but stopped, bringing Tark to a halt behind him.

Tark scowled. "What are you stopping for, boy? I told you there is a camp a little further up."

Kito surveyed his surroundings in the darkness. "Something is not right, Tark, sir," he whispered.

Tark searched but could see nothing. "Bhah, it's just the night's shadows fooling you, boy."

Kito shook his head. "No, Tark, someone is already there." He could feel it. "I'm telling you, Tark, someone is already there."

15 Cusaha

Tark walked his horse up beside Kito's mule and, leaning over, pulled him onto it, sitting him in front of him. He handed Kito the reins and tied the mule's lead on the pommel of his own saddle. Crossbow cocked, he placed it between them.

Tark slowly scanned the bushes in the fading light. A light flickered at the end of the track. He took his time, trying not to look directly at the light.

As they neared the clearing, a man rose so his visitors could see him. Tark kept his horse at a walk as he slipped off and put Kito in the saddle. Without a word, Tark slipped silently into the forest.

Tark's horse continued to walk down the trail into the small clearing and around the fire to the stranger, who gently reached up and patted the horse on the nose.

Ill at ease, Tark crouched in the bushes to observe.

Kito looked down at the man. It was hard to guess his age, except to say he was middle-aged. He had a ponytail and a slim moustache across his top lip and down the side of his mouth to his jawline, showing just slight signs of grey. His skin was golden-yellow, and over one eye, he sported a leather patch.

"Are you right to get down, Kito, or would you like a hand?"

The man seemed familiar. Kito was happy to slide from the saddle. He was almost as tall as the stranger and noticed that the stranger had put them both between the horse and the mule. The man winked at him before abruptly moving off in the direction of the trees.

"All right, Tark, I have been expecting you. You may come out now, please."

Tark sheepishly walked out from the trees directly before the stranger, who led him back to the campfire. The stranger then bowed deeply. "My name is Cusaha. Your father sent a pigeon to the palace and I have been directed to meet with you. Tark, you are to be commended, as you have single-handedly caught, Chan Kito. Also, Kain was right when he talked of a plan for the city of Samos. It has been discussed in the palace for some time."

Tark's stance changed defensively. Cusaha moved around behind Kito as he spoke. "Your father is an influential man in Samos, yes, Tark?" Cusaha pulled a strip of leather binding from his pocket.

"Um, yes, I guess you could say that. I now run the factory."

With astonishing speed, Cusaha grabbed Kito and turned him face-down, slamming him into the dirt. A puff of dust went up as Cusaha tied Kito's hands behind his back. He leaned in beside Kito. "I know your family history, Chan Kito. It will be my pleasure to take you to His Royal Emperor and hand you over. You see, Chan Kito," he rose to his feet, "I am a direct descendant of Ta Tuku!"

Tark looked at the boy's hands; they were already turning blue. This man was taking no chances. Calmly, Cusaha moved to the fire and sat, then pulled a large shell from the fire. Holding his head away from the steam, he blew several times over the hot shell, then used his knife to cut a cord wrapped around it. The shell opened. Grubs and small beetles swirled about in the broth. He stirred the green fluid with his knife.

Tark recoiled as Cusaha moved one half of the shell towards him. "You would like to share in my broth, yes, Tark?"

Tark's face reddened. "Thank you no, though the boy hasn't eaten all day."

Throwing Kito a quick glance, Cusaha shrugged. "I see no point in wasting food on a dead boy. Come, Tark, I insist."

Tark grimaced as he reluctantly took the shell offered to him. Finally, Cusaha spoke again. "So, Tark, as I was saying before, your father is a man of power in the city, is he not?"

Tark swallowed his last mouthful, trying not to gag as the grubs slithered down his throat. He coughed. "Yes, I would say my family is well thought of. The silk factory is the largest of its kind and we've had it in our family for many generations."

"So, it would be correct to expect you wouldn't like to see it lost from your family's ownership if the city was to come under siege."

"I *would* not, *could* not lose the ownership of the factory, Cusaha! It could not happen. Not now, not ever!" Tark slapped a hand on his knee to reinforce his determination.

Cusaha continued to eat from the large shell as Tark tried to look away. "Well, the Emperor may be able to help you with that when the city comes under siege."

Tark looked confused. "That's why I was hoping to deliver the boy to the Emperor myself, Cusaha. It is my intention to propose an alliance with our Emperor, for such a state of emergency."

Cusaha ate a little more, leaving Tark waiting. Eventually, he put aside his broth. "So, Tark, you say your family would support the Emperor if such a siege took place. Are you sure?"

"Yes, of course, we would be in full support. If the Emperor wishes something from us, he needs only ask."

Cusaha reached over for his pack and pulled out three small cylinders. Tark was unable to determine what they were, so smooth and faultless. Cusaha removed the end of one and took out the contents. Tark watched in fascination as Cusaha unrolled a delicate scroll and held it up to observe.

"They must be handled with the utmost of care. They are countless ages old and are said to be from the last world, from the Failed Generation. I have no idea what the symbols say. It is a language that is known to no one who has visited the palace. The palace has had the best scholars look them over since they were found many generations ago."

Tark looked perplexed as Cusaha looked at the beautifully embroidered scroll. It depicted the scene of a lake, as blue as a summer's day, with a tall waterfall in the background. What drew the eye, though, was the narrow, stone bridge that arched up high, disappearing into a column of dense fog, perfectly round and extending upwards off the scroll itself.

Tark looked on until Cusaha, taking the utmost care, rolled it up and returned it into its cylinder. Picking up a second cylinder, Cusaha removed another scroll. This, too, was strange. It depicted a beautiful young woman with a glowing smile. She was wearing a long dress of the most vibrant, sparkling orange. The bottom of the dress seemed to be breaking away, the pieces turning into butterflies that delicately spiralled up around her.

"Cusaha, what *is* this?" asked Tark in a somewhat frustrated tone.

"At the palace we all agree that she must be someone of great importance. Maybe a Princess or such like."

"Yes, I can see that, Cusaha, but I also see she is not of this land, and so it has little relevance to anything."

Cusaha noted the pompous tone of the impatient man. He rolled it up and placed it in the tube before Tark could ruin the moment further. Picking up the third cylinder, Cusaha slid out the final wall hanging. It was his favourite. Holding it up, he gave Tark a moment to take it in. Tark tilted his head, looking at the picture. It was a heavy-set man dressed in grey. The man had a hood up, so all you could see of him was his hand clutching a large bag at his side.

Tark couldn't figure it out. "What a strangely dressed man. What's he standing before?"

"I like to think it's the Sacred Crystal." Cusaha gently fingered the delicate cloth.

Tark frowned. "Why would he be standing before a crystal?"

"But that's not the point. I think this may be the mythical Crystal of all Knowledge. Where this Crystal is, I don't know. Though, is this not proof that it *really* exists?"

Tark scoffed. "Well, no. These are clearly just pictures. A bridge that disappears into the fog, some woman wearing a fictitious dress and the last one is simply a strange man in oddly dressed attire." Tark picked some dust from the corner of his eye. "It's all a bit ridiculous if you ask me."

Cusaha refrained from responding directly to Tark's ignorance. He feigned a smile. "These are gifts from the Royal Emperor himself. Do you have an office that you work from, Tark?"

"Why yes, I work from a very fine office." Tark puffed up with his own self-importance.

"Good. When the city of Samos comes under siege, and it will, you must have these hangings on your wall. They will give you immunity. You have three, so you can protect three establishments if you wish, though it would carry more power to have them together."

Tark looked less than impressed.

Cusaha had one more thing. He went back into his bag and removed a piece of cloth. He looked up into Tark's dim eyes. "This is a token of gratitude from the Emperor directly for you, Tark Fly. When he handed it to me, he said, 'Please be sure to inform this brave individual that I am in his gratitude. Please ask him to wear this for my honour of him.'"

The mention of his merit had Tark charmed as Cusaha laid the cloth in his palm. Carefully, Tark pulled back the corners. In his cloth-covered palm was a circular locket, the gold glistening brightly in the flames of the fire.

Cusaha took it from him and carefully opened it. The lid hinged back and stayed up. It showed a glass vase with a small, black stem in the middle. Inside was a white, flaky substance. For Tark, it was the long, gold chain that held his interest. In the light, it looked as if it was on fire.

Cusaha took the end of the chain where it finished with a 'T'. "Tark, sir, on behalf of the Emperor and the palace, may I?"

A little bewildered, Tark merely nodded. Cusaha reached up and slid the chain's 'T' link through the top buttonhole of Tark's tunic, allowing the chain to hang down. He slipped the golden locket into the pocket opposite.

He sat back and looked at Tark. *If the guards don't notice that, then they really do need hanging.* "Tark, sir, you really look smart."

Tark looked down. "Well, yes, I suppose I do. But what's it for, Cusaha?"

Cusaha closed his eyes in frustration, taking a deep breath. "Why, Tark, sir, it is a showpiece! If you see the Emperor's Guard, you take it out and look at it. They will see you and know you are Tark, the one who captured Chan Kito."

Tark reached into his right pocket, pulled out the piece and looked at it. Cusaha told him to put it back, then take it out once more and flick open the lid. Tark tried but had it upside down.

"Try it again, Tark."

After a few attempts, he got it right. "I will practise this all the way home."

"Yes, Tark, I'm sure you will. Now, we both have big journeys ahead, best we get some rest, do you not think, Tark, sir?"

"Yes. I thank you for saving me the entire journey. I will leave at first light to get back to my business."

Cusaha watched as Tark brought out the gift three times during one sentence. He turned away, rolling his unpatched eye.

The two men made ready for sleep. Tark went to the edge of the camp to relieve himself, and on the way back, he stopped before the boy, who sat in the dirt.

"You just remember who you are dealing with, Chan Kito. Tark of the chain!" To emphasise his point, he kicked dust into the boy's face. Kito turned his head and spat on the ground to clear his mouth. Indifferent, Tark kicked Kito in the chest, knocking him over and laughed as he walked back to the fire. Cusaha laughed with him as he lay down for the night.

The two men settled reasonably quickly.

Unable to sleep, Kito sat upright. He wondered if Baako was okay and if he would ever get to see the *Shiraz* again. He looked at the sleeping form of Tark by the fire. If he could just get hold of a knife, he could right now avenge the old man Que's unnecessary death at the factory. He uncrossed his legs and steadied himself as he stood with his hands still bound behind his back. He walked over to the snoring Tark.

He checked his balance. Carefully, he reached out with his right foot and picked up a fold in Tark's cover with his toes. He lifted the cover a little higher. Tark was asleep on the sheath, but luckily, the knife's handle was protruding behind his back.

Kito began the delicate task of lifting the cover clear so he could retrieve the knife. Tark snored on rhythmically. He was about to move the cover further when the hairs on the back of his neck began to stand up. He froze. For the longest time, he didn't move. Ever so slowly, he peered across the fire. Cusaha was sitting up, looking directly at him, his face impassive.

Kito looked at the knife again and felt for his hands. Numb. They had been tied for too long. He looked back at Cusaha. The man could clear the fire and take his life before he had the knife out of the sheath. Slowly, he lowered the cover and stepped back. Cusaha still looked on impassively. With barely the crack of a twig under his bare feet, Kito went back to his spot and sat.

Cusaha lay down again, and Tark snored on, oblivious.

16 The Young Apprentice

The following morning, Tark was up before sunrise. He didn't wait to speak with Cusaha but packed his things, including the three tubes and left.

The moment he'd gone, Cusaha stood abruptly and threw some wood on the fire. He walked to Kito, knelt on one knee and looked directly at him. The boy showed no fear. He couldn't feel his fingers anymore, yet the man didn't frighten him. In fact, there was something about him that Kito actually liked.

Cusaha spoke softly. "I'm about to have breakfast, Kito, would you join me?"

"Yes."

With a whisper of a smile, Cusaha asked, "If I cut you free, will you give me any trouble?" Kito shook his head. "Then so be it." Getting up, he cut the binds.

At first, Kito couldn't bring his hands around to his front, his shoulders ached so. His hands felt like they were on fire, then they stung like needle pricks. Eventually, they began to look and feel like his hands again. Tentatively, he started to walk around, but when he returned, he was surprised to see Cusaha turning a rabbit over the fire. Curiously, he wasn't sporting his eye patch either.

Kito looked at Cusaha for the longest moment. "Cusaha. May I call you this?"

"Yes, for now."

Kito pondered his strange reply. He looked at the rabbit. "Did you have this in your pack last night?"

Cusaha didn't raise his head, though Kito did detect the hint of a smile. "No, I caught it this morning."

"You mean you set some snares last night?"

"No, I mean I called the rabbit to be caught this morning."

Another strange comment. Kito's mouth watered at the aroma of the rabbit. He watched intently as Cusaha took the meat away from the flame and broke it into parts. He licked his lips and swallowed. Cusaha handed him a piece, and he ate greedily. When they'd finished, Kito sat back holding his belly. He dipped his head in thanks when Cusaha handed him the water container. "So, if you are to deliver me to the Emperor, we might as well make a start."

"Do you even know why you are to be delivered to the Emperor, Kito?"

"Well, yes."

"And when you are there, do you know what he is to do with you?"

"I heard some talk at the factory about the Pit, wolves, dogs and things."

Cusaha raised his eyebrows. "And what do you suppose will happen in this pit, Kito?"

Kito sat, confused. "Well, I don't expect to come back out, not in one piece at least."

"This bothers you not, young Kito?"

Kito shook his head. "I would rather not die in the middle of someone else's family war, in a land that is not mine."

Instantly angry, Cusaha jumped to his feet. "What's this nonsense about someone else's war and not your land, Chan Kito?"

Kito was not deterred. "I have no idea what my family name is, Cusaha, but I do know I have never been on this land before." He looked about at the forest and back to Cusaha. "But it is very beautiful."

Cusaha raised his eyebrows again. "Well, if your food has settled, it's time to be moving." He put on his pack and doused the fire, then began to walk down the same track Kito had arrived by the night before. After some time, Cusaha broke into a run.

Kito simply followed suit. It wasn't long before his lungs began to burn, and he had to slow down.

Cusaha backtracked to see the boy bent down with his hands on his knees, wheezing badly. He scoffed. "When I was your age, no one in this land could catch me. Not even my own brother. What is your problem, boy?"

Kito spoke between breaths. "It was not my choice to leave my family or to sit on a vessel for so long. It was not my choice to be in the silk factory *and* it was not my choice to sit on a mule for so long, to see *you*." Then, with his hands on his hips, he strode past Cusaha, walking off the ache in his side. Chuckling to himself, Cusaha walked behind him for a while. Soon after, Kito moved into a jog. It was easy to know the way, Kito followed the hoof prints left by Tark's horse, and Cusaha didn't say otherwise.

***

They kept running for several days. Kito's breathing improved greatly, and before long, he was able to talk as they jogged for long periods, stopping only to replenish water or have something to eat. He started asking questions, learning which fruit to peel, which could be eaten whole and their growing seasons.

They came to a stream that Kito remembered crossing with Tark. *I don't know why we're still going back towards Samos but as long as I'm not heading to the Pit, I'm good with it.'*

The water in the stream was as cool as it was crystal clear. Cusaha replenished his water bladder and began walking upstream. They waded out to a small waterfall and climbed up to the highest point. It was a little slippery, but the handholds were plentiful. At the top, another pool led to another waterfall. Beyond that, another pool and one more wall of cascading water. This was the tallest one yet.

Kito peered back down the stream as it disappeared over the crest. There was jungle on both sides of the rapidly flowing water, and in the distance, across a mighty valley, Kito could see rocky outcrops with the jungle breaking them up into islands. Huge waterfalls cascaded down into the deep valley below.

Kito breathed in this enchanted land. He thought about the tracks he'd seen from the mighty elephant, the curves of the snake, some too big to believe. He saw gibbons and baboons. He listened to a wondrous number of birds; some he knew, some he didn't. And then there was the roar of the big cat, which cut him to his core.

He pulled himself from this vista only to notice Cusaha was gone. Kito moved quickly to catch up. There was no track here and the thought of a big cat had unnerved him somehow. He waded through the pool, feeling the cool, smooth pebbles underfoot. They felt nice after the long, dusty trail. He reached the last waterfall and began the climb once more. This one was more challenging, the rock smooth, the handholds not as abundant. At last, he crested the top and walked forward onto dry rock. With the waterfall behind him, it was suddenly quiet.

Kito stood spellbound at the lake before him. In some places, smooth rock formations bulged out. Some soared up vertically fifty feet or more, others were only just out of the water like giant turtles basking in the sun. The jungle came close to the banks. Tall, shady trees hung over the edge, and the jungle floor was so flat it seemed it would flood if the lake rose. To the far side, he could just see the stream coursing over a low but wide waterfall.

He searched for Cusaha and found him over to the left on a long, pebble beach. Kito turned and took one more look at the mighty valley behind, then went to join Cusaha, who was now disrobing and heading into the lake.

Kito laughed as he waded through the stream onto Cusaha's pebble beach. As he began to run, he took off his shredded shirt. Getting to Cusaha's clothes, he stopped, took off the rest and ran into the water. It was refreshing. Diving under, he saw an abundance of fish, some rather too big to like, but Cusaha seemed unperturbed. He relished the feel of cool water over his dusty body. He almost wished not to surface.

Cusaha had swum out to one of the smooth, rock islands and was walking up the gentle slope. Kito swam to join him.

Cusaha's eyes twinkled. "I had never seen you swim. You are quite the fish, I see."

Kito thought his statement odd, but in his excitement, answered, "I was not sure I could swim either, but it looked so inviting I just had to!"

Before Cusaha could question his response, the boy ran to the other side of the rock. It sloped up well above the water. After a quick look, Kito dived in. Cusaha watched as the boy dived and swam with the fish. *Youth is a wonderful thing.*

Kito swam until it was dark enough to notice the fire Cusaha had made. Feeling a little guilty, he headed to it. Brushing his body off by hand, he was almost dry by the time he was at the fire's edge. "I'm sorry, Cusaha. This place is something very special. I do believe I lost myself this afternoon."

Cusaha waved a dismissive hand. "I'm not bothered about you acting your age for a change, Kito, though you could put on some clothes and go and fetch me some bigger pieces of wood to keep the fire going overnight, if you desire."

A little relieved, Kito whipped on his pants and headed for the jungle. After half a dozen paces, he stopped. It was twilight on the small beach, but dark in the jungle. He waited and allowed his senses to adjust. This was not his jungle, and he knew nothing about it, but the hair on his neck stayed down. Reluctantly, he pushed on and started gathering firewood.

With a few good chunks of wood, he headed back, pleased to see the fire in sight now. Cusaha had spread it out so it was mainly hot coals.

"Cusaha, were you a little worried about it getting too big and attracting attention?"

Cusaha flung his head back and roared with laughter. It was full and without reserve. It was the sort of laugh that made you at least smile, then laugh with him even if, like Kito now, you didn't know why. Eventually, Cusaha simmered to an occasional chuckle.

On the hot coals was a mud pack. Kito pointed to it. "Cusaha, why do you have mud in your coals?"

"I have been waiting for you to spot that. You will be pleased to see it's our dinner." With that, he reached in with two sticks, gently rolled it out, then rebuilt the fire.

Remembering the grubs in a shell on the first night they'd met, Kito was now concerned about the mudpack.

Cusaha battered the mudpack about on the pebbles. "The mud holds the heat. It doesn't need to be in the fire for long, as it's still cooking as we speak."

Kito resisted asking what 'it' was as Cusaha dealt with the hot mudpack. Cusaha rubbed his hands together like a mischievous child, his eyes sparkling in the firelight. The food must be very close to done though Kito elected to sit quietly until it was ready. He looked at Cusaha, who in turn, was studying him.

Cusaha returned his attention to the mudpack. Holding it between his two palms, he looked for the join along the edge and, placing his thumbs on either side, he pulled. With a crack, it popped open revealing half a fish. He took his knife and carefully lifted out the tail and, with it, the spine and all the bones. The fire crackled, sparkled and spat with the fish oil as he flicked them in.

Kito was hungry, but that was no excuse for bad manners, so he waited for Cusaha to start. He had never seen such a thing. Cooking with mud and how the fish had parted right down the spine, leaving no bones. He tried to remember how they cooked in his homeland but couldn't. He just couldn't.

That night, the boy cried himself to sleep.

***

It was dawn when Kito awoke. He searched for Cusaha and found him standing in a loincloth on a large, flat rock at the water's edge. He was facing the sunrise, his eyes closed and his hands clasped. Though fascinated, Kito felt he shouldn't intrude. The fire was low, so he added to it and sat quietly. The jungle was changing from night to day. The night hunters and fossickers rested and the day brought a change of wildlife.

Cusaha began to sway in almost imperceptible movements, turning, twisting, bracing, pushing and pulling. Soon his lean, muscular body was dripping in sweat.

The sun was well up when Cusaha finished. He went to the deep side of the rock and sat with his legs crossed, his hands on his knees. With his palms up, he closed his eyes. Kito waited, watching. It happened so quickly that Kito almost missed it. A large fish jumped out of the water and into Cusaha's arms. He calmly turned and put it on the rock then put his hand over the fish's eyes. The tail spasmed and then relaxed.

It was dead.

As Cusaha returned to the beach, Kito made sure the fire was good, and stood. "Good morning, Cusaha."

Cusaha placed the fish on the beach then bowed deeply and stood. "Good morning to you, Kito and what a beautiful morning it is." Kito looked about. It was a nice day, but so had most of the others been. "Kito, I'm going to prepare the fish. Would you like to watch?"

"Oh, that would truly be great, if you wouldn't mind, Cusaha."

"Well, that would be why I asked, Kito."

Cusaha fetched his knife and headed a short distance into the jungle. He showed Kito every cut and why he did it. At the riverbank, Cusaha broke away some of the mud and moulded it into a bowl shape. He placed the pad of mud on the pebbles then put some of his herbs on it. He laid the fish on half of the mud, placed the rest of the herbs on it and a few inside also. This was how the delicious fish they'd eaten the day before had acquired its flavour. Kito watched as Cusaha pressed the two halves together, completing the mudpack.

"Shall we, Kito?"

"My belly is already rumbling in anticipation." Kito eagerly took the lead back to the fire and by the time Cusaha had strolled along the beach, he'd spread the coals ready for the mudpack.

Cusaha smiled to himself. *The boy has only seen the process once.* "We must be careful. The pebbles underneath are already hot; they alone could cook this fish."

"How will I know when it's cooked?"

"Look at the dark colour of the mud. When it becomes lighter, you can tap it with a stick. It must be firm to the tap, but if it cracks, it's already too late. Then you tip it over carefully and give it half the time on the second side. You take it out to cool, as you saw me do last night."

The two walked to the edge of the water where Cusaha waded in and dived under. Kito bent down and washed his face. Taking some water in his mouth, he rinsed and spat it out. He did this several times before going back to the fire.

Cusaha swam strongly through the maze of rocky outcrops to the far end. Holding onto the rocky bank near the stream that fed this oasis, he paused, admiring the beauty and gave thanks. As he returned to the beach, he couldn't see the boy. He had thoughts of dry, burnt fish, then he remembered the crayfish he'd seen swimming. When he returned to the fire, he saw that it was burning quietly, as a small fire should, and, placed to one side, was the cooling mud pack. Kito was just coming back from the flat rock in the lake.

"Do you think the fish had enough time, Kito? It was a fat one."

"Yes, it was as you said, and I think it still cooks as it cools, does it not, Cusaha?"

Cusaha held out a hand. "Would you do the honours, Kito?"

Kito's eyes lit up. He knelt and tested the temperature of the mudpack. It would be possible to hold it, just. He placed his thumbs as Cusaha had done the night before and pulled. Nothing. He tried again. He put the mudpack on his legs and, with all his strength, he pulled. Cusaha put up a hand to stop him but was too late.

The mudpack gave way with a crack. Hardened mud and fish scattered everywhere, the fire hissed as some of the fish landed in it.

Kito froze. Earnestly, he searched for the fish. Some was in the fire, some was on his lap and up his chest, the rest was on the beach. Slowly, he looked up at Cusaha, wondering what was to happen next. *The sea anchor, the salt well, the pit of dogs and wolves? What?*

Cusaha looked at Kito's blank face with fish all over it and burst into laughter. He turned away, laughing, then faced Kito again. This time, he fell to the beach holding his belly.

Kito hung his head, ashamed and unsure of what to do next. Trying to ignore Cusaha's continued laughing, he looked about. In front of him were the biggest pieces of some of the fish, still clinging to the mudpack. He went about collecting them, then laid them down, right side up. Cusaha was still lying on the beach holding his belly. By the way he was shaking, it was obvious that he'd not stopped laughing. Kito picked the pieces off his chest and tasted them; they were good. He felt about his face, picking at those pieces as well. He looked at the pieces in front of him. The fish was mostly there, so he took what he wanted and began to have breakfast, doing his best to ignore Cusaha who was still lying on his back, wiping the tears away.

Kito finished his half and put the leftover dried mud on the fire. Cusaha rolled over, then sat back on his haunches and looked at Kito. Still embarrassed, Kito just waited for Cusaha, blank faced. This only made Cusaha laugh a little more.

With a huff, Kito decided to go for a swim. He walked up the big flat rock and dived in. Cusaha moved to where Kito had left his pieces and sat down. Then he remembered the blank look and fish stuck on Kito's face and chuckled again. He saw Kito pausing only for a moment before diving in again. The dive was perfect. Cusaha enjoyed his fish and was grateful that it had been a large fish that chose him.

He went to Kito who was busy in the shallows, washing his clothes on a rock. He glanced at his own clothes, bundled them up and walked out to work opposite Kito. They worked in silence. Cusaha looked at Kito from time to time, but the boy didn't reciprocate.

When at last Kito did glance at Cusaha, their eyes met. Cusaha's face bore a wide grin, though Kito was still a little peevish.

"Oh, come on, Kito. It was funny."

Kito scrubbed his ragged clothes intently. "Do you always laugh so much?"

"No, but it's good when it happens, Kito." He lowered his head, trying to make eye contact with Kito.

Kito worked a little harder on his clothes. "Is everything in your life funny, Cusaha?"

"No. Which is why when I see something funny, I laugh. It is said to be good for the soul."

Kito scoffed, stern-faced. "Well, I don't know where you heard that but it sounds silly to me."

"So, you do believe in a soul then?"

Kito stopped abruptly. "Of course, we all have a soul. It is from this that we are all connected to the universe." He tutted and continued to clean.

"So, is there anyone in this universe, someone watching over us, do you think, Kito?"

"Well, yes, I think some of our ancestors do. We all get to spend a little time on the other side, after this life."

"It fascinates me, Kito, that even though the two of us have lived a world apart, our beliefs are the same. Do you think they see our mistakes, hear our non-truths and watch our behaviour?"

Kito slapped his hands to his side forlornly. "Yes, Cusaha, I guess they do."

"So, do you think that they try to send us messages, to try and help us from time to time?"

Kito frowned. "No, I think not. You can't talk across the worlds. That's ridiculous."

Cusaha's eyebrows rose. "Well, I hope they had as much fun this morning as I did."

Kito stopped still at this new thought. His young face emphasised the hurt in his eyes. "Do you think they laughed at my blunder this morning, Cusaha?"

Cusaha leant over the rock and put his hand over Kito's. "I think you did exceptionally well this morning, cooking the fish to perfection. Your hands are too small to reach over the mudpack as I did. I should have offered you the knife to open it. That was my oversight, as well as your blunder, Kito. We all make mistakes in this life. It is why we are here."

"We are here to make mistakes so the universe can laugh at us?"

"No, we are here to learn. No one died, no one got hurt, and we still got to eat the fish. No harm came of it. We both learned a lesson, and if we got to laugh, then that was a bonus." He winked and picked up his clothes and wrung them out, then threw them onto a rock with a splat. He held up his hands and yelled, "Bull's eye!"

Kito grabbed one of his garments to do the same. He threw up his arms. "Hey, I got it too!" In no time at all, they had thrown all their clothes. They spread them out properly to dry on the warm rock, and Cusaha lay down to rest.

Kito was lost in thought. Cusaha waited, watching him, thinking through his question. Finally, Kito tentatively approached the question that had been burning since they'd met and started heading the wrong way. "Cusaha. What are we doing, I mean *actually* going to do today? The morning is half gone already."

"Well, I thought since we were in such a beautiful spot and we are about halfway, we would have a lay day."

"A lay day, Cusaha?"

Cusaha smiled at the boy's good manners and gentle nature. "A lay day is when you take a break from whatever it is you are doing, just for one day."

"And then we're going where, Cusaha?"

A smirk slipped over Cusaha's face. The boy was bailing him up. "What makes you ask such a question, Kito? You are new to these lands, and I've been sent to guide you on your journey. Is that so hard to understand?"

Kito shook his head. "Not at all, Cusaha, but was I not meant to be sent to the palace? Tark took me some of the way, and now you are taking me … where, Cusaha? It's not to the palace, this I worked out a few days ago."

"What makes you think we're not headed to the palace, Kito?"

A fleeting look of frustration washed over Kito's face. "Because, since we left Tark, we have been heading back towards Samos." He grew more agitated. "I have just *come* from there, Cusaha."

"Well, you are the astute one, aren't you? Well, we are actually heading for my own cabin."

Kito's eyes lit up. "Is your cabin in Samos, Cusaha? Is it?"

Concern furrowed Cusaha's brow. "No. And you can never again go into the city of Samos, Kito. Never. Do you understand me? Never." The boy nodded, but Cusaha wasn't convinced. "This is *very* important, Kito. If you are seen, with me or without me, it will spell death for us both, and it will not be a pleasant death, I can assure you of that." He'd kept his voice low and steady, but even compared to being yelled at by old Captain Tarrant and by Tark, it carried a stronger message, and Kito's shoulders slumped.

He took a moment to recover. "So why, when you said to Tark that you were sent by the Palace to get me, are we not going to the palace? Your cabin, it is nowhere near the palace, Cusaha?"

"Oh, Heavens, no Kito. My cabin is nowhere near the palace, not even close." They stared at one another for a moment, then Cusaha asked, "You feel comfortable in the jungle, yes?"

"Yes, as good as any place, I suppose."

"Well, if you wish to take a look around, over the western side of the lake, you will find fruit trees. Some are poisonous, so don't eat any fruit. Just collect them and bring them back for our next meal. There are some good trees up near the stream coming into the lake. You should get some nice fruits there."

"Very well, Cusaha." Kito went to leave then paused and turned back to Cusaha. "What is your real name, Cusaha?"

Cusaha drew back. "Why do you think it's not what you call me?"

Kito remained transfixed on Cusaha's face for a moment, then, without responding, turned and left. Cusaha watched Kito's every step as he walked across the beach and into the jungle. Once the boy was out of sight, he sighed and lay back on the warm rock.

Sleep came quickly.

17 The Awakening

A middle-aged man sat at his table. His hair was grey and long, as was his moustache and beard. A rap at the door brought him smoothly to his feet. He had been waiting for it. He took a breath to calm himself then opened the door. Two spears were thrust at him.

Grabbing the two spears in his left hand, he pulled the would-be attackers off balance and rammed their heads into the door with his right fist. Both men instantly collapsed, laying still. He thrust the butt of the spears into the belly of a third attacker who bellowed as he fell onto the upcoming foot. He too would see no more of this battle. The man swerved and parried his attackers, kicking them all to the ground without spilling a drop of blood.

A group of men were within the edge of the jungle on their horses. They watched this battle unfolding, unbelieving. The one in the centre was dressed in black suede, as was the young man to his right. The young man was getting restless. "Emperor?" The Emperor held his hand up. The young man's horse was skittish. One after the other, the Emperor's Guards fell. The man's smooth, rhythmic moves showed a speed and grace never seen before.

"Emperor! Now?"

Still the Emperor held up his hand. The young man could see the Guard falling while the older man was untouched. Soon, there were only a few Guards left. The young man could wait no more. He drew his horse whip back and drove it with all his might.

The older man dispatched another two guards. As they fell away, he sidestepped the whip, letting it wrap around his spears, then pulled it *from the hand of the would-be attacker. The brass butt hit one of the Imperial Guard in the back of his head. He dropped like a stone as the whip coiled across his back. Everyone stopped and looked at it. Only one person had such a whip, the Commander, Chenghou.*

The older man turned to the Emperor. "Have you no more …?"

***

A small voice came back. "But, Cusaha, this is all I could carry. How many did you want?"

Cusaha pulled himself from his sleep and sat up. He felt drowsy, but Kito appeared to not be paying him much attention; having put down his load of fruit, he was stretching his back. Cusaha looked about, reaffirming his location in the here and now.

Kito went for a swim, giving Cusaha the time to ponder his dream. He looked at the rough basket the boy had fashioned. He had woven in shoulder straps, and it was loaded with fruit. Cusaha leaned forward, choosing a kashia, his favourite. It was plum-like, bigger than an apple, firm and red throughout. Kito returned from his swim, climbed the rock and sat opposite Cusaha. He too chose the kashia. Biting into it, he looked at Cusaha and they both smiled.

"Do you want me to get some more fruit? I can, but I thought this was more than enough for the two of us."

"More? What makes you think we need more, Kito?"

"Because when I put the basket down, you said, 'Have you no more,' so I thought you wanted more. I would've thought this should keep us until morning, Cusaha."

"Oh, pay no attention to that, Kito, it was a jest. The basket is more than plentiful."

Kito lobbed the kashia pip over his shoulder into the water. "It was not hard to get so much. There were so many ripe ones. The ground was covered, so I chose only the best."

Cusaha pondered the fruit-laden basket. "I told you not to eat any because some are poisonous, yet you haven't picked any poisonous ones. How did you know?"

Kito took out a passion banana. He carefully cut it around the centre with his thumbnail, then split it in half, revealing the contents. "It was not that hard. Any of the fruits that had a bite from the primates, and there were plenty, should be fit for us, would you agree?"

"So, Kito, what do you think we could have for our evening meal?"

Kito drew back a little. "Um, I don't know. We have had fish twice here." He listened to the jungle teeming with life. "Should we go for a walk and see what comes, Cusaha?"

Cusaha slapped his knee. "Yes. We have plenty of time. That's a fine idea."

Kito jumped up to tend the fire. Picking up Cusaha's pack, he offered him his knife, and Cusaha led the way into the jungle.

The walk was easy, and there were plenty of animal tracks. Kito identified antelope, boar and a herd of elephants that had passed only a day earlier. Then the hair on the back of his neck prickled. One of the big cats. He breathed deeply a few times. "Cusaha, what big cats roam up here?"

"Tigers mostly, but some cougars, and on a rare occasion, a panther may be seen, although they are normally further south because they like the dense jungle. I think the paw prints you see are those of a cougar."

The information was less than assuring.

Kito asked many questions, and Cusaha answered in detail. As they moved on, some primates moved through the lower canopy. Kito thought they may be gibbons.

They came across a bush with orange berries. Cusaha stopped and picked some. He held them in the palm of his hand and sniffed. Kito followed his lead, swirling them around in his hand as Cusaha had. "They smell like … like rotting leaves. Like when you dig rotting leaves over to get worms for fishing."

Cusaha paused. "You use worms for fishing?"

"Yes, but I saw how you caught the fish. I have no idea how you did that."

Cusaha's teeth gleamed from his broad smile. "Oh, yes you do. You just haven't awakened your potential yet."

Kito frowned.

"Don't look at me like that, Kito. You have already started. The first time, out of desperation for your crew." Cusaha straightened up, dropping the berries on the jungle floor. He placed his hands on his hips. "Have you forgotten already? You will do it again, and soon I think."

As expected, the boy couldn't let the matter rest. "Cusaha, I have no idea what you are on about and I am quite sure 'it' will not happen again." With his bare foot, he shuffled the dirt around on the jungle floor, a little puzzled and pondering his own words.

Cusaha held a fresh handful of berries and looked intently at Kito. He held up one finger. "Shhh, can you hear that?" There was a faint hooting from far above. "That's the wood pigeon. They make a good meal. Follow me."

They walked out to a cliff edge and stopped, facing the edge just a few paces short of the drop.

The valley below took Kito's breath away. It was the mightiest drop he'd ever recollected, a thousand feet or more. He could see more ranges and rocky outcrops in the distance, some with the most majestic waterfalls. The valley was so big, so grand. Kito couldn't hear the waterfalls, but he knew they had great power. Cusaha coughed. Kito scurried over to Cusaha, who sat cross-legged with his hands on his knees, palms up. With his head slightly forward, he closed his eyes and began to rock gently.

Kito watched intently, waiting quietly. He heard the call of a wood pigeon, then another and another as he watched them descending to the lower canopy. He noticed the ground suddenly covered with worms and beetles. One by one, the wood pigeons flew down and fed before them.

A pigeon walked over and sat in front of Cusaha. It was a fine bird, light grey with a smooth body. It had broad shoulders and would be a strong flyer. It was a proud bird with its huge, pure-white chest. No doubt it would be more than enough to feed them.

The bird put its head under its left wing. Kito had seen ducks do the same thing. He wondered how they could sleep like that. Before long, many birds had landed on or around Cusaha. They rested, making low cooing noises, like a murmured conversation, then, one by one, they took flight and headed out into the great valley below – except the one before Cusaha. It was still resting. Cusaha opened his eyes and blinked as if he'd been asleep.

Kito waited for Cusaha to snatch at the pigeon before it flew off, but he didn't. Instead, he got up and stretched. Kito was poised, ready to pounce on the bird. Cusaha gently bent over and picked up the pigeon. It was already dead.

Not a word was spoken back to camp.

A tree stump on the way back made a perfect spot to cut the pigeon. Cusaha gutted it, removed the outer wings and the head, all of which he buried. He wrapped the rest in green leaves and put it in the pack. Further on, he picked some fresh herbs and stopped at a bush with bright yellow berries. He picked some, rolled them about in his hands then held them out for Kito to smell them. "Sweet." Cusaha agreed, and they moved on.

They got back to the beach late in the afternoon. Cusaha led them to the mud bank where Kito took the bird from the pack and handed it to Cusaha, who proceeded to dunk it in the lake. Taking care that it was properly cleaned, he put it aside and did the same with the berries and herbs. Kito removed his own pack and collected some mud.

The fire had burnt low, only ash and a few timber remnants on the outer edges remained. Cusaha took a stick from the woodpile and pushed aside any leftover wood. He dug a hole under the fire. "The stones are more than hot enough." He held his hand out to Kito, who placed a mudpack in it, which Cusaha positioned in the hole. He placed hot pebbles back over the bird, leaving a small mound on the beach. "Kito, I don't know about you, but I need a swim." His smile alleviated Kito's serious face.

The two swam to a cluster of rocks toward the centre of the lake. Cusaha stretched out to the sun whilst Kito climbed up on a higher rock to peer over the edge. It looked deep.

"It is more than deep enough ..." Cusaha could barely finish and Kito was gone, making no more than a small splash. Before long, he was doing back flips from the ledge. Cusaha shook his head in wonder at the boy's energy.

When he finally returned to the fire, Kito searched for Cusaha. It didn't take long to spot him basking on a rock, apparently after another swim. Kito chose to leave him be. Checking that he had Cusaha's knife, he trotted off into the shady jungle to fetch a little firewood.

After a little way, he found a fallen tree. It took a little effort to get to them but he managed to break away dry twigs and branches that poked above ground. He thought about the deep cliff and those uncanny pigeons and wondered why the proud bird had chosen to die.

Something snatched Kito's entire attention. He stood motionless. He didn't have to look up; he could sense what was before him – a king cobra, a full forty feet long and towering over him. The cobra's tongue flicked the air, tasting Kito's scent. Its girth was wider than Kito's shoulders. *It could swallow me whole,* considered Kito.

The cobra began to sway from side to side. It opened its mouth, exposing long fangs. Kito couldn't outmanoeuvre this king of serpents. Not knowing what else to do, he sat down.

The cobra's swaying had made him feel nauseous. With his legs crossed, he put his hands on his knees, and closed his eyes. His forearms began to tingle as he began to mimic the cobra's swaying. The tingling extended up his shoulders and into his head, then his whole body. Colours exploded behind his eyes, forming different patterns. The colours faded, but the changing shapes continued. Hazy, fog-like, Kito strained to look through it, but it was too thick. His body felt numb.

The fog cleared with the colours returning.

His vision returned, and he could see the jungle again, but now it was as if he was fifteen feet tall. He looked down and saw the pile of wood he'd dropped and, there before him, was himself! He was sitting on the jungle floor with his legs crossed, hands on knees, at one with the cobra. They were one and the same. He felt hungry, the cobra was hungry. Kito had to kill it.

Blood coursed through his veins. With a mighty surge, he headed the cobra on its way, over logs and under debris as he went. He felt the power of it. *How to kill a king cobra when you are the cobra? Can a cobra consume itself? Can I get the cobra to bite itself and then return to my own body?* The boy put distance between his own physical being and the cobra.

He stopped the cobra at the edge of the mighty cliff. He checked behind, the tail was a long way back. He wrapped the tail, his tail, around a tree, then edged forward over the daunting drop. He pushed the cobra's body out further until most of the cobra was suspended over the cliff.

He marvelled at the cobra's ability to hold itself. He looked back at the cliff. *This view must be what a bird would see as it flies in,* he thought. The serpent knocked some rocks from the cliff edge and Kito watched them fall away. *Such a long way.* He felt the strength of the serpent as it held itself, poised. It was calm.

Kito pondered the situation. *Though, is it necessary to kill it?* He pulled the cobra back from the edge and redirected it into the jungle, well away from his physical body. He closed his eyes, allowing the fog to envelop him. He could feel his spirit pulling, soaring free of the serpent. He felt his own body nearby and made his way through the fog.

Tentatively, Kito opened his eyes and the jungle was as before, and he was alone.

A burst of joy tore through him as he jumped to his feet. Knowing the king cobra was not yet too far away, he leapt about, silently punching the air. Adrenaline raced through his veins as he tried to shake it off. Finally, he calmed himself enough to pick up his firewood and scurry back to camp.

The sun was low in the sky when Cusaha awoke to the rhythm of a strong swimmer. It was pleasant to have his silence broken by the sound of company. Down at the beach, the fire had already been tended to. He smiled at the replenished wood pile and searched for Kito, who had now reached the rock near the top of the waterfall. He was diving again and continued swimming until near dark.

Arriving at the fire's edge, Kito saw the smirk on Cusaha's face. "What do you find so amusing, Cusaha?"

"It may be the twenty lengths of the lake you just swam and then the run up the beach."

Kito busily put his clothes on. "Did I really do twenty lengths, Cusaha?"

Cusaha waved a hand. "Well, I don't know, Kito, I didn't count. I see you have taken the pigeon out."

"Yes, I think it should be done."

"Well then, don't look so worried, Kito."

Kito thought about the mist and the king cobra but decided not to speak of it. He didn't know why, but he felt it might be dark magic; he was certain it wasn't allowed.

Belly full and exhausted, that evening he easily drifted off to sleep.

***

The two awoke at daybreak for their last wash in the glistening lake. Once packed and having doused the fire, they headed back to the waterfall, eating fruit as they went.

After negotiating the three waterfalls, they were back on the track, Cusaha jogging with ease and Kito happily following him towards Samos. He couldn't help but wonder if the *Shiraz* was there.

The two ran in silence, stopping only to have a piece of fruit by a stream, a drink and then were on the track again. Sometimes Kito would take the pack and be on the move again as Cusaha drank.

They spent that night nestled at the base of a huge, burnt-out tree.

The next day, they entered dense jungle where a good stride warmed their muscles. Before long, they broke into a strong run.

Kito again set to wondering. *Where have I come from? Where am I going? Why is this happening to me?* He hadn't done anything wrong by anyone, at least not that he could remember. When he was on the *Shiraz*, he had grown to like many of the crew and, of course, Baako. How he missed his brother. Then there were all the people in the silk factory who were so good to him. He hadn't been able to say goodbye, let alone give thanks. He was gone for the price of three strange tubes and a gold object that had no purpose.

Cusaha followed behind Kito but watched him closely. He could sense his woe. There was so much that he wanted to say, *But I can't, at least not yet.*

Kito kept the pace strong all morning, anger and frustration driving him on. He wondered how long Cusaha could keep up with him. It was not his desire to lose Cusaha, although, at the moment, he didn't care either way.

Cusaha called out and Kito turned to see him duck into the trees, heading down into the jungle again. He hurried to catch up along a steep decline and a track puckered with small hoof prints.

The fast decent took its toll on Kito's legs and he struggled to keep up. The man moved with grace and power, moving with ease, not like a man of his years. He seemed to be ageless.

There was the growing sound of a dull, distant roar, but over the wildlife noise of the jungle, his own steps and breathing, he couldn't make it out. The track had become more slippery underfoot and he let out a sigh of relief to see Cusaha standing on a large rock ahead. He stopped to get his breath then walked out beside him.

Sprays of water dampened their bodies. Before them was the cause of the noise, and the moisture: a waterfall that seemed to descend from the heavens themselves. The top of it was hardly visible and the fall thundered past them, dispersing into heavy rain. Shards of rainbow light fragments danced as they caught in the sunlight. Cusaha leaned in close to him and yelled. "I have been here on a windy day when the waterfall lands a long way from its base. It does actually have a pool under it."

It was hard to even imagine a pool at the bottom. Kito struggled to draw his eyes from its magnificence. Cusaha chuckled, grabbed some food from his pack and sat down. Kito accepted a piece of fruit, still mesmerised. Again, Cusaha laughed and Kito couldn't help but smile at his sparkling eyes. As he looked at them he stopped eating and pointed. Cusaha's smile dropped as Kito tried to speak. Cusaha raised his eyebrows expectantly.

"Your eyes, Cusaha, they … are different colours! How … when did this happen, Cusaha?"

"Well, I expect I was born with one yellow and one green eye, Kito."

Kito leaned in for a closer look. "But we have been together for many days now. Why have I not seen this before? I saw you'd removed your patch after Tark left but assumed it was merely a temporary dressing or something."

"Indeed, it was temporary, Kito. There are many things about others we don't see at first, my friend. It's not a bad thing. It simply means we focus on trying to get to know someone before we truly see them as a physical person."

"I have not seen such a thing, ever."

"Well then, Kito, aren't I the special one." The comment was tinged with a hint of sadness.

Kito stared long at Cusaha who continued to eat his fruit and gaze at the waterfall. He was used to people staring at his eyes, his biggest giveaway whilst hiding his identity. When he was in Samos, or as with Tark, he wore a patch over his green eye as yellow eyes were not uncommon. He also used a cane and walked with a limp and made sure he kept his hat on and his head down. With a big bounty of fertile land, new homes for the extended family and no taxes for life for the successful hunter of Cusaha's head, even the best of people might be tempted.

A hand reached out to his shoulder. "You look sad, Cusaha. Can I help?"

Cusaha looked up to his compassionate new friend. "Kito, you may not have noticed my eyes but you can read me so well." He patted Kito on the shoulder and smoothly stood.

As Kito pulled the leather pack straps over his shoulders, he watched Cusaha move back onto the track. 'I don't think anyone has to be great at reading faces to see your pain, Cusaha.'

The two continued on down the steep slope, the track cutting back and forth. Kito had neglected to ask about the strange hoof marks but now was not the time, and besides, it was Cusaha's turn to set a strong pace now. Kito needed to focus. One false move on this precarious track could result in a tumble. Only if you were lucky might you get hooked up on a tree below. More likely, it would be a tumble to the death.

Kito's thoughts were about the thousand-foot cliff, the cobra and the big cat prints. He thought about the view from the cliff top and the lake. The beauty of the land was intoxicating but it was also a place of danger. He looked to the man leading him down this endless mountainside. *How long have you been walking these trails?* he wondered. He tried to remember about his village and his people and found he was looking forward to meeting them again, *One day*.

Eventually, they reached the valley floor, the waterfall still a constant rumble in the distance behind them. They moved on, following the wide river where repeated mounds of gravel made it coil left to right and back. Mighty branches from the high canopy reached across the river and rays of light burst through to the river below. Cusaha's easy pace through the water sent droplets sparkling through the air with every stride. Kito drank briefly then rose to make chase of his new companion in this extraordinary land.

Without word, they moved on.

The trail was pitted with many different animal prints, all of them coming to the river to quench their thirst. Kito felt the jungle's eyes watching their progress. More than once the hair on the back of his neck tingled.

He kept close to Cusaha.

Steadily they made their way up the track, the river falling away below. Above them, white rocky outcrops and dark coves scattered the landscape. They pressed on until they reached a small stream that bubbled out from a pond. Kito frowned as, curiously, Cusaha didn't stop to quench his thirst.

They passed over the stream by a small, level wooden bridge to a flat, grassy clearing. Cusaha moved to the right, to a simple, lean-to cabin built into the side of a cliff and disappeared inside.

Kito stopped, surveying his surroundings, and waited.

18 Trina

Kito walked out onto the grass clearing and looked at the tall, white cliff with the cabin nestled into it. The sloping roof of the cabin covered a wood stove and neatly stacked firewood. With no other cabins in sight, it was far from being the village he was expecting.

Cusaha reappeared from inside followed by a large, very dark woman so black, she contrasted with Cusaha's brown, yellow skin. Kito watched in fascination. The woman moved with the elegance of a noble person. Tight curls framed her round face. Her nose was prominent and her eyes as dark as her skin. They walked arm in arm though Cusaha was considerably shorter and lighter than her. There was an alertness and intelligence in the woman's face. As they approached, Kito thought they made an odd couple. She didn't take her eyes off Kito.

"I have had to wait for this moment for far too long, Kito," Cusaha said as he gestured to the woman. "I would like you to meet my dear friend, Queen Trina. Queen Trina, this is the boy that I've told you so much about. They call him Kito."

It was a strange introduction and Kito chose, instead, to stand silent.

The woman's ample body jiggled as she laughed a full belly laugh. "Kito, it is my privilege to meet you but please, don't call me Queen. That was in a different land and time. Trina will be just right, thank you. He is such a joker sometimes, would you agree?"

Kito gave a curt bow. "It is my pleasure also, Miss Trina. I have found him very helpful. I believe he may have saved my life."

With a look of surprise, Trina glanced at Cusaha. "He saved your life, you say. Well, that must make him a hero, wouldn't it,

Kito?"

Kito shook his head, unclear if this stranger was making fun. "No, Miss. I think he is a man of good heart, that's all."

Trina smiled in amusement but there was no sarcasm. Speaking quietly, "Hasuca tells me you don't remember a thing about where you've come from. Is this so?"

Kito looked at Cusaha, who rolled his eyes at the slip. He'd been too eager to introduce the two and now, the distrust and fury in Kito flared. He levered his right foot to strike Cusaha in the chest but quick as a flash, Cusaha deflected the foot with his right hand, catching Kito off balance and putting him down to the ground. Kito cried out and struggled but Cusaha had him pinned.

He screamed out his frustration. "You … you lied to me also! Why? Why does everyone from this land lie? I hate it, I hate you, I hate life. I hate *my* life!"

Shocked by the outburst, Trina prodded Hasuca. "Hasuca, what just happened? What's the child saying?"

Cusaha struggled to hold Kito. It seemed strange for anyone to call Kito a child. He was almost as tall and had the strength of a young man. Kito wriggled until he came to realise it was of no use. Cusaha whispered in his ear. "I am sorry, Kito, I am sorry. If I let you go, I will explain. Can I let you go, Kito?" Kito sobbed quietly. "I will let you go and you will not run off, Kito?" Kito shook his head.

Cusaha loosened his hold and the boy spun around. His elbow caught Cusaha in the ribs, winding him and leaving him helpless on the grass. Cusaha heard a thump next to him but was helpless even to look for the moment. Finally, he slowly rolled over. On the ground was Kito and over him stood Trina, her arms crossed and a self-assured smirk on her face.

"You all right down there, Hasuca?"

"Be silent, you!" he groaned.

Trina's ample bosom wobbled in rhythm with her chuckles. Cusaha got to his feet and watched Kito struggle to do the same.

"I thought a little of his own medicine wouldn't go astray, just to slow him down, and it will, for a bit at least."

Cusaha straightened up with a struggle. "Kito, I gave you my apologies, now you will listen."

Kito tried to get up but couldn't. He settled back to a kneeling position. His anger had left with the kick to his chest. *Some Queen she turned out to be.*

Cusaha took a breath. "It was a disguise to Tark, rather than a lie to you. My name is Hasuca. It was never Cusaha. If I had given my real name, Tark would have taken us to the palace where we would both have come to an untimely death. Instead, I chose to lie to Tark and bring you back here, Kito, to live with me. I also sent for Trina to meet with you so we might be able to work out where you come from." He looked at Trina, who took over the story.

"Kito, what was the name of the vessel on which you came here?"

Kito eyed Trina with distrust. "I don't remember."

"I'm sorry I had to kick you, Kito, but I didn't see many options and perhaps it evened the situation. Would you not think that to be fair and reasonable, Kito?"

He thought about how he'd tried to kick then elbowed Hasuca and nodded.

Trina continued. "You don't realise just what is at stake here. That's not your fault but it is your time to learn, if you wish."

"I don't understand!" He stamped his foot in exasperation. "I have no real idea where I'm from or what I'm doing here, let alone where I'm meant to go!"

He scowled at the two watching him, then relented. "It would seem the two of you know more about me than I do. I would like to learn all you have to teach. If you can give me some direction in this life of mine, I will take it."

Hasuca offered a hand. For a moment Kito pondered it then reached up and clasped him by the wrist. Hasuca pulled him to his feet, held him by the shoulders and looked into his eyes. "If you are open to it, I can show you a whole world you have not known but have the spirit for."

Kito was puzzled.

"When the *Shiraz* had no food, you summoned the fish. You also sent the king cobra on its way."

Kito gasped.

"You need to be patient, this can't be done quickly but you *can* do it. Many lives depend on it, Kito."

Kito looked back, blankly. *How does Cus … Hasuca know about the cobra? And the fish on the Shiraz? I'd forgotten about that.* He simply nodded.

The three of them walked over to the lean-to where Kito had seen the wood stove. In the shade, he and Trina took a seat on stumps of un-split firewood as Hasuca gathered tinder to start a fire.

Trina began to talk. At first, Kito didn't realise that she was speaking in different languages. Surprisingly, he understood all of them. *Maybe from listening to all the men on the Shiraz,* she pondered. She asked him how far back he remembered. A flash of anger crossed her face when he mentioned Captain Tarrant, but when he talked of Baako, who had looked out for him, she softened again.

Hasuca left with a large metal pot and returned a moment later with water overflowing the container. He dunked some strange leaves in it, placed the lid on and put the pot on the wood stove. He turned to Trina. "I didn't understand all you said, though I kept up with most of it. How many languages does he know?"

Kito sat, straight-faced.

"Well, Hasuca, this remarkable young man knows all the languages, from my homeland and other dialects too. So, I couldn't really say where he's from." She squinted and thought for a moment. "But with the skin tone, he may well be from the land of sands, Audun. Maybe he's the son of a merchant, which would work with the languages."

Kito looked at Hasuca and back at Trina, who were both studying him. "Well, I guess that makes me somewhat special then … doesn't it?"

"Yes, Kito, you are something special alright," chuckled Hasuca. "Kito, why don't you go for a walk and get to know your surroundings? Explore a little, if you like."

"Very well, so you wish to talk about me further." He stood with a huff. "Are there fish down in the river?"

Hasuca walked over to the edge of the lean-to and grabbed a spear. Pulling off a few cobwebs, he handed it to Kito. "Take this and go right over the grass to the far side. You'll see a track down the hill that will bring you to a good fishing spot. Here, you'll also need my knife. Are you feeling lucky today, Kito?"

Kito tried the spear for balance and weight. "I'll be back before dark has descended." He paused for a moment. "Every day above ground is a lucky day …" and with that, he scampered across the grass clearing.

Hasuca stood motionless, his eyes affixed on the boy as he disappeared over the crest and into the jungle.

"My dear Hasuca, what *is* the matter?" Trina rose to stand beside him. "What's the matter, Hasuca? You make me nervous, my friend. What is it he said?"

Hasuca dragged his sight away from the jungle beyond. "It was a saying that my father used on occasion. I thought he'd taken it to the grave with him."

Trina frowned. "What? 'I'll be back before dark has descended?'"

Hasuca's face relaxed with a wry grin. "No, you crazy woman, my father always said, 'Every day above ground is a lucky day.' I've never heard it since he passed over." He exhaled loudly. "So, my dear friend, what do you *really* think of Kito?"

She noted the change of subject but let it be. "Well, it is as I said, he has an amazing head for language and speaks all the dialects of my homelands beautifully, though his entire look is wrong. I think he is from Audun, but his bone structure isn't right for there either." She shook her head.

Hasuca couldn't let it pass. "What is it, Trina? What troubles you?"

"I can't put my finger on it. There is something powerfully familiar about that boy, as if I have looked into his eyes before." Her voice trailed off, searching to get the answer to her puzzle, though she found nothing.

Hasuca readied the tea and poured it into wooden goblets.

"Ah, my favourite, Hasuca. Oh, and that reminds me, I'm sorry I dropped you in a sticky spot with Kito, you know, with your name. I should have realised you had to have a cover to get him."

"Ah, I don't know, Trina, I think had I not worn my patch at all, that ignorant fool Tark wouldn't even have noticed. Even if I'd used my real name, it wouldn't have registered for a handful of days. It has been quite a number of years now, you know."

Trina spoke firmly. "By the Gods above, Hasuca, why must you take these risks? If your name passed over everyone's lips again, it could change all that we've waited for. Some of us only waited this long because you said so."

"Forgive me, Trina, you're right. It was foolhardy and reckless. It won't happen again."

She shook a finger at him. "It had better not, or by the Gods I will ..."

Hasuca jumped up and bent over, peering back over his shoulder with his coloured eyes and cheeky smile. "Oh, Queen Trina, will you spank me?"

In mock frustration, she took a swipe at him, and he leapt forward, holding himself as if she'd hit him. She frowned, again pointed her finger. "Aw, you are incorrigible, Hasuca. No wonder your brother had you banished."

Hasuca turned on his heel and pointed back at her. "Ah, but he didn't, though, did he? He would have had me thrown into the pits, but he couldn't catch me. I kept one step ahead."

"Well, if you keep running risks like that, my friend, he *will* get you and you will be two steps *under*. Then where will we all be? What will become of this great nation then? Your father's gone, and with you gone, it would leave the rest of us with the Emperor and his halfwit son, Desora." Hasuca held up his hand as if to push away the thought. She realised her blunder. "I'm sorry, Hasuca, I get carried away when talking of politics. You know this."

"So, what is the latest concerning my nephew?"

Trina took a moment to consider her words. "He is a good-looking boy."

"You have seen him, Trina?"

She placed her hand on his knee. "Hasuca, I know how you have missed your family and the huge sacrifice that you've made for your people. Most will never know it, let alone appreciate it. Though you are hard to read, I know how much pain you suffer every day."

Hasuca's eyes dampened. "And?"

"Yes, Hasuca, I have seen him. He is still the show pony all the way. He's always immaculately dressed, his shoes clean and not a hair out of place. Always parted down the middle, jet black and cropped over his ears and down his neck. I once saw him run his hands through his hair, and it sprang right back into place." She shook her head, smiling at the memory of the arrogant youngster.

Hasuca broke her train of thought. "I, too, have seen this in my visions, but when you look at him, what do you think? What do you feel in your heart, Trina? Tell me truly."

"I wish I could tell you different from what you know, Hasuca, but truthfully, I must not. He has his father's blood pumping through his veins, his father's head on his shoulders, and his father is teaching him all his own ways. I fear he is not learning, nor caring to learn, of the ways of our Gods at all."

She patted his knee. "I wish I had some good news to bring, but I know, as do you, Hasuca, the boy's heart is shrouded in the same evil as your brother, Hannu Koe. Without any true teaching of the Gods, this entire nation must be on the brink of collapse. We will surely have little hope."

Elbows on his knees, Hasuca held his head in his hands. "I know you are right, Trina. I had hoped that what I've seen in my visions was wrong but my visions are never wrong, although I have, on the rare occasion, misinterpreted them." He gazed at her. "Why is it you spend so much time speaking of politics with me when this isn't even your land? Why should you even care, Trina?"

She leant back and folded her arms. "I could tell you it's because the people of your land will suffer if this evil is left unchecked. I could tell you that the evil that festers over your land will seep through to mine. I could tell you that it helps me to keep my mind sharp and that, one day, I will return to my rightful place, my rightful land. I could even tell you it is what friends do for each other. But the truth is, I am just a busybody."

Hasuca scoffed, spitting out his mouthful of tea. "No, Trina. I think it's all the first reasons but not the last. I have always admired your mind, sharp as a thorn, and dare I say, you are here and not in your rightful place for good reason. In life, as in death, there is always good reason, Trina. Always."

He rose to put another log on the fire, and felt Trina's eyes on his back. He'd said too much. It always happened with Trina.

"Hasuca, what is it you haven't told me? What have you seen?"

"I can't give the answers to life, I can't even get them for myself, Trina, but I can tell you to hold your faith. For you, it will work out right. As always, there are surprises, even some good ones, but you must hold strong and be patient. You will get to play your part. Be wary of the Oasis and know you are necessary to the plan."

The crackling of the fire was the only sound for quite some time.

The silence was interrupted by the sound of Kito ripping through the grass at speed. In his left hand was a huge fish, in his right, the spear. He dropped both as he approached the lean-to. Without a greeting, he grabbed the double-headed axe and ran back out onto the grass clearing, holding it as if he were expecting war.

Hasuca moved swiftly, picking up the spear on his way to stand beside Kito. "How many, Kito? Who are they?"

Standing perfectly still, Kito considered Hasuca's question. "About thirty, and it is not *who* but *what* are they?"

"Well, what uniforms did they wear? It's important to know your enemy before you engage in war so you can engage them correctly."

Kito straightened and looked confused. "Uniforms? No. These are evil things on four legs with horns out of their heads and cloaks of white. They don't like to touch the ground, and they move from rock to rock, making strange noises."

Just then, there was movement on the edge of the jungle, and the group of white forms emerged. Hasuca looked at the boy with a smirk. "Kito, have you never seen a goat before?"

"You *know* these things?"

Hasuca handed the spear to Kito. "Not by name, no, but they sure do like a nibble on this grass. Did you think I cropped it by hand?"

Kito looked about the clearing; it was indeed tidy. He scowled at Hasuca laughing at him – again. Not knowing what else to do, he walked back to the lean-to to return the axe and spear, then went back to retrieve his fish, eyeing the 'goats' carefully as he went. Kneeling beside the small brook, he pulled the knife from its sheath to wash the fish blood from the blade. He dipped his hands into the water then leapt to his feet, startled.

Boisterous laughter came from behind him, and he spun to see Hasuca and Trina surrounded by goats. Hasuca pushed his way through. "Is there something wrong with the water, Kito?"

Kito pointed. "The water … it's hot like in a pot, Hasuca. Put your hand in it, look!"

Hasuca tried not to laugh any more. Kito was having a confusing day. "Yes, it is hot. It comes from deep in the ground.

Some days it smells like a rotten egg. Never drink it unless you boil it first. Oh, and if you have a wash in it, and you will, Kito, don't put your head under. Other than that, I drink it boiled and use it to cook, clean and, of course, bathe."

Kito put his hands back in. It was not really that hot, only warm but not what he'd expected.

"Come, Kito, now I will introduce you to some of my friends."

Kito tucked the knife into the small of his back and followed him reluctantly into the herd of goats, attempting to conceal his nervousness of these strange creatures. The one with the biggest horns rubbed up against Hasuca and then stepped towards Kito, whose hand instinctively moved behind his back.

Hasuca spoke quietly. "No, Kito, he just wants to rub himself on you so the rest of the herd know that you are safe for them. Everything the herd does is first approved by him. If he accepts you, they will follow his example."

Kito allowed the goat to nudge against him. It was warm and soft. It leaned against him and he couldn't resist patting it as he'd seen Trina and Hasuca do. It made a strange rumbling noise. "Is it trying to communicate?"

Hasuca shrugged. "Maybe."

"Do you think he likes me?"

"With horns like that, Kito, if he didn't, you'd know it by now."

Chuckling together, they ambled back through the goats towards the lean-to. Trina giggled when he gave a small bow. Bewildered, he wasn't sure why. *Did I not bow enough? Should I have not bowed at all?*

The fish was laid out flat on a small metal grate over the fire so she could bake it. He watched as she checked the fire but didn't add any more wood, clearly wanting the coals to do the baking. However, she reached up the cliff wall and pulled out a wooden wedge and slid the fish into the hole in the cliff and replaced the wedge. After wiping her hands on her apron, she opened the stove and pushed in generous amounts of tea tree leaves. Kito was about to protest when, with a bang, she closed the door. He pondered the wood stove with no chimney. The smoke began billowing from every crevice of the old cooker. He rose quietly and moved outside, expecting to see great clouds of smoke, but nothing. He looked back at the cooker still billowing smoke. Trina was waving her hand back and forth, coughing as she came out.

The two watched Hasuca talking in a silly, high-pitched voice with the goats, then Trina asked, "Kito, if you remember nothing, then who gave you your name?"

He continued to watch Hasuca fuss over his goats. "On the boat they called me, 'boy.' It seemed reasonable, but when I was at the silk factory an old lady named me Kito."

"Why did she name you Kito?"

He shrugged his shoulders. "Because she said I deserved to have a name. Will the fish dry out if we leave it too long?"

"The cliff cools the smoke up where I put it. It will be all right for a while yet, Kito. Did the lady tell you what it means, the name she gave you?"

"No. I didn't ask." He walked back to the lean-to.

Hasuca was sat on the grass with the goats clambering all about him. *He is just a kid himself,* Trina scoffed to herself. Kito returned and handed her a mug of fresh tea. She took it and watched him disappear through the cabin door.

Having had his fill of the young goats' sharp hooves, Hasuca brushed himself down. He saw Trina drinking her tea, and she indicated to the cabin. Hasuca entered quietly to see Kito standing in the middle of the small room. He cleared his throat.

"Is this where you live all the time, Cus - Hasuca?"

"Well, yes, Kito. Is it not to your liking?"

Kito looked out of the window, pointing. "*They* are not to my liking, but I think your cabin is very handsome. But where is everyone else?"

"Everyone else who, Kito?"

"Everyone else, meaning your tribe, Hasuca."

"Ah, them, the tribe. No, I live on my own. Sadly, I have done so for a long time." He looked down at the dirt floor for a moment. "Way too long a time. Sometimes I may seem a little vague, please don't think of me as rude, I'm not much used to having people visit."

"You travelled from afar to save me from being sent to the pit, so no, Hasuca, I will not think of you as rude. I am in your debt." Before Hasuca could respond, Kito continued, "But if you live alone, why did you build a cabin for two? It couldn't have been a small task. Were you not on your own before, Hasuca?"

"Yes, I was on my own then, Kito. And you are right, it wasn't easy." He saw Kito observing a large deer pelt hanging on the wall of the main room. "When I left my home, it was far north of here and the middle of winter. I had little food and not enough clothing to keep myself warm overnight. I think the Gods gave me this gift for my survival, and I thanked them for it. I didn't need the pelt and had eaten most of the meat by the time I was in the jungle, but I have always kept the pelt to remind me of their gift and the deer's sacrifice."

Opening a door, Hasuca entered another room. "Kito," he motioned, "This is your room. It has had a guest or two over the years, though it was always yours."

Kito's mind turned over. *It was always mine?*

The room was modest but pleasant. It had a large bed on one side and a smaller one on the other. In between was a small table with an unused candle, some tinder and a flint. The table and bed headboards touched the cliff face. Kito pondered the effort involved in fitting the timber into the cliff.

Hasuca answered the unspoken question. "It was a bit of work, but it saved me a whole wall of timber to log from the jungle."

To the other end of the room was a wide window with open shutters. Kito frowned at the sight of those goats again. Beneath it was a table and a chair, and to the left, a closet and a chest with drawers. With a pang, he realised he had nothing to put into them. His eyes reflected his sorrow.

Hasuca shook his head. "Don't you worry about such things, Kito. All that is needed comes to those who wait. Be patient. Now, how about something to eat? I think I can smell smoke."

Kito sniffed, and tears trickled down his golden cheeks.

"Kito, whatever is wrong?"

Kito struggled to breathe between sobs. "You … you have done all this for me and I, I have not a thing to offer in return."

Hasuca put his hands on Kito's shoulders and looked into his eyes. "But don't you see, Kito? All I wish for is your presence. You, being *here* is all I need." He shook him gently as if to emphasise his words. "You have to offer nothing but to do as I ask, even when it seems silly or you don't understand. I will show you many things to help you along your way in life, and there will be times when you believe you've had enough. There will be times when you want to stop, but I must push you. You will listen to what I say and do all as I say. Can you do this for me?"

Through glassy eyes, Kito muttered, "But for how long, Hasuca?"

Hasuca thought for a moment. "For the longest time yet, Kito. Will you agree?"

Kito rubbed his eyes, nodding. Hasuca gave him a gentle squeeze then led the way out of the cabin.

Trina was sitting on a wooden block in the lean-to, her hands in her lap and her chin resting on her full chest. Hasuca coughed softly, and she opened her eyes.

"Well, it's about time. I think the fish will be nicely cooled. Shall we?" Without waiting for an answer, she pulled pieces off the fish, placed them on copper plates and handed them out. She noted Kito's puffy eyes. He picked up a piece of his fish, studying it. It was golden brown, not at all like the fish's white flesh. It smelt like the wood stove. He couldn't help frowning as he drew back. Hasuca and Trina laughed. "Oh, I'm sorry. I haven't seen such a fish before.”

“Kito, it’s not the fish but the way Trina cooked it. It’s a bit of a specialty down in the city.”

“They pay good money for smoked fish in Samos, Kito,” agreed Trina.

Kito looked at the two of them with their greasy fingers and decided, if it was good enough for them, it must be good enough for him. He took a bite. The open flesh was a little firmer than the rest but never had he tasted a flavour like this before. He could see why it was a delicacy in the city and that the people would pay good paper for it. He took little time to devour his portion.

Once finished, the trio made their way to the small stream, the warm water helping to remove the fish grease from their hands and the blackened plates.

Kito noticed his strange plate. “Hasuca, these are very good dishes. You must have sold a lot of your smoked fish in Samos to get these.”

Hasuca burst out laughing before Trina jabbed him in the ribs. Over Hasuca’s laughter, she explained, “The jungle gives Hasuca all he needs. From time to time, I take a little to Samos and sell it for him. He can indeed get a good price for it.”

Kito stood up, letting his plate drain. “Are you his servant? I thought he said you were a Queen. Why doesn’t he take his own goods to the market?”

Hasuca’s chuckling stopped abruptly. Trina gathered the tableware and gave them to Hasuca, who, with a blank face, took them. She motioned towards the cabin, and he duly went to put them away.

“Kito, in my lands, your name means ‘jewel.’ To have such a name is a privilege.”

Kito looked at her calm face. “Is it beautiful, Trina, your land?”

“Oh yes, the land I come from is in some ways not unlike this jungle, though we live differently than our neighbours.”

“Your land is next to this land? Why do you not walk home to where you belong? There must be a lot of people who miss you very much. You must have family, a King even?"

"Kito, one cannot just walk there, and besides, it has been a long time since I left my home. Things at home are … different now. The King has a new Queen and she is well-loved in two lands. She is the daughter of the Pharaoh to the north, so it was a good joining for the King." She was careful to keep her composure. "Kito, could you tell me about the woman that named you? It is important, so please, take your time."

A frown crossed his brow. "Haung was the eldest lady in the factory. If you have been in Samos a long time, you must know her."

"It is a big city, Kito."

"She, Haung, has been in the silk factory since she was just a girl. It was not a good life for her, I think," he said, his sorrow evident as he recalled Huang's pain.

"Kito, all things happen for a reason. I believe we live for three lifetimes, and in that time, we have lessons to learn. We don't choose our lives but are given them by the Gods, to learn what they know we need to learn. For whatever reason, she had to live this life to learn a lesson … her lesson."

Kito thought about this for a moment. "But why three lives?"

"Well, because if we didn't have a deadline to live up to, we would squander the time we are given. These lives are a precious gift from the Gods and should not be taken lightly." She watched Kito absorbing it all.

He raised his head so he could look Trina in her big, dark eyes. "But what could Haung learn from being locked up in that factory for her whole life? It doesn't seem right to me. Is this not a waste of a life also?"

"Maybe she had done wrong to others in a past life. Maybe she has served a purpose in the factory that we don't know or understand. Maybe the plan in this life changed, and the Gods had to rewrite her path. It is not for us to know, or judge, Kito. It's our place on earth to do our best for our lives and the lives of all around us, and if all around us do the same, we would all be happy.

Would we not?"

Kito agreed.

"Kito, why do you care so about the people of the factory?"

"They didn't know me. I am much different from," – he waved his arms, "everyone, but they didn't judge me. Instead, they took me in and helped me. I should be doing the same for them. I should take care of Tark and set them free."

"Take care of Tark? Kito, no! I don't think it's your place to take care of Tark. The Gods don't like it when we commit crimes on their people. You may believe you have the freedom to kill him, but the Gods know *everything*. When it's time for Tark to face his Creator, he will know all and he will pay the price in full."

"So you think Haung has committed murder in her past life, now she is locked up for it in this one."

Trina smiled. "I have no idea. The Gods have their plans, and it is not for us to question but simply to do the best we can with what we have."

Kito's face tensed. "So, do you think I must have done bad in my former life to be cast away from my homeland? To have no memory of my name, my family or my life?"

Trina was quickly learning the depth of this boy. "No, no. I cannot know, Kito. It is not for me to judge. I told you that, it is ..."

It was as if Kito had reached boiling point. All the heartache and suffering, the longing for a home he couldn't remember and family he didn't know. "*No!* This is not my life! There has been a terrible mistake! The Gods need to rewrite this chapter of my life. I would never desert my family. I would never desert my land. And I would never desert my King and his people!" With that, he rushed off into the jungle, swiftly clearing the brook as he went.

Trina turned to Hasuca who stood at the lean-to, arms crossed. "Don't you start!"

He held up his hand. "No, Trina. You did really well with the boy. He's just going to be difficult to work with. Come, I've warmed some tea, please, would you like to join me?" Trina looked to where the boy had headed down the trail, and Hasuca spoke gently. "Don't worry for him. You can see as clearly as I that he will be all right, for now. Come, sit with me."

Trina appreciated her dear friend. "If ever the Gods had made a mistake, if ever a chapter needed to be rewritten, it would be about you leading the strongest nation on earth. I have accepted my walk in life, the loss of my Kingdom, my family. I only get to see one son and that is not nearly often enough, but it is enough to keep me going. But why, Hasuca, why was Hannu Koe allowed to lead this nation? No good could ever come of him – or of Desora."

The two talked until dark. When Kito returned, he apologised for his outburst. Nothing more needed to be said.

***

At first light the next morning, Trina said her goodbyes and left for the city of Samos. Hasuca went about his morning exercises. Kito asked why he did them, and Hasuca explained, 'Positive energy and bad chi.' It was from the old times, he said. He told Kito he could join in if he wished.

From that day onwards, when the sun chased away the mantle of darkness from another night, out on the lawn, they did the exercises together.

***

Many seasons came and went. It was the best of times for Hasuca, watching the boy grow and learn. He taught Kito how to meditate. The talent was strong in the boy, almost unnaturally so. They would go out and track, hunt and live off the jungle. Hasuca knew it would not last forever, and before he knew it, Kito wasn't a boy anymore.

He was now a young man.

19 Desora

The Emperor clasped his hands behind his back as he strode through the palace, the issue of taking Samos burning in his mind.

Since the disappearance of Hasuca so many years ago, he had pondered the problem of who was to lead his army. Everyone said Hasuca was dead. The record cold winter of that year would have finished him, as it did his bastard son. But the Emperor didn't believe it. Hasuca was alive; he could feel it. Neither the body of Prince Desora's twin, nor the tin bucket had ever been found either. It never felt right with the Emperor. That spring, a large wolf had been seen near the palace, *but a wolf would not carry away the bucket*, argued the Emperor.

The Emperor hesitated as he passed a classroom and, feeling an impulse, he looked through the back doorway at the students. He decided on an impromptu visitation.

The students were paying attention, reading aloud in unison. Shu Memottu, their teacher, silenced them and gave the signal for them to pay their respects. The chairs clattered as they quickly stood to attention and bowed.

The Emperor tapped the back of his hand. "Ah, yes, good decorum indeed. Please be seated. Continue."

Shu Memottu glanced at one of her students, Tanica. There was fear on the teacher's face, and Tanica saw it. By contrast, she felt calm, though she would not look towards the Emperor. Shu Memottu instructed the class to sit and work on their arithmetic sums, causing a flurry of activity as they drew out their rice papers and began their calculations.

The Emperor walked around the tables as the students worked, Memottu close behind him. He lifted the heads of the boys and looked into their eyes. Memottu wasn't sure if she was breathing as he passed Tanica's desk, but she did momentarily stop when he halted and turned back to her. He stood behind her and placed his hands on her shoulders, gently pulling her back into her seat so to look down on her. Memottu trembled as his hands gently massaged Tanica's shoulders. He pointed to one of her sums. "Are you sure this is correct, my dear?"

Memottu stepped forward to intervene. Without looking up, the Emperor raised his hand, silencing her.

Tanica checked the sum. "Yes, Your Excellency, it is indeed correct, I am sure. But if you wish to teach me otherwise, then I must listen."

The Emperor smiled at Memottu. "I congratulate you, teacher. That was a perfect answer. Anything less and I would have taken her for myself as she is clearly of age, but no, she can stay to study, for now. A sharp brain, even a female's, should at least get a full education." He peered down the young woman's developing chest. "Although, she is …"

One of the boys behind him forced a cough. The Emperor turned and glared at the boy. With his head down, he made two more fake coughs. The Emperor marched to the boy's desk, grabbed him by the chin and wrenched his head up. The boy let out a squeak, fear in his narrow, dark-brown eyes. The Emperor, with the back of his hand, slapped the boy, who spun back over his chair and crashed to the floor with a whimper.

The Emperor gave him a kick. "Where are your testicles, boy? Do you even have any?" No one laughed. The Emperor stood glaring at the classroom, waiting. A forced chuckle was followed by a gentle clap. Satisfied, he left the classroom.

Memottu reached out to Tanica, who pushed her hand aside and hastened to the boy lying on the floor holding his stomach. She knelt beside him, putting a hand on his shoulder. "Dai. Dai, will you speak to me, please?"

The boy opened his eyes and gave a forced smile. "I will be good soon enough," he croaked.

The Emperor walked on down the hall, the thought of the young female student thick on his mind. Because of the wimpish boy's feeble cough, he'd neglected to take the girl's name. For some reason, he couldn't even remember her face.

He continued on to the stairway leading up to the garden room. There was his lifeblood, his only child and son, Prince Desora. Now turning into a young man, he wasn't going to have his father's height though he was broad and thick set.

The Emperor watched as Desora practised. He was between four experienced guardsmen with their makeshift two-handed wooden swords. The first man lunged and Desora parried. The second and then the third came at him. He parried them both, smacking one of them hard on the back. The fourth man stepped forward and made a cutting motion on Desora's shoulder. Desora grabbed the sword by the blade and ripped it off the man then cracked his own sword into the defenceless man's knee. The man cried out as he stumbled to the floor, clutching at his leg.

Desora threw the man's sword at him. "No! No! Not until the first man has had his second attack do you step in." He foamed at the mouth. "After the *first* man has had his *second* attack! How hard can it be?"

No one noticed the Emperor as they hustled back to their positions, intently focused on the prince. To harm him, even accidentally, would spell death for all involved and their families. Desora, by contrast, seemed oblivious of their contempt.

The first man lunged forward and was parried. The second and then the third came at him. He parried them both. The first came again. Desora spun on his heel and slammed his sword across the man's back with the full force of a strong, young man. The fourth man lunged, as best he could with a bad knee, and Desora parried him and kicked him in the groin. The guard dropped his sword as he went down, holding himself.

The prince tucked his sword under his arm and removed his custom-made leather gloves with an arrogant, smug grin. "Well then, old boy, how hard was that, eh?" He spat on the squirming guard.

Clapping from behind surprised them all. Desora gave his father a curt bow. "Father, did you see me? I cut down your Guard. Four, no less!"

The Emperor looked at the guards splayed on the floor. "And one can't stand, it seems. A grand show of your skill indeed, Desora." He clapped again. Desora drew himself up with pride.

The guards collected the swords and helped the last one to his feet. They bowed to the Emperor first, then to the prince, and waited for Desora's dismissal with a flick of the wrist.

Desora walked with the Emperor. "Yes, it is quite exhilarating when it all comes together, Father. Quite exhilarating indeed."

Hands clasped behind their backs, they ventured to the indoor garden. The warm summer breeze of the south had given way to the cold winds of the north, the first signal that the snow was imminent.

"Yes indeed, Desora. I shall now put you under Master Xiang's charge. He really *is* a Master of War."

Desora stamped a foot. "But Father, I am doing well enough as I am. You just saw me, did you not?"

The Emperor put a hand on Desora's shoulder. "Yes, I did. As I said, you are showing some skill. Force and speed together are the makings of a worthy opponent, but, Desora, Master Xiang sparred and fought beside your grandfather. He taught me to fight all manner of battles. It is said that during the time he has led the Imperial Guard, we have never lost a battle. Never. You cannot learn from better, son."

Desora tutted as he rolled his eyes and brushed the non-existent fluff from his tunic. "If it pleases you, I shall spar with this old legend of the past. But if he can't keep up, Father, then we must re-examine the issue."

"Ah, and now the negotiator, my prince. Very well, Desora, if you think he can't keep up with you, then it shall be so. I will discuss this with Master Xiang when I see him later. Will you join me at the Dome mid-afternoon, Desora? The Pit will be entertaining today. Some fresh meat has come down from the rift."

"Have I ever passed up the chance to try my luck at the Dome, Father?"

"Indeed, no, Desora. And may I add, you do have a gift for picking your winners."

"Yes, I do seem to be one of the best at it, don't I? I shall freshen up and have my post-battle rub-down, Father, then join you at the Dome."

The two bowed to one another, and the Emperor watched the prince stride away.

20 The Sports

It might have been midday but the winter sun was noticeably lower than in summer. The Emperor wore his black silks with pearl buttons and, to withstand the bitter northerlies, he had donned his long, black coat. The black, lace-up boots finished his attire.

Hands clasped and deep in thought, he made his way across the cobbled courtyard. He shared with the prince, the excitement at the prospect of fresh meat. *Handy thing, the battle of the rift,* he mused.

Purpose built, the grand Dome surrounded the central pit, providing undercover entertainment throughout the cold winter days. Some of the nobles and Assets from the outer regions had begun to gather, bowing deeply with the Emperor's arrival. Heading directly downstairs, he paced back and forth through the cave system, watching the Barbarians preparing for their fate.

A rat scurried along the dirt floor. Keeping against the stone wall, it passed through two pens before it was seen, and three more before it was caught, then eaten alive. Impressed, the Emperor stood before the pen where the big Barbarian was eating the last of his good fortune. He saw the Emperor and, still chewing, he walked to the bars.

The Emperor drew back slightly at the pungent body odour. "What's your name?"

The Barbarian picked at his teeth with the rat's bone splinter. "They call me the Devourer."

"I see, Devourer."

The Barbarian shook his mane of red hair. "No, you don't understand. They call me the Devourer because I have slaughtered so many of your Guard." He continued to chew.

The Emperor's body stiffened. "Well, I will look forward to you *devouring* your own tribe in the Pit."

The Barbarian spat a bone, narrowly missing the Emperor. "No, I think not."

"Barbarians deserve to be removed from this earth by the Gods' hands – *my* hands. So why would you not slaughter them, Devourer?"

"Because, Emperor, this is not my clan. I don't see a face I know. Besides, I don't think I will fight today."

The Emperor's face darkened. "So, what is it that you think you *will* do today?"

The Devourer reached up and tapped one of the bars. "These bars, they are round, you see?"

The Emperor looked in disdain. "Yes, round as you say. And?"

"Being round they have no sides. Yet, you are there and I am here. Today I am to die and you are to profit from it, only because of what side of the bars we are standing. It's a strange life, don't you think?"

The Emperor's composure returned. "No, Devourer, I think not. You are on that side because we caught you and now I will send you to meet your Maker, to face all the lives you have *devoured*."

"No. You have the better land and therefore you have more people. What's more, it has been built on a lie. Your father took my land because he thought we did wrong by him, but he was mistaken. It was your *own* people that attacked your father, killing Ta Tuku in the process."

For a brief second, the Emperor pondered if there was any truth to his story. He narrowed his eyes, his growing temper evident. "Our people? Why would we have done that?"

"Well, let me explain, *Emperor*. One from our tribe got one of your women pregnant. The only way her father could hide the catastrophe of his daughter falling in love with a Barbarian was a distraction of the fact. So, he faked the ambush and even got their land. Talk about a win-win situation." The Barbarian stood back, his hands on his hips and a broad smile on his face.

The Emperor was now beyond caring for composure. "You dare come down here and feed *me* such a bunch of lies! You will pay for this!"

The Barbarian made no attempt to conceal his contempt. "Oh, but this is not the greatest land. Like these bars, the world is round. It has no sides, no top or bottom. It is a perfect sphere, and some of it is not yours to inhabit. No one can own the land. We merely look after it for our children. Nor did I come down here to visit — your people caught us, remember? Anyway, that wasn't the worst of it."

The Emperor's fingers twitched over the short sword on his belt. "Oh, and what would be the worst of it? Do tell."

The big Barbarian put his face to the bars. "As the Emperor of Middle Kingdom, you're well known to have the Sacred Skull of Magnar, *our* Sacred Skull. It was a gift of peace and trust from our people to yours."

"Guard!"

The Organiser of Games was right behind him. "Yes, yes, sire. What is it you wish?"

The Emperor spun about, catching the Organiser of Games under the chin with his elbow. The Organiser dropped the board he was holding in the commotion. Hastily, he bent over to pick it up. He didn't see the boot coming down on the back of his head and the cobbles come up to crush his face. The Emperor glanced around. There was no one else about.

The Barbarian scoffed. "My name is Tzu Hsi. Now you know everything, as do the Gods. This is all I need before I meet them, Hannu Koe."

The Emperor turned ever so slowly. "*I* am the only God you need to concern yourself with, Devourer. Before this day is out, you will beg me for mercy, as you should have from the day you were conceived."

Satisfied, he strode away through the poorly lit cave.

***

Arriving at his double throne in the massive Dome, the Emperor snatched a goblet and downed the wine, gazing up at the beams some eighty feet above. Suspended from them were three chains with a twenty-foot iron wheel covered with oil lanterns. Dozens more lanterns around the Dome lit the great hall.

The Dome itself was a stone-sided pit. Around this was raised seating, creating cushion-covered benches. Heavy railing made sure the Emperor's overexcited Assets were held safe.

The prince took his seat. "Father, did I hear we may have a little surprise tonight?" The Emperor turned to his son. Desora had seen this look before. "Father, what has happened? Are you not yourself this afternoon?"

"Yes, Desora, some of our fighters are not well enough to fight today, so I have decided to hold them until another day. It will be good to keep a little sport for the winter, would you not agree, my son?"

"They looked fine to me, Father."

The Emperor closed his eyes for a moment, then turned to his pride and joy. "Yes, you do have a good eye, Desora, but you must consider the plan well in advance. It will be winter very soon. If we use all the sport today, what shall we do for the rest of the winter?"

Desora was taken aback. "Well, Father, I will do what I did last winter, study, practise, smoke and try to impregnate the incubators. Is this not enough for a winter?"

"You do seem to like the smoking and impregnating, don't you, my son."

Desora blushed, breaking eye contact. "So, which sports will be participating today then, Father?"

"I thought I would put Sport Nine against Sport Three."

"That would be a good match, but I feel Nine, who is a little older and carries a little weight, would be outmanoeuvred by the younger, leaner, Sport Three."

The Emperor smirked. "Don't dismiss Sport Nine because of his age and weight, Desora. You don't get to his age without learning a few tricks."

"Yes, of course, Father, but I'm just saying that when the match goes the distance – and it will – youth will win in the end."

"Very well. If Sport Nine wins, you will spar with Master Xiang until I say otherwise. If Sport Three wins, you will only spar with him until you feel there is no longer a need for the old warrior."

The Emperor looked across to Master Xiang in discussions with the Assets. They seemed to pay as much respect to him as they did the Royalty. A vein in the Emperor's forehead pulsed with hatred. Getting the attention of the new, younger Organiser of Games, he'd almost forgotten the earlier incident. "Be so good as to fetch Master Xiang to my side, boy." The man bowed and moved away in haste. The Emperor leant back to Desora in time to hear his reply.

"Well, Father, when my Sport Three takes out your older Sport Nine, I will not have to endure your old Master Xiang at all, will I?" Smug and confident, the young prince sat back, satisfied.

"Don't count your chickens before they hatch, my son."

Desora's forehead puckered. "What does that mean, exactly?"

"A chicken might lay twelve eggs. You can count them when they are laid, twelve, but four may be unfertilised, and two chicks may die of the cold before they hatch, so only six eggs hatch. A long way from your first count of twelve, don't you think?"

"Yes, but you can eat the four that are not fertilised, and you could take all of them into care, to ensure nothing gets left out in the cold to die. So, then you have eight chickens and a good breakfast. All twelve eggs accounted for, Father."

The Emperor rolled his eyes and was about to reply when he was disturbed by a faint cough on his left. "Ah, yes, Master Xiang, good of you to appear here today, as always. Who is it that you have put your money on today, if I may ask?"

"I have been honoured by the Emperor's invitation to enjoy the Emperor's company and, may I add my good wishes to the prince also." He bowed to the prince directly, before continuing. "I believe I will be backing Sport Nine, sire."

The prince sat forward. "So, just how much of the Palace's paper have you put on the old man, Xiang?"

Master Xiang eyed the prince directly. "I do not have the paper to place a bet, my Prince."

The Assets went quiet as the prince raised his voice. "So, you lied to my father, the Emperor of the most powerful land?"

"No, my Prince, I said I will *back* Sport Nine, not bet on him."

The prince sat back in his oversized throne. "So, you admit you will back Sport Nine, but you would not put your paper where your mouth is? Is this so, Xiang?"

Master Xiang's calm expression remained unchanged. "Not quite, my Prince. My brother has an extended family that I help with, so I can ill afford to lose paper on a fight."

Not content with this, the prince persisted. "So now you are saying that the Palace is underfunding you, is that so, Xiang?"

Master Xiang kept his tone natural and composed. "No, my Prince. As I said, I have a large extended family and I can ill afford to lose paper on a fight." He was aware that some of the Assets had become intrigued with the discussion. They were men of wealth and power, unlike him.

The prince spoke with the stubborn insistence of a spoiled child. "Well then, Xiang, think of how much you could win on a round of fights here today." He waved his hand over the Pit as if he were responsible for having built it and sat back in his throne again.

Master Xiang didn't take his eyes off the young prince. "When one gambles on anything, he must first ask not what he can win here today, but what he can afford to lose. I, my Prince, cannot afford to lose. I also do not hold my Emperor in any way responsible for my large, extended family," he smirked, "which was not your father's doing." A chuckle moved through the listeners. "I have discussed such matters with His Excellency, and he has given his blessing. This was before your birth. Now that you are coming of age, we could revisit the matter if you wish, my Prince."

Sniggers were heard, but the look of thunder on the prince's face cut them off sharply as he jumped to his feet. "*Coming* of age? I *am* of age, you blind old coot!" He shook with rage in the face of the old man. "And I will show you as much before this week is out with a one-on-one battle, just me and you!"

"My Prince, knowledge is a most powerful tool and can only be learned with time, an open heart and mind. I have had the pleasure of learning and sparring with your grandfather and your father. If you think I am a deserving opponent for yourself, then I am most honoured." The master's calm manner remained unchanged.

The Emperor studied Master Xiang. He had indeed been instrumental in the training of his father, himself and Hasuca. Though now of a respectable age, his ability to train the best of them was far from over. Internally, the Emperor seethed over the affection Xiang had held for his traitorous brother. For a moment, they locked eyes as everyone silently waited for one of them to speak.

Master Xiang returned his attention to Desora. The prince was about to answer when the Emperor stood, bringing a curt end to the conversation. Like a young stallion yet to be broken in, the prince struggled to rein in his disdain for the old Master.

Emperor Koe addressed the greater gathering. "My loyal people, I have invited you all here today for a real treat. As always, we will enjoy watching the Barbarians doing what they do best – killing." Polite clapping and laughter filled the Dome, although most would rather for the discussion to continue. "After that we will have a very special person here for a real treat that I, your Royal Emperor, will be personally involved in." The Emperor clasped his hands behind his back and puffed his chest out, revelling in the clapping and cheering. He held up one hand for quiet then gave the signal for the performance to start.

Drum rolls sounded from the labyrinth of caves below, growing to a thundering climax.

The Emperor clapped his hands as he sat down, waiting for the fun to begin. His son continued to glare at the Master of the Guard, who ignored him, peering expectantly into the Pit. Master Xiang then dipped his head to the pair and moved away.

Sport Three and Sport Nine were in opposing cages, ready for the gates to rise. Sport Three was pacing and breathing hard. He glared at Sport Nine, who seemed unperturbed, as if he were watching his daughter picking flowers.

Then the gates went up. Sport Three rushed forward, Sport Nine side-stepped and pushed the young man from his feet. Landing hard, he tumbled and sprang to his feet, charging again. This time, he was ready when Sport Nine stepped aside, and the young man grabbed him with both arms, sweeping him from his feet and slamming him into the stone wall. They wrestled, but neither gained any advantage. Sport Three threw the older man to the dirt floor. Rolling twice, he rose effortlessly to his feet and beckoned at his young opponent.

Sport Three lunged again. This time, Sport Nine stepped forward, shoving his knee into the young man's chest. The air hissing from his deflating lungs was audible to the entire crowd. He slid to a halt on his back. Sport Nine glared up at the throne. Quickly, the young prince rose to his feet and gave a signal. The chains rattled, and a steel door rose behind Sport Nine. He spun round and stepped forward, placing a foot either side of Sport Three.

The first dog leapt. He dispatched it over his shoulder and into the stone wall. The second received a fist straight in its snarling mouth. The third dog was airborne when he grabbed it by its throat in his left hand, crushing it as he tossed it to the side.

Using both hands, he grabbed the fourth and last dog as it charged at him. With a fist of skin and fur on either side of the dog's head, Sport Nine spun around twice in the Pit and, with all his remaining strength, heaved the snarling dog straight up at the thrones. He spun once more before bracing himself against the open door to the dog cage.

The prince screamed at the dog landing on top of him as the two fell from the throne.

In an instant, Sport Nine received a cluster of short arrows. He gazed down at his punctured chest. The Dome faded away and, as he looked, it was now a wide field covered in flowers. He heard singing and turned his head to see his daughter, who had died two winters earlier. She was more radiant than ever and was picking the flowers as she walked towards him. He smiled as he breathed his last.

The Emperor lunged forward and grabbed the dog by its tail and the back of its neck. It was already dead. The Emperor was about to throw it into the Pit when he saw one of the courtiers pointing at its throat and the two knives lodged in it. He pulled them out before he dispensed of the large dog.

Master Xiang strode towards the Emperor, holding out his hand. "I thank you for retrieving my knives, Your Excellency."

The prince was brought to his feet with the aid of a stunned entourage. He dusted himself off as the Emperor approached him. "Are you all right, my son? You have blood on your face."

A flash of panic ran over the prince's face. "Someone get me a mirror, now!" No women were allowed in the upper Dome, so it fell to the Assets to settle their prince. After a flurry of activity, a polished silver mirror was produced.

The Emperor turned back to the Pit. Sport Three was back on his feet, flexing his chest like a conqueror. The Emperor turned to the Organiser of Games and gave a series of signals. The Assets once again gathered around the Pit. This time, there were four wolves.

Sport Three backed against the wall as they came leaping through the open cage, snarling. He ran forward to grab the first one, but misjudged and his arm was snapped on by the wolf. A second latched onto his calf muscle. The two remaining wolves quickly overpowered the man. He couldn't scream through a crushed throat.

After they'd fed for some time, the guards came in and warily dragged what was left of the bodies into the wolf enclosure. One of the dead dogs was cut into quarters and pushed through the bars of an adjacent cage. The guards backed away as the snarling began. Their job was done and, closing the pen, they made a hasty retreat.

The Emperor stood and raised a hand for silence, which ensued quickly. "And so, my dear friends, after all this excitement, I now bring on your surprise." With that, he descended the steps into the Arena.

21 *Tzu Hsi*

The Assets watched transfixed as a blacksmith dragged a brazier into the Pit. Inside it, the hot coals glowed red and white-hot, and several handles protruded from it. Four men followed, wheeling in a large frame in the shape of an X. They turned it around to face the cage filled with the white fangs and eyes of ice. A large paw shot out, swiping the ground with a speed that sent dust wafting through the Pit.

The crowd muttered and passed their paper bets to one another as they sighted the large, naked Barbarian strapped tight to the X frame.

He spoke boldly. "Greetings, gentlemen. Judging by the commotion, you are having quite the day." He shook his long, flame-red hair. "So then, what do you think of my new look? Not really appropriate for entertaining, though, is it?"

A voice came from behind. "No, but that's why we call your lot Barbarians, isn't it, Devourer?" Around into full view came the Emperor, pulling on heavy leather gloves.

Tzu grinned, revealing his yellow, stained teeth. "Aren't you looking forward to seeing me, Emperor? And there I was thinking you were having such a good day."

The Emperor smiled thinly as he took the red-hot poker from the coals. "Oh, I *am* having a good day. What's more, it is about to get even better." Without warning, he prodded the poker into Tzu's side. It hissed as smoke rose with the raw smell of burning flesh. The man's head snapped back, though he made no sound.

The Emperor returned the poker to the brazier to reheat. He removed his coat and rolled up his sleeves.

Tzu lifted his head. "Well, that was ill-mannered, my dear Emperor. You didn't even show me the brand before we began, but then, you're not a very noble lot, are you, Your Imperial Excellency?"

"Of the two of us, you are the Barbarian. It has always been so."

"Are you certain about that, Koe? This may not seem to be the most auspicious time for me to offer an opinion, but I merely point out that there is always a time of reckoning. Do you not think so?"

"You are deranged. *I* am the only one you need concern yourself with." His sentence trailed off to a mutter as he turned back to stoking his brazier with another iron.

"Are you going to give me one of those tattoos? I do like them, you know." The Emperor held up the oak-leaf-shaped brand for Tzu to see. "Well, that looks like a nice one. Where should we place that one, Koe?"

The Emperor gazed over Tzu's hairy body. His eyes came to rest on his chest. He turned the brand around and held it like a long sword. Tzu smiled at the Emperor as he pressed it down. Tzu lost his smile, but he didn't lose the Emperor's gaze. The brand continued to hiss, and heavy smoke rose. Eventually, the Emperor stepped aside, momentarily putting the back of his leather glove to his nose.

"Well, you gave me no opportunity to bathe, Koe. Such poor hospitality for your star guest."

The Emperor thrust the brand back into the brazier whilst Tzu looked up at the nobles. Most of them, too, held a purple cloth over their noses.

"You are a hard crowd to please. Look at your Royal blood down here, putting on a show for you. Look at him, breaking a sweat for your entertainment and not one of you have uttered a word of encouragement." Tzu spoke quietly. "Say, Koe, they are a little withdrawn. Is everything as it should be? You know, with the

Palace and all that?"

The Emperor grabbed a branding iron in each hand and shuffled them firmly. He side-stepped quickly to avoid the glowing coals that shot out.

"By the Gods, you be careful with that – a man could burn himself," scoffed Tzu.

A suppressed snigger came from the crowd. The Emperor glared around, but all he saw were impassive stares.

"Oh, there you go, Koe. That *is* encouraging, isn't it? A little humour from your lot after all."

The Emperor used a set of tongs to gather the runaway coals. He picked up the first and returned to Tzu with menace. Tzu looked to the glowing coal and followed it as the Emperor slowly led his gaze down to his feet. Under each foot was a board so the victim could stand whilst he was being moved about. The X was then laid back so the Emperor could walk about and reach any part of the victim he wanted to. Tzu knew where this coal was going. The Emperor's eyes bored into the Barbarian's as he carefully pushed the tongs between the board and Tzu's foot and released the coal.

Tzu's training had prepared him. This was his destiny.

As he began to recover, Tzu lifted his head and grinned at Koe. "So, tell Tzu all about it, Koe. I know your father was a good, fit man, but suddenly, he up and died. Then, against all the odds, the heir to the throne, Hasuca, vanishes, leaving it all to you. What do you think of that, hmm, Koe? All a bit strange, don't you think, *Emperor?*"

The Emperor picked another coal off the ground and placed it under the other foot. The smoke from the first foot was still thick on the air as the second began to smoke too. Tzu looked at the two remaining coals on the ground behind him. "My feet are cooling now, be a good Emperor, would you?"

The Emperor carefully picked up another of the coals.

"This one is a little dull, I think, not worthy of a Barbarian." The Emperor walked around the back of the 'X' as Tzu looked up into the crowd.

"Well, come on, good people. Help the poor Emperor with a little suggestion. Where should he put it? In the small of my back? Under my tongue perhaps, to stop my talking."

The Emperor moved to the other side. "Oh no, you will be able to beg for your soul right to the end of your time here, Barbarian." He carefully took aim and pushed the tongs under Tzu's left knee, being careful not to burn the rope. Tzu was sweating but stared back impassively until further adrenaline kicked in. He took a few deep breaths. "So, where is Hasuca these days? Does he come by from time to time, Koe? He did get all that training from your father whilst you were, by all accounts, left outside the purple circle. You were, weren't you, poor little Koe."

The Emperor's face reddened to rival that of the hot coals. He stormed around to the brazier and fetched another, driving the tongs under Tzu's right knee. Both knees emitted smoke. The left leg began to spasm as Tzu's eyes now glazed over.

"So, Barbarian, you are not all animal after all." The Emperor looked up to the crowd. "Well, come on, my friends. Maybe the smoking pig is right. You have been rather silent. Come, my Noble Assets, what would you like to see next?"

A small voice called. "If he smells like a pig, bleed him like a pig."

The Emperor nodded in agreement. "He does smell like a pig, but we bleed a pig, so to make it a better feast. We shall not be eating this pile of excrement."

Roars of approval came from the upper Dome.

"Well, I never, Koe, you do have a little character after all. When you took, or should I say, *stole* the throne, the majority believed you didn't have the merit to rule it. We may have been wrong, just maybe."

A shout came from above. "If you won't cut his lying tongue out, cut his thieving hands off." The crowd cheered. Another voice cried out. "Put a poker up his anus."

Tzu looked at the Emperor. "I don't know if I would turn my back on a man who would suggest that, Koe. How bizarre." The Emperor found himself nodding in agreement. Another shout came. "Crush his testicles so he can never spawn another pig like himself." Again, Tzu looked to the Emperor. "Well, there's another one. What do you lot do in the palace when the lanterns are down?"

Eager to participate, the prince shouted out. "Give him the keyhole." He turned to the rest of the Assets and began to chant, his voice low to start, shaking his fist with each chant. "Keyhole. Keyhole. Keyhole."

Before long, all the Assets were chanting with him.

The Emperor hesitated. There was more fun to be had, but there was no backing out now. He pulled out his short dagger and held it up for the crowd to see, then placed it in the hot coals of the brazier. He turned back to the Barbarian. "I would have preferred to do this much later, but they have asked for it, so I will deliver. It is what a good leader does, you see, Barbarian."

"Thank you, Koe. It's good of you to say as much at this juncture."

The smirk disappeared from the Emperor's face. "What does that mean, Barbarian?"

"Juncture? Well, it is ..."

"I know what juncture means, you imbecile! What is it you think I complimented you on?"

Tzu's voice dripped with sarcasm. "Oh *that*. Well, I let your people capture me so I could deliver the message I gave you earlier. I did the same for your father, although we never actually met. It was not a message many wished to carry on behalf of Magnar, or the Barbarians as you call us, to the Emperor. So, I am the one selected. Now all my people know that you know the whole truth, they'll wait to see what you will do next."

The crowd was still chanting, eagerly waiting for the dagger to heat.

"What makes you think your lot will *know* you gave the message directly to me?" He stood back with a smug smile.

With two fingers, Tzu beckoned the Emperor to come in close. The Emperor leaned in. "Because when they wheeled me out here, I gave the signal."

Panic flickered across the Emperor's face as he spun to search about his Arena. He glared back at the Barbarian. "You lie again!"

"I can only tell you now because the message is well on the way."

The Emperor snatched the glowing red knife and held it above his head amid wild cheering and chanting. He stepped in between Tzu's quaking, smouldering legs. The Barbarian smiled as the crowd above still chanted, "Keyhole! Keyhole! Keyhole!"

"Well, this is it, Barbarian," gloated the Emperor.

"What is a keyhole anyway, Koe?"

"Keyhole? Well, it's a locking device."

The Barbarian's face turned almost as red as his hair, sweat and tears ran down his face, leaving tracks through the dust and grime. He threw his head back and laughed, deliriously. His whole body shook as the Emperor stepped back a pace.

He regained his composure and pushed his knife in the Barbarian's navel then, with the care and patience of a surgeon, he began to cut a small ring right around it. He eased it out with his finger and the point of the knife and put the navel on the Barbarian's chest. Stepping back to the brazier, he chose one implement he hadn't yet used and drew it out slowly. He nodded to himself, satisfied it was the right one, a small rod, thinning out down its length, with a hook on the end.

The Barbarian had settled a little, though it was still off-putting to the Emperor.

Tzu hissed for the Emperor to look at him. "Well, there you go then, Koe, you will actually send me off to the next world in a good mood. I do thank you. This may not have been my best day, but at least I have delivered the message, and by now it will be well on the way back to my people in Magnar, so my solemn oath to my people is true."

The Emperor studied the big red man for a long moment. "So why is it that *you* had to deliver the message? I send messages all the time, but I need not die for it."

The Barbarian's legs had now stopped quaking. "It is not about pride or anything like that … we simply felt it would not be taken for its full value if not delivered by me, the King, to the Emperor. Besides, a thing so big is worthy of such sacrifice for my people. There is good in you, Hannu Koe. I can see it even when you try so hard to hide it. Your problem is your ego; it defeats you. I'm sure you have tried to overcome it but you have failed and submitted to it. Now tell me, Koe, what is a keyhole? And not the one in a door, thank you. You may think of us as Barbarians, but we have good homes with doors, though we never had any need for keys."

"What happened to all your great homes then, man?"

"Your lot took them. Remember?"

"You did have a need for keys then?"

"No. We never saw any profit in thieving from one another. If I need an axe, I go to a blacksmith and ask for one. While I'm there, I will ask what he needs and I will get that for him while he is making my axe. However, if I go out one night and steal one from my village, then the village is still short of an axe, and I will wake up in the morning a smaller man. But if I get the blacksmith some furs and meat, I am the bigger man for it."

The Emperor found himself agreeing.

"Psst," beckoned Tzu. "The keyhole, Koe. It's time." His eyes motioned up around the Dome and then back on the Emperor. "Your entourage await their treat, Koe."

The Emperor held the hook up like a trophy and the crowd cheered wildly. He turned back to the man of iron and spoke in a low voice. "Farewell, Tzu Hsi, leader of your clan, *this* is the Keyhole." Without hesitating, he pushed the red-hot hook in through the small opening he'd cut and drew it back out slowly.

The Barbarian looked down to see his stomach pull out then snap back. Over the hook was an intestine, *his* intestine. He shook his head slowly.

The Emperor walked over to the wolves' cage, pulling the intestine along with him. Once more, a paw shot out. Putting the hook down on the ground, he continued dragging out more intestines. Soon he had enough to make some loops which he picked up with the tongs. He cautiously eased up to the cage and swung the hoops through the bars. He jumped back at the speed of the wolves. He turned back to Tzu and pointed at his missing navel with his tongs. "And that, my nemesis-to-be no more, is what we call a Keyhole."

Tzu's belly tightened as the intestines pulled into the dark of the cage. "Besides my demise, what exactly happens at the end of the line?"

The Emperor sneered. "All of your internal organs will bunch behind the keyhole then, either your skin will tear, or your organs will shred." Tzu scoffed at the indignant Emperor. "What, could you possibly have to mock about, Tzu?"

Tzu noted that the Emperor had used his real name. "I'm happy my message has been delivered. If only it were to your father, things may have been different for my people. My comments about your late father and brother, I was out of line and I apologise for my indiscretions. Pain my only excuse. I'm allergic to it, you know."

"On the contrary, you have taken a ridiculous amount of pain and not lost any of the direction of your original plan. You must have a mind and determination of true steel." Both men looked at the 'keyhole' as it made a gurgling noise and began to pull the skin out tight.

Tzu looked up to the Emperor's entourage and called boldly. "We are but ONE PEOPLE!"

His skin tore and out splayed all his internal organs. Just for moment, they stopped at the Emperor's feet then, with the heart still beating, they slithered through the bars, disappearing into the snarling, dark abyss.

22 Fate of Samos

The two huge, black beech doors opened and the Emperor and his entourage entered the Den. In the room's centre, a blazing fire welcomed the guests, whilst opium pipes and canisters of wine were placed about the room by topless concubines.

Changes had been made to the traditional seating. They were now in an arc, shaped like the shoe of a horse. The Emperor was in the centre, facing out directly to the hearth in the middle of the room. Between seats, small tables held the goblets. Eagerly, the Assets sorted themselves into rankings that indicated a who's who of the realm.

The Emperor glanced up at the smoke-damaged rafters and thought of the terrible fire. Several concubines and a eunuch never made it out. It was said that Hasuca and Senior Matron, Sen Ya San had also perished. He had made a minute inspection of the bodies, looking for his brother. They were all burnt beyond recognition, though it just didn't add up to him. Master Xiang, no less, had sworn that he saw the Matron and Hasuca enter the burning room to help as best they could. It was clear that Master Xiang had also gone in to do what he could. He'd very nearly perished himself, receiving many burns and suffering smoke inhalation. He'd made it back to the door, carrying a young concubine before collapsing and being dragged clear of the fire. The concubine died later that night.

The Emperor brought himself back to the business at hand — today was to be the day to play his first of many hands. He strode to his throne where a concubine carefully plumped the final touches to his cushions. He pushed her aside abruptly and swiped up a goblet, gulping the contents and placing it back on the table with a slam. A concubine moved quickly to refill it, looking nervously at another who acknowledged her, then stared at the floor. The Emperor was in a particularly dark mood. The Assets made themselves comfortable. There would be time for the Emperor's gifts later. It was business first.

The Emperor leant over to the prince and whispered to him. The prince rose and began a circuit of the room. As he did so, one by one, the Assets came over and sat by the Emperor to discuss what was happening in their provinces and how much produce they had for the supply of the Palace.

He studied each of the Assets' traditional purple, silk gowns, their condition and the care taken before they presented themselves to him. Each man also wore a coloured belt which indicated what area he was from. Blue indicated north, red was south, green indicated west, and yellow was east. The more belts an Asset wore, the lower his standing, unless one of those belts was black. The Emperor himself always wore black and purple. Those deemed to be from strategic areas, such as Samos, would wear a black belt with any other colour, so everyone would know their business was of Royal importance. If this person made a request for his City, it would be the word of the Emperor himself.

Finally, Prince Desora returned, and the Emperor waited for the murmur of light conversation to subside and stood. "Thank you for your journeys to this gathering. For those of you from the northern provinces, this will be your last visit until the spring, no doubt."

He began to pace the centre of the seating, one hand behind his back, his head down in thought. "I am thinking it is time to show my authority over this nation. I don't like to have to demonstrate to any of you who is leading this great country. It is known. It is taught from birth to every child who has the good fortune of being born to these, my homelands."

He paused, pointing at each man in turn. "None of you, bar Master Xiang, and of course, your Prince, are aware that I have concerns about the loyalty of the most important province …" He came to a stop in front of the one empty seat, drawing attention to it. "But there comes a time to let one know where he actually is – not where he *thinks* he is."

The Assets all mumbled their support of the Emperor's comments. One of the Assets sat forward in his seat.

The Emperor studied him momentarily. He wore three belts. "Yes, Ish Wa. You may speak."

Ish Wa stood. "On behalf of my colleagues and myself, I would like to thank you for the entertainment this afternoon, Your Excellency, as well as for the impending feast." There was a small clap to support Wa. The Emperor soaked up the attention. Ish Wa waited for it to settle before continuing. "I do concede it is very disappointing to see an absent colleague. There has been no message at all from Samos, Your Excellency?"

Ish Wa sat down as the Emperor contained his annoyance at the stupid question. He needed the support of everyone for his plan to lead his Imperial Guard against his major city. He'd been waiting for a reason, and now, as the prince was coming of age, the plan had been put in place. The time was now.

"I verified just before coming to this meeting, no effort seems to have been made. It's not the first time this particular Asset has proven not to be … an Asset." The Emperor tried not to smile as an angry murmur swept through the meeting. He allowed it for a moment before holding up a humble hand. "All right, do settle, my good men. I am still sure that there is a good explanation."

He let his words hang for a moment before he got what he was waiting for. A slender man, not much older than the Emperor, with a mean scar through the bridge of his nose, slipped forward in his seat. The Emperor waved for him to stand. "Yes, Norinko, what is it you wish to add?"

Norinko stood and acknowledged the Emperor first, then the prince, and bowed to Master Xiang as well. He cleared his throat into a loose fist. "I have known Kain Fly a good many years, Your Excellency. I plead we give him time. There will be an explanation of reason, I'm sure." He held firm in his support of Kain Fly. "I couldn't say he is the most refined man, but there is no question about his loyalty to the throne. He would never waiver."

It was not what the Emperor had wanted. Out of the corner of his eye, he noticed another Asset turn to one of his colleagues and mutter angrily. He walked back to his throne and stood in front of it. "La Chun, is there something you would like to add to this meeting?"

Chun looked about, his chubby forehead heavily wrinkled. With a grunt of effort, he slipped his short body forward in his seat. Around his wide girth, he wore a red and a green belt. Chun wanted a black belt more than he wanted his next meal. His hand didn't cover his mouth as he coughed.

The Emperor waved him to stand.

"Thank you, Your Excellency." He also dipped his head to the prince. "I was in Samos just one day before coming away for this trip myself. Now, I know most of you would realise I am not the most athletic type …" The group chuckled and Chun nodded his bald head, his neck wobbling in waves as he did so, "… and yet here I am."

Norinko studied the Emperor, who was smiling at him, as Chun continued. "I have also seen the horses Kain keeps in his stables, and I think that most of you know they are second only to the Emperor's fine stable." He raised his fat arms. "And yet, where is he?"

A cheer erupted. The Asset had to call over the ruckus. "I saw his son, Tark, whilst I was there, idling about, as he does." Chun paused as another small chuckle rippled around the room. He tucked his stumpy thumbs into his red belt. "Yet he's not here either. I have received so many messages from the great city that I have wondered if he has every boy in the city on his payroll as a messenger …" He punched a fist into his palm. "… and yet, where are they now?!"

Angry men turned to one another, nodding in agreement. The slender Norinko slipped forward again. The Emperor made eye contact. He couldn't refuse Norinko another chance to speak. Reluctantly, he waved him up.

"All I'm saying is, it may be a little hasty to make a decision just yet. His messenger, or heaven forbid, he himself, may have taken a fall on the trail up here. We have all passed over it at some point in our lives. It's not a walk in the field now, is it? One false move … it could happen to any one of us." Norinko took his seat, catching Master Xiang's gaze, signifying an understanding between them.

Chun was quick to slide forward in his seat again. The Emperor waved him up. "I use, for the most part, the very same track. I didn't see a stricken horse. I didn't see a fallen rider. I didn't see either Kain, Tark or a messenger, for which I, *Norinko* …" He glared at him as he spoke, "would have stopped immediately to help." Chun pointed at Norinko. "Your Excellency, I resent the implication that I would not have stopped to help!"

The gathered men were in all sorts of angry debate. Now divided, the meeting had not gone according to the Emperor's plan. He'd wanted to take control of all the wharf rations now, before winter.

He held up a hand and the men settled. "I can see reason in Norinko's wise words, and I will heed them. But, as a cautionary measure, I ask all of you to return here at the first opportunity after winter. I do hope it is a stricken horse, of course with no one hurt. As Norinko has pointed out, it is indeed a difficult track and one of the longer journeys, but also, as Chun told us, *he* has made it."

Chun's cheeks wobbled as he proudly agreed, and the Emperor concealed his desire to boot the fat Asset from his chair.

"So, after considering your comments, I will leave it until the spring before I make any move. Every one of my Assets deserves reasonable doubt, would you not agree?"

The men muttered and clapped gently until the Emperor held up his hand. "I know I can call on any of you if the time comes. Heavens forbid I will need to, but make no mistake, if I am given reason, I *will* act on behalf of the Sovereign." He held up a tight fist and shook it. "That is my duty of care to the people of my Nation!"

He still wished to make his move right now, but it seemed a few of the group were leaning more towards Norinko's argument than Chun's. He didn't wish to press his luck. After all, he knew well that there would be no messenger. Kain's demise had already been taken care of. All of them would have to give their full support so he would have the momentum to move as he wished. Once in play, there would be no turning back. This was a plan that had been on his table for almost two decades. *One more winter to get the full blessing of these simple Assets then they will see me conquer a lot more than the City of Samos.*

He sat back down and watched the politics play out in front of him. Some had gathered around Norinko, mostly the older Assets, but Chun's group was larger. The Emperor knew he would be a good ally in this, as Chun did have more than his location to Samos on his side. He wanted that black belt too much for his own good. Most of all, Chun's arrogance, selfishness and overinflated ego clouded his reason. *I could lead this man like the carrot leading the donkey. It would not be the fastest journey, but as long as he got a reward from time to time, this donkey would get him there — and carry the load all the way.* The Emperor smiled to himself. *Yes, this will be my last winter to wait. Besides, with a change of Asset for the city of Samos, the game could be played even better.*

The prince had joined in conversation with Norinko's group. The Emperor frowned. So much was at stake in the plan that had been put into play this autumn. One wrong word and all would be lost — perhaps irretrievably lost. The Emperor believed that he'd already proven that there was not a problem too big for him to solve. It was merely a question of timing.

He almost flinched when Master Xiang spoke from his left. He'd completely forgotten about his presence. Still keeping an eye on the young prince, the Emperor leant over to listen to the Master of the Guard.

"Your Excellency, you must be pleased with our Prince. He is growing fast."

The Emperor relaxed, radiating pride as he observed his son. "Yes, Xiang, he has come a long way these last few years."

"Indeed, he has, my Emperor. He has a good eye for whom to look out for in a fight, and now we witness his ability to move from crowd to crowd and command the respect he deserves."

The prince was now involved in conversation with Chun's group and they all seemed to be reasonably attentive. A small knot formed over the Emperor's brow, but he was mindful of Master Xiang's uncanny ability to discern his thinking.

"So, Your Excellency, what is next for the young prince, if you do not mind my asking?"

Of course I mind you sticking in your unwanted nose, you used up old coot. He drew a breath. "You have served this family for two generations and are now caring for the third. Your dedication to this family is second-to-none, Xiang, your influence of wisdom, immeasurable."

Master Xiang didn't wish to see the Emperor's lying eyes. He lowered his own. "You are most kind to me, Your Excellency. And the prince?"

The Emperor frowned inwardly. Xiang had not forgotten his question. "I shall wait and see what is to come of Kain. I shall be asking you to accompany us to the city of Samos in the spring, Master Xiang. We shall have much work there, I feel."

The two watched the prince, who was continuing talks with the Chun group.

"So, you have already made up your mind that we are going, Your Excellency?"

The Emperor slowly drew his attention back to the Master. "What?"

"Well, from what you say, it suggests to me that deep down, you already have a plan for Samos. May I be of help for one last time, Your Excellency?"

"Firstly, you are reading too much into my words, Master. Secondly, the city of Samos will not be your last time, Xiang."

Master Xiang could discern the venom on the Emperor's tongue. He knew not to say another word. He hadn't known this man all his life to not learn how to read the words as they fell off his forked tongue.

Just then the huge double doors opened and a messenger hurried across the room to whisper in the Emperor's ear. The Emperor whispered back, and the messenger left as hurriedly as he came. He stood and clapped twice, drawing attention to himself. "My good friends and Assets, leave the business for now. Please enjoy a well-earned meal, and as always, my concubines are yours for this night." He lifted his left hand, patting the top of it with his right. The group responded, applauding as he stood to leave.

Master Xiang rose to follow, but the Emperor held up his hand for him to stay. He stopped and watched the Emperor ascend the steps out of the Den. A quick glance confirmed that Norinko was also watching, his face bearing a pained expression.

Xiang frowned. This was all wrong. Wrong like the sudden death of this Emperor's predecessor – his father, Emperor Gauxi. An ominous feeling crept over the old Master.

23 Kito's Message

Kito watched the signs closely as he jogged through the jungle. Now a young man, his body was fit to its every fibre. A broken branch, a trampled fern, they were all signs that the wild boar had gone this way. Hasuca already knew Kito had been a naturally skilled hunter in his former world, but for Kito, it was a lost memory that simply needed refreshing. Focusing his attention, he could call flying fish or redirect the mighty king cobra and command his prey.

It wasn't uncommon now for him to be away for an extended time, but this trip he'd strayed farther than ever. The boar he was hunting was not aware that Kito was following, though it was moving in a specific direction, and at pace.

He'd followed the boar for days, and it had barely stopped. Both had been climbing for the entire time. Kito had become increasingly curious about what would drive a boar against its instincts, climbing in autumn, away from their winter home in the lower, warm jungle.

He refreshed himself at a stream. The jungle had given way to bush. The cool, thin air brushed his bare chest and burned his lungs. Before he'd left, Hasuca had argued that he should never go hunting at this time of the year without his pack of warm clothing. Kito didn't need it right now, but he most certainly would tonight. He lifted his head and looked around. At this rate of climbing, the boar would have them both up in the snowline by nightfall.

He slowed down at the sound of pigs grunting and squealing. They were feeding on something. He got closer and paused. A rocky spur ran down to his right, and the source of the noise was just beyond that. The spur would give him the advantage of height. Careful not to loosen any rocks, he climbed up through the bushland until he found an ideal place to peer over into the next ravine.

Kito gazed down at the sight below and gasped. There were more than a hundred wild boars feeding. It took him a moment to take in the scene before him. An ornately decorated coach lay on its side, ruined. He could only make out one of the four wheels. It had been drawn by at least six horses that lay amongst the scattered ruins. In their feeding frenzy, the boars had consumed most of their remains, and those of the coachmen.

With the coach on its side and fresh meat abundant, none of the boars had yet bothered with the passengers inside. Kito tried to figure out where the coach had fallen from. Broken branches from a large oak hung over the coach, indicating where it had crashed down. It could only have been going to or from the palace.

The coach had come to a halt partway down the precariously steep and slippery shale ground. Kito just had to look inside. Taking great care, he walked onto the huge oak branch. His toes gripped the gnarled, broken branches hanging directly over the coach as he eased down them then dropped onto the side-turned carriage. The pungent smell of death hit him and he breathed through his open mouth as he crawled through the splintered door into the coach.

There were only two men. The bodies were relatively well preserved. The thin, cold air had taken its time aging them. Confirming his expectation, one of the men was dressed in purple and wore two belts around his waist, one red, one black. Kito peered into the man's open eyes. Two things struck him, one was the fear on his face and the other was a sense of knowing, the unfortunate fellow. He continued to stare at him for a while, then, with a start, he jumped back so quickly that he inadvertently landed on the other victim. The coach slid a little. The man dressed in purple was no less than Kain Fly, the Key Keeper of Samos and Asset to the Emperor himself.

Though Kito carried little sympathy for Tark, the Emperor ought to be informed of this horrific accident immediately. He removed the two belts to verify his story, then closed Kain's eyes and those of what must have been his bodyguard.

The coach slid again as wild boar surrounded it with renewed interest. Gingerly, Kito climbed out and looked up at the hanging branch, now out of arm's reach. He knew he would only get one shot at this. He took a moment, then leapt in the air, catching the branch. He swung out and back, then used the momentum to flip himself up onto the broken branch. It creaked and splintered a little more. Quickly, he moved further up to the more solid branches of the fallen oak.

Below him, the coach gave way to the sliding shale beneath. Kain's body now lay on the shale. He was feet-first to the cliff, his hands at his side as if he'd lain down to admire the view. Some of the boar grunted and squealed as they tried to get in close though the shale proved too unstable. For now, Kain's body was safe.

Once back on the road, Kito looked to the sun; it was well past mid of day. He verified the contents of his pack – ribbons, fruit and plenty of water, at least more than enough to get a good start. He swung it on and jogged away. He'd never been to the palace, but if the coach was going this direction, the road going up must get to the palace, eventually.

As he ran, he pondered Hasuca and his affiliation to the palace. Hasuca had not directly talked on the matter other than that Kito must never mention Hasuca. He knew that the Emperor played evil games because that was where Tark had planned to take him. Hasuca had warned him never to go there, but this situation was different. He was taking an important message to the Palace, and this would win him favour with the Emperor. And since the Emperor would have no idea who Kito was, what harm could it do?

***

It took a few days run, but Kito pushed himself hard and made good time getting to the Palace of Middle Kingdom. Large gates loomed across the ridge of the trail he was on. On either side, the contour dropped away sharply. Tall, stone walls running all the way out of sight in either direction told Kito he was going the right way. Up here, the first of winter's snow had already settled on the ground and from the tracks along the stone wall, he could see that the Imperial Guard had been patrolling day and night.

The mighty gates were at least forty feet high, each supported by equally enormous hinges. Heads poked out from the covered-in platform across the top of them.

Kito took a breath. "Hello. My name is Kito. I have an important message for the Emperor."

The heads disappeared and he waited for the gates to open. They did not. A guard called back. "Where are you from, Kito?"

Kito pointed back down the hill. "I came across an accident several days back. It was the Keeper of the Key for the City of Samos."

"Are you from the City of Samos then?"

"Well, yes, I am. I found the accident while hunting wild boar."

"If you were hunting wild boar, where is your crossbow or spear, Kito?"

Kito pulled his knife and held it up. Without warning, there was a flurry of activity, and a mass of crossbows were now pointing at him. He slowly took off his pack, then heard the *pang* of a discharging crossbow.

He closed his eyes.

His toes held firm on the frozen cobbles for balance. The bow had loosened from his right, and in his mind's eye, he could see the bolt coming his way. The tip turned, slicing its way through the crisp air, the feathers whispering in pursuit of the quivering bolt. He could feel his knife, light in his right hand, and he heard Hasuca's instruction, *Focus on the bolt, hit the knife with the bolt.* He stretched and flexed sideways as he watched the knife strike the bolt, breaking it into two pieces that bounced over the cobbles behind him. He didn't look at the men on the wall who'd stood transfixed at the impossible scene just played out before them. He pulled the ribbons from his pack and held them out in his hand.

"Here, I took these from the Keeper of the Key. I can give them to you if you wish. I just thought the Emperor should know what happened. I think he was murdered."

A hesitant voice responded. "Oh, really?"

"A tree fell and spooked the horses."

"Doesn't sound like murder to me."

"The tree was cut."

"Keep this between the Emperor and yourself."

There was a clambering of chains as guards worked to unlock the massive gates. Slowly, they opened to the biggest man they'd ever seen. They'd all heard stories about the big, black men that came into Samos from time to time, but none of them had ever been to the port to see for themselves. He towered head and shoulders above any of them. His long, wavy hair hung over his open fur jacket, revealing his powerful chest, still wet from his run.

Kito walked forward with all eyes upon him mean, repulsed and resentful. Tension filled the air and, for a moment, he felt like a child again, being dragged into the silk factory, wrapped in chains.

With an air of defiance, he strode through the gates, a nervous entourage following.

It was quite a walk before they came to a flight of stairs. He ascended and crossed a cobbled patio then up another flight of stairs and then another. *What are all these steps about?* He could see no good reason for them.

Finally, he reached the top step to the most magnificent building. Its base was all stonework and the rest was made up of heavy timber. He was awestruck.

The building towered over him as he walked forward through the grand entrance to the enclosed courtyard. The numerous balconies overhead all faced down onto it, its centre dominated by a large grassy area with tall trees reaching to the glass roof.

The discreet cough from behind didn't startle him. He'd heard the man approach and assumed it to be one of the gate-keeping guards that had followed some distance back. Judging by the footsteps, the man had modest training.

He turned to see a young man, about his own age, wearing a black, long-sleeved silk shirt with matching trousers. His hair was parted down the middle, impeccably presented. Kito immediately dropped to one knee. "I do beg your pardon, my Prince."

A whisk of a smile came over Prince Desora's face. "Ah, you did not hear me coming then, Barbarian?"

"No, my Prince, I heard you some distance off, but I didn't realise it to be you." Kito bowed again, not seeing the prince's face turn to thunder. He added, "And I'm not from the north, so I'm not one of your Barbarians."

Without hesitation, the prince drew his sword. In Kito's mind, it was not provoked. The prince wasted no time attacking with a quick lunge. Kito slapped the side of the sword with the palm of his hand and stepped back, holding up his hands.

The prince snarled. "You are not of this land so you *are* a Barbarian!"

Kito continued to back around the grassy area with his hands up. Bows were again raised and pointed at him as the prince rushed forward. Kito swayed smoothly, the blade missing him by a whisker every time. At one point, Kito caught the blade between his palms and winked at the prince. He knew this would anger him and invoke clumsy mistakes. Hasuca had pulled no punches in his training. It was reassuring to spar with someone different. Kito understood his training was for his own benefit, but if the prince had received the training one would expect, and he could deflect him, then he must surely be ready to find his way home.

The thought made him smile.

On the balconies above, the servants had been going about their evening round of chores. One by one, they stopped to watch the exhibition taking place in the mini forest below. A young woman with big green eyes was amongst them. She wore her hood up and walked with her head down and her back slouched so as not to make eye contact or show how tall she was. When she saw the big man catch the prince's sword, she drew her breath and lifted back her hood in amazement.

It was a strange kind of fight, the prince and all his training, armed with the long, curved sword and this man with bare feet, a scruffy coat and not a weapon in sight. Yet for every move the prince made, the dark man had an answer without being slashed to pieces. The fight went on. Then she saw the dark one flick the blood from his hands. She put a hand over her mouth, grasping the railing to steady herself. He was tall, masculine and moved with the grace of a swan on a smooth lake. His turns and swift moves kept her enchanted.

Kito continued to sway and volley, but the prince was skilled, and Kito knew it might be only a question of time before he made the mistake that would be fatal. The prince was putting on a show that was taking too long. He needed to look masterful to his watching Guard. More than once, Kito tried to catch the blade, but the prince was not about to be shown up like that again, twisting it to cut Kito's bleeding palms. Kito had to allow the prince to take him out, or take out the prince. *Death either way.*

He waited for the right moment. The prince's lack of experience meant that Kito could predict when the prince was going from one combination to his next. He waited for the slightest hint of hesitation before the next combination, for when he would step in and finish the fight, and his own life. With so many bows pointed at him, it would be a quick death. He watched as the combination came to an end, so he could step in.

"STOP!"

Kito stepped back, not removing his eyes from the breathless prince.

"*What* is the meaning of this!?" demanded the Emperor.

Kito bowed deeply and stood proud, if not a little defiant. "Ruler and Commander of this magnificent land, your son, my Prince, was giving me a good workout, Your Excellency. We were having a friendly match, as it were."

"Hmm, is that so?" The Emperor clasped his hands behind his back and began to walk around the two. "Friendly sparring, you say?"

Kito stood taller than the Emperor, and much broader and heavier. "My name is Kito. I have come to bring you these." He reached in under his heavy jacket. The Emperor's eyebrows raised as did countless crossbows. Kito paused for a moment, then continued slowly, checking the bowmen as he did. "Easy, men. Easy. Nobody needs to get hurt. I am finding the message for the Emperor." He eased out the ribbons, watching the realisation flash across the Emperor's face.

The Emperor slowly took the two, blood-stained ribbons. "Where did you find these, Kito?"

Kito kept his voice low. "I found them on the road from the City of Samos, or more to the point, just *below* the road."

The Emperor frowned. "Just below, Kito? Did somebody fall from their horse?"

Kito shook his head. "No, I'm afraid it is more sinister than that, Your Excellency."

The Emperor looked around with genuine concern. "Guards, you may return to your post now. With the protection of the prince, I will take care of this." He looked up to the balconies and the servants quickly headed back to work. There was no comment as the guards released the tension off their crossbows and made their way back out into the cold, though some couldn't resist looking back.

Kito's hands still bled, forming two red blotches on the green grass, though the prince had not managed to cut a thread of his clothing.

The Emperor inspected the ribbons. "Kito, it's getting dark. Would you stay as my guest at the palace?" He held up his fist, clasping the ribbons. "You have come a long way to deliver an important message, and I am grateful. By morning, I shall have a message of great importance that I need to be delivered. I believe you may be the man for the job. Would you be prepared to do this, Kito?"

Kito was taken aback. "It will be my pleasure to serve the Palace. In the morning, I shall run your message."

The Emperor seemed satisfied. "Good. We shall talk then. I will have a servant show you to your room."

23 Messenger

The palace truly was a place of wonder. Kito could feel the history in its walls. A maid opened the door to his room but didn't step in. Instead, she backed into the wide hall and bowed. No one had ever bowed to him like that before. He wondered what sort of a life she must lead, to bow to *him*.

Closing the door, he checked over the large room. To his left, an open fire blazed with more than enough wood for the night stacked to one side. To his right was an elaborately handcrafted bed. He walked over and sat on it with a bounce. It was soft and silent. No crunching straw, this was a bed of feathers.

He drew the full-length curtains, and the vision took his breath. He was surprisingly high off the ground. The full moon lit up the snow-covered valley below. The deciduous trees carried a thin layer of snow, whilst the evergreens were wrapped in their white, winter cocoons. He noted the clear sky where the stars twinkled as if in competition with the bright, full moon.

There was a rap at the door, and Kito turned. Another knock. He opened it to an elderly woman, bent in reverence and holding a food-laden tray in her outstretched arms.

He waited for the servant to stand and bowed back to her. "My name is Kito and I thank you for this food."

For a fleeting moment, her eyes lit up and she reciprocated his enchanting smile as she reached in to close the door.

Kito finished the meal and gazed into the fire, wondering what Hasuca would be doing. The door opened without forewarning, and the Emperor strode in. Kito rose to his feet and bowed. Behind the Emperor, the maid came through and quickly retrieved

Kito's near-empty tray.

"You serve the finest food. I am grateful, Your Excellency."

The Emperor looked him up and down. "Had you not eaten at all today, Kito?"

"Only a little fruit and a lot of water, sire. I have been in a hurry for the last few days, Your Excellency."

The Emperor moved to the window. "Kito, where did you say you come from?"

"I did not say, sire, as you did not ask. The truth is, I don't know. I was brought here on a vessel and then sold into bondage. For some years since, I have been living in the jungle near the City of Samos. I got a bump to the head when on the vessel and have no memory before that, sire."

"Grief, man, what a sorry tale you tell."

Kito stood beside the Emperor, sharing the magnificent vista of the valley below. "I have a good life, sire. I have seen bad things happen to others. I have seen bad things done to others. Yet I am still just a boy and have much to be thankful for."

"I had a brother, Kito. He lost his life in a fire right here in this palace. He used to say such things, just as you did then. You said you were sold in the City of Samos. As the Emperor, it concerns me that boys are sold like animals. Who sold you and who bought you, Kito? Can you remember?"

Kito was careful of the Emperor. He wondered what might ensue if he could expose the injustices of the silk factory and the boats. He might free Baako; he might free Baako's mother. "As I said, sire, I don't know who sold me onto the vessel, though I can tell you that I was bought and used by Captain Tarrant of the vessel *Shiraz*. He sold me to a silk factory in the City of Samos. Tark was the owner's name. He treated all his personnel very badly. I once saw him put a man down his salt well. The people in the factory cried. They said it would sometimes take days for someone to die in there."

The Emperor continued admiring the view. "He doesn't sound like a very savoury character. To whom did he sell you then, Kito?"

"We were out hunting when I gave him the slip. I have lived in the jungle ever since."

"What? All alone, Kito?"

"Yes, that is correct. The jungle is full of good food if you know where to look, sire. Ironically, it was Tark who taught me this."

The Emperor faced him. "I heard that a man, a little older than me, and a dark-skinned boy about your age, had been seen in the City of Samos from time to time. Did you come over with any brothers, Kito?"

"No, sire. As I said, I got a bump to the head. I'm afraid I don't even know if I have any brothers – or indeed any family." Kito lowered his head.

The Emperor squinted. "So, when you say that the accident you saw was more sinister than a riding accident, what exactly did you mean by that?"

"My Emperor, it was not a riding accident. The travellers were in the carriage when it was driven over the cliff, sire."

"Driven over the cliff! Who would drive a carriage over a cliff? Even if you did hate your Master, you wouldn't just drive him over a cliff, Kito."

"No, but if you wished to get rid of him, you might fell a tree so the horses would spook and run over the cliff."

"So, you don't believe it was an accident?"

"No, sire. The tree was cut."

"You know the tree had been cut by hand, Kito?"

"Yes."

"And how do you think they had it fall at precisely the right time?"

"I thought about that for some time, Your Excellency. I believe they tied it back with rope then made the cuts. They just waited for the carriage to come along and cut the rope."

"Did you see this tree and the rope with your own eyes, Kito?"

"Yes, I did, Emperor."

"This would still take skill and timing to get it right. I mean, just how long would it take for a tree to fall?"

"As I headed up to deliver my message, I found another tree of the same type and felled with the same technique."

"And you think it was, say, a trial?"

"Yes. It was felled in the same direction. It was also on another blind corner. If they had somehow missed with the first tree, the carriage was nevertheless doomed."

The Emperor turned back to the window. "Well, I must say you have been thorough in your investigation. How did you happen to be there, Kito?"

"I was hunting wild boar, which led me there."

"Really, Kito? How far had you chased this wild boar?"

"Several days, though it's not unheard of when a boar smells blood, sire"

"Really, Kito? You believe it smelled it through the jungle several days away?"

"No, sire. I think everything in the jungle is connected. The jungle wanted the chaos cleaned up and called in experts. When I got there, there were over a hundred boars in the chasm. The horses had almost been completely eaten already. The men inside the carriage were more difficult to get. I am sorry for your loss." Kito dipped his head again.

"Kito, this is murder of the most serious degree, and it is of national importance. It must never be spoken of again. Do you understand me?"

"Yes, sire. It is why I brought you this message myself."

The Emperor saw in him the expression of a devoted follower. He put his hand on Kito's shoulder. "I will send for you in the morning, Kito. Until then, please enjoy my hospitality."

Kito bent low before the Emperor. The Emperor's eyes narrowed, though he resisted his urge to drive his knife into the man's spine.

***

235

The Emperor burst into his office where the prince and Master Xiang were talking of battle plans using a large map on the wall, covered in blue and red pins. He poured from his decanter and drank the first goblet in one gulp then sat at his writing table and sighed heavily as he poured another.

Master Xiang pondered the Emperor and the goblet he now drank from. Recently, he'd used a white cloth to clean one of the Royal goblets. No matter how much he rubbed inside it, a blue smear continued to discolour the cleaning cloth. Tarnish was leaching from the silver. The Master had seen the mysterious gypsy who'd dropped off the goblets. Hasuca had suffered terrible headaches at the palace and now the young Prince drank from his same goblet.

He brought his train of thought back to the Emperor. "Is the young, dark fellow of particular interest to you, sire?"

The Emperor drank some more, glaring at the Master. "Yes. I think I would like to tear the lying heart out of his ridiculous chest *but* ..." He wagged his finger. "... he may be of help to me if I'm to flush out the cheating Hasuca."

It took all Xiang's self-control to remain inscrutable as the Emperor glared at him. "What, after all this time, makes you think that Hasuca is alive, sire?"

The Emperor let the silence burn the air. "For many years, there have been consistent reports of a man fitting Hasuca's description with a boy of brown-milk skin. Every time I begin to dismiss it as a fable, the whispers happen again." His voice rose with the flare of his anger. "Yet when I have it investigated, it is like finding a silhouette without a person to cast it!" He hit the table with his fist.

The prince flinched. Both men turned to him as he averted his eyes.

"And as for you, young man, he was about to break your nose had I not stopped the fight." A few drops spilled from the overfilled goblet as the Emperor waved it at Prince Desora.

The prince sprung from his seat. "Father, *I* was about to kill him. It was *his* certain death you prevented."

The Emperor leaned his elbows on the table. "He was waiting for you to come to the end of your combination. He was going to step inside on your left and plough his elbow into your nose. If he had done so in a downward stroke, it would have broken your nose, given you two black eyes and further bloodied my garden. If he had done it in an upward stroke, it would have killed you instantly."

The prince folded his arms tightly as the veins in his forehead pulsed out his fury. "No! I had him where I wanted him. I had already cut him – twice."

The Emperor batted his hand as if swatting the prince's nonsense away. "Yes, Desora, but not before he'd caught and held your blade. For a moment, I thought he was going to give you a kiss on the cheek."

The prince now trembled with rage. No other man would live after talking to him in this fashion.

The chair creaked as the Emperor sat back. "You have had no lessons with the man that taught your father and his father before him, yet you think you know better than I, Desora? You have my blood, which is now raging through your veins. With training, I know you have the ability to at least equal me with a sword. You will begin training with Xiang in the morning, and you will do it *his* way. You will truly learn why he is called Grand Master. Now, go and have a hot bath and get some rest. Master Xiang likes to work hard." He filled his goblet yet again.

As the prince ascended the stairs and reached the door, the Emperor added, "Oh, and Desora, the young man is staying in the visitor's room on the seventh floor of the east wing."

The prince looked confused. "Father?"

"Just so there is no question of where he is. I wouldn't like it if he were to have an accident overnight whilst in my care."

The prince barely dipped his head. "Yes, Father." The door slammed shut.

The Emperor and the Master turned their attention to the grace of nature through the window before them. The Master silently thanked Father Creator for making it and Mother Nature for keeping it in forever-changing perfection.

The Emperor drank heavily and sighed. "Xiang, the prince has been telling his teachers of the arts, how *they* are to train him. I have but one son. You will not do the same. He must live to lead this nation in my absence or be my representative in other nations to be led. I must be able to know that I can rely on his backbone and right arm when I need it."

Master Xiang continued to admire the view. "If that is to be my duty through this winter, then it will be my pleasure to work with my Prince."

The Emperor turned to him, stone-faced. "It's not about your pleasure, Xiang. The dark one was playing with him, yet he still believes he was in control. You will *teach* him."

The Master remained silent as the Emperor swayed a little by the window.

"Xiang, it has just occurred to me that you have served the throne your entire life. You have never condoned the plans I have for this great nation. You don't have the imagination to see where I'm going with it. I can't have you holding back my destiny, and so I think it is time for you to step back from the appointment you have held for so many years. It is time I put you in a responsibility more fitting your experience." The Emperor paused, but the Master remained inscrutable. "I will have you train the Imperial Guard from here on, at the palace."

The Master didn't speak, but the Emperor believed he saw hurt in his eyes. "Master Xiang, you are to have a life inside the palace. You will keep all your privileges without the need to travel or go to battle. Enjoy this. You have earned it."

The Emperor had misread Master Xiang's sorrow. It was not for himself, it was for the nation to which he'd devoted his life. He smiled. "It has been a special life for me. I have had a gifted life serving the throne. I have seen things I wished I had not, and I have been in battles I should not have lived to talk about. When will you make the announcement to replace me, sire?"

"It is time to bring some new blood into the fold now, rather than later. He will need to be prepared. As you know, I wish to make my first moves at the time of spring. I will quietly build allies where I need them and strike late in the autumn. I will hit them hard and fast so I have the port in Samos tied up by next winter. From there, I can begin my quest to my rightful destiny." He emptied his silver goblet and placed it on the table, the thickening blue smudge inside it clearly visible.

The old Master drew his eyes away from it. "And if I am to stay in the palace under your care, under what name will I be summoned, sire?"

"After I have made the announcement, you will be known as *Grand Teacher* rather than *Grand Master*. Fitting, don't you think, Xiang?"

The Master dipped his head. "Of course, it will be as you say. I thank you, Your Excellency. What is it that caused you to think we need a full-time teacher within the classifications we have always maintained here, sire?"

The Emperor stared blankly out of the window. Finally, he faced the Master. "The dark one has a certain way that is like no other I have seen. It must be of his people but his moves were all too familiar. His palace etiquette is equal to any. Xiang, he didn't grow up alone in the jungle. He lived with someone who knows us. Desora said that he bowed at the first sight of him. How would a boy who grew up in the jungle know what the prince looked like? I need to keep this dark one. I am so close to the traitor of the throne, I can taste it." He punched the timber window frame several times in quick succession.

Before the start of daybreak, maids were engaged in their chores ahead of everyone rising. The cobbles were swept, the windows cleaned, and cobwebs removed. Everything always had to be impeccably maintained or they would fail to see nightfall.

The green-eyed woman made her way through the moonlit balconies overlooking the indoor forest. She caught her breath as his movement took her attention.

Kito wore nothing but long trousers, his long, wavy hair in a topknot. She noted his sweat-covered chest as he worked out on the grass clearing. He moved with grace, power and extraordinary speed. Never had she seen a man do splits or leap and kick so high. Eventually, he stopped for a series of stretches before mopping his brow.

The young woman almost squealed when a maid whispered beside of her. "Tanica, isn't it the most grotesque thing you have ever seen? I know he's not a Barbarian, but he is so big. They say he is only a boy. It's vulgar, I say."

Tanica frowned. She certainly wasn't about to confide that she had not slept for thinking of this captivating creature.

"Come, Tanica, we have much to do."

Reluctantly, Tanica followed, but not without glancing over her shoulder.

***

In Kito's room, a large bowl of warm water and a towel had been prepared for him. He was just about to get to the food set out when the Emperor walked in.

"Ah, Kito, you are up then, very good. I take it you slept well."

Kito bowed. Without waiting for an answer, the Emperor continued. "Kito, as I suspected, I do have a message for you to deliver. As soon as you are ready to leave, please meet in the entrance where you arrived yesterday. I will have a map, directions and food for you to take. For the first part, I will send you on horseback with some of my men. As soon as you can continue on foot, you will be on your own."

"You have been most kind, Your Excellency."

"Yes, this is true. It is also my duty to my people." He turned to leave. "I will expect you shortly, Kito."

The door clicked shut and Kito was left alone. He ate quickly, clearing the large plate in no time. He was on a Palace mission and he would need his strength.

24 Tarim Caves

Two young men were riding bareback. They wore their uniforms in the last warmth of the shortening days, their furs rolled up behind them for the cold nights. Though they were heading south, they wouldn't beat winter rolling in behind them. The dark green clouds, heavy with snow and ice, had been slowly gaining on them. The smell of snow wafted in on the gentle breeze. They had little food and no provisions for a winter but neither spoke of it. They had to rely on the Gods' help to survive winter this far up on the steppes.

Bolli, the stockier of the two, always wore a fur hat. During the day, he tied the sides up. When it grew cold, he let them down to cover his ears and the back of his neck. His shoulders were broad and he was heavier than his taller travelling partner.

Hao was the Legion's hand-to-hand combat champion. He wore his long hair in a plait down his back. Only Bolli could make the occasional jest about the tail. With his broad jaw and sparkling eyes, Hao was popular with the ladies. Not that Bolli had any trouble with the girls, his confidence and Hao's striking good looks made it so the two never lacked company. They carried crossbows and short swords and were competent in their use. A longbow was also strung across Hao's chest, but both would rather avoid trouble than shed blood getting out of it.

They stopped their horses just short of a crest. As they studied the gentle slope of the steppe below, the horses nibbled the dry stubble. They scrutinised the area, looking for movement of people. Nothing.

After a long silence, Bolli pointed at the tracks to their right; Hao agreed. It would be slower travelling and they didn't have time to spare, but there was something not as it seemed ahead of them; they could sense it. They backed away from the ridge and headed for the forest.

Numerous animal prints puckered the tracks approaching a stream. Hao nodded at Bolli, who rolled his eyes and let out a small chuckle. Hao did so love to hunt. At a flat clearing, they dismounted to lead the horses for a drink and refilled their water bladders in the near-freezing water.

Bolli lifted his head when the horses stamped their feet. Something was crashing through the bush, heading their way. They quickly loaded crossbows then split up, crossfire their small advantage.

They could hear breathing, heavy, harsh and desperate. The noise was too loud, too much to be made by one beast. Whatever was coming was big, powerful and numerous. One of the horses neighed nervously. The men lifted their weapons to take aim, crossbows held firmly into their shoulders, hands relaxed, breathing even.

Three boars broke free of the bracken and both men stepped from behind the trees to get a clear shot. The first two pigs stumbled and fell. The third animal swerved around them, running at Hao. Not having time to reload, he ran forward, diving headlong over the pig and grabbed it by its back legs as it passed under him. The pig dragged him a short distance before Bolli came in from the side with his knife. The pig let out its last squeal. A third, clean kill.

Hao pulled the mud and fermenting leaves from his face. On seeing his companion, Bolli roared with laughter, releasing the twitching pig and falling back.

Hao stood, trying to brush his uniform clean. "Oh, ha, funny, Bolli. Let's all laugh at the man who just single-handedly brought down a large wild boar."

Bolli rolled over onto his knees. "Well, yes, but you did have some help, and it is the smallest pig." He looked up at Hao's muddy face and burst into laughter again.

"You are as blind as you are delusional." Hao flicked away the mud and pointed to Bolli's horse. "That pig is no smaller than that donkey of a horse you ride!" He took the last bit of mud from his hair and flicked it at Bolli, who was still laughing.

Hao strode over to the stream. It was late in the afternoon to be getting wet, but he was not prepared to put up with Bolli's jibes all night. He was finishing his ablutions when he heard a whistle. In a reflex, he snatched his crossbow off the bank and drew his knife in one fluid motion.

Staying low, Hao moved downstream to find the reason for Bolli's whistle. He was surprised to see him talking to two men, one young, the other old with white hair. Kneeling in the icy water, he cocked and loaded his crossbow. He climbed back up on the bank to find a clear shot. It made sense to shoot the younger one, but the old man was standing in the way. He slipped back into the water and made his way further downstream to get behind the two strangers. He saw a large oak tree just ahead, a perfect spot to exit the water and get right behind them.

When Hao reached the oak, he put the bow on the bank so he could climb up the roots out of the stream. A hand came down to help him. He looked up to see the old man smiling at him.

"It is a pleasure to meet you, Hao. My name is Maki."

Hao turned to Bolli, who was approaching with the young man; they were in relaxed conversation. He looked back at Maki, his voice was just not right. The old man's face was weathered, and his skin was like leather. An outdoor man, but the voice was like a woman's. Seeing his confused look, Maki stepped back, giving Hao space to not feel threatened by the two strangers.

Maki turned to introduce the younger man. "And this is my son. Yaan, this would be a cool, if not frozen, Hao."

Yaan and Hao clasped wrists in greeting. "It is a pleasure to meet you, Hao, but I suggest we prepare these fine pigs and get inside before the storm hits and you freeze."

Bolli scoffed, but Hao shot him a glare that ended any more jesting. The four of them made their way to the dead pigs.

Maki pulled a knife, the blade was thin and well-used. As he went to work, there was no doubt about his ability to butcher the carcass. Hao walked past the second pig as Yaan was making short work of that. He reached for his knife when Bolli slapped him on the shoulder. "Why don't you go and get your things before you freeze? Nor will a walk to fetch the horses do you any harm."

"Well, thank you, *Mother*. And I was beginning to think you didn't care."

Clear of the three men, Hao removed his wet clothes to wring them out as best he could. After gathering the horses, he returned to join the others. He considered the work they'd done.

Maki walked over to stand beside him. "We keep the brains to cure the skin. We eat all internal organs except the heart and lungs, which we bury in the garden as an offering to the Father and Mother and as the beginning of the next wild animal. The snout and trotters will make a soup you will be grateful for."

Hao agreed. They testified of a high understanding of the order of the Gods. Hao liked these two men already – and there was the mention of soup. With the cold setting in, he couldn't help the sporadic shivers now.

They loaded the pigs onto the horses as they stamped their feet at the smell of blood. Once loaded, Bolli removed his llama skin from the rear of his horse and walked around to Hao. "Your shaking is getting bad; take my furs."

Not feeling his toes, Hao conceded. "Very well, Mother." A thin veil of a smile smeared across his blue lips.

Yaan was already striding out in front, and Maki fell in behind. "Let us find shelter before the storm strikes."

The two horsemen laboured to keep up with Yaan's pace, and Hao's teeth now chattered incessantly.

By the time they broke out onto a grassy plain, the weather had closed in over them. It was snowing heavily as Yaan led them into blinding whiteness. Hao looked at Bolli, who simply shrugged his shoulders and slapped Hao's horse on the rump to keep it going.

They crossed the plain for some time until Hao's horse stopped. Bolli led his up beside him, but Maki was already tending to Hao, now slumped in his saddle. Together, they laid him over his horse.

Bolli looked at Maki. "How did you know to stop and look back at him?" Maki just smiled and took the reins of Hao's horse.

They followed Yaan's footprints, and before long, they were moving downhill. There was a change in the snowfall, and just to his left, Bolli could make out a high bank. They descended along a wall that grew in height. The long, grassy vines that hung down from it offered more shelter for the men were now covered in snow. Bolli too shivered, and he couldn't imagine how cold Hao must be, being wet from the stream. He'd seen many a good man battle on the Wall all summer, only to die in the freeze of winter.

They came to the bottom of the hill and, to Bolli's surprise, turned left into the bank. A stream bubbled to his right. His jaw dropped as Maki pulled aside the grassy vines like a curtain. They stepped through an opening just large enough to take the horses and their cargo and entered a huge cavern, the light and warmth of it hugely inviting.

People swarmed around, taking his horse. Bolli pushed them aside. "Hao!"

Maki stepped up. "Here, young man, stop your bleating, they're working on him now. We have some of the best hands here. If your friend has the will to fight, he may still make it."

Bolli pushed the old man aside and made his way through the crowd, stopping abruptly on the edge of a pond. A small waterfall fell opposite, and countless candles lit the cavern. The air was heavy with steam. An old lady and some younger women were holding Hao in the water whilst they slowly removed his clothing until he was completely naked, floating. They began rubbing his limbs.

A woman spoke in a soft voice beside him. "You should join him. Look, your hands are blue."

Bolli held up his hands to see that she was right. He had experienced blue hands before and not lost a finger, though he knew some who had. He saw Yaan and Maki getting into the water, and the sight shook him. Maki's manhood was not complete, and he now understood the voice. They sat down, and some other women entered the water and began to rub their arms. It looked inviting. He turned to the stunningly beautiful woman holding his hand. Without thinking, he nodded. "Yes, er … thanks." She led him around to where the pool led into the stream and began to undress him. He hadn't thought of that ... too late.

Hao awoke to a room full of light. He looked at the ceiling but couldn't quite focus. He frowned; it appeared to be sand, but it was above him. The room had been carved, apparently also from sand. The room was simple, apart from the unusual building material. The bed was a raised platform cut into the wall, the mattress made of leather and stuffed with wool or something similar. A real contrast with the bedding supplied to the Imperial Guard.

To his left, an elderly woman rocked herself in a chair, eyes closed. Almost blinding light poured in from two open doors. He pushed the covers back, the cool air gaving him an appreciation for the bed and its warmth. He considered slipping back in; he could sleep some more, but no, he wanted to see outside. Bolli had clearly abandoned him for now, so it was up to him to work out where he was.

He dragged a fur from the bed end and wrapped it around himself as he stood. A dizzy spell made him lean on the bed, waiting for it to pass. He reached the doors and put one hand on the doorframe for balance, waiting for his eyes to focus. Finally, he stepped forward onto a balcony. The scene astonished him. Below, he counted four more balconies. There were many more balconies to the left and right. All sheltered by the large, overhanging cliff.

Down to his left, the hot stream came out from the cliff and meandered through the snow-covered field and into the tree line that sloped down from his right. There, just short of the trees, was a small stone bridge.

It had been a good storm. Even the forest had a generous dusting of snow. The deep blue sky above was scattered with tufts of white cloud as if a reminder of where this beauty had come from.

Hao could hear children and adults laughing and playing. Naked children were running up and down the steaming stream, the adults throwing snowballs. To escape the missiles, the youngsters would dive under the warm water, so the adults were hitting each other more often than the youngsters. With every misfire, a shouted promise of revenge came back across the babbling stream. Hao laughed aloud, then flinched as a woman spoke beside him.

"I have watched them play this game at the beginning of every winter. I still haven't worked out who it is played for. Good morning, Hao. My name is Sen Ya San. They call me San."

Hao stepped back to bow. "How long have I slept? I feel as weak as a fawn."

She put a hand on his arm. "From what Yaan has told me, you should have been dead, and Maki backed every word of his story. Looking into your eyes, I can see you are a remarkable young man, and you have suffered greatly. When you get your strength back, you can share your story with us."

Seeing his doubtful gaze, she added, "Don't you worry, I have more to hide than most, but everyone here in Tarim Caves knows my story. It is easier to live free of secrets." She patted his chest gently with a chuckle. "I'm sorry. Listen to me ramble on and you have just woken. Sit back down and I will fetch you some soup. Come, I will walk you back to your bed."

Hao leaned over the balcony, searching for Bolli, but San dragged him away. "Come on, my boy, you can go and throw snowballs with the rest of them soon enough, but not before I give the say-so to leave your bed. You hear me, young man?"

They made their way back to the bed. Hao's feeling was not unlike the times when his mother had caught him out playing after bedtime.

There was a knock on the door. Not waiting for an answer from him or San, Bolli barged in. "Are you still in bed, man? It has been days already."

Hao smiled. It was good to get some prodding from his companion. "Listen to you. If I remember right, I was the one walking down the stream to save you. Isn't that how it went? You were the one caught with your hands on your hips, Bolli."

Bolli raised both his hands in the air. "Oh, come on, who's talking it up now? We both know that I could have taken them both with one hand behind my back."

San studied Bolli. "If you wish to go into the forest and kill supplies for the people of the cave, be my guest, but you will not bring your soiled sword and aggressive ways to these peaceful people."

Hao understood. Too much blood had already been spilled.

"San, I must tell you that without fighting machines like us, you people ..."

Although a great deal shorter than Bolli, San stood directly in front of him. "I might look like a cave dweller to you, but let me assure you, I have served in the palace for longer than you have walked this earth. If you think I have no idea what I'm dealing with, you can think again." Defiantly, she pointed to the open door.

Embarrassed, Hao was not sorry to see Bolli leave.

***

Hao spent several days in his room, although he did enjoy soaking up the sun on his balcony. Bolli talked with him every morning, mostly stories of what he'd seen and done the day before. Some days, he was pleased when San told Bolli it was time to leave. Bolli would protest, but he was no match for the old lady.

When the day came, Hao was pleased to leave his room. As they walked into the hallway, there were a lot of doors. He noticed everyone left their doors open to let the light into the hall. The hall's ceiling was high and evenly curved. He marvelled at how warm it was, knowing there was now several feet of snow outside.

San held his arm as they descended the oak-covered steps, neatly cut into the walls on either side of a curved stairway. He stopped and braced himself against the wall, gazed down some thirty feet below that led to a huge, cavernous room. Several fire pits held red, glowing coals and big pots simmered away. On the far side, a hot spring bubbled. As it overflowed, the water cascaded down pink, white and yellow rocks into a large, hot pool. From there, it ran through a hole to the outside.

San let him take in the scene before she urged him on down the stairs.

Maki was there to greet him. "Well, good morning to you, Hao. San said you were coming along well. Good to see you on your feet, young man." He gave Hao a firm slap on the shoulder. Hao bowed politely and continued to take in his surroundings. The pots were up against the back wall, leaving the bulk of the floor space open, for what he couldn't say, except there had been fires there in the past.

Maki followed Hao's gaze to the ceiling of the great hall. "Ah yes, you have a good eye, my friend. There was no outlet for all the steam when this natural wonder was first found by their ancestors many generations ago."

"*Their* ancestors? Not yours, Maki?"

Maki gazed at Hao with a smile. "Like I said, Hao, you don't miss much. San and I have been here for almost two decades now. They are good people, Hao. They asked no questions, just gave us shelter when we needed it."

After a pause, Maki looked up again. "So, they made an opening at the top, as you can see. When the summer storms came in from the south, it got too hot, and if they closed it off completely, it got wet from all the steam. So, being as smart as they are, they made up adjustable shutters.

Maki pointed to the doors. Other than a few columns supporting the rest of the rock, the wall was open. They had boxed in the door frames with heavy timber and put through more big timbers across them for additional support. Hao was beginning to appreciate the engineering ability of these unusual people.

Between each door, on the columns, is a handle. Push it up and the shutters close, and if you pull it down, it will open, as it is now with the shutters at an angle so that sunlight can enter."

Hao shook his head. "Well, I never. What fantastic innovators."

Maki proudly clasped his hands behind his back.

A beautiful woman came in from outside, her cheeks flushed; she shook the snow from her hair, her laughter childlike and captivating as she threw her arms around Maki and gave him a big hug before standing back. Tethered to the woman, with a cord tied around her waist, was a younger woman. Clearly, they were mother and daughter. The daughter had her mother's dark brown eyes, rounded chin and finely chiselled cheekbones. The mother giggled and slapped Maki on the chest with her hand.

"Oh, Father, I love the snow. It is a time when the men can stay home and we can all be family."

"Yes, my dear, I too love the joy and companionship. Tammirie, I would like to introduce you to my newfound friend, Hao." He turned to Hao. "Hao, may I introduce my daughter, Tammirie."

Hao and Tammirie held hands, looking at each other for several moments. Eventually, Hao bent over and kissed the back of Tammirie's hand. She looked over his broad shoulders at the dark locks of hair spread across his heavily muscled back. The stubble on his face tickled her soft hand. When he stood up, his magnetism captivated her.

Reluctantly, Hao released her hand. "It is a pleasure to meet you, Tammirie."

As Tammirie gazed at him, Maki raised his eyebrows and gave a small cough. "Tammirie, would you like to introduce your daughter?"

Tammirie took a few moments before turning to her daughter. "Oh, yes. Hao, this is my daughter, Jeng."

Jeng took Hao's hand and gasped as he kissed it. Suddenly, Jeng smacked him over the back of the head with a closed fist, making agitated grunting noises. He sprang back in surprise as she waved her hands about, shrieking. Tammirie stepped in front of her, making hushing noises to soothe her.

Maki grabbed Hao by the arm and hustled him outside. Once clear of the doors, he turned to Hao. "And what was that, may I ask, young man?"

Hao held out his arms. "How would I know? I thought I did everything correctly. What did I do wrong? Maki, tell me."

Maki waved a dismissive hand. "Not that. I'm talking about my daughter. What was *that*, Hao?"

"Oh, that."

"Yes, that!" Maki stepped back and pointed to the great room. "*That* is my daughter. She had a difficult start in life, and Jeng has problems, but they are my kin. You get me, boy?"

Hao pondered the old man. Double his age, half his weight and the high-pitched voice was disconcerting, but Hao didn't doubt the strength of the man's feelings.

"You must understand, Hao. I failed to protect my daughter in the past, and that other precious soul is my granddaughter. I will not fail either of them again. Not on this earth, not in this life." Before Hao could say another word, Maki strode back inside.

Hao sighed at the bad start to the day. He moved his attention to his temporary home. Like vines, long grass hung down the cliff face, tied between each balcony to let in the sun. The ties could be undone to hang down, keeping the weather out. He understood now why the great hall was below the bedrooms, it would ensure warm air would make its way up.

The stream ran only a few hundred paces into the woods and from there joined the icy cold river that ran down the valley. It would become a formidable waterway as it flowed down towards the far coast. Most mountain people never went to the sea, only travelling as far as necessary to barter furs and produce.

He decided to take a walk along the bush line. The snow hadn't covered everything and the sun was high enough to shine through. He purposely headed uphill first; the easy bit would be the return.

He had walked for some time when he heard a horse coming his way. Turning, he saw a woman riding along the snow's edge, her long, wavy hair drawing out behind her. The horse's hooves sent the snow flying in icy rainbows. Hao's heart skipped a beat as Tammirie came to an abrupt halt and slid from the horse's bare back.

"Well, I wouldn't like to be you right now, Hao."

Hao couldn't hide his surprise. "Oh? What have I done now, Tammirie?"

She took the bridle and held it behind her back with both hands. Stepping in beside Hao, they began to walk. "Well, you've upset Sen Ya San just a little by taking off. I shall be pleased not to be in your shoes when you get back." Her chuckle made Hao smile.

"Your daughter, Jeng, did I do something to upset her, Tammirie? Please, if you do not wish to talk on the matter ..."

She shook her head. "No, it was nothing you did, but ... well, yes, it was what you did, actually. You acknowledged her."

"But I was trying to be polite. I wanted to greet her and pay my respects. What is wrong with that?"

"There is nothing wrong with that, Hao." She stopped the horse and faced him. "I was a concubine to the Emperor. We all smoked opium and drank a lot, and I remember little of those times. One day, my father, bless him, stole me away, and we all left for good. If the Emperor were to find us, we would be executed, though he believes we all died in a fire at the palace. I was pregnant. Jeng came early and underweight. It is only thanks to San and her potions that Jeng and I survived at all."

Hao gently reached out to hold her face with his big hands. He wiped her tears away with his thumbs.

Tammirie smiled. "What is it with you?"

"I don't know what you mean."

"First, I can't take my eyes off you, then I tell you my life story, and yet I don't even know your family name."

Hao's smile slid away. "My family name is Ta. I am Ta Hao."

"Ta Hao, it is my pleasure to meet with you."

"And it is my pleasure also, Wan Tammirie." They both bowed at the same time, bumping heads. Holding his head, he looked at her. "The men bow, the women just dip their heads, ouch."

"Yes, but it is polite to let the women dip their heads first, then bow back to you." They laughed together, then continued to walk.

"Hao?"

"Tammirie."

"Yaan told me that the day you arrived, you had shot two pigs and that you caught the third by hand. I saw the size of those three boars …" She stopped to face him. "Is this true? You caught one of those by hand?"

He shrugged his shoulders. "Yes, but not without help from Bolli."

"How does one catch a wild boar that size by hand?"

"Without fear and with a great deal of respect for Mother Nature." He looked about. "Say, Tammirie, it's getting dark. Just how far are we from your home?"

She checked the sky then bit her bottom lip. "It will be nighttime shortly and freezing."

Hao turned to the horse; it was sturdy enough. He took two steps and leapt. He had mounted many horses this way as a child; his father used to have bets with him about how fast he could mount a horse bareback, ride out and around a nearby stump and back again. He had it to a fine art with his own horse. Not so

Tammirie's. This running stranger startled the horse, which moved sideways when Hao was barely half on. He slammed down into the frozen earth.

Tammirie tried not to laugh out loud. She failed.

Hao got himself up, his limp adding to Tammirie's amusement. He bent over, hands on his knees. "Why is it, when a man hurts himself, a woman has to laugh, and the more he is hurt, the more she will laugh?"

Tammirie, with one hand over her mouth, couldn't say a word. Hao moved over to the horse and gently took hold of the reins, making soft sounds to calm it. Slowly, he reached up to let it smell his hand. The horse reared up and kicked out with its front feet. Hao pulled hard on the reins. Again, it reared up, kicking out and stepping forward as it did. Hao stood his ground. As the horse came down, he gave it a swift nudge in the chest and pulled on the reins. "Whoa! Stop now, whoa, stop." The horse shook, wild-eyed. Hao stepped in close.

Tammirie was dumbfounded, saying nothing but watching in fascination. Hao whispered to the horse and blew gently into its nostrils. He walked around the horse checking its legs, picking up one of its front hooves and inspecting it. He stroked its flank then gracefully swung onto its back.

The stallion stamped its hoof in protest but otherwise didn't move. Hao reached down to Tammirie. "It is your horse. Would you like to sit at the front or the back?"

She looked at the horse now standing still with Hao on his back. "I don't know what that was about, Hao, but I'm thinking it is not my horse anymore." She took his hand and swung in behind him as if she'd done this a thousand times before, though she never had. With a light kick and a 'Ha!', they were on their way, hooves throwing up snow into the setting sun.

Maki was pacing on the spot just outside the cave's entrance, San beside him. "Why don't you come on inside, Maki? It is freezing already." Maki studied the tree line, not replying. San looked but could see nothing. "You silly old coot. If that boy is destined as you say he is, then he will be fine, won't he?"

Maki looked at her. "If he is not inside shortly, all the wanting in the world will not bring him back safely to make his next journey. And stop calling me an old coot. I am younger than you and you know it."

San's eyes twinkled. "Well, stop behaving like an old coot. It's about time Tammirie let a man into her life, even if it is just for a bit. Anyhow, what makes you the authority on the scheme of things all of a sudden?"

Maki stopped his pacing for a moment. "You know damn well what I'm on about and you know damn well how important it is."

San was lost for words, though not for long. "Very well, but there's no need to swear at me, you old coot. I'm going inside to warm my *old* bones. If you want to stay out here and freeze, good luck to you. Just don't think you're going to come to me in the night to warm yourself, even if just for a little bit." With that, she went inside.

Maki mumbled and began to jog on the spot. "Yeah, well, just don't go saying things like *'a little bit'* to a eunuch. It's cheap and unfeeling," – the door closed with a thump – "you old hag."

He was about to relent and go inside when Tammirie's horse came into view at full gallop. His jaw slackened and his eyes narrowed when he saw who was riding it, Tammirie holding tight behind him. "What on earth ..."

They rode down the tree line then turned towards the cave. The horse struggled through the deeper snow but appeared to enjoy the run as much as the riders. They came to an abrupt halt, sending a plume of snow flying over Maki.

Tammirie swung down on Hao's arm, walked over to Maki and gave him a big hug. "Maki, you silly old coot, you should be indoors before you get a chill," and with a peck on his cheek, she strode inside.

"Well, Hao, what do you have to say for yourself now, young man?"

Hao slipped down off the horse and rubbed its nose. "Maki, please know when I say we, Bolli and I, are very appreciative of the hospitality you and the cave people have shown us. I think we would have perished by now if it had not been for you and Yaan coming along when you did."

Maki went to speak, but Hao held up a hand. "Tammirie is more than old enough to do what she thinks is right, as am I, Maki. Do not misunderstand me, I wish no harm to her, or Jeng."

Not waiting for an answer, he led away the heavily breathing horse, leaving Maki silent.

Hao walked the horse into the winter stables. It was a simple but effective setup. Each of the pens had an arched roof and a flat floor covered in straw. Manure was gathered each day and dried outside then brought back in and stacked by the fire for fuel. The straw was taken outside and spread over next spring's garden, dug in when the ground thawed.

He was tending to the horse as Tammirie came in with Jeng. This time he was careful to look at Jeng but not touch her. "Hello, Jeng, how are you?"

Jeng eventually mumbled, "Good, ta."

"I am going to brush down the horse now. Would you like to stay and watch?"

Jeng swayed a little, holding her mother's apron. "Yeah."

He set about brushing down the horse. "Good, Jeng."

Halfway through his grooming, it occurred to him that he hadn't paid his own horse any attention since they'd arrived. He made a mental note to take his horse for a ride the following day. A goat bleated. Through the hole to the next pen, an elderly woman was milking it. He looked at Tammirie, who was plaiting Jeng's hair. "Do you drink goats' milk?"

Jeng giggled; Tammirie looked puzzled. "Don't you?"

"No, never. We have house cows. We make cheese too."

"Really, how do you do that?"

Hao kept brushing down the horse. "It's not that hard, really. You put the milk into a machine we call a churn, add salt and churn the milk until it goes firm. It must sit and drain for a time. We put in some herbs and churn it some more, then we put it in moulds and place them on a shelf in a cool room to set." He stood up and glanced at Tammirie, who still plaited Jeng's hair. "The trick of it is knowing how much salt to put in and not to stop churning too soon. It's hard work, but the rewards are great."

"It sounds disgusting. Wouldn't you say it is just rotten milk?"

"No, it's a great way to preserve milk. It doesn't go off, it sets. It's not really milk anymore. It's a food product that everyone can enjoy at a much later time."

"Oh, very well then. Have you just about finished the horse? I think it may be time for you to have a rest."

"Yes, but I will be fine until mealtime, you know."

Tammirie pointed her brush at the entrance, and Hao saw San hobbling over in their direction.

"Ah, yes, I see what you mean. I think it may be my sleep time now."

Maki watched from a distance as San led the big northern man upstairs. He walked over to the stable. "Tammirie, Jeng, has the stallion settled down now?"

"Yes, he is fine after his rub-down, but that's not why you've come over here to speak with us, is it?"

"I just don't think a horse should be run hard like that at the end of its journey. I thought I had taught you better, Tammirie."

Maki's scolding didn't take away Tammirie's smile as she linked his arm and they walked back inside. "You are right, Father, but I was more concerned about Hao being out than I was for my horse. He had wandered a little further than he'd realised."

Maki's eyes narrowed. "Wasn't it you who walked him so far, Tammirie?"

Tammirie's head tilted a little. "Father, the sacrifice you have made for me is one I would never ask of any man. My gratitude is immense, and you know this, but please do not cosset me like this. Why so protective suddenly?" She drew in a sudden breath. "Father, you've had one of your visions, haven't you?" She put her hand over her mouth as her eyes welled up.

Maki reached out and put his hand on her shoulder. "In the spring, for reasons I cannot foresee, Hao will have to leave us. Bolli and Yaan, too. I am sorry, my daughter, but it must be so."

"Why does Yaan have to go also? Will they come back, ever?"

Maki stared at Tammirie. "For some time now, I've had visions of Yaan leaving with two strangers. I recognised Hao and Bolli as these two men the moment I met them in the forest. When Yaan returns, he has only one companion."

"Father. Which one?"

"It is the one that wears the hat, and the two of them are connected. Connected, like they have reason and purpose – like brothers."

Tammirie struggled to hold back her tears. She looked over at Yaan. As always, he was helping with the cooking. None of the old girls minded. He was such a striking young man, and those eyes. She turned back to Maki. "Sometimes I feel like I am just a small piece in somebody's bigger game." She stood up and wiped her tears away. As she strode out with Jeng beside her, she added, "San always said that from the day of his birth, there has been something special about that boy."

Sitting alone, Maki ran his fingers through his thin beard, eyes still on Yaan. "You should have met his mother …"

25 Strangers

As Kito stretched and leapt in the small forest of the palace forum, he could hear the voices of cleaners several levels above him. He was used to being watched. Tall, dark, and with presence, people looked at things that were unusual or different. Here in the palace right now, it was him. So, focusing on his workout program, he continued.

His concentration was broken when the Emperor arrived with Desora, followed by an elderly man a few paces behind. For a fleeting moment, Kito and Desora locked eyes. Kito bowed deeply, then stood.

The Emperor smiled and handed Kito a message satchel which bore the Palace seal. "Kito, it is very important that you deliver this to the person named on the cover. No one else is to open it. Do you understand this?"

Kito dipped his head. "Yes, of course, Your Excellency."

The Emperor studied him for a moment. "Here are the maps you need to help you on your way. Master Xiang will take you downstairs and show you to your horse and guides."

Kito acknowledged the man beside the Emperor, who nodded.

The Emperor continued. "He will give you some more suitable clothing also. We don't want you dying in the cold."

"Thank you, sire, you have been most kind. I feel fortunate to be on your land, Your Excellency."

The Emperor indicated for Kito to follow Master Xiang. Kito dipped his head and followed the Master. They walked down a corridor and into a wide flight of stairs that descended deep into the palace. They made another turn, and Master Xiang opened a door. Kito walked into a small room, which had one little window up high. The room had no furnishings of any kind; it was stone and featureless. Kito swiftly spun, facing Master Xiang.

Master Xiang held up one hand. "I know you as a good, young man. Believe me when I say, I mean no harm whatsoever. I think you know this. I simply wish to ask of you one favour. For this favour, I will give you one in return."

Kito's posture relaxed. "You can ask. If I can help, I will."

"The Emperor tells me you grew up in the jungle south of here. I have known many a good man go into the jungle only never to return. Kito, may I ask, how old were you when you went into the jungle?"

"I cannot say as I don't know my age, Master Xiang. The answer I believe you want is that I have been in the jungle for around eight years."

"I see. The jungle out from the city of Samos … it is said that it has many animals, from big cats to the king cobra. Is this true, Kito?"

"Yes."

"And you found the broken carriage hunting wild boar, I believe?"

"Yes."

"And you grew up in this jungle on your own? Is this what I am to believe, Kito?"

"That is not the entire truth, Master. I had made acquaintances from the silk factory. From time to time, I went down into the city and they helped me keep on the right track. I hope that I will find them well again, once I have run this message for the Emperor."

"So then, why did you not just stay with your friends in the city, Kito?"

"Because I had given the Chain Man, Tark, the slip as he transported me to here. I believe I was to be some sort of gift to the Emperor, for his pit of wolves. Tark and his father hold a lot of power in the city."

"I saw your face, Kito; you immediately recognised my name. Will you tell me, how is my dear friend?" The reference rolled off the old Master's tongue as if he were speaking of his brother or son.

Kito studied the man for a moment. "I have no idea who it is that you are referring to, Master Xiang."

"So be it, Kito." The old Master paused then, "Of the three men guiding you on your trek, one is not to be trusted. Mind your back, my friend."

The comment struck Kito. Whilst he'd been protecting his only father figure and had given nothing away, the Master had still given him the warning.

"Kito, I am of no use to the Emperor anymore. I shall not be of this world much longer." Master Xiang lifted the latch and listened for a moment then opened the door abruptly and walked out with Kito following.

Down in the horse stables, the Master led him through a labyrinth of caves where servants were working. Kito could hear murmurs and caught references to his fighting unarmed with the prince. He didn't look at anyone but held his head high, following the Master.

Just as Kito could see daylight again, they came upon three men with horses already packed. Master Xiang dipped his head and made the introductions. "Kito, these will be your guides for the next few days. This is Wongue." Kito bowed but Wongue's responding bow was cursory. "Wongue will be the group leader. His word is the word of the Emperor. These are Shue and Ginta. They are here to assist Wongue."

Kito considered the three men. Shue was just a lad. Kito didn't doubt his ability with weapons of war but in his eyes was self-doubt. Ginta had a wiry goatee and oozed arrogance. Kito could see malice in the young man's eyes and decided this was the one he would not be turning his back on. Wongue had the demeanour of a warrior who had spent at least some time on the war field. He moved with confidence and grace. Not a man to be unnecessarily challenged.

"Grand Master Xiang, I thank you for your guidance." Kito bowed deeply then paused for a long moment. "If you have time to do some hunting in the jungle, I recommend the area to the north east of my home town. There, all things seem at peace with all around."

The old Master looked deep into Kito's eyes and nodded his gratitude.

Wongue mounted his horse then headed out with Shue. Their horses were packed with supplies. The three men were dressed warmly for the winter's bite. By contrast, Kito was still wearing his own clothes, more suitable for the jungle. He didn't mount his horse, which had no pack at all.

Ginta stared at him. "Is there a problem, Kito?"

Kito inclined his head. "I do believe the Emperor said that I would get clothes to be suitable for this journey."

"Oh, did he, Kito?"

"Yes Ginta, he did."

A voice cut the tension between the two men. "Is there a problem, gentlemen?"

Ginta took on a lighter tone. "No, Master Xiang, the boys have simply forgotten to pack Kito's horse for him. Is that not right, Kito?"

Kito's eyes remained firmly on Ginta. "I could not know. You will remember I arrived with Master Xiang."

With a thin smile, Ginta replied, "Indeed you did, Kito. If you look in the room behind you, everything should be there ready for you." He backed away and mounted his horse. "But don't be long, we have a lot of ground to cover." With a slap of the reins, he turned his horse and galloped out of the cave.

Kito packed his horse and caught up. He stayed a few lengths back and they, for their part, ignored him. The pack had food and sleeping furs but there was no extra clothing.

***

263

At night, Kito slept with his hunting knife in his right hand. They had good weather as they descended but he overheard Wongue saying that they would pay for that on the trip back. As the weather was building up to the north, it would come down with a fury before long. Soon after that, Ginta began dropping hints that they had taken the *'dark one'* far enough and should turn back. As the trees became denser, even with a sprinkling each night, the snow didn't settle underneath. Kito could make his own way soon enough.

The next morning, they came out onto the tip of a high spur. Their travelling order had changed. Ginta put himself to Wongue's right, pushing Shue further out. It appeared they wanted Kito to pull up his horse to Wongue's left, so he did.

The view was breathtaking. Down a long, shale bank before them was a bush line that followed a stream. It seemed to get bigger as the eye followed it.

Kito spoke to Wongue. "I will be fine to follow that bush line on foot from here."

"Yes, I think you will, Kito. You have your message in safe keeping I trust?" Kito patted his hip to indicate the bag tied to his waist. "You are an unusual kind of man, Kito. I would have liked to have known you better."

Kito smiled and slipped from his horse. Shue took the reins from him and Kito bowed to the young man but Shue didn't look at him. The hair on the back of Kito's neck prickled up. He turned to bow to Wongue who dipped his head. Ginta smiled and turned his horse to follow the other two.

Kito didn't turn his back and Ginta didn't take his eyes off Kito.

Slowly Kito took off his furs to move more freely. Ginta trotted his horse only a little distance and turned side on towards Kito. Kito shook his head and spoke quietly. "Behind you is the storm Wongue has been speaking of, Ginta. It will probably do the job for you. You know this to be true."

Ginta slowly lifted his right arm from under his furs. In his hand was a loaded crossbow. He smiled as he took aim.

Kito saw himself as a boy wearing a blindfold on Hasuca's lawn. He was holding a wooden sword as Hasuca sprinted around throwing knives at him, the boy catching them with the side of his wooden sword.

Kito watched as Ginta's finger squeezed the trigger. He saw the latch release and the string pull on the rear of the bolt. The bolt bowed as it struggled to take the force exerted on it, turning as it sliced through the thin air, quivering side to side. The fletching lay back as the icy wind massaged it.

He breathed deeply, remembering the words of his teacher. *Still the mind; focus.* Silently, he prepared himself to catch the bolt.

With his right hand, he snatched the bolt, spun on his left heel and released it with all his might back to Ginta's contorted face. Ginta was not prepared. The bolt hit its target with a *thock*. Wongue turned just in time to see Ginta fall from his horse, the bolt poking from his right eye. Wongue kicked his horse, his sword gleaming in the sunlight and galloped straight at Kito who just had time to sway to one side, feeling the wisp of air from Wongue's blade fall just short of a fatal cut to the neck. Kito tumbled and sprang back to his feet. Wongue and his horse couldn't stop at the end of the spur and plummeted into the precipice.

Shue, panicked and confused, sat wide-eyed on his horse.

"Shue, quick! The Emperor must be told what has happened immediately."

The boy didn't glance back as he galloped off in the direction they'd come. The low, dark-green clouds rolled in from the horizon, heavily laden with ice. The chance of the boy making it were slim to none. Ginta's horse made chase after Shue and his own was long gone. Kito would now have to make it on foot.

He walked over to Ginta's lifeless body. "Arrogant fool," he whispered as he took the extra furs. He would face serious trouble without them.

There was no time to waste so Kito carefully descended the shale spur to where Wongue had tumbled to a halt and took a few more items and cut some meat from the horse carcass. He took no weapons. He had his hunting knife and could see no point in carrying anything else.

Wearing all his furs and with the meat strapped to his back, he broke into a run. He followed the stream for the rest of the day. As it grew later in the afternoon, the poor light made visibility difficult in the forest. There would be a near-full moon that night, with some food and a rest, he could go out to the forest edge and run by the moonlight reflected in the snow. To beat the storm, he had to stay on the move.

Kito's plan worked for most of the night but when the moon set, it was too dangerous to continue. Even an ankle sprain would spell death.

***

Over the days that followed, Kito made good time. Light snow was now falling and the storm would eventually run him down. He ran on the outer edge of the bush until he found a trail. Travelling by moonlight made it easier and he was grateful for that but with each night, the moon was fading.

As he moved further along, horse tracks appeared on the trail. He followed them for a good half day until he smelt a fire and noticed a camp ahead.

Kito moved slowly towards the fire and the hair on the back of his neck began to prickle. He could see the camp clearer now, one horse and possibly a man tending the fire. He looked at the horse and kneeling, he closed his eyes and allowed himself to relax. After his first time blending with the king cobra, he had worked on this with Hasuca although he'd not yet reached Hasuca's mastery.

As Kito had become the cobra, he now became the horse.

From its position, he saw a second horse lying down by the fire. He turned the horse's head back to look at himself kneeling on the forest floor. Hidden from him were two men, the one wearing a hat had a crossbow, the other a longbow. Both were ready. He plotted his route away through the forest. If he went to his left, he could get in some ground away from the tall man's longbow.

He carried out his plan, not looking back as he moved away as quietly as he could. Neither man followed him.

***

Kito ran hard for several more days, the heavy cloud that had been gaining on him had dissipated.

The next day, he came across the beginning of what looked to be the Colonial Dig and, following the route traced on the map, he turned east and continued to run. There was a message of great importance to be delivered.

26 *Tammirie*

Every morning for weeks, Bolli would go to Hao's room. The two would go downstairs, chat with the women while they gathered food from the night before and enjoy a hot drink, mostly made with manuka leaves.

Whilst Hao had been recuperating, Bolli had spent his time exploring. He'd discovered many a good fishing spot and Hao was keen to try his hand, so today they left before most were up. Carrying food for the day and taking borrowed fishing tackle, they walked along the hot stream, turned left over the stone arched bridge and headed down river.

Hao noticed that Tammirie had become distant. It bothered him, even more so as Bolli had begun talking about how he was befriending her. Bolli couldn't know about his feeling towards Tammirie, *But she did.*

Now well downstream, they walked out onto a large boulder, water cascading down a huge waterfall beside them. Standing shoulder to shoulder, they could hardly make themselves heard above the water's thunder. A long distance below them, the river ran out through a narrow gap, the stone walls on either side reaching up almost as high as their standpoint. Beyond, the river flattened into a wide expanse of blue water with big round rocks jutting out intermittently. This was where they were to fish.

They hadn't been fishing together before. Up north on Magnar Wall, they hadn't even known each other – not until *that* night when everything changed for them both.

They made steady progress down to the river. Hao could hardly wait, but the ground was frozen and both men knew better than to rush. When they got to the river's edge, Bolli put down his fishing rod and lifted the bag off his shoulder.

"Well, Hao, is it everything I said it was?" Hao stood wordless as he took it all in. Bolli laughed. "I'll take that as a yes, then."

Through the crystal-clear water, the pebbled river bottom glistened as fish swam in the weeds. Hao stood back, feeling the sun's rays on his face, watching the mighty river rushing over submerged rocks. "Where do these trout come from?" He walked along the river's edge. "There are so many."

"You remember when we left the North and you suggested we head for the coast? Well, that's where they've come from, all the way up the river."

"I imagine, if these fish came from the coast, it must be flat all the way down." He looked about. "There are plenty of trees right here to build a good raft."

Bolli's response at the suggestion was emphatic. "What? Do I look like a fish? Heck no! There's bound to be lots of white water from here to there, I can assure you of that."

"Have you asked, or are you just assuming, Bolli?"

Bolli's eyes opened wide. "I don't need to ask if I'm intent on drowning. Wasn't it you who nearly died from your last dunking in a stream?"

Hao laughed. "I'm not talking about pushing off this afternoon, you bonehead. But in the spring, we'll be able to fish and hunt all the way to the coast. Did you know they say even the air smells different there?"

Bolli sniffed, shaking his head. "I can only smell the *cold*, Hao. I like your enthusiasm, but we have no idea what's downriver. The fishing is so good here because the trout cannot get up that waterfall. They come all the way up here to breed, but I have also been told that a great many don't make it through all the rapids and waterfalls. These here are just the best of their species. Trying to raft down there would mean we are the dumbest of ours. Forget it. I don't even want to talk about it. I came here with you because I thought you would like the fishing, now I almost regret getting up this morning."

Hao ducked as Bolli made his first cast without checking that Hao was clear. As Bolli fished, Hao couldn't help but think of Tammirie; they didn't have fine women like her on Magnar Wall.

Bolli flicked another fish onto the rock and looked at Hao. "How can your ears and nose be so blue when your cheeks are so red?"

Hao scoffed. Shrugging away his discomfort, he kept his head down, cleaning the fish. Before long, they had as much fish as they could carry. He was happy to be out for a time, though his thoughts were back at Tarim Caves, wondering what he'd done wrong to be so inexplicably rejected.

With the catch strapped to the ends of the rods and carried over their shoulders, the men steadily began the journey back. Tomorrow was the shortest day of winter, celebrated with food and festivities. Fresh fish would be a welcome contribution for their hosts.

The two men returned with little light to spare. They put the fish in the cold room, which was an easy walk up the outside path under the overhang. Entering through an outside door, the room was spacious but dark, so they had to leave the door open to let in enough light to stack the fish. The temperature in the room was the same as outside – freezing.

They picked up their rods, and Bolli opened a door into the hallway lit by candles. As Hao was about to follow, he heard another door open and saw Tammirie give Bolli a one-armed hug. They exchanged words, laughed and departed together down the hall with Jeng in tow.

Dejected and alone, Hao took a deep breath. The door where Tammirie had come from was ajar. He pushed it open. It was not as cold as the room next door, and he was fascinated to see fruit, sweet potatoes and vegetables obviously harvested during the last season. When he looked to the back of the room, he laughed out loud. Cheese. Lots of cheese, some blocks with holes in them, some solid, some dark and square or blue and round. These people didn't just make cheese, they were experts at it!

That night, Hao sat, as always, with the hunters. He could talk and swap stories all night. The young men would ask him about life on Magnar Wall, which he answered as best he could, but he couldn't bring himself to tell of his last night of fierce battle. It brought up unwanted emotions.

***

He would always make time to sit with Maki and San. He enjoyed seeing the spark between the two and liked them both immensely. They seemed to be constantly ragging each other, which always ended in raucous laughter. This night, he noticed that Jeng was holding her hemp rope tied off on San's waist. Neither Tammirie nor Bolli were to be seen. He struggled with his emotions as Maki moved over beside him.

"I have to say, I was up in the frozen room earlier doing a stocktake for tomorrow's festivities. That is a powerful effort you and Bolli have made, especially for a feast you have never been to before."

Hao gathered himself. "We are both very grateful for your hospitality through the winter. To contribute is the very least we can do."

"It has done you no harm either. You are stronger than when you arrived. You know not many men suffer such cold and live."

Hao smiled briefly. "I think I owe it to that amazing spring you have here."

Maki nodded in agreement. "It was a great find, Hao, a true gift from the Father Creator and Mother who keep it hot. Did I tell you that it saved me in a similar manner?"

Hao looked with surprise. "No, Maki, you didn't."

"Well, Hao, I am not going to tell you now either." Hao frowned as Maki leaned in closer, a serious look on his face. "When you and Bolli left the North, did you do so with the Emperor's permission?"

Hao hesitated. "No, we did not."

Maki kept his voice low. "You have a story to tell, and you will tell it tomorrow night, Hao." Noticing Hao's hesitation, Maki continued. "You will tell the whole story tomorrow night, and not one soul will condemn either of you. Be open, tell all, and you will be all right." Hao began to shake his head, but Maki held up a finger. "Listen to me. I have a story just as bad. I only told it after being here for a long time, but after I finally told them what I'd done, they loved me more for it. I then slept a full night for the first time since I'd arrived. You are younger and stronger. You need to let this go, and you will, Hao. Tomorrow night, a child will ask me to tell my story again, and I will. Then I will ask you to tell yours, you *and* Bolli. I feel it is as much his story, as it is yours. Let Bolli start it, but you must tell your part also. Only then will you sleep quietly, Hao. Only then." With that, he slapped Hao on the thigh as he stood.

Hao remained seated, staring blankly at the table as Maki walked around it and seized San in a bear hug. "Hey, you old battleaxe, how about a rattle of the bones?" He said it loud enough for everyone in the hall to hear.

Her reply was just as vocal. "Half a chance would be a nice thing I say, Maki, but we both know you are not the man for that job."

The room erupted in laughter. Hao looked about for the two familiar faces, though he knew they wouldn't be there.

***

The next morning, Tammirie awoke first. Moving out from under Bolli's arm, she slipped away quietly. She walked to the end of the bed, grabbed a soft leather over-garment and wrapped her naked body before pulling aside the heavy leather skin hanging over the door opening. She opened the shutter doors – it was barely dawn –and the crisp air hit her face. Stepping out onto her balcony, she watched her breath drift up in the freezing air.

Everyone was sleeping, except one. Her smile fell as she watched a man walking out into the dim morning light, his horse trotting behind. She knew that walk. It was the walk of a man of strength, a man of confidence. He flicked up the hood. It was the same overcoat he wore the night he came in, all but a frozen corpse.

He mounted his horse and walked it up the tree line, slowly cutting into the forest as he headed away. She wanted to call out, but what could she say? She knew what Maki had told her. She knew what was right. *It must be so.* She looked to the sky in search of an answer, or at least some comfort. Then she heard a stir behind her.

"Hello, beautiful, come here and keep me warm."

She wiped her cheeks with her hand and did her best to smile before going back in.

***

The caves were a hive of activity, today being the shortest day and a time of family. Tammirie was to help with the cooking, but first she would go out with Jeng and play with everyone. It was one of the few times that Jeng didn't need the tether.

Tammirie threw a snowball at Bolli, which struck him on the back of the head, falling down his neck. Bolli was a trained fighter and took no prisoners. Tammirie couldn't run fast for laughing, and it took Bolli no time at all to catch her and tackle her into the snow. Maki noticed it took some time for Bolli to let her up.

With smiles and jokes, watching people playing in the snow outside, the cooks worked their magic for a feast. The cooking began to fill the great room with smells that promised to make even the most fastidious lick their lips.

When the fun outside simmered down, some of the younger children were ushered upstairs for their afternoon nap. Tammirie came back in to help. She could feel San's eyes upon her as she approached the cooking area. Putting her apron on, she tried to ignore the burning stare.

"Why, Tammirie dear, you look positively flushed."

Tammirie didn't look at San but chose to add water to the

silverside as it bubbled away. "Well, San, you know how hard those children like to play. You know what? I just don't think I'm as young as I used to be."

"On the contrary, my dear, you appear younger than you have in a long time."

Tammirie glanced at San. "Thanks, San, it is just a little fun. They will leave in the spring. We all know that."

San smiled and continued to work her pots. "Yes. Only I don't understand why you are with the broader, when it is the taller you want."

Tammirie stopped. "I don't know what you mean, San. I will have you know Bolli is fun, caring and polite."

San's eyes sparkled. "Yes, I can see that also, my dear, and so handsome. Not too long ago, I would have chased you away to have him for myself."

"Oh, how could you even say such a thing!"

San waved a dismissive hand. "Settle down, Tammirie, I might be old, but I'm not dead. I'll have you know, your father and I have a very healthy life in the furs." She stood with two hands firmly on her hips and a mischievous smile on her face.

Tammirie held up one hand and put the other over her eyes. "San, please! A daughter just does not need to ..." Suddenly surprised, she said, "But wait, Father's a eunuch! How does that work?" The hand went up again. "No, sorry, I don't want to know. What sort of a conversation is this anyway?" The two women laughed and continued with their work.

Through the open door, San caught a glimpse of Maki. She tutted. *I bet you had something to do with this, you old coot.* She shook her head, but he'd taken great risks for them, so she could never be truly angry with him.

***

Preparations continued until dark. San stood up and rubbed her aching back. She felt the rigours of a full working day and reflected again that she too was not getting any younger. She joined Maki and Tammirie at a table with some of the other men.

A boy came running down the stairs with his mother close behind, calling him. "By my word, boy, if you don't slow down around here, I'll be talking with your father." By this time, the boy was going faster than ever, crying out, "But Mother, he has the biggest moose I have ever seen!"

Most of the group of people got up and followed the boy outside. Hao, covered in snow with icicles hanging from his bristled chin, was walking his horse along the stream edge. He stopped before the crowd. "What's going on? Have I missed the celebrations?"

They pointed at the moose with a full head of antlers lying on the crude sled Hao had fashioned. He turned to his horse, pulled the hemp rope off one end of the sled, and said, "Stand clear!" before letting go. The rope whipped over the horse's back and the sled hit the frozen ground. Startled, the horse stamped a hoof. Hao rubbed its muzzle, making low whispers of gratitude. "I would like to tend my horse. Could some of you help me deal with the moose?"

Eagerly, the men responded, touching and admiring such a trophy. An older man spoke up. "How would you like us to prepare it for you, Hao?"

"I got one shot just under his jaw, so the pelt will be worth keeping. He had bled out by the time I caught up with him, so I only needed to gut him. All the offal will still be there. Prepare it as you prefer. After tonight's feast, there will probably be space in the cold room."

He turned and walked away. His horse simply followed.

27 Storytellers

The feast was said, as always, to be better than the winter before. In the great room, the noise of excited conversation made quite a din and, as the night wore on, the stories of fish catching and bear hunting became more and more glamorous.

Everyone now gathered around the centre fire, the focal point of the room. Children and a few mothers sat at the front, elderly took the seats behind them, and the rest were happy to stand at the back.

It wasn't long before one of the children called out. "Maki! Maki! I want Maki to tell his story like he told it last year!" Groans, followed by a laugh, and clapping ensued.

"But Maki told us that story last year and every year before that."

"Yes, Mother, but I have only been here –," he held down his thumb and one finger, then raised his hand up for everyone to see, "this many years."

Maki got up and shook hands with the boy. "Well, how could I resist that, hey, you little monkey." He bowed to the greater room and held up both hands until the clapping stopped. "Well, here we are again, my friends. I think some of you will be happy to see me go to face my Maker, just so you don't have to sit through another telling of this story."

A chuckle circled the room.

Maki had left out a few simple things to disassociate the timing of the incident. If the story ever got back to the Emperor, it would tell him everything he needed to know.

He cleared his throat. "It was a bitter cold night, and the Emperor had just left his favourite place, the Den. Someone, in their wisdom, threw another log on the already loaded fire. A spark flew out, no one noticed it until it had caught and became a fire no one was going to stop. The palace was on fire! Unthinkable! People were running everywhere searching for loved ones, and old Maki here was right in the middle of it all. I was in search of my own dear daughter, Tammirie." He held out his hand as if to introduce her to everyone.

Tammirie smiled and waved, as she had so many times before, but the crowd loved it and just a few had not heard the story before.

"So, with her draped over my shoulder, I headed down into the horse stables far below. There, I met up with a very dear friend of mine, Sen Ya San. She'd caught up with us to make sure we were okay. She had with her a young newborn, rescued from the perished arms of one of the serving maids. Since I was the damn fool that put the extra log on the fire, everyone said I shouldn't stay. It was not a good day for the Emperor, after all. So, with a little help, I put together a crude snow sled. I saw no harm in using the Royal family's famed black steel skis. Only the Royal family knows how to get that shiny black finish. Prince Hasuca was truly an artist at it. It was a finish that was to save my life before the journey was out.

"The snow outside was deep – real deep – and it was still snowing hard. So, there we were, me, my daughter and a newborn just a few hours old. So, how was I to flee the palace in the middle of winter? Well, any normal person would simply not have gone, but I had started the fire, and I was not going to leave my family there to deal with it, so it was on the makeshift sled we went. I strapped on my skis, put snowshoes on my back and headed out."

A fake cough sounded behind Maki. He turned to see San sitting, as always, behind him with one stern raised eyebrow.

"Oh, and with us, insisting we couldn't possibly make such a trip without her, was San to care for the baby. Tammirie was still unconscious. I wrapped them under all the furs I could find and strapped them in."

Pausing like the skilled storyteller he was, Maki gazed to the ground, letting the tension build, then resumed his tale.

"The thing I remember the most about this moment wasn't the cold sting on my face, not even the deep snow – it was my friends, helping me at great risk to themselves. Two of them had lived at no other place for their entire lives. They risked it all for this one moment of my craziness.

"So off I pushed and what a ride it was. I had done some skiing with my father, bless his soul, but that was on wooden skis, not these flash metal things belonging to the Emperor. Well, they can fly, let me tell you."

Laughter broke out, and Maki had to raise his voice to speak over them. "And what's more, I now had a load in tow, but I was not towing it, it was pushing me!" More laughter erupted. "If I could have opened my mouth, I would have screamed all the way down, but I had lockjaw, and my locked jaw was frozen shut! So, with my frozen lockjaw, I realised I wasn't really up front leading the way, I was just the first passenger on a horror ride of our lives. All I could think of was if we all lived through this by some miracle then we were making good distance on any would-be pursuers!"

Everyone listened intently to Maki's dramatics.

"We had been riding this crazy ride the best we could for far too long. I knew we had pushed our luck and was pleased to see it flatten out and slow down. How we were still alive was beyond me. We came to a crest and I turned a little uphill to slow the ride. I wanted to get some control and have a look at every crest as I did. But I didn't know I was aligning us with a cliff face. A very, big, cliff! I saw my error as we crested the top, but it was too late, and we were too close to the edge. With a loud crack, the entire ledge of snow broke away and we tumbled uncontrollably down the mountainside until we came to an abrupt stop."

Maki looked at the floor again, but this time no one was laughing. His eyes shut, he shook his head as he tried to control his emotions. "I felt responsible for the lives of my three passengers, but when the avalanche came to a stop, I was buried under snow. I didn't know which way to dig. I couldn't work out up from down, and now I just wanted to go to sleep. I couldn't keep my eyes open." A gasp went around the room.

San stood and moved in beside Maki. She clasped his hand in hers as she took up her story.

"It was pitch-black. I felt I had the weight of the world on me, but to stay put was to quit and die. That was not to happen to me, not there, not then. I pushed and shoved. I could feel the snow and ice giving way. I could hear it tumbling away. Finally, I emerged from the top of the sled, which had its front well out of the snow, but the back was completely buried. Under the furs, I could see Tammirie and the baby. They were both breathing, both alright. I looked around for Maki. He was nowhere in sight. I slipped out of the furs and began to climb down the slope. I stopped and listened. Nothing. I peered back up the mountain. It seemed so high it was hard to believe we'd fallen so far and were still alive. It could only be with the hands of the Mother and the Father under us that we survived it.

"Desperate and not knowing what else to do, I fell to my knees. I gazed to the sky and I said, *'Please, please, help me this once. Please help me deliver Maki from the ice and snow just as he risked his all to help deliver us from the hands of evil.'* I don't know what I thought was going to happen really but, just as I turned to look down the valley for our way out, the clouds parted for a moment and a stream of light shone on the snow. And there it was. A cross in the snow, shining so bright it was almost blinding."

San held up her forearms in an X to demonstrate what she saw.

"Holding my hands up to shade my eyes from the cross glaring so bright, I made my way down to it as quickly as I could. I had no idea what it was, but I thought it was not of this world. As I got there, I realised what it was. Two black skis poking out of the snow, crossed over one another, shining in the now dissipating sun. With my bare, blue hands I began to dig and dig. Maki was face down, squashed up like a ball. I pulled and pulled on his hips until he rolled into my lap. He blinked twice and spat out a ball of snow. Then he looked up at me and said, *'Well you took your time, woman, where have you been?'*"

Maki feigned a look as if to say *'what?'* He held out his hands and shrugged his shoulders. Everyone chuckled. San shook her head and gave him a little slap on the back.

He continued the story, San being happy to sit again. "When we got back up to the sled, I could see it was not in good shape. What's more, the mountain was too steep and rough to ski. I had to make a decision. Going to the fur shelter on the sled, I pulled out the baby and handed it to San to keep warm. I then pulled out Tammirie, she was in poor health. I got all the furs out and made a shelter in the snow then put them all back under the furs. Going back to the sled, I had some work to do."

"Digging under the front of the sled, I could see both front skis were twisted inward. I can remember shaking my head, was it even worthwhile digging out? But without the sled, there was no other way I could get them down the mountain to safety, wherever that would be. I just kept digging and digging and digging."

San stood up again and put a hand on Maki's shoulder. "At last, Maki did manage to free the sled and get it over to the side of the avalanche. Everyone back on board and tucked into our cocoon of furs, we were off again. We continued down the mountain at speed. I had no idea he was such an accomplished skier, but when he dug in the skis, he'd disappear behind big plumes of snow, and when he came back out, he would be skiing in the opposite direction. It wasn't long before I could feel us slowing down, then with a thud, we stopped. I waited for Maki. I could hear him fossicking about. It was difficult to make anything out as the light was fading and we were on the dark side of the valley. I couldn't step off the sled, the snow was too deep. I couldn't see Maki anywhere. I called out for him, when a large blob of snow fell on my head." San laughed with the children – they always got a kick out of that part.

"I looked up and in the fading light could see a cone shape reaching way up into the evening sky. I tell you, it was reaching for the early stars themselves. I realised it was a grand old fir tree covered in snow."

Whispered comments circulated as Maki took over again.

"The fir tree was truly impressive. Heavy snow clung to the branches, making them arch downwards. Inside, there was a clear area from under the snow-laden branches to the trunk, and this would be our impromptu covering for the night. Once I had dragged the sled inside, I asked San to get the flints, as I busily went about breaking off small, dead branches from the trunk of the tree. Fortunately, they were aplenty. As soon as San had a fire lit, I could see some bigger dead branches and went to work fetching them. Soon we had a good fire going."

Maki paused, pondering his spellbound audience. "It worked so well and tree shelters were abundant so for many days we travelled and camped like that every night. But our next problem was food. We had nearly finished the little we'd taken with us."

Four young men struggled to carry in two logs. They came around to the fire and dropped them on. The blaze hissed and sparks flew upward like red fireflies towards the ceiling. San stood up beside Maki once more. She took a silent moment to thank the Gods, Mother Nature and Father Creator for providing them with the necessary things to be warm and comfortable in their dwelling before she spoke.

"One night, we made camp and agreed to stop for a rest day. Maki took off his boots, the first time since we'd left." She covered her mouth with her two hands. "His feet were dark blue and his toes were black! I don't even think he noticed me massaging his feet, trying to get the blood to circulate. Can you imagine how angry I was when I came out of our camp the next morning to see him knee deep in the freezing stream? I gave him a piece of my mind, let me tell you. I scurried down to the riverbank only to have a salmon thrown at me! It did stop me in my tracks, though. There was fish for glory. When he left the water, his face was as blue as his feet had been the night before, but he was beaming with pride. He knew we would be all right, at least for now."

"Maki slept right through the rest of the day, and from time to time, I massaged his feet. I really didn't think there was much hope for them, they seemed to be getting darker. But, for the first time in my life, I felt like I was truly my own person. I felt that I was free! Already, we should have died several times over, and we could still die at any given moment. I have always known how fragile life is. I had seen many people die at the palace, and it never seemed to be necessary, but they were there one day and gone the next, and no one would talk about it. Out there, I could die, but I would die a truly free woman and breathe my last breath by nature's rules, not some unworthy leader's. For this, I had but one man to thank." She leaned on her chair, a little choked up but too proud to let on.

Maki squeezed her hand and took her place. "I awoke to see it was just getting light. *'How long have I slept?'* I asked. *'A day and a half,'* she replied. I didn't believe it. *'How could that be, the sun is just rising, you silly old fool,'* I said. She just smiled, *'No, silly old fool yourself, that would be the sunset.'* I could only manage a feeble, *'Oh.'*" A few giggled.

"I noticed she was rubbing my feet. A chill went up my spine when I realised I couldn't feel her hands. We didn't need to talk on the matter, we both knew what it meant. Just then I heard footsteps. San looked up and I followed her gaze. I called out, *'Who is there, friend or foe?'* He was quick to answer, *'Well friend, of course.'* It was to my surprise when he said, *'We have come for you. When we saw the smoke from the fires we knew someone must be in trouble, it is just too cold to be out and about at this time of year.'*"

"Our new friends camped with us overnight, and the next morning, at first light, we all left together. I couldn't ski anymore so, wearing snowshoes, five men fitted a rope and dragged the sled. It was mostly downhill and we made good time. We couldn't believe this place when we arrived. Needless to say, I stayed in the hot spring for quite some time." Maki held up his hands to signify the end of his story.

A woman called out. "If I remember right, it took two days and three of our most beautiful women to entice the old fella out!" Raucous laughter erupted around the room. Someone else said, "That's an amazing story, Maki."

Bolli was captivated, not just by the story but by how the old couple had told it. He'd never seen two people share such storytelling. As the festivities resumed, he got up, leaving Tammirie to find Hao.

Hao was deep in conversation with old Maki. "I just don't like to talk in public, Maki," argued Hao.

"This is not about talking in public. This is about sharing a story with your friends." Maki invited Bolli. "What about you, Bolli? Would you get up there and tell your story? The ladies always enjoy a good yarn. It could work to your favour."

Bolli could see the pain on Hao's face. "I will do it if Hao will help. What do you say, Hao? These people have only heard rumours. Shall we tell them the real thing, our thing?"

"No, Bolli, I don't think this is a story that everyone would understand. What about we tell of our journey down here, when we saw that black fellow? Now that was strange, wasn't it, Bolli?"

"Yes, but it's not a story with an ending. It was just weird."

Maki's curiosity was piqued. "What black man?"

Before Hao could answer, Bolli waved a dismissive hand. "We were being tracked by a stranger, so we set a trap. Just as he was walking into it, he stopped, knelt for a moment, then backed out and made his way south. It was uncanny how he did it. He was huge and yet moved with grace, like he almost floated over the ground. We couldn't quite get a good look at him, and we never saw him again. He was on foot, and the storm that got us would surely have taken him. He is a dead man now."

Hao wasn't happy; to him, it was a great story, but Bolli had just made small of it. Without thinking, he blurted out, "Anyway, Bolli, you don't need any help with the ladies now, do you?"

Bolli and Maki both looked at him.

"Hao, what are you on about?"

Hao knew he'd overstepped. He had no right to a free lady; his opportunity had passed. Quickly changing the subject, "Well, I still don't think it's a story that we should be sharing, but if it gets the pair of you off my back, I will just this once, help to tell our story."

Bolli stood back, grinning. Maki slapped Hao on the shoulder. "You need to do this, you'll see."

Hao replied as they headed for the feasting tables. "Yeah, and you are like a dog with a bone, you just don't let it go, do you, Maki?"

On cue, the women came back down the stairs, the children were in bed, and everyone returned to the fire and settled in again. Before Hao got cold feet, Maki stood again and raised his hands. "All right, all right, settle down, you unruly lot." He didn't need to raise his voice. He had everyone's attention already.

"We've all heard the rumours of what goes on in the Bad Lands of Magnar, but tonight we get a real treat – we get to hear a story from the horse's mouth, as it were. We get to hear this story from our new friends and winter guests. These two men have had their toes on the fringe of Magnar, fighting the Barbarians. I give you Bolli and Hao!" Stepping back, Maki raised his hands, clapping.

***

Loud applause welcomed the two men as they walked forward. Bolli, in his element, took centre stage. Hao averted his eyes, choosing to stare into the fire as Bolli began.

"We'd had several hard frosts and so we knew the war was about to end for another year. It had been quiet for a few days. Some said it was over for the season but my gut told me otherwise. I was right. There was to be one more fight and it was to be the last big push for Magnar Wall. It was only just dawn and we were under attack."

Some of the women gasped as the men leant forward with elbows on knees, not wanting to miss a word.

"I headed outside and up the frozen steps. The hot blood was already running down to meet me. The Wall was chaos. It was the biggest attack I had ever seen. Arrows rained down in constant arcs of death. Grapples clanged as they were thrown over the Wall, blindly scraping over the stone pavers looking for a hold. I had my own short sword out and lunged forward just as a twin-horned helmet came to the top of the Wall. He got one foot over, and I knew if he got the other foot up, I was beaten."

Some of the men murmured at his candid admission.

"These are Barbarians. They would throw their own daughters into wolf pits just for entertainment. They love to fight, the more blood the better for them, and so it was blood I gave him. He was a giant of a man, but I was quicker. We parried, blocked, dodged and ducked before I got in a deathly cut to his throat."

Women held hands over their mouths and the men waited intently for more of Bolli's account of that frozen morning.

"The battle raged all day. No one could remember an assault lasting all day. Three times the Barbarians breached Magnar Wall and three times we overran them, regaining control. It is incredible what you can do when you have no other options. Once the day was finally done, we were pleased with our efforts. Though we had lost too many good men; we had killed more than our share of theirs too."

"I headed down the stairs once more, this time to find my mother, who would be worried about me. I couldn't find her. She had been going up onto the Wall to tend the wounded. I'd told her time and again not to. It was just too risky. But mother was not good at being told what to do. She always said, the sooner the wounded got treated, the better their chances. When I returned up the stairs, I remember thinking how grand it was to have this season over. I was bone tired. I walked along until I found a group of men looking intently out to the Barbarian camp over the other side of the rift ..."

For a fleeting moment, his voice quivered. The silence was as strong as the anticipation in the room.

"In the middle was Zavec, Master of Magnar Wall. He is a great warrior. The sight that struck us would change my life forever. There, strung out tight between three poles, was my mother and one other man. The Barbarians began to tear off their clothes. I went forward to Zavec, calling out, *We must stop this! What can we do?*' Zavec turned to me and said, '*And who might you be?*' I pointed. '*She has worked on this Wall for many seasons nursing your men back to life.*'

"Zavec held up a hand, '*Easy, boy, I am well aware of who she is. I asked who you might be. Has she saved your life?*' I said, '*No, sir, she gave me life,*' and Zavec raised his chin. '*I am sorry for your loss, son, but I will not be sending out a party on a suicide mission.*'

"I was beside myself. I didn't ask him to send out a party on a suicide mission, I asked, what he was going to do! Zavec turned to the scene over the rift and placed his blood-covered hands on the freezing stone wall. '*I will not leave them on their own though I see little that anyone can do,*' he said. I couldn't just stand there and do nothing. I would not!

"Zavec turned and stared me down. He spoke with power and wisdom. '*Sometimes we win, sometimes we do not. Today we won them over, three times. This was our war, won for the season but, as always in war, there is a cost. And sometimes, the cost hits so very close to home. Those are two of my people there also, but many more died right here today, last week and the weeks before that. It is all I can do right now, to have them see me stay until their time is over.*' He pointed to the two people over the rift who, for the most part, were now naked. Every time a piece of clothing was torn away and thrown onto a bonfire, a cheer of drinking Barbarians went up."

Bolli shook his fist. "I was furious, but I also knew he was right, that it is the cost of war. Then a stranger jabbed me in the ribs; he gave me a nod whilst walking away. I saw no value in staying there so I followed him as he led me away from the group." Bolli held out his hand to Hao. "That's when I met this man, my new friend,

Hao."

A polite clap went around the fire as Hao shook Bolli's outreached hand. He took a deep breath and began. "I had a simple plan that might work. I knew that sometimes you had to be prepared to risk the ultimate sacrifice in order to achieve the ultimate goal. I had listened to Bolli's plea and knew he was a man who would not hesitate to try my risky idea."

The room was silent as Hao continued. "First, we eased down off the Wall on ropes. We took clothing from dead Barbarians and crossed the rift to the bottom of the other side, keeping in the shadows like thieves. We made our way along until we were directly under the bonfires. I touched Bolli's arm and pointed to a ravine that ran into Barbarian territory. He saw it and agreed. We had to go together. There would be no finding each other afterwards."

Intrigued, everyone waited with bated breath.

"First, we made our tedious climb up the embankment. This wasn't easy, not because of the shale bank, not because of the thorn bushes, but because we could hear the prisoners screaming. There may only have been two people being tortured, but all our people were feeling the pain."

Hao took a calming breath before continuing. "We climbed until we were just under the light of the bonfires. From there, we could get a clear shot. We looked at one another and agreed on our plan. I saw the pain on Bolli's face as he wiped the tears from his eyes and took aim with his crossbow. I had offered to shoot his mother, but he declined, saying, *I could never ask another man to do such a thing. It should only be me, her son.'* I agreed."

Everyone stared at the two brothers-in-arms, some women tearful at the thought of their situation.

"We fired at exactly the same moment. There was dead silence as we turned and slid down the shale embankment. Once at the bottom, we made for the ravine, hanging our bows and drawing our knives as we went. Chaos erupted in the Barbarian camp.

Some of them, in a drunken rage, had grabbed their weapons and now charged blindly down the shale embankment. Up the ravine, we heard horses stirring and wasted no time in going that way, pleased to be wearing Barbarian garments."

"We headed straight to where their horses were kept in a large makeshift pen. Quickly, we dropped a few rails and mounted. Several Barbarians rushed forward with short swords and crossbows, screaming at us. I turned to Bolli, who was digging his heels into his ride. Almost knocking me over, he charged directly at the screaming Barbarians. I kicked my horse, which leapt into a full gallop after Bolli's. Arrows whizzed past us as we cantered blindly into the dark, hurtling down the ravine, unable to see a thing until we neared the end. And there before us were hundreds of Barbarians, carrying torches as they yelled abuse at the defiant Wall above. I thought Bolli had lost his mind when he turned straight into them, but there was nothing I could do except follow him. Sticking together was everything."

He paused a moment. "Some of the Barbarians stood fast, trying to draw swords, but most turned to run, tripping over each other. What I had not realised was that all their horses had followed the first two, ours! Hundreds of them, in full gallop right behind us. We cut a path of death through the Barbarians."

Gasps broke the silence. "As we broke free on the other side, I looked up to Zavec and our brothers, they were waving swords and torches in the air. Some stood on the Wall as they cheered, not that we could hear them above the stampede and the cries of death behind us. I really hadn't expected to be breathing at this stage. We just kept galloping."

"After some time, we slowed to a canter. I rode up beside Bolli. *Where are we going?* I asked him. *As far away as we can get,* was his reply. I told him he would have no arguments there. We couldn't go home, not after this, not after what we'd seen and done. Besides, both our villages would never be the same. We had both lost too many loved ones."

For just a moment, Bolli struggled to hold back his emotions.

"We took off the Barbarian furs and rolled them up, showing our uniforms to get back through Magnar's gates. The guards knew nothing of what we'd just done, and they welcomed the extra horses. We told them that we had stolen the horses and were heading back to our unit. Leaving the other horses behind, we took the valleys and lowlands heading south, away from Magnar Wall. And now, here we are."

The two men grabbed wrist-to-wrist and shook firmly. Everyone sat in silence. Hao felt cold as he looked about at the critical eyes staring back at him. He'd known they wouldn't understand. He himself struggled to come to terms with it. No one said a word. The muscles in Hao's shoulders began to tighten.

As Bolli opened his mouth to speak, Hao marched away, pushing through the crowd. All at once, chatter started through the group, the gap in the crowd closed off, and it was as if Hao had never been there.

A heavy-set man sat up straight. "Bolli, am I to understand that the woman you shot was your birth mother?"

"Yes."

"Your true birth mother?"

"Yes, she was my true birth mother, and she and my father raised me with one sister and one older brother."

"Do I have this correct? You went over the Wall on this suicide mission to murder your own mother?"

"I was not going to stand there and watch the Barbarians have a drunken night of torture at the expense of one of the most giving, caring and experienced healers the Wall had ever seen. I knew if I had asked, there would have been ample volunteers to do this mission for me."

The big man sat back with his arms spread. "Well, why in the name of the Gods, did you not let one of them do this?" The big man slapped his hands down on his knees with his elbows turned out.

Bolli's voice was soft, unthreatening. "My mother had saved many, many lives by working on the Wall itself. But it was I who had the true right for such a task. It was my responsibility and mine alone." He stood directly before the big man, who now had his arms crossed.

Tammirie stood up to speak. "The man who was also killed, he was your father, yes?"

Bolli shook his head. "No. I have no idea who he was, except to say he was one of ours, and his was going to be an undeserving death. We went for one, we went for both."

A man spoke up. "Where is your father now? Will he not be wanting you to return?" Before Bolli could speak, the big man spoke again. "Yes, my point also. Your mother may be dead, but didn't you say you had a sister, a brother and your father, who would be waiting for your return? Have you not deserted them all as you ran away?"

Without waiting for an answer, everyone began voicing their own opinions, some to each other, some calling out their own questions. Tammirie was standing still, staring at him.

A voice called out. "*Dead!* They are all *dead!*" The room fell quiet as Hao walked back to the centre. "I had never met Bolli before we took on the mission, but from that moment to when we arrived here, we have never left each other's side. You can learn a lot about a man on a journey such as the one we have endured together."

The big man waved an arm. "*Endured*, endured together! I don't care if the two of you fell in love. Hao, you must still have family and if that was not *your* father, Bolli, it had better be yours, Hao!" He pointed an accusing finger. "Otherwise, you did not have the right. It was plain murder."

Hao spoke quietly. "One night, it was snowing heavily. We were holed up in a shallow cove. Huddled up to a small fire, we swapped our experiences on Magnar Wall. In one conversation, Bolli told of how, in his first battle on the Wall, some of the other men were getting overrun by a barrage of Barbarians. He went in to help but couldn't break through in time to save his own brother. By the end of that battle, his father had also fallen to the Barbarians."

"Another time when we were watching a waterhole for game, we talked about how men would come to the village looking for fresh women for the Royal 'stock.' Bolli's father and brother were already at the Wall. Bolli was just a boy. A fight broke out between his mother and the Imperial Guard. When his mother was slapped to the ground, Bolli jumped in and attacked the guardsmen. He wears his beard to cover a badly healed jaw and other scars from that day. His sister was taken anyway. He never heard from her again."

"A few years later, Bolli got the call to go to the Wall to serve the Emperor. Having no one left at home, his mother went with him." Hao looked directly at the big man. "And on the night we scaled up the shale bank, as we crested it to see our two targets, I saw the man strung out, naked. His skin was blistered, his head was smouldering after he had been lit up as a human torch and the smell of burning flesh hung heavy in the air. His genitalia were a melted mass of skin and sinew. The Barbarians were just getting started. Whether he was my son, brother, father or my worst enemy, I would have ended it for him. So, you see, my friend, I do not need to answer to *you,* and nor does Bolli."

The big man sat still, the room, once again, silenced.

Bolli put his hand on Hao's broad shoulder, turning back to face everyone. "Hao didn't want to share our stories with you. He knew you wouldn't understand such decisions a person has to make. All I could think of was standing up here and talking to you all and being a hero. Sadly, you are ready only for fairy tales, not for the raw truth as we lived it."

Together, the two men turned and marched their way out of the circle.

28 Emperor's Revenge

Making his way through the palace, the Emperor passed several of his maids but did not lift his head to register their presence. Like so often now, he had only Samos on his mind. The taking of Samos was so close, it consumed him.

He thought back to how he had wanted it long ago, before his son was born. The plan had been set, but the loss of his cheating brother was a major loss to the plan. Then the birth of his son was the fitting replacement. Now at last, he was of age to fill that loss. A few adjustments needed to be made, then he would strike as early as the coming spring.

The Emperor lifted his head and breathed in the crisp air. *Ah, it's good to be me. And soon I will be on my way as ruler of the world. A Demi God to these ignorant peasants.*

The Emperor stepped into the morning light. It was warming, though the air still had a bite. It was not usual to have the Dome working at this time of year, it was just a little risky for his Assets to get here. They did lose Kain last autumn after all, he mused.

The doors to the Dome opened just as he reached them. Inside, he paused to remove his long coat, flinging it at a nearby attendant to hang. The servants had worked all night to be sure it was warm for this event, and indeed it was quite pleasant.

The Emperor took his seat and made himself comfortable. The prince was already working the crowd, excitedly waving their tickets and placing bets for the upcoming games. Desora was right in the middle of it all, in control, it seemed. The Emperor nodded in satisfaction as he searched for Master Xiang, who was talking with the other Assets from Norinko's group.

It was time. His time.

***

Today would see the remainder of last season's Barbarians used for sport. The Emperor waited for the wagering to subside, then stood with his hands raised. The room was quickly silenced.

"Welcome and thank you for your effort and hardship to be here today. As always, we have plenty of entertainment on offer for you all." Through the ensuing cheers, the Emperor held up his hands. "However, it is not all about the fun now, is it?"

He lowered his voice, drawing their attention. "There is much work ahead of us. We still have the Barbarians to the north, though they will be weaker than ever with their leader coming to an unfortunate and abrupt end." He clasped his hands behind his back and let the gentle laughter circle the room. "I have reliable information that a major breakthrough was made in the closing moments of last season's fighting. The Barbarians' losses were substantial …" A cheer went about then subsided. "… probably because they knew that I, your Emperor, had their leader here. This would have weighed heavily on them; there will be other threats to our borders to consider. As the biggest and most advanced culture on earth, we are a target like the tall poppy. And we all know what happens to the tallest poppy now, don't we?"

His words trailed off through the murmuring crowd. "However, we are not that tall poppy waving with the wind in the field. We have culture, we have structure, and we have leadership with vision! A vision to grow, to prosper and to rule! We must not sit idle. We must not sit on our hands when others are all seeking to take what we have, or it will be the fault of ourselves for not preparing, not being ready and not taking action!"

The Emperor watched the room full of greed, wanting, and in the eyes of Asset Chun, desire – desire for the opportunity to rise to power. The power he had always dreamed of. The power he felt he deserved. The Emperor was careful not to give Chun anything at this point; he would come to the Emperor on bended knee for what he wanted because he wanted it too much and, for the Emperor, that would be just enough.

The Emperor continued. "Like the moose moves from green field to green field, they, the outsiders, peer over our borders and see our economy growing; they see our river systems being developed and they see our strength." He stopped and lowered his voice. "And what is wanted the most right now? What is now the most valuable thing to us? I ask you, where is all the world trading done at this time? THE CITY OF SAMOS!"

A gasp swept the room.

"Samos is the hub of the world economy today, and if we do not move to protect it, we will lose it to the wandering moose! It is our duty to our people, the people of this grand and great land, to act and to act NOW!"

Chun's face reddened with excitement. To Norinko's left stood Master Xiang. Neither one of them shared the level of enthusiasm of the others.

The Emperor paused. His talent lay in leading them to do what he wanted, without them even knowing it. "I saved just a few Barbarians for your entertainment today, enjoy." He stayed standing until the clapping subsided, then gave a subtle wave and 'Sport one,' walked boldly out into the Pit. The wolves immediately began to snap and snarl through the steel bars, and the dogs did the same from the other side. Another cheer erupted, and the people surged forward, waving their tickets to spur on their bet, as if it would make a difference.

Master Xiang moved around the outside of the yelling Assets and stood beside the Emperor's seat. Neither man looked at the other.

The games went better than they had for some time. With everyone's attention on them, they hardly noticed several guards grab Master Xiang from behind. A leather rope was looped around his neck, holding him tight, then a knee to his back pulled him backwards towards the floor. The prince leapt to his feet in front of the Emperor and kicked Master Xiang's half-drawn sword, snapping it off in its sheath.

In moves befitting his title, the Grand Master of war retaliated as best he could. Before being overcome, several men had gone into the Pit and another was lying on the floor, a snapped off sword up to the hilt in his sternum. However, all war has consequences, and the aging Master was no exception. He hung precariously with his left arm over a rail, dangling over the Pit. His right arm hung useless, a bone poking out through his leathery, tough skin, just below the shoulder.

He looked at the Emperor through the rails. "Do you believe in the Gods, sire?"

The Emperor rolled his eyes. "I have seen many people pray to the Gods. I have seen many people 'do the right thing' by the Gods." A smug smile washed over his impassive face. "I have even had them call out to the Gods for help when their lives hung by a thread, or in your case, just one, old arm." He leant forward and held out his hands. "And yet, I am here, and where are they, Xiang? All dead is where they are. Dead and buried. With their forgotten names and no headstones to remind us of their existence."

Master Xiang did not back down to the man he had served for too long. "Check behind you, Hannu Koe."

The Emperor did as he bid, checking left and right, then back to Xiang with a sarcastic grin. "Yes, and what is it you expect me to see, old man?"

"Can you not see him? Why, it is your own father. I have a message for you from him, Koe. He says, *'You have broken a millennium of successful traditions.'* He says, *'If you continue on this path of destruction, you will lose the very thing that is most important to you. The one with the eyes will be your successor. The different one cannot die.'"*

The prince stood rubbing his forehead. He held the handrail to steady himself then stepped forward to the Master, but before he could do anything, the Master spoke. "I let you live, boy. You will be your own demise in a fashion more suitable than today." The

Grand Master who had served the royal family into its third generation, released his firm grip.

The Emperor sat wide-eyed. He couldn't hear the wolves feeding on the man who had never lost a battle for the palace. He didn't see Norinko glaring with disgust and rage, nor the Assets turning their heads away at the ghastly scene in the Pit. It was one thing to serve your Emperor, but the truth was, they all loved and respected Xiang, who to most seemed immortal, until today.

The Emperor shook off the last words of the man that had been there more than his own father had when he was Desora's age. He looked at the prince, leaning over the rails, watching the wolves. The noise in the Pit subsided as they settled to feed. Other than the prince, no one glanced down.

The Emperor stood, holding up his hands to draw attention. If ever there was a hint of doubt about the Emperor's iron fist of leadership, there wasn't now. He took a breath. "Today the wolves have won, I believe." He clapped, and a meagre clap ensued. "Now, my good friends and Assets, it is time to go over to the palace and enjoy my generosity."

There was a murmur of thanks as the Emperor headed for the door. On his way, he turned to the prince who had already taken up his new role on the Emperor's left side. A large bruise had begun to form on his forehead.

"Do you need to have that checked, Desora?"

The prince immediately stopped rubbing it. "No, Father, I have nothing needing attention, though if the old fool has scarred me, I shall never forgive his uncouth manner here today. Good riddance I say."

"Well, if you are up to it, then I shall ask of you your first task in your new role. You will let the wolves feed till they have had their fill then you will have them caged and taken to the Wall. There, the wolves will be set free on the north side. Understood?"

The prince dipped his head and nodded. He turned to leave for the stairwell when the Emperor spoke again. "Are you sure that head will be okay, son?" The two locked eyes for a moment.

The prince dipped his head again. "If it pleases you, Father, I shall have it seen to just as soon as I have followed your instructions. I feel any leftovers from the floor today should also be tipped on the north side of the Wall." Without further word, he turned and left.

The Emperor went to leave but almost bumped into Asset Chun. "Beware where you stand, Asset."

Chun immediately stepped back, bowing deeply. "You must surely be proud, Your Excellency. I do believe our prince is becoming a young man of great power and strength."

The Emperor frowned further. It was not the business of Chun how the prince was growing, though many had not appreciated the loss of the old man, so he ought not to push anyone else away right now. Annoying as he was to the Emperor, Chun was to have his uses. "Yes, I do believe he is going to fit his role well. You, Asset, would do well to try and keep yourself to *your* role and not keep me from fulfilling *mine*."

Chun faltered. This was not the beginning that he had wanted for himself and the Emperor. He took a step back as the Emperor snapped, "Now let me through!"

29 Colonial Dig

Kito awoke at dawn and stirred the fire back into life. Pleased to have beaten the storm, he began to think beyond. *Maybe I'll be able to begin my journey to the coast and catch a vessel, maybe to the* Shiraz. *Maybe I'll be able to free Baako on my way back to my birthplace.* However, first he had to deliver the message.

After eating, he did some stretches and began to run, taking easy strides along the Colonial Dig. It was a strange scene, this man-made thing, straight lines and regular, even curves. In his mind, it did not belong in the Gods' garden.

He had lost weight on this trip, but it would not be much further. He would be able to rest and set an easier pace for the coast, though his longing was no less than on the day he had awoken on the *Shiraz* and he knew he was getting further from home with every step he took.

Now moving at a strong pace, it did not take long before he saw his destination. He slowed to take in the scene. *Never rush into any new situation,* Hasuca had taught him.

Kito slowed to a walk. There were people in a huge trench, digging out clay. Another group put the clay into bags, which were slung over a pole, carried on young men's shoulders, two bags on each end. It was heavy work, and sweat flowed freely on the faces of the carriers. They walked out of the dig, up a track and onto the wall, where the bags were emptied. Women raked the clay out on the ground and packed it down with their bare feet.

Kito looked for the man in charge. It was not hard to work it out, it was the dumpy one sitting in the raised shade shelter.

Kito slid down the side of the Dig, crossed the bottom and made his way up a steep track on the other side. He headed towards the man in the shade. The dumpy one was also short, but from the raised platform, he could look down over the workers.

Two guards stepped forward. "What is it you want?"

After so long in solitude, it was a rude reminder that he was different to those in this foreign land. "I am Kito. I have come from the Palace with an important message from the Emperor himself."

The dumpy man sat up. "What is this nonsense about a message from the Palace? Come, strange one, come here before me."

Kito stepped forward, forcing the guards to back away. Once before the overseer, Kito bowed, then stood. The dumpy one walked forward on his platform; he was still only chest high to Kito. He looked him up and down. "What is this message from the Palace, strange one?"

Kito eyed the dumpy one carefully. "My name is Kito." He handed over the note with the seal intact. The fat little man read it once, then studied Kito. He read it again and stepped back as he finished reading. "Kneel before me, strange one."

Kito opened his mouth to repeat his name, when two guards kicked his knees from behind. Another slammed his knee into Kito's back, and a whip was pulled tight around his neck. He was quickly swarmed with guards, who tackled him to the ground.

Stepping down from his platform, the dumpy one slammed a foot onto Kito's chest, waving the message in his face. "Now tell us, won't you, what happened to Wongue and his two helpers, Kito?"

Kito was choking, unable to speak. He poked out his tongue. The fat one waved a signal at the man holding the whip. Kito coughed to clear his throat. "I was taken several days south, then they returned to the Palace, or I hope they did."

The fat one tilted his head. "What do you mean, you hope they did, strange one?"

"When we parted company, I wished them luck. Luck, because there was a terrible storm bearing down on us. I moved south from it, but they turned back into it."

The fat one raised one eyebrow, "Well, is that a fact, strange one? Do you know what an Honourable Servant of the Palace is?"

It was not a term Kito had heard before. "No."

"Well my strange friend, it is the wish of the Emperor himself, that you be made one. Do you know what a privilege this is, strange one?" Kito shook his head, and the fat one smiled. "Then it is my pleasure to greet you here on the Colonial Dig. I am the Superior Commander around here. If you have a problem, you ask to see me; if you have a question, you ask to see me. Do you understand, strange one?"

Kito pondered the note still in the man's hand. The fat one bent over to get right in Kito's face, waving the paper. "Oh, I see you would like to read this letter." He slapped Kito lightly over the face with it. "This personal note is from the Emperor himself, to *me*, Superior Zekec. Understand? It is addressed to me, not you, strange one, but as I have already explained, it is my job to see the wishes of the Emperor are carried out to the letter – his letter. You will call me, Superior Zekec and I, in return, will call you anything I like. Clear so far, *strange one?*"

Kito's mind reeled at his betrayal, again. He thought back to the other betrayals. Tarrant had become a friend, of sorts, that was until he tried to drown him, then sold him to Tark. Then Tark tried to sell him to the Emperor, even Cusaha wasn't who he said he was.

Zekec waved the letter over his face once more, and Kito watched the hand wash by. He saw the sparkle of a large diamond and looked at Zekec. "When you have finished the Dig, you will feed the needy, as you will be needing nothing yourself."

Zekec drew back, first in shock, which quickly changed to mirth. His neck and a multitude of chins wobbled. Kito wondered how it was under the Gods' grace that a man could let himself get like this.

With effort, Zekec staggered back up to his platform and sat down in his makeshift throne. He waved a hand and finally said between laughs, "Take this fool to the cage and put it out so all the peasants can see what happens to those who even think to defy Superior Zekec. Go!"

Within moments, Kito was dragged to a cage on the edge of the Dig. It was made from bamboo, lashed together with leather strips. Bodily fluids smeared the bottom of the cage and the putrid smell hung heavy in the air. With his hands tied behind his back, he was prodded with the sharp tips of a multitude of spears. He stepped in and lowered himself into the lotus position. The lid was slammed onto his head and spears prodded his shoulders until he had bent over enough. Two guards feverishly secured the lid.

He was hungry and already had a raging thirst. His muscles began to cramp. He twisted in the cage so he had his head to one corner, his narrow waist to the other. It was a little better, at least he didn't have the bamboo bars denting his head.

His thirst intensified as the day grew longer, hotter.

Kito had left Hasuca to go hunting and now Hasuca had no way of knowing his fate. Kito felt even more guilt for this emotion. He had never returned to his own homeland either but it did not give him the same feeling of remorse. Although, he hadn't had a choice in leaving home.

The cage stood where the labourers were carrying up the sacks of clay. Kito could hear their breathing and see them sweat. The men did all the digging and carrying of clay. Along the top, the women worked just as hard spreading out the clay and walking it in. In groups of eight, they carried what appeared to be a water barrel fastened with ropes. They used it to compact the clay. The thump, thump, thump resonated from where he was. It was hard work, and no one looked even remotely happy. *What type of land is this?* In his travels, he had seen so much unhappiness. At the palace, the people did not make eye contact. Hasuca always said it was poor character not to do so, especially when you had just met.

Then he thought back to the misery of the silk factory. No one there was happy either. They were kept against their will. He thought about the *Shiraz*, where most of the crew were chained to the floor. Their human spirit was not free. This was not the will of the Gods. Hasuca had taught him, *We are one of God's creatures, as are the simple goat or the magnificent eagle. We can wander and feed at will, taking only what we need and giving back all that we can. Only when we are at one with the earth, then in spirit, we can truly fly.*

Kito thought about the man in his dreams, the one Kito knew was his father. The other tribesmen loved this man; they sang to him; they sang with him. He hunted as one of them, and they hunted with him. They sang and danced in the jungle, free and at peace with all things. *How Hasuca would have loved my people.*

***

The night passed and the next day began as the last had finished, no food or water. He was dizzy at times now, and it was hard to differentiate between what was a dream and what was thought. He began to think back to when he was dropped onto the *Shiraz* in a sack. He knew the two voices. One was Captain Tarrant's, but the other voice he knew. Somehow, somewhere deep in his memory, he did know the other voice.

Kito could feel the sweat dripping off his nose. He resisted the urge to lick it, knowing the salt would make him thirstier and dreamier. If they left him in this way, soon he would slip into unconsciousness, then death. Thirst was a horrible way to die. He had heard Tarrant talk of it when vessels were lost at sea, all that water and nothing to drink.

A strange noise pulled Kito back into the present. He opened his eyes to see an elderly man hissing at him. He was on the track below the cage, stretching up with a ladle of water. "Drink it, my friend," he whispered.

Kito rolled his head over to look at Zekec, who had men at his side, waving large fans for his comfort. Then Kito saw a guard coming his way. He looked back to the old man. "I am not to die like this, but you will if you do not leave before that guard gets here."

The old man's face showed just a hint of confusion but, taking Kito's advice, he made a quick retreat. Just as the old man got to the first digger down in the pit, the guard began to urinate over Kito. His voice threatened the workers below. "If any of you even so much as stop to look at this ogre, you had better be prepared to take his place. It's no fun taking a piss without a target."

Zekec's high-pitched laughter carried over the Dig. "Good idea, Nikko. How about you stay there until the next man needs to use the target." Jeering swept about the guards.

The day drew long. As planned, the guards took turns at urinating on Kito. Zekec had a brass bowl so he didn't have to get up, but now, he too walked over. One of the guards brought a chair so he could stand on the cage. Kito thought it funny that he needed a stool to get up on the cage, though he kept his amusement to himself.

Later, when Kito opened his swollen eyes, he realised it had grown dark. Lights flickered in the distance, and he could hear the sounds of a village. He could even smell cooking now. Looking to his left and then to his right, he saw that he was still on the wall but had been turned around so that he was looking down on the camp. He knew that without water, tomorrow he would die.

Just then, he thought he could see people below him, shadows moving in amongst the bushes at the foot of the wall. He concentrated his energy the best he could. Directly below him were two young men, one carrying a sack, the other what looked like a skin filled with water. Kito sensed two guards behind him as the two figures emerged from the tree line below.

Kito could see about forty feet of clear land; if the guards saw them, it would be certain death. He suddenly let out a massive cry, like that of a caged animal. It echoed over the village.

The two men ducked back to the cover of darkness just as a guard came and gave the cage a firm kick. "Hey, you do not want to be responsible for waking Zekec, mongrel."

Kito heard another guard laugh. *So there were two guards*. He felt pleased that he had not lost all his senses. The guard urinated over the front of the cage, then sat on the rear of it. Kito looked down to the tree line. Now that the guards were settled in, it was too risky. Eventually, Kito sensed that the men had left. He sighed, both pleased and remorseful at the same time. He remembered Hasuca saying, *If you look, you will always find the good in people, you just may have to look harder with some, than others.*

Kito settled in for the night. Hasuca had shown him that deep breathing slowed down time, one of the many ways to move beyond three, to four dimensions. Everyone had the ability to fly with the eagle, though most had lost their way or forgotten.

***

The following morning, Zekec climbed into his mobile shelter. The guards slowly lifted it and carried him to the Dig. As they headed up onto the wall, the labourers stood immobile.

Zekec picked up his stick and slammed it on the shelter. "What is the meaning of this? We have not finished yet, imbeciles. Move. Move out of the way!"

The carriers stopped and put down the shelter. Zekec rose from his seat as, there before him, was Kito, motionless, sat on the cage with his eyes closed, facing the morning sun.

Slowly, Zekec moved forward towards the cage. No one made a sound. Not a whisper. Zekec was about to slam his cane onto Kito's head when Kito opened his eyes and sprang down in front of Zekec. Startled, Zekec staggered back.

Kito bowed. "I would like to work now, if that is acceptable to you, Superior Zekec. It is acceptable to you, isn't it?"

Zekec stood open-mouthed with Kito towering over him then nodded weakly. "Er, well, strange one, yes. I do believe it is time for you to earn your keep, but we are nearly finished here. You need not think you are to have anything other than the food you eat and the water you drink and, when the Dig is finished, the

Emperor wishes to see you."

"It will be as you say," Kito responded calmly, and he walked through the silent people, down the steps and into the Dig. He took up the heaviest hoe he could find and began to dig. He dug from the bottom, into the heavy clay that never had any breeze and where rainwater would back up. He found it was not unlike being in the hull of a vessel. It reminded him of his old friend.

***

After hours of labour, Kito checked the afternoon sky, wiping his brow with his forearm. *Yes, Baako is still out there somewhere.* He went back to work, singing one of Baako's songs, his voice low and deep. The people around him were beaten and abused. They were withdrawn and quiet but, little by little, they listened to Kito's song, a ballad of crossing the ocean, of a vessel in a storm and of the crew working to keep her upright and free of water. It told of how the lightning crashed into the ocean around them, but they did not stop, eventually coming out the other side of the storm, victorious. One by one, labourers on the Dig joined in, and after a time, everyone was singing.

Kito stopped when the old man came along to give him some water. "I am Jong, Master Kito. Where did you learn storytelling?"

Kito drank deeply. "Firstly, I am no Master. But to answer your question, I learnt from a good friend on the vessel that brought me to this land." With that, Kito returned the ladle to the bucket and went back to work.

"If you are no Master, Kito, how did you get out of the cage? It is still bound."

30 The Commission

As always, Patch rose first. He pressed his temples trying to relieve the pain of last night's overconsumption of wine. Every time he awoke with a headache, he promised himself he would never do it again. Another broken promise, it seemed. *Personal note: a real man keeps his promises, especially those made to himself.*

He went over to the water basin and peered into the polished brass mirror. *Oh, it looks worse than I thought.* He turned back to his bed. The double doors on their third-floor balcony were open, the polished timber floorboards reflecting the morning sun as the cotton curtains wafted on the summer breeze.

On the bed, not really covered by a single sheet, was Alexa. She had become the revered centre of his life. Her small waist and pert breasts were enough to make any man look twice. But she could drink as much as he could, most of the time. Best of all, she had an uncanny knack for business, though this was not a place or time for a woman to be in business. It was forbidden for a woman to have, or even manage a business, but then Patch was not from this part of the world either. Somehow, although he had no knowledge of his homeland, it seemed a ridiculous way of doing things. Alexa was a living testimony of this. Still, it worked for him to be the cover for their success. They were a great team. She never got an ounce of limelight but Alexa never seemed to need it.

Patch was a respected vessel builder. The business had been handed down to him after the death of his second father when he was still very much a boy. Despite his tender age and against the odds, he had spent the past few years accomplishing what most had deemed impossible. He didn't just pride himself on building the biggest vessels, but also their finish was second to none. By contrast, his business sense was not strong. He was a little soft on his men according to Alexa, who would say, *It is human nature to take advantage.* He knew she was right, she was also right about his underquoting. He would prepare costings for a new vessel only to have Alexa go over his calculations, then add as much as thirty per cent. She acted as his secretary-come-tea-lady. During meetings, she would drop him notes, guiding him through negotiations. They always got the jobs.

After drinking copious amounts of water, Patch wrapped a towel around his waist and headed out onto the balcony. It was the highest building in the city of Samos. From there, he could gaze down over his own dockside. There were two vessels in at this time, one having its hull scraped clean of barnacles and mussels for better sea-slip and the other being modified to increase its cargo capacity. For both commissions, Alexa had increased Patch's figures significantly. They already had more than enough work.

Arms wrapped about his waist, and he turned so he could hug her back. "Hey, Alexa, you need to cover yourself, it's broad daylight, you know."

"What's wrong, my Patch? Scared someone is about to move in on your territory?"

"Ha! With my dark skin, long eyelashes and broad shoulders, you could never leave and you know it!" He leant back and put his hands on the balcony railings, looking confident.

Alexa backed up. "Yeah? Watch me!" Snatching away his towel, she ran back into the room. Naked, he made chase, tackling her as they got to the bed. The two rolled together, giggling like children.

***

Later that morning, Patch sat at his desk looking over notes that Alexa had written on his pricing for another job. He could not fault her comments. He smiled at the good fortune they had to be with one another. He thought back to the day she'd walked into his office. It turned out she had done her homework, finding out who was the best in the business and what shipyard was the biggest and, just his luck, he and his yard were both. She had said if she could improve his business in just three months, she would stay for a slice of the difference of those three months. She wore tight leather pants with long boots and a cotton blouse that did her justice in all the right places. Truth was, if she had asked for all three months' earnings just to sit on his desk, he would have agreed.

They made an agreement, but the moment she began working, she dressed down quite dramatically. She even made herself scarce in meetings. This suited Patch. He felt no pressure, but he was also no fool, and he had been aware of some bogus deals offered to his father by competitors. The biggest and best in the business was also the biggest and most wanted target.

Alexa spent time on the workshop floor talking and working with his staff. At first, he was wary of this, but he soon came to realise that she simply liked people, plus her suggestions to improve their workspace were practical and beneficial for his staff, and so too, for his business.

Like Patch, Alexa was different from this nation's people. Not only was she taller and well-tanned, but her eyes were rounder and her cheekbones weren't as high. Her hair was wavy and light, not straight and dark like the hair of the local women.

Patch had got his name because as a toddler, he'd been left on the wharf anonymously. Wrapped in a patchwork quilt, a staff member had found him at first light and brought him into the office, presenting him to Bua, the man who was to become his second father. His second mother, Pang, loved him like her own.

Whilst growing up, Patch knew that he was different. He looked different, he sounded different. Even his name was different. Bua and Pang had two daughters, and so the business became his when Bua died. This didn't bother the sisters — it was simply part of their culture. Patch saw to it that his sisters never wanted for anything, and they truly loved him like a brother. They had grown up seeing the endless hours Patch spent with their father, learning the business of building vessels from a very young age. Every moment Patch was out of the monastery for the day, he made for the yard and often stayed there till late. Never had Bua's patience with the energetic boy faltered; theirs was a powerful bond.

When Bua died, Patch did something unexpected: he cleared out the shipyard attic and converted it for himself, leaving his two sisters and mother with the home. His attic was not the usual home, one room with a large bed, a bath and a flushable toilet, never seen before.

The day Alexa walked through his front door, a blind man could see what was to happen. Patch and Alexa had one of those relationships surely shaped by the Gods.

Patch had left the office on the second level exactly like his father before him – one big room. It had a large desk across one corner and to its left was a set of windows so he could stand and check the works in progress in the workshop. The desk faced both the entrance and the large opening doors at the end. In the summer, he liked to leave the doors open as he worked at his desk. His father had done the same thing.

Directly under the office was the front room where vessel owners came to order ropes or new oars and anchors. Patch let one of the older men who had grown up with his father run the front room. Some said he was mad to trust someone else to run it, but Admasin was like another father to Patch. There was nothing and no one the old man didn't know about the business. There had been more than one occasion when Patch was talking with a prospective client and Admasin would walk in behind the client, giving Patch a cut-throat signal as a warning. The man may not be good for his word, or for his notes. The warning could save Patch the old man's entire annual pay. Word invariably came back later that one of his competitors had suffered a loss. On occasion, Patch would slip the old man a bit of extra something. Once, Admasin received a master-crafted, fish filleting knife that had been delivered to his home, anonymously.

***

The carriage made its way out of the jungle into the edge of the city of Samos. As it progressed through the outer suburbs, the Emperor opened a window so the people could see him. Frowning, Prince Desora held a scented pocket cloth over his nose.

"Well, you could at least give them good reason to bow, Desora." Desora stared blankly at his father. "Wave, son, wave. It will not hurt you."

Desora gave a lame wave with his spare hand; he was not going to let go of his pocket cloth. The Emperor shook his head, knowing how stubborn the boy could be. It was not an issue worth fighting over.

"I thought we were going to the Colonial Dig, Father."

The Emperor continued to wave. "Yes, Desora, but first I wish to lay some foundations. I need to find an ally in this town for the future of the nation. My nation." The Emperor watched the peasants some more. He didn't need to see the scowl on the prince's face at the *My nation* comment, though it was good to remind him of his place.

"But we have no army to spare to take this city right now, Father."

The Emperor was pleased with the less demanding tone. "Yes, that is quite true, but before you strike out at something, it pays to do some homework so you know exactly what it is you are fighting with. Some old Master taught me that." The trace of a smile washed over Desora's face at his father's sarcasm. "Besides, if I am to rule the world, then I will need ships to move my army. Would you not agree, my young apprentice?"

"I am the son of the Emperor, not some damn apprentice."

"Hey! Language."

"And I do wish you would not call me that, you know it annoys me so!"

"There, there, don't get uptight. Poor control of one's temper is an indication of a lack of confidence in one's position in life. Do you question your position in life, son?" The Emperor eyed Desora carefully. No one else could question him like this, but once he was in a position of leadership, he *would* get questioned. It came with the role.

Desora stared coldly. "I am born of the throne, for the throne and I will cut down any man, woman, child or Barbarian who ever *dares* to question or stand in the way of my own destiny!"

The Emperor clapped. "Bravo Desora, bravo. You may have the spine to rule beside me after all."

The carriage hit a hole in the road and Emperor lurched forward, slamming his fist into the front wall of the carriage. "I have killed peasants for less!" he bellowed, before sitting back down with a huff. The carriage slowed a little. Neither driver spoke.

"So, tell me, Father, exactly why have we come here, surely not to order some vessels? We must have someone in our court that could have carried instructions for commissions. It's so time-consuming, if not somewhat uncomfortable."

"Indeed, I do have better things to do, but I do not want just any vessel. The Emperor of the most important nation does not have *any* vessel. This man is said to be the best of the best. Do you get my meaning, son?"

"Yes, I believe I do, though I hardly think at his age he could live up to that reputation. So just how big do we get this new vessel to be?"

The Emperor shrugged. "I will find out how big the biggest one is, then add a little. We are journeying to visit the maker of the biggest vessel to date. He will know how well it travels and from that, how much bigger we can go, Desora."

***

Patch's concentration was broken by a rap on the door. "Come." Alexa entered, and Patch pushed himself back from the desk.

"Alexa, how many times do I have to tell you, *you* don't have to knock."

She put some papers on his desk and walked around it, leaning on the edge facing him. "It is *your* office, and I will always respect that. You should demand it of everyone around you. *You* should command that kind of authority of your staff." She flicked her hair and smiled as she slipped up onto his desk.

He looked at her legs swinging either side of his and put his hands on her knees. "Is that so, woman?"

She smiled coyly. "Well, yes, sir. We are just here to serve you, as you please, sir."

He slipped his hands up her thighs. "Well, yes, I do suppose there is truth in that. You have not been working to the usual standard of late, woman. I do believe you need to add some, shall we say, extras, just to show your commitment to your job. That is, of course, if you wish to keep your job. Do you wish to keep your job, woman?"

She slid forward on the desk so that she was right before him and rolled a lock of hair around her index finger. "Well, yes, sir, I could not be without my job. If I have not been a good girl then you must punish me, if you need to ..."

***

The Emperor and Prince arrived at their destination, unannounced. They waited for the coach door to open and a stool to be placed outside for their exit. The Emperor was pleased to see the prince had put his pocket cloth away. Stepping out, they both looked about the harbour. It was humid, with a taste of salt on the tongue. Neither liked it.

The Emperor gazed up at the tallest building in the city. He thought he heard a woman cry out, and studied his company, but apparently no one else had heard it. One of the palace servants came before him and bowed.

"Well, if you have something of importance to say, then say it," growled the Emperor.

312

The old servant looked weary after the long journey. "Yes, of course, sire. This is the residence of the one you asked for. I believe he is known simply as Patch, sire."

The Emperor frowned. "Patch? How very uncouth." He took off his riding gloves and slapped them in the old man's face. "Hmm, this should not be too hard then. It has been said that the uncouth and their money are easily separated. Shall we, my Prince?"

The young prince followed his father's lead by removing his gloves and took pride in also slapping the old man in the face. "Indeed, Father, should be no problem whatsoever."

The Emperor headed straight for the entrance into the front room, where he saw an old man hanging up a new grapple anchor. The Emperor coughed into his hand. "Could you be so good as to point me in the right direction to find a … Mr Patch?"

Without turning, the old man pointed to the stairs to his left. The Emperor tilted his head and looked to where the old man had pointed. Without further word, he scaled the first flight of stairs, where he was confronted with a large, oak door. He stopped before it as one of his servants quickly stepped around to open it. The Emperor strode in, with Desora in hot pursuit.

Patch was leaning back in his chair, up close to his desk. Abruptly, he moved to sit forward, whispering, "Gods! It's the Emperor," as he tried to stand to bow. There was a knock under the desk as Patch cried out and fell back into his chair, grabbing at his groin. Finally, he stood and gave a deep, awkward bow. "Your Excellency, if you had given me warning of your impending visit, I could have had the place tidied up appropriately." He bowed again, still somewhat awkwardly.

The Emperor looked at the desk. "I like to call unannounced on a business that I intend to do business with. It lets me see how that business is run on its day-to-day basis, rather than a fool's front, if you get my drift, Mr Patch." The Emperor stared at Patch, still awkwardly bent at the waist. "Are you all right, Mr Patch? You haven't done yourself an injury, have you?" He strode towards the open doors onto the balcony, not caring for an answer.

"Ah hum, no, no, you see I have an old hernia problem, too much lifting when I was an apprentice to my father." He gestured about. "My father built this business up to what you see before you today." Regaining his confidence, Patch then bowed to the prince. "Please be welcome to my humble business."

Desora acknowledged with a small dip of the head and moved to stand with his father on the balcony. Patch, now standing upright, joined them. The bright light made his eyes squint and his head thump. "So, how is it I am flattered with a visit from not just the prince, but also the Emperor?"

Desora's chest puffed slightly, but the Emperor cast a sly eye over Patch. He was about to respond when Desora spoke. "They say you have built the largest vessel ever. Is this so?"

"Yes, it is so. She was launched ..."

"We do not care how old she is, just that she is still afloat. She is still afloat, isn't she?"

"Yes, she is ..."

"What is the length of this vessel then?"

"She is one hundred and twenty-five feet and ..."

"Well, we want some vessels one hundred and thirty feet long and no less. When can you deliver these for the Palace?"

Patch bristled at the prince's commanding tone. He needed to stay calm. "The *Shiraz,* is the biggest ever built. No one has challenged Captain Tarrant, who, together with Mensa, now controls all the cargoes to and from Zimbali in the jungle lands. There is word on the water that Captain Tarrant is contracting with the Pharaoh to tie up the entire west coast."

Intently, the Emperor studied Patch and what he had said about Mensa controlling the waters. The Emperor now knew *he* must control Mensa. He let Patch continue.

"I understand that since his daughter went missing, the Pharaoh is building arms to attack Zimbali to avenge her loss."

The Emperor did not know this either; he spoke a little less demanding. "What my son is trying to say is, we wish to know how big can we go? The experience you have with, what was the name of the biggest you built?"

Patch noted the change in the Emperor's demeanour. "Her name is the *Shiraz*, after the grape. The captain is a lover of wine, you see. She is not just the biggest that has come out of this city, she is the biggest ever made."

The Emperor frowned. "Why is that?"

Patch realised he was dealing with two people that had no knowledge of large vessels. "Well, you see, sire, it becomes a problem with the building technique itself. After a certain length, most builders just can't build a bigger boat because they do not have the skills, the experience or the equipment. The sheer size intimidates them. Some may assure you that they can build it, but in reality they don't have the yard space or the facilities to pull off such a commission."

Desora stared blankly at Patch, who was watching the Emperor calculating something more.

"And what makes you so special then, Patch?"

"Nothing, sire."

The Emperor was clearly irritated at the plain answer. Calmly Patch continued. "My father was a man of great vision, Your Excellency. As this city grew, every new vessel building business tried to get better land further downriver. This drove up riverbank prices. He told me, once you have earned a reputation it does not matter how far away your sheds are, clients will come to you for your workmanship. So, he purchased this cheap bend well upriver and worked very hard to build a reputation that would exceed others."

The Emperor nodded, though Desora intervened. "Yes, quite the business decision maker then. And where is your father now, Patch? Retired no doubt but still there to guide you?"

Patch held the Emperor's gaze. "No, I am afraid he died some years back."

Desora pressed on. "But he was here to build the *Shiraz* I take it?"

"No, he was not here to oversee the biggest vessel this world has seen being built. And what is more, my Prince, I had to develop new techniques to allow the building of such a vessel. I designed these techniques in this very room. If you wish to have the best builder to make the biggest vessels for the Palace then it is here in this room, that you begin, and end, your search."

Alexa was at the desk, making out to be tidying up his papers. Never had she heard Patch talk to any prospective new client in this manner, yet there he was, speaking like a man with confidence and gumption, and with the Emperor. With shaking hands, she went to the cabinet and poured a shot of white port. Her head thumped as she breathed out and threw it back. Quickly she poured three more and scribbled a note for Patch.

She went out to the balcony with her tray. The Emperor was a little startled to see her arrive. He checked the large oak door. It was still firmly shut.

Alexa bowed deeply. "It is a privilege to have you both here in Patch's modest business." She raised the tray for the drinks to be taken. Patch opened the note, read it then folded it and gave it back noticing the Emperor eyeing Alexa. "Your Excellency, my Prince, this is Alexa. She cleans and helps out around here."

The prince barely bowed though the Emperor took particular interest. He held out his hand to take hers and kissed it. "Alexa. And where did such a beauty come from?"

Patch was about answer but the Emperor raised his hand. Alexa smiled calmly to the Emperor. "I was sold from captain to captain until I was considered too old for that use any more then Patch paid a modest price for me to work for him."

Patch could all but keep from bursting into laughter as the Emperor promptly withdrew his hand. The Emperor stared coldly at the floor as Alexa dipped her head and walked away.

***

Patch moved the conversation on. "So, you wish to build a vessel of no less than one hundred and thirty feet – is this to be my understanding?"

The Emperor was abrupt. "No, Patch, this is not to be your understanding."

Alexa was back at the cabinet preparing three more shots of port but the Emperor's brusque response made her stop. She watched a blank-faced Patch as the Emperor continued. "It is your understanding to build a vessel two hundred feet long and twice as wide as the *Shiraz*. It will have separate top deck rooms fit for the Emperor and the Prince with his servants."

Patch did not blink. "Very well. I see the Emperor knows what he wants and it will occupy my every waking moment of every day to deliver this for the Palace." Alexa stared wide-eyed. "And is there anything else I need to know about this, *Conqueror of the Ocean* you wish to commission, sire?"

The two men locked eyes in a battle of egos.

"Yes, if you make it as well as you say you can and it floats, I will commission fifty more just like it." Without waiting for an answer, the Emperor turned and strode up to Alexa and swiped up two of the drinks. He threw them back in quick succession. Breathing out hard, he turned to Patch. "I will have the correct notes sent for you to formally commission this *Ocean Conqueror*. Also, I will have one of my Assets, Master Chun, deliver timber to your requirements. He will be in touch with you shortly." He turned to leave and as he approached the large oak door it opened for him. He turned back. "Oh, and Patch."

"Your Excellency?"

"I will pay a good fee for as much of that white port as you can deliver. See to it." And with that, he and Desora were gone.

31 Family

The solid oak doors were left open by the departed Emperor's entourage. Alexa and Patch stood still until they heard the carriage leave. Alexa ran forward and threw herself at Patch who twirled her around. When he stopped they both held their heads for a moment, reminded of last night's drinking.

"Not the best move, sorry," Patch apologised .

She put her hand on his chest. "All good, just don't do it again." She laughed out loud, that gorgeous laugh Patch adored. Today he needed no help in rejoicing at their continued good fortune.

Unannounced, Admasin barged through the doors. "Did you …" he pointed to the doors, "That was him, you know, the Emperor and the Prince!"

Patch grinned. "Admasin, I hope you aren't going to tell me that *he* is not good for his papers."

Admasin swallowed hard. "By the Gods, no, Patch. Did he?"

Patch went over to the decanter and, pouring three shots, he returned to serve Alexa then Admasin and holding his own drink, declared, "To the best and biggest vessel building yard in the world!"

The three of them threw back their drinks. Patch took the decanter to his desk and motioned Admasin to sit with him. Alexa left without a word. Admasin went to the window and signalled for someone to care for the front room as Patch refilled their drinks.

Admasin sat. "May I speak my mind, Patch?"

"Admasin, you know in this room you are as I, and I am as you."

"Patch, on rare occasions your father would say, 'it would be a great day if the Emperor was to visit.' Today, the Emperor visited. Did he commission us – this yard, a good vessel, a good one like the *Shiraz*?"

"It will be longer, wider and bigger. My first job will be creating a design then I will have to create the capacity to build it here." Wide-eyed, Admasin sat silent. "Admasin, if your eyes get any bigger, you will look like one of *my* kind."

Admasin blinked several times. "Bigger than the *Shiraz?* No one has ever built anything like that. What if we can't do it, Patch?"

Patch gazed out of the doors into the bright, midday sun. The curtains wafting gently on the breeze. "Admasin, everyone said the *Shiraz* would not float. Even when she was nearly finished, they said it would not handle a good sea but the *Shiraz* has come through some of the biggest storms. Furthermore, Captain Tarrant claimed he would have not survived on anything less. Admasin, I think we can do this."

Admasin poured himself another drink. Patch was right about the *Shiraz*: it had never been done before – or after.

Patch spoke with a gentle tone of authority. "I will need you to return to the workshop floor. It is now my task to design it. It will be yours to deliver it, firstly to the floor and just as important, to report back to me all works, good and bad, so I can make any needed adjustments. You are not to pick up one tool yourself. Do you understand?" Admasin was about to object, but Patch was firm. "Not one tool. Clear?"

Admasin was still for a time then agreed and poured himself another drink.

Alexa returned, clutching large rolls of drawings. "I found these upstairs. I knew I had seen them but I couldn't think where. Look, the real beauty of this design was how you bolstered the sections together. Truly genius. If we apply this design, in principle we can build a vessel any length."

She reached for the white port decanter and picked up her glass. The decanter was empty. She eyed Admasin, who motioned in Patch's direction; he was deep in thought. Alexa looked back to Admasin who again indicated Patch, then faked a sad face, shaking his head. Alexa smirked.

Patch was oblivious. "Yes, it's true, we could build to any length in principle but realistically it must be seaworthy. Any longer and a vessel would cross straight between the waves."

Alexa frowned. "Though it would get a smoother ride, yes?"

Admasin understood Patch's train of thought. "Half of the oars would not reach water. It would not be productive."

"Exactly. Captain Tarrant spoke of this. He said the *Shiraz* could be no longer but I interpreted this as his ploy, that he would not have me build anything longer than *his* vessel. Up until now, nobody has asked for it so I never thought it further." He sat back in his seat. "There must be another way. There is something out there, waiting. We've just not seen it yet. I can *feel* it."

Alexa faced Patch. "Can we make it wider and give him the extras he asked for and just a few feet longer ..."

But before she had finished, Patch objected. "No Alexa, the Emperor rules this nation with his ego. His vessel must be way bigger or he will leave us both wishing we *had* been sold from one vessel captain to another." He stared at his drawings.

"What exactly do you mean ... there is something out there just waiting, Patch? Maybe there really is a limit for the length of this style of vessel and you have reached it with the *Shiraz*."

"There is truth in that, Admasin, so we have to find the next style of vessel, that's all."

Admasin was confused. "What in the blazing fires of lightning does that mean, Patch? Now you sound like you've had too much of that fine port. Speaking of which, would the house have more, by any chance?" Alexa lifted one eyebrow at the old man. He quickly jumped to his feet. "Well, I think I have said enough for now and I heard a customer come in some time ago so best I go check all is okay.”

Not making eye contact with Alexa, he made a hasty exit.

“Patch, what *did* you mean with something out there, just waiting?”

Patch, entranced by the curtains wafting, talked almost under his breath. “You know what it is like when you can’t think of a name, but you know it’s right there, like on the tip of your tongue but you just can’t say it? Honey, that’s me right now.”

Alexa sat on his lap, drawing his gaze from the curtains. He smiled up at her with her hair blowing in the breeze. She bent over, pressing her forehead to his. “I love it when you call me honey.”

“Awe, go on with you,” Patch scoffed. “I’m sure many a good man has called you that before.”

***

A momentary chill ran down Alexa’s spine. The two sat gazing at each other then Alexa spoke. “What are you thinking about, right now?”

“I was thinking that I’ve had *that* feeling just of late and with this commission, it has come to a head.”

“Ah, here we go. You have a problem and you feel you need to solve it right now or life will never be the same.”

“Is that sarcasm I hear? The lowest form of wit, they say.”

“They say a lot of things though, don’t they? I say, if you haven’t seen or heard it yourself, then talk means very little. You never answered my question though, did you, my Patch?”

“*My* Patch? You make me feel like some piece of land or furniture you have just purchased.”

She reached down and grabbed him by the groin. “Oh, but you are *my Patch* and you know it.”

He clutched her by the arm. “Easy, tiger, there are better jewels in there than on the Emperor’s throne.”

“That’s true, my love, but you still haven’t answered my question.” She lifted her hand and gently pulled his chin up so he had to look her in the eye. “What is *that feeling,* Patch?”

He lost his focus on her as he spoke. "Just lately, I've had this weird feeling that we're on the brink of change, real change. Not bad, I don't think, just big changes and I think this new vessel is the key to it all. I just can't see how, yet."

Alexa brushed the back of her hand over his cheek. "Don't you go taking on too much, Patch. You know it drains you. Then it is not worth it, is it?"

"We are a funny couple, aren't we? I have no idea where you've come from, who your family is or even if you have any, and that is about as little as I know about mine too."

"But you do know your family, Patch, as do I. They may not be of your blood but everyone in town knows the love and respect they have for you. You haven't just continued your father's business, you have built the world's biggest vessel from this yard. Then today the Royals came and you have a commission with the Emperor! It is probably all over town already that the Emperor came here today."

Patch shrugged. "Yes but none of them are your family, any more than they are mine. All that is known about mine is that they are not of this land, and they left me on the wharf. It's a wonder I'm not called *Jetty*."

Alexa was taken aback; never had she seen him like this. She wanted to tell him about her family; it was all so close she could feel them sometimes, *But how do you tell someone you care for the ugly truth of your own family?* No, it would stay where it was, how it was.

Gently, she raised his chin and kissed him deeply.

32 The Journey

Hao was outside, packing his horse with supplies, when Wan Maki approached, sorrow etched deep in his forehead. "Are you sure you wish to leave, my friend?"

"You said yourself, Maki, it was Yaan's fate to leave with us."

The young man was right. No matter how difficult it was to let Yaan go, Maki's dreams had told him it was to be so. "Yes, Hao, it is true I said this, but now the winter has broken, I do not wish for you to leave."

Hao stopped packing to hold Maki's slight shoulders. "I will promise you this, I will care for Yaan as if he is my very brother."

Maki could not doubt Hao's word. "Yes, I know you will, Hao. You are a man of honour and wisdom beyond your years. Though I am a man who has had no sons, I have lived to see two men leave my house with my blessing, honour and heart."

Hao paused at Maki's comment, then heard his companion coming.

"Good morning to you, Maki. How are you on this fine spring morning?"

"Ah, Bolli, I am fine and so are you, I trust?"

"Indeed, I am, my friend. We are blessed with another beautiful spring day."

"So we are, Bolli, and I must add, the Gods have blessed us all with your kind and seemingly never-ending, positive attitude." Maki turned to Hao. "Is he always like this, Hao?"

"Yes, Maki, and sometimes it depresses me," scoffed Hao. "But now we will have a new companion to share our time with. And where is our new friend? I do hope he does not think we are going to wait on him like he is royalty or something as ridiculous."

Maki smiled as he considered the irony of it. Just then Tammirie and Yaan came over arm in arm, holding each other close. Yaan placed his two hands on Tammirie's cheeks and looked into her eyes. "Apparently, this is a journey I must make but, my sister, I will return. Until then, you will have to keep these two under control." He motioned to Maki and Sen Ya San, who had just joined them along with everyone else.

Tammirie reached up and kissed Yaan on both cheeks. She then went to Bolli. "I will miss you and your bold manner. You have become dear to me. Please take care, and when the time is right, you must return." She reached up and kissed his cheek as well. Hao was looking up at the numerous balconies, most with people waving coloured ribbons. He flinched when she reached up to demand all his attention. "You are the one I know least but wished to know more. You will return with Yaan." And she kissed him on both cheeks before leaving to join Maki, San and Jeng.

Without warning, Jeng ran forward and hugged Hao so tight, he had to step back so as not to fall. She then kissed both his cheeks and, as quickly as she had arrived, she was back with her mother. Everyone laughed. Hao blinked back his emotions and, not knowing what else to do, mounted his horse.

Yaan was finishing his goodbyes when Bolli called out boldly. "You know when Hao mounts his horse, you have two options. One, mount your horse and try to keep up, or two," Bolli leapt into his own saddle, "you wave him goodbye."

The crowd roared with laughter. Hao did not join in. Instead, he turned so red he thought his cheeks would ignite. He sat shaking his head at Bolli, who beamed at everyone with that wide, confident grin. Everyone waved and laughed. All but one.

As Hao turned his horse away, he saw Tammirie, who was not laughing, as she waved Bolli goodbye. He saw her tears glitter in the morning sunlight. As he headed for the small bridge to go south, he heard Bolli say, "See, now we have to try and keep up!" Everyone called their farewells as the trio made their way off.

Hao resisted the urge to turn and look back. He enjoyed winter in the caves, perhaps not as much as Bolli, but it was an interesting experience of an alternative way of life. The caves with their neatly carved rooms, so warm in such a harsh environment, the main gathering room with communal cooking arrangements, the hot bath bubbling up from the earth – these were gifts from the Gods themselves, for sure. He would miss the clean feeling of frequent bathing in the winter without the risk of hypothermia, a privilege indeed. Even the animals in their attached stables were well-to-do. Hao had, on occasion, lain down with his acquired horse and slept like a child without a care in the world.

He leant forward to give his horse a couple of slaps on the neck. Turning its ears, it neighed and almost seemed to prance. Hao could not refuse the urge to dig in his heels. With a husky voice, he called, "Ha!" and he and his ride were off across the plain at full gallop. Bolli and Yaan made chase, but Hao had his elbows up, his shoulders bulging under his trailing furs as he drew away, leaving his chasers in a hail of flying frost. Bolli and Yaan could do little more than hold to a canter and wait to catch up.

***

When they came to a small stream, Hao and his mare were taking a drink. Bolli slipped from the saddle. "Very well, Hao, maybe I did get a little carried away back there with the joking. You know how I'm always having a joke, anything for a laugh, but there was no need to gallop off like that."

Hao stood up from the stream, cool water dripping from his chin. "As always, Bolli, you have caught the bull by its tail. After a winter in the caves, I'm just happy to be out in the open again."

"Too many people for your liking, Hao?"

"No, not at all. I am just pleased to be out in the open and free again. Nothing more, nothing less. Now would you just let it be, man." He slapped Bolli firmly on the shoulder and led his horse back up the small slope to where Yaan stood, having overheard the conversation.

"Yaan, please do not think I am ungrateful for the time in the caves."

Yaan stepped in close. "It does not matter what I think, Hao. You are a man of your own mind. Please excuse me as I water my horse." He brushed past Hao, who had to step aside to get out of the way of Yaan's horse.

Hao waited on the embankment where he could hear the two men talking as they took their time to drink. He could not make out what was being said, but he heard his name. *Bolli's right, people aren't my thing.* It was not that he didn't want to be part of what was going on; it was just that he always seemed to be misunderstood, and then, like now, would lose trust in those around him. It was when he befriended someone that he seemed to get hurt, and it was when he was in the biggest crowd that he could be the loneliest. He kicked up the dirt with his boots, wondering what he had done to have his two companions turn their backs on him so early in their journey.

Bolli called out. "Well, come on, slowpoke. For someone so happy to be free, you sure are lagging behind." Yaan laughed, giving Bolli a nudge before swinging into his saddle.

Hao mounted and followed. He looked around the forest and smiled. The warm sun cut its path through the trees. Evidence of spring was everywhere. Pockets of green grass were bursting out of the rich soil made by the fermenting leaves from last autumn and countless autumns before. The snow was now mainly in small, sheltered pockets. The trees had an abundance of small shoots, breaking through, reaching for the spring sun. It occurred to Hao that they were witnessing one of Mother Nature's many wonders, the rebirth of a forest.

Yaan was talking when Bolli pointed. "Look at him now. Is he too good to ride with us?" He shook his head. "Just when I thought I knew the man."

Yaan watched Hao trot off through the woods, his head down. "Does he intend to come back? Should we wait here for him?"

Bolli shrugged his shoulders. "I have no idea. Anyway, as I was saying, I think toward the end of every winter, instead of just waiting for the first Barbarian attack, we should send out scouts to see where the Barbarians are advancing, so we would be ready in the right place along the Wall."

"That is a good strategy, Bolli, but what if we were to make contact with them and try to find out if a resolution could be found before any more blood was shed?"

"No, I have looked into their eyes – there is no life in them. It is like they are a curse of nature, born without a soul."

Yaan remembered the winter story Bolli and Hao had told. It was a sensitive issue, and he tried to tread carefully. "Yes, it is difficult for me to imagine what you have seen up there. So, where do you think they go for the winter months?"

Bolli lowered his voice. "That is a good question. Some say they go into a cave and hibernate; some say they go way up north and huddle up in a group on the ice. That's just another reason to send in snipers. If we knew more about how they lived, we'd be better prepared to wipe them out." The bitterness in Bolli's voice was evident.

"Yes, these are some interesting ideas, Bolli. Can you tell me *why* we are at war with them? It was not something that was talked about at the caves. Your arrival has given us all some interesting insight."

"My grandfather always said it was a misunderstanding over who killed Ta' Tu tu...ka...ha or something like that," he responded, waving a dismissive hand. "We all know it is just the will of the Gods. They made a mistake when the Barbarians were created, and they wish us to wipe out their mistake for the good of all mankind."

Yaan made a subtle change in subject. "One of the downsides to living in the caves is that we don't have contact with anyone else. The elders do not talk of it, but we have had a few deformed births in the last few seasons." Bolli's eyes burned the side of

Yaan's face. He moved on quickly. "Some say that it is a curse of the Gods, I think we just need to make an effort to come out and mix with other people of our own kind."

"So, what is it with Jeng? Did she get a bump on the head at birth?"

Yaan replied sharply. "No, Bolli, she was a little different from birth. Maki said that it should be a lesson to all, because Tammirie had not cared for herself properly when she became pregnant."

"And what about you, Yaan? Your eyes are not really the way they are meant to be, are they?"

"You are taller than Hao, aren't you?" countered Yaan.

"Hao is not related to me."

"And I am shorter than both of you, aren't I?"

"Ah, yes, Yaan"

"And you like to wear that hat, but neither Hao nor I wear a hat."

"So you think we are all just made different, do you?"

Yaan waved a finger at Bolli. "Exactly, my friend. There does not always have to be a reason or a sign from the Gods. Much stuff is just there to make us an individual, wouldn't you agree?" Yaan waited patiently for Bolli's reply.

"Then, would this freedom to choose not in itself be God's will, Yaan?" Bolli sounded smug in his reply. He enjoyed having such a discussion, a man of the sword *and* philosophy.

Yaan remained silent. It was only their first day, and they had already had a minor confrontation with Hao, then lost him altogether. For the most part, Yaan had enjoyed his conversation with Bolli throughout the day, but it would not be for much longer. Now in the late afternoon, they would soon stop for the first night as the sun dipped behind the Great Eastern Rages..

Suddenly Bolli grabbed Yaan by his sleeve. Yaan froze and followed Bolli's gaze ahead. At first he couldn't see anything then his eyes discerned the smallest flickering of light on the dark side of the trees.

They rode slowly. Then the smell of meat cooking reminded them that they'd had virtually nothing to eat all day. As they drew closer, Bolli found himself wishing he had taken more care on their approach. Yaan pointed to some movement at the fireside.

Bolli smiled. "Hao! Where are you hiding, old friend?"

"There is no need to hide from the two of you."

Yaan spun about in his saddle. Standing behind them was Hao, unstringing his hunting bow, his steel-barbed arrow glinting in the fading light. Yaan whispered to Bolli. "How did you know?"

Bolli stepped down out of his saddle. "Ha. I know this trick," pointing at the fireside where Hao's horse was eating some straw. "The horse gives the impression of life and movement at the fire and by the time you can see what it actually is … well, he would have had us, wouldn't you say?"

***

By the time they'd unsaddled the horses, it was almost dark. Yaan had grown up around life in the caves. It was the only existence he knew. It did not come without its dangers – bear, big cats, wild boar – not to mention being caught by a winter's storm. There were many ways to die up there, but here in the wilderness, the hot pools and the way of life in the caves meant nothing.

Yaan got to the fireside to see Bolli lying back on his saddle. Hao was tending a goat's carcass over the fire; he had also placed his saddle beside his horse. Following their lead, Yaan put down his own saddle. He was strangely happy to see Hao, not only for the fresh meat and fire, which was right on time, but there was something more, something comforting about Hao's presence.

After a satisfying meal, the men made small talk before drifting off to sleep, comfortable in their ample supply of quality furs to protect them from the cold night. Though spring was approaching, the nights were still below freezing. As one of them woke to relieve himself, he would crack away the ice off his furs and add another log to the fire.

At one point, Yaan looked at Hao, reflecting on how well he knew what to do. He was asleep, close to his horse, sharing the furs. *How could one sleep with a horse and not be concerned about getting crushed?*

The next morning, Yaan awoke to find Bolli had stoked the fire and put the goat back over it. He watched from the warmth of his furs. Bolli had some water on the boil and had picked some tea leaves that had been left on a bush sheltered from last season. It promised to be bitter but was, nevertheless, tea. How good it was to start the day with hot food and tea.

"Morning to you, Yaan, I trust you slept well?"

"Ah, life is good, Bolli."

Bolli handed him a steaming cup. The woollen flaps of Bolli's hat were done up, and his smile was as big and warm as ever. "I hope you know how to get us down onto the next steppe. It is still a little cool for me up here; your caves have made me soft."

"Yes, I think we are on the right track. If my memory serves me right, it is treacherous going down, and we will have to walk the horses."

Pushing back his furs, Hao now joined the conversation. "Yes, Yaan, I found a way down yesterday and then followed the track back to find the two of you. It is just as you and Maki told us before we left. We will indeed have to walk the horses, and possibly will not do it in a day. It is a mighty way down for sure."

Bolli took a steaming cup for Hao. Yaan sat up, almost spilling his tea. "That's right, Hao. I remember we camped on a ledge one night. Yes, it is a long way down, two days of walking the horses."

After their morning meal, the men packed up camp and dropped snow over the fire. Leading their horses, they went on the downward trail together. In their concentration on the difficult surface, they hardly noticed the day passing. Down at the halfway point, Yaan checked the cave he was looking for. It had clearly seen a lot of fires over countless years. To one side, a small spring bubbled up through a small fault in the rock.

That night, tucked inside and quite comfortable, the men sat and gazed out past the fire to watch light snow fall outside.

Yaan gestured. "This is quite beautiful."

"It's winter taking its last stab at holding," Hao suggested.

"I hope it leaves us enough track for tomorrow," Bolli added.

The snow only fell for a short time, and hardly any settled on the ground. Soon enough, they could see stars again.

"Tomorrow, we'll be fine," Hao said as he patted his horse and settled for the night.

***

The next morning, Hao took the leftover wood and stacked it at the back of the cave for any passers-by. They broke camp just after sunrise, eager to get to the valley floor. The track was a little slippery, but it seemed to widen and flatten out as they descended.

Dark clouds rolled in and thunder made the horses flinch. More than once, the horses faltered on the icy track. Wisps of mist caressed their faces as they descended ever more carefully. It began raining and grew bitterly cold so the men stopped to put on as many furs as they could carry. Hao looked at Bolli's hat with more than a little envy, not that he would ever admit it.

It was late in the day when they reached the bottom, the three men and their horses drenched. Hao was surprised to see that the track did not break away from the cliff into the forest. Instead, it went along the cliff edge. He withstood the urge to ask exactly where they were going. He might have grown up in the north, but right now, he was beyond cold. All he could think about was fire and food. He knew the consequences of letting the chill take hold.

It was getting dark when Yaan finally slowed, and there before them was another cave opening. With a large grin, Yaan turned to his two companions. "This will be worth it, my friends. Let's get inside."

The three dismounted and led their horses inside. The cave had a sandy floor that sloped up as they walked in. Yaan handed his reins to Hao then went about flinting some tinder into fire. This gave him enough light to locate some torches stacked against the cave wall. He stayed with the little fire until it was hot enough to light the torches. He handed them out then stood back proudly. "Well, what do you think? Pretty handy, hey?"

He pointed at the large stack of firewood to one side. "And look, we can dry our clothes on those racks." Impressed, the two men nodded. "Also, we have another spring here, so no need to worry about water." Hao and Bolli looked down and saw the water draining off their clothes; no one was thirsty.

The three unloaded the horses and hung some of their furs to dry on the racks. Yaan's teeth began to chatter.

Hao frowned. "You going to be alright?"

Yaan smiled bravely. "It's the draft through here. I just need to get some tea into me, that's all."

"We can't close the door, so we need to make the room smaller."

Bolli frowned. "What nonsense do you speak, Hao?"

"Have you *ever* heard me speak nonsense? Think carefully, Bolli."

Yaan decided right there, he would never challenge Hao. It wasn't what he said, but *how* he said it. Bolli stared back at Hao as he spat in the sand. "Just out with it then. How do you make a room of stone smaller?"

Guided by Hao, they used the racks to form a lean-to, three-quarters around the fire. The open side, towards the wall of the cave, was where Hao put the horses. There was ample room inside and a small hole to expel the smoke.

Yaan took the pot off the fire. "Ha, right on time." The warm drink helped repel some of the cold, and they had little trouble demolishing the last of the goat.

Bolli sat back on the sand. "Ah, nothing like a hot meal to warm the blood, hey, Yaan?" Yaan looked to Hao, who gave a wink in reply. It was good to have something hot to eat, but it was plain to Yaan that Hao's lean-to in the cave was pure genius.

Hao smirked. "Hey, Yaan, are the boys blue?"

It took a moment for Yaan to understand what Hao was on about, though a quick look over to Bolli and his sarcastic grin was enough to realise.

"I have been horse riding since about the same time I could walk. The *boys* are fine, but thank you for caring."

Hao and Bolli chuckled together, and the three settled in for another night.

33 White Light

Hasuca sat cross-legged in the centre of his neatly trimmed lawn, looking to the stars, meditating on the Gods' work. In his meditations, he had wanted to travel far and wide, though without knowing if he could return to his mortal body, he did not roam too far. Following Kito through his own lands was one thing, going out to new lands was quite another, *And besides, there will be time for that, after death.* Flying free was such a beautiful experience, he could not help but go from time to time.

Like a small child, he sat admiring how many stars he could explore after death. In his eagerness, he had considered hastening that freedom, but he did not have the right to make such a decision. The Gods would decide when he had served his purpose in this life, and it was then that they would release him.

Hasuca was mesmerised, as he often was when staring into space, pondering life and what more he might do for his fellow man. Even with his brother's meddling, Kito had done so well that Hasuca was not sure he was required any more.

Movement broke his train of thought, drawing his attention. It was a star gently weaving its way, getting brighter as it fell from the sky.

Hasuca stood fearless, the star was now just high enough to illuminate the jungle as it passed over, moving closer. Then the white light slowed and came to rest on the lawn before him. The light dulled, and before him stood Grand Master Xiang.

With tears in his eyes, Hasuca bowed. *"My dear friend."*

"What are you doing, bowing to me?"

Hasuca held out his hands. *"Do you still not see, Xiang, I might be the one of Royal blood but you are the Master that taught me, along with my father, everything I know today."*

"Never did I enjoy my time better than when we worked together. Never did I have a mind as sharp and as open as when I worked with yours. Please Hasuca, you must never bow to me."

Hasuca's face lit up almost as bright as the star that was. *"So, you will spend some time with me then. This gives me joy."*

"See, there is that sharp and open mind."

Both men chuckled.

Many eyes had followed the white light. From inside the tree line, they watched and listened. Insects, birds and animals of all sorts, all enjoying and understanding these two exceptional minds, pulsing goodwill together.

"Agreed then, we have a truce and I abide by the wishes of my teacher and life mentor." The two men sat as Hasuca considered his next words. *"Yaan must be growing into a fine young man. Have you seen him?"*

"Yes, he was my first stop, though he took a bit of finding."

"Maki and San have done a wonderful job in raising him, don't you think?"

Xiang scoffed. *"If you plant the seed of a tiger lily, care for the waters and see it gets the right amount of sunlight to grow strong and bright, it is still the tiger lily it was meant to be. Don't be too humble, my friend."*

Having Xiang serve him in the palace was seductive. Hasuca had almost forgotten what a great mentor the man was. An invaluable gift to the Palace, in such contrast to his own brother. *"Would you forgive the actions of my short-sighted brother, Xiang?"*

The old man smiled. *"I served the Palace to the best of my ability. I had nothing more to give and was of no more use, so it was my time."*

Regret etched across Hasuca's face. He sighed. *"No one gave more or as willingly. Everyone, all but my brother, will remember."*

"Why do you keep saying that Koe is your brother?"

"That is what he is."

"Yes, we know this. Why do you insist on repeatedly saying it?"

Hasuca considered his answer carefully. *"Because I feel responsible for his actions."*

"Did you ask Koe to do the things he has done, the things he is planning?"

"No!"

"Did you, at any time, try to talk him around, to go in any other direction?"

"Yes, you know I did. I still see no point in him attacking his own port. Samos belongs to him."

"Then why are you taking responsibility for his actions?"

Hasuca leant forward, despair in his voice. *"If I had fought for my rightful place on the throne, our lands would be at peace. You would still walk the corridors as you should and the people would want to serve their Emperor because they love him, like they did my father."* Hasuca rested his hand on his knee and looked about as if searching for further answers. Xiang saw the frustration and anger in his friend and waited silently.

"Why must he do this to his own people? I see no logic, no point. It is against the will and laws of the Gods." He waved an arm in anger at the Gods in their carpet of stars. *"And what are you doing about it? Why do you let your own people be punished under the iron fist of repression? Your own people are suffering and for what?"* He pointed towards Xiang. *"This man served you with all his heart, and you let him be fed to the wolves. And the Emperor, loved by more than just his own people, poisoned at his own dinner table, poisoned by his own son. Tell me! Explain it to me! How is this just?"*

Xiang sat impassive at the rage Hasuca had held back for too long. Hasuca, with his hands on his knees, head tilted back, stared into the heavens. In the starlight, Xiang could see tears running down his neck. When Hasuca lowered his head, Xiang spoke.

"The Gods have their own plan. We just act our part the best we can with what we know on the day. That is how it works. If you had risen against Koe, your lands may even today still be in a bitter, civil war. We just can't know." Hasuca took a deep, laboured breath as Xiang continued. *"Your father sends his best wishes."*

"You have spoken with Father?"

Smiling broadly, *"Well, yes, Hasuca, your father and I talk a lot about the past and about the fate of our lands in the future."*

Hasuca broke in. *"You have seen the future? You know what is to happen next? What should I be doing?"*

Xiang held up his hands. *"Yes, Hasuca, though we only get little snippets, not unlike what you have seen yourself. You know there is talk of you on the other side."*

"Really, why?"

"Because you have such a strong vibration. You get to see more than any mortal alive today. Just quietly, I think you keep the Gods on their toes." Xiang winked and the two enjoyed a gentle laugh.

Hasuca sat up straight. *"I do miss our conversations, my friend. I am pleased you took the time to look me up."*

"I was not sure if you would allow me to stay. You never sent an invitation, so in the end I just invited myself."

"How did you know where to look?"

Xiang smiled. This would make Hasuca proud. *"We had a visitor to the palace some time ago. I believe you know him as Kito."*

Hasuca was beaming before Xiang had finished. *"Ah, yes. Is he not something extraordinary?"*

"Yes. And he will need to be."

Hasuca's eyes narrowed. *"Just what have the Gods planned for the poor boy? Has he not suffered enough already?"*

"Settle down. I think your boy can handle anything the Gods throw at him, having learnt from the best." Hasuca grumbled as Xiang continued. *"When he was leaving the palace, he said for me to try*

hunting here, in this area. I knew what he meant but in the end it was simply a case of following your vibration."

The men sat quietly for a moment. Hasuca grinned. "*Well now that you know where I am, you have no reason to be such a stranger.*" He laughed, then saw something in Xiang. "*What is it, Xiang?*"

"*What is what, Hasuca?*"

Hasuca waved a finger at Xiang and continued with a more serious tone. "*Please do not pretend. You just realised something and I want you to tell me, or I will feel insulted. You know this to be true of me.*"

"*You have not asked about your daughter, Hasuca.*"

Hasuca sat bolt upright. "*My daughter? I … have a daughter?*"

Xiang blinked. "*You did not know?*"

"*I had no reason to ask. I took great care in my meditations to keep up with Yaan. Where is she … my daughter?*" Hasuca's tone was demanding, insistent. "*Xiang, you cannot begin this topic and not finish it. How old is she?*"

The question shook Xiang. Hasuca's eyes narrowed again. "*What was that on your face again? Oh, the Gods! She is … she is Yaan's sister?*"

Xiang looked about as if he was hoping the Gods would physically remove him from the spot. Hasuca's voice was low and firm. "*Xiang. You will now take me to her, as you know I will find her anyway.*"

Clearly shaken, Xiang looked at Hasuca. "*I fear I have changed the course of things, I have jeopardised the young woman's life.*"

Hasuca sat back. "*Young woman? Yes, I suppose she is, if she is Yaan's sister.*" He studied Xiang. "*Jeopardised? Jeopardised how, Xiang? Is she in danger?*"

"*She lives in the palace.*"

Hasuca's eyes bulged. "*What? How was this done without Koe killing her?*"

"She has been brought up by working peasants in the Palace. She works there still."

"My daughter, a concubine?"

Xiang, quick to clear up the confusion, said, *"No, no, heavens no. She had an education like any other and is now a cook and cleaner."*

"And Koe is happy with this?"

Xiang waved his hands about once more. *"Wait! Settle, my friend."* He held up a stern finger. *"Listen! Sha'Doe' died giving birth. Not to twins but triplets, bi-paternal triplets, one mother, two fathers."*

The news took Hasuca some time to digest.

Xiang continued. *"Maki, bless the man, had one taken from the birthing chamber before the Emperor arrived. Unfortunately, the Emperor did get to see the eyes of our favourite son, Yaan. As you know, he was thrown out from the birthing chamber to certain death had it not been for the quick thinking, again, of our good friend Maki. The Emperor believes there is just one child left, Prince, Desora. The girl was taken downstairs and brought up by all the staff working together. It is a wonder the poor thing did not look like a goat for all their milk she drank."*

***

Hasuca grumbled again, though Xiang could see his pride returning. Xiang went on to tell how the girl grew up with the staff, how the staff treated her like one of their own, though she was clearly her mother's daughter, evident by her large green eyes. And how, nevertheless, she formed her own personality and was loved by all.

"One night, this girl approached me as I went about my duties; she asked me to teach her how to protect herself with some of the arts of a Master. At first I was shocked by this request. Girls are not taught such skills. No female had ever become a Master."

Hasuca smiled as Xiang explained how, in this, she was her father's daughter. Her mind was as sharp as her body was fit and nimble. *"At times, it seemed I was teaching you."* Xiang hesitated at Hasuca's frown. *"What is it you fear, my friend?"*

"You have done all this at great risk to yourself. I forbid it to continue."

Xiang burst into laughter. *"You foolish man, have you forgotten my place?"*

Hasuca looked sheepish then joined in the laughter. *"Oh, this is not fear, it is my foolish pride. It is I who should have been teaching her."*

"Well, maybe you can take up her training to become a Master, Hasuca."

Hasuca shook his head. *"No, that would endanger her and the other Masters in the Palace. How has my nephew come along?"*

Xiang held Hasuca's stare for some time, he would have to tread gently. *"I am afraid he is his father's son, Hasuca."*

"Yes. I have watched him many times over." He leant forward in earnest. *"In the name of the Gods, why? Why do people like my brother and his only offspring exist? What do they add to enrich the lives around them? What purposes do they serve?"*

Xiang felt a presence surround him. He would not answer.

Hasuca's face was solemn. *"Do they come to challenge our lives? Is life about being tested? If we were not tested, would it mean there is little purpose to it?"*

"Why must you have the answers to all of life's questions, Hasuca? You ask more questions than all my other students put together. Hasuca, you ask questions that no other students, or adults, ever asked."

Hasuca tilted his head. *"Really?"*

Xiang chuckled until a memory came to mind. *"No, actually, there was one other with a mind like yours. Her questions made me sad."*

"Sad?"

"She reminded me so much of you. We have all missed you, Hasuca."

"You understand why I left?"

Xiang was silent for some time, then responded. *"I do not understand why you didn't challenge the throne when your father died. Nor did anyone else, Hasuca."*

"But how could I?" Hasuca shook his head in despair. *"Koe came to me the very morning he died, together with all his followers. I had not even taken Father's Imperial belt. As I mourned, he took it. Right before my eyes, he just assumed it. You said yourself, Xiang, had I challenged, the lands may still be in civil war, you know he would do that."*

"When you were both growing up, he was the faster, but you were smarter and more patient. You could have won at any time, but you never acted. Why was it so, Hasuca?"

"I could never strike my own brother. It just ought not to be done."

"It would never end as a fight to the death."

"I do not care. I would never strike my own brother."

"But your brother took every chance. Many times, I could see he really tried to hurt you."

"Yes, but I would not."

"Why?"

"Because he is my brother."

"Yes, and your brother is now running and perhaps ruining the country, and you hide in the jungle."

Hasuca was taken aback by Xiang's blunt comment, though it was a valid point. *"To whom was Sha'Doe given?"*

Xiang hesitated at the ambiguous question. They both knew the official answer to that. *"She was a gift to the Palace."*

"Yes, but the gift would not have been made if Father or I ran the Palace. She was a gift to Koe, a gift to impress and to promote him as Emperor Apparent. Father and I would not have approved. Our people knew this, but Koe ..."

"So, you would not have a son and his twin sister to Sha'Doe, if you were in power?"

"Exactly. They, my children, have claims to the dynasty of another land. Have you been to seek it out, Xiang?"

Xiang smirked.

"What is it now, Xiang?"

"I came down here feeling like a guardian angel and you propose to send me off with homework like a school child. Have you been there yourself?"

Hasuca shook his head. *"No, my friend, I have not. I do not go beyond the Great Eastern Ranges. I am not of strong enough mind to go further and then return. Though I have learnt a lot about our own lands since I have been 'hiding in the jungle.'"*

Xiang grinned at the sarcasm. *"Oh? Would you like to share what you have learnt?"*

"Yes, though I would have thought you'd have looked already, Xiang."

"You would not believe what I have understood since I have been where I am now. I have answers to questions I did not even know to ask. Please, what have you learnt for us?"

"When my father was a young man, he went north to settle a dispute about the work of some assassins. You know the story of how they were set upon and that Father's good friend, Ta Tuku was killed by the Chan family?"

Xiang knew the story well. *"And what did you find out about this well-known tragedy?"*

"Tuku was indeed killed in that assault. What everyone has missed, though, is that the killers were not representing the Chan family at all. In fact, they were not even Barbarians. It was a decoy to implicate the Barbarians, drive them out and hide a family shame. Ta Tuku was merely caught in the middle. However, Tuku was such a close friend of Father's that it inadvertently set into motion events that the real killers

had not anticipated. Father was so enraged he acted wholly out of character. He launched an assault on the Barbarians so fierce that it drove them out of the farming lands they cared for, and now, with the stone wall up, they have no chance of putting things right – right as the Gods had it."

Xiang was horrified. *"Did we get all this so horribly wrong, Hasuca?"*

"I believe so."

"I fought for all those years. I believed that what I was doing was not just the Palace's work, but the Gods' intention also. Now you are sitting here before me saying we got it all wrong?"

"Apparently, yes. I am sorry, Xiang."

"All of those men! Dead because of a misunderstanding! Men are still dying. Have you any idea how many people I alone have killed for the wrong reason? That makes it murder, Hasuca. It makes me a murderer!"

Hasuca had never thought of Xiang as a murderous person, and still didn't. *"Xiang, you dwell in the presence of the Gods. Have they punished you? No. Have they spoken of your countless attacks and countless defences of the Barbarians' failed attacks? No. Why? Because you were doing what was expected of you and furthermore, you were acting on the information you had on the day. A man can do no more than that."*

Xiang looked dejected. This had cut him deeply. *"I saw how the Barbarians dwindled in numbers, Hasuca. I understood their suffering without land for wintering their stock. We have more land than we ever needed, much is not even being used. Yet men are dying defending it. Defending land that is not ours. How do I justify this? How do I undo this?"*

Hasuca urged. *"You do not have to justify this because it was not your doing. You simply did as you were told, following your Emperor's orders. No Master has ever served as well as you served. It should be you, before me, demanding an explanation as to why your life was taken early and so brutally.”*

“Why would I demand this of you when it was not your doing either? This was not your fault, Hasuca.” The old man’s chin lifted as the corners of his mouth turned up ever so slightly. *“You think this is the same as me not knowing the truth about why the war against the North began?”*

“Yes, my old friend. What is more, maybe the gruesome end to your life was the Gods’ way of washing your own bloody hands. You have nothing more to pay, my friend. You did no more than your duty.”

“So how do we right this wrong, now that we know of it?”

Hasuca smiled. *“Now, you Xiang, forget your place. You have nothing more that you can give. As for me, however, I have spent much time pondering that very question, just as I have spent time searching the future.”*

“What is it you have seen?”

Hasuca rubbed his hands over his tired eyes. *“Only fragments. They do not make sense to me now, but maybe as time goes on, it will come together. It is like the question of Samos. Koe is going to do what he wants. Fairness and reason mean little to the man. Why does Koe want to invade Samos and why has he taken so long to go there?”*

Xiang sighed. *“I had pondered this before my death, I see no harm in talking about it. The Samos dispute is a farce. Koe is obsessed with his power. He thinks if he has power over the waters, he will find all the Crystal Skulls. He believes they will give him the ultimate power. I believe he will crush everything in his way to get it. When you left, all his efforts went into attempts to shed your blood, though he could never get past the love the people had for you, for your father also. No one wanted Koe as Emperor. When asked, they would lie to his face, but no one wanted him. He was searching for someone of your calibre to lead, but he could not replace you. Then, he believed that his son, Desora, was developing into an acceptable choice, so he decided to wait for him. Sadly, they do make a formidable team. I have seen small portions of what is to come. The danger of him is that he does have two Skulls and will get ..."*

Suddenly Xiang began to glow, like he was fracturing into light. His light became too strong for Hasuca, who held up an arm to cover his face. He heard Xiang's dwindling voice.

"I have said too much ... your daughter ... Tanica, go to her ... go ..."

Hasuca lowered his arm and cautiously looked up. The man and the star were gone. *"May the Gods love you as I, my friend."*

34 The Dagger

The next morning, Hao and Bolli were up and stoking the fire when Yaan woke. The three men were keen to move on after some hot tea and the last of the goat. Yaan led the way out of the cave into the light, after burying the torches upside down in the sand for future visitors.

The day was bright and sunny, the ground underfoot soft and a little mushy. The butterflies were out, and bees could be heard humming their endless tunes of energy as they went about their duty of pollinating the glorious wildflowers, signalling the first tentative signs of spring.

As they settled into their saddles, Bolli wondered if he would return to Tammirie and the caves before winter. Yaan picked a grass stem and began to chew it as he thought about finding the next campsite correctly, while Hao wondered if the Gods had planted all the wildflowers just for their pleasure.

They passed the morning at a leisurely pace, chatting and admiring the country around them, thankful for the scattered sunrays on their faces.

The forest edge came upon them unexpectedly. The woodland had been cleared, and the ground fell into a short, steep ravine towards a fast-flowing, muddy river.

Yaan spat his grass out. "I do not remember this. No, there was no river crossing here. Never."

Hao gave him an expectant look. "Well, Yaan, there is now."

"I'm telling you … there was no river crossing here before!"

Bolli closed his mouth and swallowed. "Damn, boys, it looks cold."

Yaan swung down. "I have not made a mistake. This was not here last time we came through, I swear."

Bolli stood with his hands on his hips. "Well, it's here now, and what a dirty mess the Gods have made of it. Look at it, see how much dirt there is in the water. Hao, have you seen the likes of it?"

Hao was at the edge of the bank. "No, Bolli, but don't be too hard on the Gods, they are not responsible for this."

Yaan lifted his head. "What?"

Not taking his eyes off the river upstream, Hao pointed. "In all of the Gods' beauty that I have seen I have never seen them lay a level or use a straight edge."

Bolli crouched down. "Well, I never, it *is* perfectly straight. What could have done this and why?"

"I have no idea, and I see no crossing either." Hao looked back into the forest. "There was some dead timber back a little way. I won't be long."

"Very well, Hao, we'll have a scavenge and see what we can find."

Without another word, Hao swung into his saddle and trotted away. Bolli saw some flax and tied his horse to a small oak. Drawing out his short sword, he checked the cutting edge. "You know, Yaan, I never thought I would ever get to use it for this. My late comrades will be rolling over in their graves," he scoffed, "as well as some of the poor bastards I have slain with it."

Yaan kept his distance. Bolli might have considered the weapon to be in appalling condition, but there was nothing wrong with the smooth, easy confidence in which he slashed his way around the base of the flax. In no time at all, there was just the green tuft of new growth standing upright in the middle.

The moment Bolli had finished, Yaan moved in and began to gather the flax, putting it aside in bundles. He followed Bolli's lead, picking up a large bundle and dragging it over to where the horses were tied up. Hao returned, dragging a bundle of timbers. He slipped off his horse as it came to a halt and, taking the rope off the saddle, he slapped his horse on the rump. Yaan watched it wander off some distance and then stop.

Hao nudged Yaan on the shoulder. "Hey, Yaan, if you are not too busy daydreaming, could you make some cords from the flax?"

Yaan took the hint and got busy.

It did not take the men long to fashion a crude raft with the dry timbers as a backbone. The flax was woven and tied on top. The furs came next, carefully placed, skin down. The three men stood back to admire their work.

Yaan frowned. "It is not really big enough for all of us, though, is it?" Hao and Bolli burst out laughing. Yaan held out his hands. "What?"

The two big men took off their shirts and threw them onto the raft. They then undid their boots and threw them on, too.

Yaan's face dropped. "Oh, no, no, no, you can't be serious? It's freezing." He walked forward to the bank and pointed emphatically. "Look! That's ice, I tell you … ice!"

By now, Bolli and Hao stood practically naked. Yaan looked everywhere else but at his friends. "Don't you boys from the north have any sense of propriety at all?"

"Yaan, there is only one way across. Bolli and I are going. If you wish to return to the caves, I will not blame you. I never wanted to leave."

Yaan and Bolli looked at Hao. "What? You were the first to go. We could hardly keep up with you, as I remember."

Hao ignored Bolli, holding Yaan's intense gaze. Then, to Bolli's surprise, Yaan strode forward, taking off his shirt. "Very well, boys. If this is how it is to be, then this is what we must do. It is only cold water after all."

Hao picked up the rope and whistled for his horse, which pranced over. He tied the rope onto the saddle, then leapt on. "Ready, Bolli?"

Unleashing his own horse, Bolli leapt into his saddle, Yaan followed close behind. With loud cries, Hao and Bolli kicked their horses, galloped over the bank, right into the icy water. Letting their horses swim freely ahead, the men held on to their manes swirling out behind. The horses' hot breath steamed over the icy water. The men kicking the horses' sides strongly was more a reaction to the shocking cold.

The bank on the other side was steep, though the horses made short work of clambering over the soft clay. Once at the top, Bolli and Hao were quick to dismount and pull the rope to retrieve their clothes. With the raft recovered, Hao waved to Yaan to follow. Yaan's shrieks were less than impressive as he kicked his horse into full gallop.

Hao drew back, and Bolli muttered. "Oh, no …"

Yaan's horse faltered right at the top of the clay bank. It was too late to stop and both rider and horse cascaded into the river below. The horse made an ungraceful dive, Yaan splashing into the river with his legs splayed in an undignified manner. The horse surfaced and headed straight for the first bank it saw as Yaan came up with his face contorted, gasping for breath. Hao wanted to tell him to grab the horse's tail as it went by but failed for laughing. Yaan swam like he had never swum before, happy to eventually reach the other side. As he began to leave the frozen river, he realised the bank was soft, wet clay. The horses got up all right but they had four long legs. By the time Yaan dragged himself to the top, he was as yellow as the bank itself.

As Hao and Bolli dressed, they had to stop at intervals, laughing at Yaan's efforts of scraping off the yellow mud, cursing as he did. Hao swung onto his horse, glanced at Yaan once more and burst out laughing again.

Instead of making a mud-coloured mess of his clothes, Yaan left them on the makeshift raft and wrapped himself in furs. He decided to walk, leading his horse, behind Bolli to help get his blood pumping.

Soon they came to a small clearing, where Hao already had a fire crackling under a large oak tree. "Yaan, you need to come over here and warm yourself up." He kicked away some of the leaves near the tree trunk and laid down another fur. Yaan hesitated.

"Well, come on, man, I'm not doing up an invitation."

Yaan frowned as he wandered over and sat himself on the fur whilst Hao swung another one over his shoulders. A tree had fallen across the clearing and the men had placed the three saddles and one bridle on it, tying two horses on long leads to it. Hao had left his horse free. They all grazed contentedly.

Bolli had been gone some time, and when he returned, he was carrying a rabbit.

"Hey, fresh food, good work, Bolli," commended Hao.

That night, the men enjoyed the fresh meat. Once finished, they sat back and watched the fire. It had been a tiring day. Hao's horse came over and lay behind him.

"Hao?"

"Yes, Yaan?"

"Tomorrow, I think the 'boys' will be blue."

The laughter made the horses flinch.

***

As the men headed south, the land sloped away and they continued to descend in altitude. The ground was still soft after winter, so at times they dismounted and walked the horses. It was a good break for the horses, and it was pleasant to stretch their legs too.

Slowly, the forest became denser, with more evergreens, like bamboo and lettok, towering over the canopy. One time, Yaan sat side-saddle, picking red berries and stuffing them in his mouth with great speed. Hao and Bolli watched for a few moments, then followed his lead. The fruit was a welcome supplement to their all-meat diet.

***

The trio travelled on with the days growing longer and warmer. The furs stayed rolled up on the rear of their horses; there was even talk of leaving them behind but they could not bring themselves to waste good furs. In awe, Hao and Bolli watched the primates swinging through the treetops. The birds were full of colour, unlike any they had seen before. Yaan enjoyed their wonderment. For once, he was showing them something new and different.

Hao and Bolli regularly argued about what was the better hunting tool, the crossbow or the long bow. Yaan was impressed with both men and their ability to shoot true and straight, game sometimes falling from high in the canopy. Fresh food in abundance was carried on the back of Bolli's horse.

Eventually, the three men rode out onto a large flat area covered in heavy jungle. So far, the trip had been exactly as Yaan had predicted, but now he stopped, looking perplexed and dismayed. Seeing Yaan's concern, Hao rode up beside him. They dismounted in silence.

They were at the side of a ravine; there was no river. Instead, there was a tiny, trickling stream at the bottom. The white rocks were smooth, and the jungle edge showed an unmistakable line, but no water. Instead, there were dried fish bones and small pools with dead fish floating upside down in green slime.

Yaan turned to Hao. "I don't understand. What has happened to the river?"

They mounted their horses and headed onward in silence. There were lots of fish bones, and something much bigger was lying over the rocks. Yaan explained about the crocodile. They walked their horses along the edge of the dry riverbed with an endless line of bones picked clean and dry. It was difficult to know how long it had been since the river had properly run.

Yaan stopped, Hao stopping behind him. "We know you are sad for the river, Yaan."

"No. Those bones are not of a fish."

Hao saw a large pile of bones to the far side. Bolli agreed. "That does look a little like a human skull. One of those crocodile things must have gotten him, poor fellow."

Hao agreed. "Do many people live in these parts of the jungle, Yaan?"

"No. Not that I know of."

Bolli walked his horse around Hao's. "Is it far to our next camp,

Yaan?"

Yaan did not answer. Hao spoke gently. "There are plenty of loose rocks about."

Yaan pointed across the river. "The thing about this limestone land is that there are lots of caves. See?"

Hao saw a dark cleft on the far side. Leaving their horses, they headed down into the riverbed towards the pile of bones.

"Hao, all the other bones are laid out as they died, but this one isn't."

"I can see what you're saying, Yaan, I guess that is in keeping with this person being eaten by a crocodile."

Yaan wasn't used to handling human remains; by contrast, Hao had experienced them while still warm and twitching. He began gathering the bones, and Yaan eventually followed suit. It wasn't difficult to tell the difference between a person's remains and those of a crocodile. Hands and feet had stayed intact. They stacked the human's bones neatly in the small cave and returned for the skull. Hao bent over to pick it up when Yaan pointed. "Hao, what is that?"

Hao drew back.

In a crevice below the bones was a gleam of light. "I don't know." He gently removed the skull. "You saw it, Yaan. Would you do the honours?"

Getting down on hands and knees, Yaan peered down into the crevice. "It looks like the hilt of a knife." Bracing himself, he reached down into the crevice but not quite far enough. He drew back and looked again. "It is a little further than I first thought." Hao watched in silence as Yaan tried again. This time, he lay right down on the rocks, took one more look at his target and reached in. "I ... have ... it." Slowly, he drew his arm back out and, just held by his fingertips, was a small knife.

Within moments, Bolli was there. "What a treasure you have, Yaan."

In the palm of Yaan's hand lay the small dagger. It was not fragile but finely wrought, likely to be the possession of a Noble.

Hao put his hand on Yaan's shoulder. "Well spotted, Yaan. This was no jungle-dwelling peasant. Fitting that you are giving this person the burial they deserve."

Yaan looked up. "All people are born equal, regardless of their birthright and position in life. All people deserve a fair burial."

Bolli had not taken his eyes off the object. "What do you think it would fetch at a market?"

"No, Bolli, this will not be finding its way onto the market."

Confused, Bolli looked at Yaan, his frustration clear. "Well, it has no value stuck in your belt. It is not even a hunting knife, is it?"

Hao intervened. "He is right about the hunting thing, Yaan. I would even go so far as to say it belonged to a female of the nobility. Look at the ornate design in the base of the handle."

Gently, Yaan turned the knife in his hand. It was still damp and clearly had been in the water for some time, though there was little sign of damage. It was of the highest quality.

Bolli reached for it but Yaan drew back. In a low voice, Bolli responded. "No need to be so protective. I was only going to point out the inscription around the butt."

Hao pointed. "He is right, Yaan, look, right around the brass butt."

Yaan held the knife up to the light and slowly turned it. Licking his thumb, he rubbed the butt. "That is not brass. It's gold."

"What does the inscription say?"

Yaan shrugged. "It's not a language of this land, Hao. I have no idea." Neither man noticed Bolli moving away.

Hao held up the skull. "This was no Noble, this was Royalty."

Yaan agreed. Sorrowfully, he looked into the eye sockets. "What a story this poor person could tell. The skull is by no means large, and given the smallness of the skeleton's hands and feet, if it were not a child, then it could have been a woman."

"Yes, a Royal woman." The two stood in silence for a moment. "I will place the skull and cover them up with the rest of the rocks so that she can now rest. Yaan, what you do with the knife is your choice."

Yaan considered the person as he studied the knife. "I will keep the knife and ask elders everywhere I go – someone will know the language. It is a handcrafted knife, fashioned for a loved one. This is personal."

Hao paused a moment. "This is determined by the Gods. They have chosen wisely for you to find it." He looked to Yaan. "And I will never call you boy again."

Hao walked to the small cave, placed the skull, and closed it off with rocks.

***

The men continued their trek in silence. They were brought back abruptly to reality with the growl of a big cat. The horses twitched and bucked as the jungle rumbled with the unmistakable sound of an ambushing cat.

The men dug their heels in and rode hard, needing no time to check over their shoulders. Yaan swore, putting in some of the best riding Hao had ever seen, affirming that the boy really had been in the saddle since he could walk. Bolli straggled but remained in his saddle, doing his best to push a horse that was used to wide open spaces covered in tussock.

Just ahead of them, sunlight shone down into the jungle. Hao wondered why there was a clearing in this densest jungle, when Yaan simply disappeared from in front.

Hao's eyes grew wide as he galloped out into thin air. He leaned back in his saddle, holding on to the reins with one hand and waving the other arm about for balance. For an instant, he could feel the sun on his skin and all around him was quiet, as he and his horse plummeted towards a large pool below. He clung to the reins. The water seemed to take its time as it loomed up to him. *This will hurt* – water from this height felt harder than soil. He was concerned for his horse, which was not known for an ability to dive.

The water would have been clear, but for all the bubbles. As the impact of the water winded Hao, he surfaced, wiping water from his face, gasping for air. Although clearly distressed, his horse seemed to be well for all its ordeal, and he grabbed the saddle and guided it towards Yaan, who was leading his horse up onto a pebble beach. Bolli was now swimming their way with his horse.

Once on the beach, a breathless Hao lifted his chin to Bolli, who looked back to where they had come from. It had been an impressive drop. Yaan jumped and danced about, trying to burn off the adrenaline, and Hao began to laugh with him. He was a little surprised, if not embarrassed, when Yaan ran forward and gave him a bear hug that lifted him clear off the ground.

Once released, Hao noticed a fig tree meadow with fresh grass and an abundance of flowers. The horses would be happy for the night. On the other side of the huge pool, a large waterfall rumbled. In all the excitement of surviving such a descent, he hadn't noticed it.

Yaan pointed to Bolli's head. "That was a lucky, but you lost your hat for it."

Bolli grasped his head. "Oh, no!" He ran back down to the pebble beach searching for his precious hat when Hao called, "Hey, Bolli, look, it's over there."

Down the river, where the pool overflowed into the rapids and caught on a log that balanced precariously on some rocks was the hat. Bolli began to remove his shirt.

Hao grabbed his arm. "Bolli, what is it you think you are doing?"

"I am going to get my hat, numbskull. Did you think I was going fishing?"

"No, Bolli. I saw you in the water with Tammirie. You can't swim well. We have not come all this way to have you go and drown over a damn hat now, have we? Think about it, man!"

Bolli snatched his arm away from Hao's hold with a ferocity that made Yaan flinch. "I can swim," Yaan offered. "I think I even swam here as a child."

The two big men turned to see Yaan already taking off his clothing and boots. He strode upstream to the river mouth then picked up a pebble and put it in his mouth as he dived in. The fast current took him with alarming speed, but Yaan was a strong swimmer, and he wasted no time in getting well out into the river.

Just as Hao and Bolli thought he was going to miss the log altogether, he reached out to one of its roots and let it bend around, landing him at the back of one of the rocks supporting it. He pulled himself up and carefully stepped onto the log.

He took a few deep breaths, eyeing the hat on the far end, then ran along the log. It immediately began to sink. From the bank, Hao and Bolli saw him fall in.

Bolli threw his hands up in the air. "I will kill the clumsy fool – if he gets out of there."

The two men ran down the river, but they lost sight of Yaan the moment he went into the white water behind the rocks. They stood, holding their breaths. Hao pointed downstream. "There!" Yaan was climbing up onto a rock. They ran towards him, yelling out, but the raging rapids were too loud for voices to be heard.

As they drew closer, they saw Yaan drop the stone into the hat then throw it with all his might. Bolli yelled, "Nooo!" To his astonishment, it flew high overhead, landing with a crack just behind them. Bolli ran over and picked up his treasured hat.

Yaan dived back in, and Hao ran farther downstream to help him, running into the shallows to grab Yaan by the arm. Lifting the young man out of the water, they walked up the bank. Hao's big stallion had come over to watch the events.

As Yaan sat on the bank catching his breath, Bolli arrived carrying his clothes. "That was an almighty swim, Yaan. You were right not to let me try. I had no idea how strong the river was running. I, um, I thank you, Yaan."

Once Yaan had caught his breath and dressed, they headed to their campsite. Hao's horse ambled behind.

***

They continued their journey through the hot jungle, predominantly following the river. Finally, they found signs of people, the first that the trio had seen since they had crossed the near-frozen river, which seemed so long ago.

All around the slopes appeared to be carefully flooded ponds. They hugged the gentle hillsides, one overflowing into another, maintaining a constant water level. Fresh green tops of a crop could just be seen growing up through the water.

"I wonder what they are growing and if it is ready to eat, whatever it is?" enquired Bolli.

"Such careful work and so well planned," Hao responded. "Is this not man and his Gods working in unison for the betterment of both? If we could utilise every square of land, we could leave the jungle to propagate the hunting game we need."

"I heard a wise man call this the balance and circle of life," said Yaan, "which continues uninterrupted, unintimidated."

Before long, the three men were on a well-used track. Yaan was sure they were close.

A long, dusty line of a large group of people and animals came into view. "Look!" Yaan said excitedly, "They must be people from the village."

At the end of their track, where it ran onto another, they stopped and sat side saddle to watch. What they saw was a beaten and weary group, making their way past. Those in the first part of the caravan were on donkeys. They led milking cows and goats. Few made eye contact or spoke, leaving the strangers feeling unwelcome.

Hao and Bolli sat impassively. Yaan, on the other hand, was shaken by the sorry-looking figures. They were not at all like the happy, friendly coastal folk he remembered. "Have I taken a wrong turn? Are we passing through a different place?" he whispered to no one.

He wondered where the proud people he had known were. He'd had been looking forward to re-introducing himself, but now he wasn't even sure he had the right people. He looked at the end of the line and scrunched his face. At the rear of the caravan was a group of elderly men and women. "Why are they not shown the usual respect given to old folk? Normally, they would walk at the front in clean air and to set the pace."

They looked on, dumbfounded. Walking with the elders was possibly the biggest man they could imagine. He seemed neither black nor white. His left hand looked to be bound in rope attached to one of the elderly men.

"I have seen the old man before," Yaan thought aloud. "Do they own the giant? I have heard of such a thing, one human owning another."

All three stared at the huge man in silence until Bolli spoke, distaste thick on his tongue. "What beastly thing is that?"

35 Muddy Waters

As spring gave way to summer, Kito put on weight and stature as he worked in the bottom of the canal. The summer days were long, and he gained strength as he worked the tools. To the people, his appearance was strange. Some whispered about him within earshot, but most of them simply ignored him. The feeling of isolation was hard.

After the hot days, the warm nights were tolerable. The camp was now on the banks of the Yellow River, where Kito swam to wash away the day's grime.

The project was now just days away from breaking through into the Yellow River. It was to flood back up, opening the Colonial Dig from the top then flow down from the distant western mountains into the Yellow River, though it was a mystery as to why.

****

Late one afternoon, Kito felt someone watching him. He continued to dig, though the feeling was quite unmistakable. He didn't feel any danger but the urge to look grew. He decided to wait until Jong was back with the water bucket, then he would turn Jong to see beyond.

Not too much later, Jong returned. He started at the other end and worked his way towards Kito who continued to work until Jong reached him. At first, he saw nothing but a high mound in the distance, at the last bend of the canal. In his concentration, he hardly noticed Jong speaking quietly to him.

"You are from a faraway land, we can see that much, but who trained you to be a Master? It is for the selected few. How is this, my friend?"

"Why is it that you care, Jong?"

"Why, Kito, when you had been in that cage for well more than one day, I offered you water. You cared more for my safety than your own thirst. This is, in my experience, very rare."

Kito lowered the ladle, contemplating the old man. This land seemed to be full of old, patient observers. "I told you the situation as I saw it. That, in my experience, is not so rare, Jong."

"We all see things, Kito, but is it real or is it what we wish to see?" Jong put the bucket down and stretched his back. He paused, like he was considering his next words. "Now, if you have seen what you were searching for, I need to return."

Kito picked up the bucket and dropped the ladle back in, handing it back to Jong, who dipped his head and trotted away. He resumed his digging, his mind running over who he had just seen, and moreover, why he was here. It was the Emperor, who was looking back at him through a sight glass.

Lost in thought, Kito hadn't noticed it growing dark, but a whistle brought him back to the here and now. He could just make out the outline of old Jong, giving him a wave. He also saw a good-sized fire up on the knoll.

The end of the dig was now a thin sliver of earth; tomorrow, they would break through.

As he walked along the riverbank, he could see trout ambushing insects. He marvelled at how clear the water was. He decided to dive in and let his body clean itself as he slid through the cool water. As always, he swam with his eyes open, clearing the dust from his eyes. Surfacing, he floated for a while in the gentle current. This was a luxury, and he took his time appreciating it, wondering what it had been like before the river was this close.

He swam back upstream to his point of entry and walked out. Everyone had already washed and left. Undressing, he wrung out his clothes. He had just pulled on his loose top when he heard a child's voice in the dark.

"Hello, Master Kito."

Quietly, Kito asked, "Who is in the dark?"

"My name is Orton. Are you well tonight, Kito?"

"I am indeed, but that is not why you've come out here in the dark, is it, Orton?"

There were a few silent moments before the reply. "What is that you do in the river for so long?"

"I swim."

"Kito, we live by the sea. We are all good swimmers in my village, we have to be, but why do you float down on the current?"

Kito was curious. "I like to float. It is when I thank the Gods for this life of mine."

"But you are here, on this Dig. Did you choose to come here, Master Kito?"

"Please, Orton, do not call me Master. I have a Master and I am not he. No, I did not choose to come here; I was sent by the Emperor."

"Then why do you stay when you could go at any time?"

"I cannot go at any time, Orton. What makes you think such a thing?"

"The cage, Kito. They cannot hold you because you are a Master."

Kito smiled at the boy's inquisitive nature. "I think if I was to leave, Zekec would enjoy making the rest of you pay for my absence, therefore, I am bound to finish the Dig." He motioned to the wall. "This will be done very soon, then I will be a free man once more."

Kito held out his hand and Orton seemed comfortable in taking it to walk back to their nomadic village. With excitement, Orton asked, "So where will you go to next, Kito?"

Kito gazed at the stars that had begun to illuminate another night. "I will find my way back to my Master. Then, after I have made my apologies for my absence, I will ask permission to travel over the mighty seas."

"Over the mighty seas! Why would you do that? You could come and stay with me and my family, Master Kito. I know grandfather would be pleased."

"Who would your grandfather be, Orton?"

"Why Jong no less, Master Kito."

Kito scoffed at his own expense. *How did I miss that?* "And why would Jong be pleased, Orton?"

"Grandfather thinks Masters can call for good seasons. Even just welcoming a Master into the village can bring good fortune."

Kito wondered what would happen when they had a bad season. He knew well that the seasons came both good and bad. Captain Tarrant had taught him about weather outside of their natural cycles. "Well, it is really very kind of you to offer but I have my own tasks in life that I must pursue, Orton. Have you considered *you* might be the next village Master, Orton?"

"That would be truly a great privilege in life but you know as I do, Master Kito, the Gods choose the Masters, not the people."

The comment struck Kito like a physical blow.

***

In the food hall, Kito had his dinner and helped clean up. All the men pitched in with any duties about the camp, which they freely shared with the women who also worked on the Colonial Dig. Even children and the elderly had their jobs, as set out by tradition and enforced, sometimes harshly, by Zekec. The only men who didn't help in the evening were the ones who went out every night to hunt. Kito was never invited. In fact, most of the men didn't even look at him, let alone talk with him, even less so as he grew into the large, dark man he now was.

Kito had a restless night and rose well before dawn. Moving from his bed, he went out into the dark and looked up, wondering if his family watched the same stars.

On the knoll, the glow of a campfire gave Kito an ominous feeling. He walked out of the camp in the direction of the knoll and sprang up onto a large boulder with the power and grace of a great cat.

Undressing, he sat cross-legged on his clothing. He closed his eyes and listened to his breathing … slower … slower … slower…

until all around him slowed, then became quiet. The morning cricket stopped its clicking, and Kito slipped away from his physical body. It had been some time since he'd been free. He stretched as he slipped through the night, heading towards the fire.

There were sentries posted about the knoll. He recognised them as the best of the best, dressed in pure black silk and not one was asleep. He continued forward to the series of tents around the fire. The cook was already preparing breakfast. Kito was surprised to smell how good it was; he was surprised to smell at all.

He refocused on the scene before him, checking all the tents. Two were large enough to house royalty. The first one was massive with no centre pole. He went in. In the centre was a very large bed with many forms under a single, silk sheet. Though the candles had burned down low, Kito could still see well enough. The room was full of the scent of burnt candle wax. *Probably better than the perspiration that would have been thick on the air last night,* he mused.

He needed to know who was here on this trip – who he was dealing with. *Two Royal tents, one will be in here.*

Kito moved in ever so slowly, closer to a form. The form rolled over; it was a woman. He couldn't help but let his eyes slip down to her chest as he eased up the silk sheet. He sighed. *It must be good to be Royalty.*

Suddenly, her eyes sprang open. It was as much a reflex as anything, but he held his hand over her mouth in a heartbeat. Bewildered that she could see him, he stared into her terrified eyes and whispered, "I will release your mouth." They nodded together. "You will not scream?" They nodded again. "Then I will leave as quietly as I came, no harm will come."

As he released his hand, another woman sat bolt upright and screamed. Instantly, everyone was up and running about. More naked, screaming women than Kito cared to count. He exited up through the tent into the night sky. As he looked down, he could see people throwing wood on the fire for light, red hot sparks rushing up into the warm night sky.

The guards gathered their swords, fearlessly checking the camp. Then Kito saw what he'd come for. The Emperor. He came out of the other Royal tent at the same time as Desora appeared from the tent where Kito had just been. Kito scoffed at him striding about without a top on, puffing out his chest like he'd just conquered the entire Barbarian tribe.

Sentries ran into camp, trying to source the problem. Kito watched all the naked women screaming deliriously. He scoffed again. *Good luck with that one.*

Kito began his journey back to his physical body, gladly leaving the ruckus behind. He scouted around and, when it was safe, eased himself into his body. Once back in his own skin, Kito stood and stretched. *Hasuca was right about the freedom of flying.*

The rock was smooth and flat, as good a place as any to do his morning stretches, a routine that he and his Master had followed since the day they'd arrived at Hasuca's cabin.

Kito was deep in thought as he approached the village. He began to sense something threatening, something bad, so bad he almost missed the voice to his right.

"Good morning to you, Kito. You were up and away early."

Kito politely bowed. "Good morning to you, Jong." He saw the old man's questioning eyes. "Yes, I did not sleep well, though I never went beyond that rock just down the track."

"No indeed, Kito. Come, let us share breakfast, I am sure my dear Quinn has enough."

Along a dirty walkway, the two men walked through the village to a small tent stained with drying mud. Inside, paperbark lay over the ground to soak up the moist dirt beneath. A low table centred the room, and a large metal pot hung over a small fire at one end.

Kito hunched over under the low ceiling. After working at the Dig for almost two seasons, this was the first time he had been invited by anyone. He usually found a corner of the common room where all unattached people ate and slept. He never had reason to enter people's personal space.

Jong offered Kito a seat at one side of the table, as he and his wife shared the other.

"It is good of you to have me in your home, Quinn. I thank you both."

Quinn peered into the boy's piercing blue eyes. "You foolish boy, you could have lived here if only you had asked. We waited and we waited, but you never asked. Why not, boy? Do you not want to be seen with old man and wife, eh? We not good enough for you, eh? You too good for us? Why?"

Kito sat wide-eyed as Jong openly laughed. Quinn hadn't finished. "Eh, what wrong you, boy? You lose your tongue walking in the forest this morning?"

Kito looked at Jong and back to Quinn. "I am deeply sorry, Quinn. I have spoken good wishes for you and Jong, but we have never really talked as such, and most people do not even see me, so ..."

Quinn was dishing breakfast into bowls. She leant over and smacked Kito on the wrist with her ladle. "So you assume? No assume, boy, no assume. Just ask."

Kito leant back, holding up both hands in submission. "All right, all right, just ask. I get it."

Jong's shoulders jiggled as Quinn put down a bowl in front of Kito. It contained at least half of what was in the pot. She split the remainder into two bowls for herself and Jong. The three ate in silence. From time to time, Jong would look to Kito then chuckle more. Kito finished his meal, politely put his bowl aside and drank water from the wooden cup before him.

As Quinn stood up to clear the table, Jong asked, "So Kito, what did you see on the mound? Was it our Emperor?"

Kito hesitated for a moment. "Yes, and the prince too. Did you follow me out of the camp?"

"No, what would make you think that?"

"Quinn had enough breakfast for all three of us when we returned."

"How many tents on the mound?"

"Seventeen."

"The usual royal entourage."

"I have no idea."

Breakfast done, the three began the trek up to the Dig. Kito headed down to the far side of the pit and, as usual, was the first to start work. He didn't want to give Zekec any reason to pay him attention, but every morning, Zekec would stand at the top of the Dig and watch him intently. Kito would just as intently ignore his presence.

***

It was the usual quiet start to the day, which began to heat up by mid-morning. Kito had started a habit of singing the songs he knew, sea shanties that were designed to help on the boats, to keep a rhythm, a good steady pace, everyone thinking of the next verse, not how hot it was, or how dry and tired they were. It also worked well on the Dig, many of the workers joined in, though it did seem strange to be singing songs of the sea so far inland.

Kito was working and singing when he heard Jong with the water bowl behind him. He put his tool down, finishing the verse. He looked to the mound as Jong put the bowl on the ground to stretch his back. Kito could see the Royal Entourage quite clearly in the midmorning light, but something was amiss; none of them were facing the Dig.

Kito took the ladle and drank deeply, then closed one eye and waved the ladle at Jong. "All you have to do is ask, boy." Laughing, he went to dip the ladle once more, and Jong saw the smile slide away from his face. Kito was holding the ladle to one side, gazing deep into the bowl of water.

"Kito, what is wrong?"

Kito looked to everyone on the mound, turning towards the Dig. They were watching something, and it was coming their way. He looked up at the wall end, the top was being breached at a few different points. Many workers were at varying heights, and some, like Kito, were right down in the hole. He saw the ripples in the bowl getting bigger and bigger.

In one swift movement, Kito bent down and, with one arm, scooped up the old man, yelling as he began to run. "Water! Get out! The water is coming! Get out!"

At first, people couldn't hear above the singing. As Kito ran across the floor of the Dig, he swiped a labourer's swinging pick and ran at the side wall. There was no time to get to the steps.

The earth began to tremble, the singing stopped and the people screamed with alarm. The terrified boy, Orton, was in the corner of the Dig, just below the top. Panicked by the sight and noise of the dirty, swirling water tumbling down the canal towards them, adults were trampling over him, knocking him to the ground every time he tried to stand.

Orton was confused as the water roared down then he saw Kito with Poppa Jong over his right shoulder, wielding a pick with his left hand to pull himself up the steep, clay bank. Kito looked right back at him, smiled and gave him a wink. Orton read Kito's lips.

"Crawl out, just crawl, Orton. You will be alright."

Orton turned and crawled. Adults still knocked into him but on hands and knees, he crawled up onto the top ledge and turned back to see at the dirty water smashing down the canal. Scores of people had not made it out of the bottom, and they were slammed into the end wall by the angry mud. As the water crashed back in a swirl of mud thundering back over itself, Orton saw the bodies tossed around in the chaos.

The boy gasped. The mud was flowing back at Kito and Poppa Jong. Kito held tight to the pick, grappling the wall as the first wave passed them; he swung the pick repeatedly until they crested the wall. Still the muddy water tumbled down the canal, rising higher with the growing pressure.

Orton watched as Poppa Jong was set down and Kito began to sprint towards him. Orton could see every muscle bulging under Kito's tunic. His straining body shook with every powerful stride. He could feel the muddy waters lapping at his feet, trying to drag him to a deep, dark world below, but Orton could not take his eyes off the dark man as he ran to the people trapped by the engulfing waters.

The canal was at the point of overflowing, the end wall could no longer hold back the angry deluge. It broke in multiple places, forming islands and washing away those in between. The torrent hurtled down into the Yellow River. Behind Orton, people shouted out to loved ones stranded in small groups, crying and screaming deliriously.

Kito ran past Orton towards Grandmother Quinn. From the moment Kito had dropped Jong on the embankment, his eyes were on Quinn, and she saw him coming. He didn't see all the screaming people standing to the side, but he could see one little boy sitting on the edge, watching his grandmother slipping away.

Kito had to try, though from the moment he set Jong down, he was but one pace too late. With every fibre in his young body, Kito did try. As her island gave way to the greater force, Quinn smiled at Kito, and his effort to reach her was lost.

The island tilted away, sliding toward the Yellow River.

Kito took two more strides before diving after the group, his arms straining to reach Quinn as the island dissolved into the muddy torrent just as he got to her. The unforgiving maelstrom enveloped Kito and everyone on the small island.

On the banks, villagers watched and screamed, hoping for a miracle, for a loved one to return from this beast that had been set upon them. They began to run downstream, screaming in disbelief, horror and anger.

Aiming with outreached fingers, Kito hit the muddy, churning mass. With eyes closed, in his mind was Quinn's arm and, as he plunged into the mud, he managed to grab her. He was tossed this way and that, almost losing his grip more than once. He put all his energy, his every thought, into pulling Quinn towards him and curled up into a ball around her, holding her, protecting her.

In the pressure of the mud, he was repeatedly tossed and thrown about. He gritted his teeth and, with bursting lungs, he held his breath. With Quinn tucked into his abdomen, they rolled uncontrollably in the muddy mass without any sense of which way was up.

He began to feel giddy. His blue lips parted as he trembled for air.

***

As a little boy, Kito stood on a large rock. Below him, men and their sons swam in a large, clear pool. They were his friends and were yelling at him to dive. Deep down below, there was a log on the bottom. He dived down to it and slipped his body under it, peering up to the surface. His friends dived down too, searching for him, but, without success, they rose back to the surface. Kito stayed calm, conserving energy. Adults were now diving down but he stayed under the log and they too, returned to the surface. Then a big hand grabbed him from behind. Kito saw his father's bright teeth shining in the water as they headed upwards. With a mighty rush, they broke the surface, and everyone cheered and laughed.

***

The churning river eased. Kito bumped on the bottom and pushed off hard. Feeling lightheaded, he broke the surface, drawing in air, water and mud. He couldn't see anything so swam towards the yelling crowd. Feeling the bank, he managed to drag Quinn clear of the mudflow. Hands pulled her away, and when she was free, he was left alone. On all fours, he gulped to unblock his airways as he gasped for air. His stomach cramped and heaved until he began to throw up. When the vomiting subsided, he took long, deep breaths to calm himself. He heard the people talking.

"She never had a chance."

"So much to look forward to."

"Just does not seem right, he survived and she did not."

"No!" called Kito. He crawled forward; he couldn't see, but he knew where Quinn was. He drew her lifeless body to his and held it a moment. Still on his hands and knees, with one hand on her chest and the other on her abdomen, he sat back on his haunches and squashed her stomach.

369

Several women sobbed out loud. "Stop him, stop him now!"

No one moved.

Mud and water spurted from Quinn's mouth. He squeezed her stomach and then her chest again, expelling more water and more mud.

Then Quinn threw up and drew a deep breath. Kito slumped forward, still holding her. She threw up again and drew another breath. Exhausted, Kito lay on his side, releasing her. He listened as she gasped and spat, then gasped again. Laboured though her breathing was, he could almost smile.

Once her breathing was settled, they washed her down, then carried her away. Kito dragged himself onto his elbows and knees, his head in his hands. Still feeling sick, he needed to drink but chose to stay and rest just a while longer. He heard people coming his way and they began to gently tip water over him as he drew himself up and sat back. Helpful hands washed the mud away.

There were no further rescues. No one else was to emerge from the muddy water.

After some time, he stared to the heavens. He was getting help, the hands were caring as they tried to clean off his broken body, but the sky was dark. "I can't see."

A little more water was poured, gentle hands washing his face. "I can't see. Is it nighttime?"

A small voice answered him. "No, Kito, it is only early afternoon."

Kito turned his head towards the person who'd just spoken. "Orton. Grandmother Quinn, she will be good, yes?"

There was silence before Orton replied. "Yes, Kito, Grandmother Quinn will be good. She had a good life, and the Gods will care for her now."

Kito could feel all eyes upon him as the crowd watched the confused, dark man who had defied the river.

"But, Orton, did I not pull her from the mud? Did I not just hear her cough and breathe?"

The silence was painful. "No, Kito, you did not. I'm sorry."

Water began to pour over his head again, then Kito heard a young man's voice.

"Come now, that is about as much fresh water as we can spare for you."

"Kai, is this you?"

"It is, Kito. If you are ready, we can go back to the village now."

"But I do not see, Kai."

"We all saw what you tried to do for Quinn, Kito. When we get back, you will understand what has happened. Let us go now."

"No, Kai, you do not understand. I have lost my sight."

Kai waved his hand in front of Kito's face. His jaw fell slack as he turned to his father. Manchu walked forward and knelt before Kito.

"Kito, I am Manchu, Kai's father."

"Yes, I know you, Manchu, you are husband to Jin."

Manchu was a little surprised that Kito knew his ties; they had never spoken. "Has this happened before?"

"No, never, Manchu. Are the Gods angry with me? Did I do something not right?"

"No, Kito, I do not think the Gods are angry with you. This will only make sense in time; we must get you back to the village to rest. Kai will lead you."

"No! Is Jong here?" Kito waited in the silence. "Is Orton here?"

"I am, Kito."

He was happy to hear the small voice. "I am sorry I failed your grandmother, Orton. If you would be so good as to lead me to your grandfather, I must make my condolences and my apologies."

Orton did not answer but took Kito by one of his big hands and placed it on his shoulder. During the long trek back upriver to the village, not once did the boy let go of Kito's hand.

Through the warren of streets, people stopped to watch. Kito bent low so he could reach Orton's shoulder. He walked with his eyes closed, the mud now drying on his dirty, ripped clothes. There was an uncanny silence as the two walked on.

Kito could feel things, things he had only experienced when meditating – the sun, now lower in the sky – high overhead, the song of a starling. He could feel the village and all its inhabitants, their sorrow, their mourning.

They crossed through the meeting place in the centre of the village. Kito sensed the tents around him; a large one off to his right was where he had been eating and sleeping when he wasn't at Jong and Quinn's place.

Then he felt Quinn, standing outside the food hall, together with a large crowd. They wore crisp, white clothes. Kito slowed to a stop, he knew when they all bowed to him. They were shining with health. Clean, happy and free.

"Kito, we are nearly there. Keep going now."

"Orton, is that the food hall over there?"

"Yes, it is. Do you see it?"

"You said it was not far to Jong's and I can smell the food, Orton."

They continued on. "Well, there is nothing wrong with your nose, Kito. I had not noticed the food hall myself."

As the two drew close to Jong's place, well-wishers were speaking with him. They hushed as the two approached. Orton stopped and Kito waited.

As Jong greeted Orton, Kito knelt before him. "I have asked Orton to bring me to you. I am sorry to have failed you. I did my utmost to reach Quinn. By the love of the Gods, I tried Jong. I have failed you both. Now I can only ask your forgiveness and offer my condolences to you and your family."

Silence hung in the air. Eventually, Kito rose and turned away from Jong to face the way they had come. "Orton, would you be so good to help me back to the food hall now?"

A few muttered before a man asked, "Why is it you need help to get to the food hall? You know where it is."

"Indeed, I do – we passed it on our way here, but I'm afraid I need a little help getting back. Orton assisted me to get here, and now I ask him to help me get back."

Orton looked up at the big, dark man, standing there helpless and covered in dried mud. "Of course, Kito, I can do this." He bowed deeply to Jong. "I will be right back, Grandfather."

Jong's face, awash with tears, lit up with pride for the boy. "I will have food ready for your return." Jong gazed at Kito, tattered, dishevelled and eyes shut.

Nothing more was said as Orton took Kito by the hand and led him away.

***

Back at the food hall, silence fell as Kito darkened the door. He could feel everyone staring at him.

"Where was your place?"

"I was in the corner to our right, Orton," whispered Kito.

"Yes, of course." Orton led him to his place on the floor, and Kito felt the sides of the big tent, sighing as he eased himself down to sit.

"May I ask of you one more favour before you go, Orton?"

"Yes, Kito."

"My throat is sore, would you be so good as to fetch me some water, please?"

Orton bowed and Kito listened to him scurry off. When he returned, Kito drank thirstily. "You have been very kind to me, Orton. I thank you. Now your grandfather needs you." Kito dipped his head and waited for Orton's little feet to trot away. He drank again before settling on his back.

Sleep came quickly.

36 Kito's Stance

Kito woke with a start. Disoriented and confused, he rolled onto his side and rubbed his eyes, but still he could not see. Like a bad dream, the events from the day before came flooding in. He floundered, fumbling to find the water container. Once in his grasp, he pulled the cork and drank several large gulps, then tipped some into his palm to rinse his face. He blinked and blinked, but there was nothing but darkness. He lay back down with his hand over his face, going over everything that had happened. Jong had told him the plan was to allow the Yellow River to gradually flood back up the canal, they would then feed the waters from the top and allow gravity to set the new river in motion.

Kito let his senses take over as he stood to get his balance. The food hall was quiet and empty. He ran his hands over his clothes. They felt foul, tatty and dirty. He needed to get down to the river and wash. People were talking outside, talking of who survived, who drowned and who was still missing. He overheard raised voices, heated conversations about why the waters came, who had sent it down too early. Then Kito heard the voices of Manchu and Kai making their way through the village of tents.

"Father, I was talking to Narpa earlier … he was saying that as many as thirty people have been killed with the collapse of the wall."

Manchu strode briskly. "I am sad for all the people that are now gone, but my emotions confuse me. With the most remarkable chain of events I have ever witnessed, I am happy that my daughter was handed back from the deluge. There is talk that the Emperor and the Prince are coming. Mother has decided to stay behind with

Mikka, so it is just us representing our family.”

The two joined the crowd just in time to see the first of the procession of guards, all dressed in black silk, with twin swords hanging on their left hip. Their black horses pranced along the street, leading the way for the grand carriage that followed. The gold, brass and silver gilding shone in the morning light. It stopped before the food hall, and guards rushed over with steps to place before the door. The Emperor alighted, followed by Prince Desora, then Zekec and Nikko. The four of them walked around to the clearing of people behind the carriage. The crowd fell to its knees and bowed.

The Emperor waved and dipped his head. “Well done, everyone, you have served your Emperor well. I would like to also give special thanks to Zekec. I know you will agree that he was the backbone in this arduous job. Without him, this would not have been done on time, and disaster may have struck.” He was interrupted by a deep voice that boomed from behind the crowd.

“A disaster *has* struck! Families and friends have been swept away to untimely, muddy graves.”

Gasps and sobs were heard among the crowd.

The Emperor’s face darkened to thunder. “And *who* said that? Come. Come before me if you dare!”

The people turned to the food hall. There in the doorway stood Kito. The crowd opened, making a path as Kito walked forward. The Emperor’s face betrayed his astonishment at Kito’s presence. He had seen him dive into the water and thought it had been the end of him. Yet there he was, walking towards him, bigger and more daunting than ever. The Emperor tried to cover his shock by starting a slow clap.

Kito walked straight towards him, but he did not bow. The Emperor stopped clapping. “Kito, I sent you here on a mission with three men who never returned.”

Kito was careful. “If my memory serves me, there was a large storm bearing down on us. I was fortunate to survive by going south, they went back north. I feel they may have perished in the storm."

The Emperor began to walk around Kito. "Yes, your memory serves you correctly, Kito. We did find young Shue frozen to his saddle. Foolish boy had tried to wait out the storm under a tree, his saddle as cover. It took my guards some time to dislodge the saddle, which was Palace property." The Emperor paused. "And what of Wongue and Ginta? Does your memory serve you to tell us what you did with those two men, Kito?"

Kito spoke calmly. "When I was lost in the jungle, one of the first things I learnt was, I have the right to protect myself. So, when Ginta tried to shoot me with his crossbow, I had the right to shoot back. He missed, I did not."

A gasp went about the crowd. Kito had just confessed to the killing of a member of the Imperial Guard.

The Emperor smiled thinly. "I see. Wongue was a man who I trained myself and chose as leader of my Palace Guard. What do you claim for him?"

"Wongue was a good man. We formed a friendship. I trusted him, but when he heard Ginta fall from his saddle, he turned and saw a bolt protruding from Ginta's eye socket. He assumed it was I, trying to be the murderer. Sadly, he charged at me. I merely stepped aside and he succumbed to his own unfortunate end. Though I will say, your training was of the finest, he did leave me with a scar." Kito pulled at a cut in his tunic over his shoulder.

The Emperor stared coldly. "Though clearly, not deep enough." The Emperor walked again. "Last night, we celebrated the completion of the Royal Dig. Zekec has told me a strange story of how you got out of a bound cage. Would you like to explain just how you did this, Kito? We would all *love* to hear."

Kito began to answer before the Emperor finished. "It was really very easy. I came to realise that Zekec was going to leave me to die of dehydration in the cage."

The Emperor, behind Kito at this point, looked at Zekec who appeared rather happy with himself. "Yes, Kito, we have it so far. Continue."

"So, at my wit's end, I used my last piece of gold to bribe your second in charge, Nikko. You need to pay your men better, Emperor. He freed me then gave me food and water."

The Emperor spun on his heel, glaring at Nikko, who stepped forward, whip in hand, eyes blazing with anger at the huge man. The Emperor quickly stepped away.

Kito heard the whip flick out behind Nikko. His mind went back to when he was a small boy. Hasuca would sit him blindfolded on a stool at a window, a candle burning before him. At first, all Kito could hear were moths flying into the candle. It would flare up and then burn down to its former size. Hasuca would talk gently to him. *Control the mind and let go of consciousness.* Then finally one night, Kito heard the wings of a beating moth making its way through the night air. Seeing the candle, it came in close, his hand lashed out and knocked the insect to the ground, the moth could still see the candle and returned. This time, his hand whipped out, catching the moth.

Kito heard Nikko exhale as he drove his arm forward. The long, whip handle rushed through the air, dragging with it the cord of plaited leather with the three beaded threads trailing behind. He stepped forward and reached out with his left arm. He heard the beads whistle through the air, and he stretched out further with his big hand. Listening, he caught them and pulled back as hard and as fast as he could, tearing the handle from Nikko's grip. With a 'whoosh', the handle flew over Kito's head, and he looped it back with lightning speed. The brass butt slammed into Nikko's chest. Winded, he bent over and fell forward, slamming his head onto the ground then slumped to the side. It happened so quickly that no one even moved.

The Emperor blinked at what had just transpired before him. "You would say you have the right to protect yourself … is this so, Kito?"

"I believe so."

The Emperor saw Zekec cower to the ground, open-mouthed and colour drained from his face. Nikko was curled up in a small ball beside him. Desora looked just as surprised and pale as Zekec. *At least he is standing,* thought the Emperor.

The Emperor glared at Kito. "And where may I ask did you learn that? Would I not be right in saying it is a trick of the Masters, Kito?"

"I would not know."

"Did you ever learn about respecting your Emperor, Kito? About bowing before him? Where was it you grew up, just north of the City of Samos, perchance?"

"I have lived in the jungle. It was in bushland just southeast of the palace that I found the coach. You recall my report of the coach, do you not?" Kito stood with eyes unfocused, unseeing.

Then it dawned on the Emperor. *My word. He is blind!* He began to walk around Kito again. Through holes in his torn tunic, the Emperor saw cuts and large patches of dark blue bruising. "Kito, I heard from a reliable source that you were in the city of Samos."

Kito's voice remained deep and calm. "I heard from a reliable source that the water was not to come ..."

Before he could finish, the Emperor kicked out his foot, landing it on a large gash behind Kito's left thigh. With a grunt, Kito fell onto his knee.

The Emperor walked over to the prince. "I believe the two of you have a score to settle, my son."

Desora's eyes lit up. "Indeed, I do, my Emperor." He made an exaggerated bow and, drawing his sword, strode into the circle of onlookers. As the prince got within striking range, Kito stood up to his full height. With the contrast between their statures, the prince appeared feeble.

Unsure, the prince darted about attempting to flank Kito, but at every move he made, it appeared Kito knew what that move would be. After a great number of feigns, the prince lunged at Kito, who moved with the grace of a cat and struck with the speed of the cobra. Pushing aside the sword with the back of his left hand, he turned his back to Desora, then drove his right elbow into the prince's face. Desora's nose burst, producing a copious amount of dark red blood. He fell to the ground at the same time as his sword, two body lengths away, motionless.

The Emperor roared for his guards, but before they could move, someone else also yelled, and the entire crowd surged forward, pulling Kito to the ground. Within moments, he disappeared under the mob. The Emperor held up his hand, confused. The guards stopped, not knowing what to do. Two villagers carried the unconscious prince past the Emperor, yelling, "Your Excellency, quickly it is not safe! We must get the Prince out of here."

The Emperor saw the mass of people, driving elbows and fists into Kito, expressing hatred with passion. The Emperor smiled and waved to the guards to return to their horses. With the crack of a whip and a whistle, the coach sped off.

Manchu and Kai watched the coach go with Zekec waving his pocket cloth in the air, running after it. Scoffing, they turned back to see Nikko, still curled up in a ball. Passing each other a knowing look, Manchu and Kai went over and gave him a few kicks of their own until the man scrambled to his feet, and chased after Zekec.

Through the hordes of people, Manchu and Kai made their way in to break the uproar. Kito lay on the dusty ground. Kai leant in and shook his foot. "Hey, big fellow, the word around town is that you need a bath." Laughter broke the tension.

Kito sat up. "I do not understand, Kai. Is Manchu there also?"

"I am here, Kito. Do not worry yourself; we need to do one more thing with you. I can see you are in pain, my friend, but you must let these people bathe you in the river now."

Kito frowned. "Are you sure we need to do this? They all seemed quite angry with me."

Manchu gave a wave, and many hands supported Kito. They lifted him over their heads and carried him towards the river, amongst light banter they sang one of his songs.

Kito was eased into the water, and a woman leaned in close to him. "The river is still a little dirty from its wound, but much better than yesterday. We will let you down, but you must trust us and breathe, Kito."

"Who are you, may I ask?"

"Yes, we have not before spoken. My name is Jin, I am joined with Manchu."

"I thank you, Jin. I do feel I need a bath." Like a nervous, lost boy, Kito did his best to smile. *These people who have not so much as bowed to me, now wish to bathe me like some sort of prince. I could quite easily have found my way down to the river's edge.*

"Kito?"

"Yes, Jin."

"We need to remove your tunic."

"What? Why, Jin?"

***

Jin could not help but smile. For all his size, this young man really was little more than a boy. "Because it is ruined. We will need all your clothes, thank you, Kito."

Reluctantly, Kito helped as he was undressed. Jin gasped at the sight of his back, covered in scars of claws, whips and chains. Now massive bruising was forming as the result of his turbulent time in the fury of the flood. She closed her eyes for a moment and shook her head. *This young man has many stories of regret, yet all I have ever done is ignore his very presence.* Now she was deeply in his debt.

Kito felt Jin's eyes on his back. Even in the sweltering heat, he had kept his tunic on to hide his many scars. Naked, he sat waist deep, hoping the water really was dirty enough to keep his modesty.

"Kito, we are finished now. Here is a towel, and there are dry clothes on the bank for you." Jin tapped his shoulder as everyone left the water.

He stood up straight, turning into the cloth as it was gently wrapped around him twice and tied off firmly. One of the men took his hand and placed it on his own shoulder, just as Orton had done. Kito stood tall and walked with his head up.

They headed downstream a little way, then turned into what was clearly a bush track. Narpa spoke gently. "Kito, would you please bend down low – we wish to keep you dead." Despite the bizarre request, Kito did as he was bid. Soon enough, they entered a tent where Narpa guided Kito to a pillow to make himself comfortable.

A second voice asked, "Kito, do you know who I am?"

"Well, yes, Manchu, we have met already. Please sit with me. This is your tent?"

Manchu sat beside Kito. "Yes, it is, Kito. We wish for you to feel at home here with us."

Kito thought for some time. "Was it your friend that I pulled from the river yesterday?"

"Indeed, Kito. Jin, Kai and I are in your debt."

"No one is in my debt. I am sorry to say it was Jong's wife, Quinn, that I was trying to rescue, and failed. I have asked Jong and little Orton for their forgiveness."

"They are in shock and grieving their loss. They know how much you tried."

"I am dry. May I bother you for some water?" Kito heard a whisper go through the room and the sound of a leather vessel being handed along. It was not Manchu that handed it to him. Kito thought at least seven people were in the small tent. There was silence as he drank. Tying the skin off again, he handed it back to the person who had given it to him. "Manchu, who is it that I saved yesterday?"

Jin looked to her daughter, Mikka, who was sleeping on cushions near where Kito sat. Kito turned and reached out towards Mikka. For a long moment, he held his hand just short of her, then, as he pulled back, he lifted his head. "Is this her?"

Manchu nodded. "Yes, Kito."

"She is strong. She will be well soon enough." He paused for some time. "I tried to save a friend who was kind to me when I was a stranger here. I got it wrong, and it was instead this one I saved, the one special to you. I am pleased for you, but I am also sad for Jong and his family."

The room remained silent.

"So, this is Mikka. May I ask how old she is?"

"Just fifteen, Kito," Manchu answered.

Jin saw the pain in Jong's eyes. He turned to leave the room, holding Orton by the hand. Jin followed, and outside, Jong turned to her. "I thank you for making us welcome to your home. Kito is right, Mikka is young and strong, she will be well soon enough."

Jin bowed deeply to Jong; he reciprocated then left. She took a moment to calm herself before pushing aside the flap and re-entering. She looked at Mikka sleeping, then to the big, young man who had leapt into what should have been certain death. He was now stretched out, sound asleep. Sitting in the opposite corner with his legs crossed, watching his sister, Kai looked as if he would never leave her again.

***

The next morning, Kito stirred then lay still for a time, letting himself wake up properly. There was much activity in the space around him. He sat up, crossing his legs.

"Well, good morning, Kito. I am sorry to have woken you. We are going to have to pack for our big journey back home. Are you hungry?"

"Good morning, Jin." Still seated on his cushion, he dipped his head. "Yes, I am very hungry."

"And how is your throat? Still a little sore, I dare say?"

"Yes, too much mud, I believe."

"I would say so, Kito. Mikka has said the same thing."

"I see she has gone this morning."

Jin turned from her cooking, her face lit up. "You can see, Kito?"

Kito held up a hand. "No, just a figure of speech, I'm afraid."

"Of course, Kito, yes, I am sure it is." She went back to fetching some rice and added some honey.

"Jin, just how good is Mikka, really?"

"She is out with her father pulling down the food hall, but do not concern yourself with her for now, young man." She knelt before him, dipped her head and held out the food bowl. Instinctively, Kito reached out and took it. Jin stood. "I shall fetch you some water to wash that down."

"I do not wish to be a burden to you and your family, Jin, but until I can work out what it is I am meant to do with myself, I ..." At a loss and confused, words failed him.

"Listen to me, Kito," said Jin quietly, "I don't know who whipped you, I don't know who used a chain on you, and I have no idea where you got those massive scratches or where you have come from, but I can tell you this. We all saw you dive into that muddy mass, and when you came back out, you had my daughter in your arms. So, I *do* know that I and my family wish for you to stay with us. When we get back to our home, we will introduce you to our village physician. If anyone can help you, she can. And you, Kito, will always be welcome in our village, our home."

Kito sat in silence for a time. "I did what I did. If I had known that it would make me blind, would I do it again? I just cannot say, but thank you, Jin. I have no family, and so I will be in your debt."

Jin gazed upon Kito sitting with his legs crossed, feet on his knees, holding his bowl. To her, he seemed to glow, God-like. Having him staying in her house would make them the better for it. She knew this to be so.

Jong and Orton were at the food hall. Everyone worked together in packing up the camps. Orton was there to assist Jong, claiming to everyone's amusement that every good job has a supervisor and such an important man would have an apprentice. And so it was Orton's job to be at his grandfather's side, chin up, chest out and hands proudly clasped behind his back. On more than one occasion, Jong was seen conferring with his bold little apprentice.

A cheer went up as the final tent collapsed and the ropes were put away. The people talked excitedly and gave thanks to one another. Part of the group prepared to drag two large poles with them, bridging the canal to get back to their home on the banks of the Yellow River, further north. The rest of the makeshift Colonial Dig village was to head south to the stone village of Kadra on the coast.

Manchu and his son, Kai, were about to head back when Narpa came over with Mikka. "Manchu, I talked to Mikka and was wondering if I could be of help in getting your own place ready, since you all came down to help with pulling down the food hall."

"That would be great, Narpa." Manchu looked at his daughter. Her brown eyes sparkled, and her hair ran down over her shoulders; never was a father so proud. Stood beside her, Narpa was leaning towards her just a little. Mikka gazed at Narpa and giggled. Manchu's face dropped. "On second thoughts, Narpa, I think you should go and help out at your own dwelling. Let your mother and father know Jin and I are very grateful for taking in Kai as we have become low for room."

The smile slid off Narpa's face, as it did from Kai's. "Father?"

Manchu looked at Kai with cool, dark eyes. Kai knew immediately not to argue. "Oh yes, Narpa, I forgot … Jin wishes to have just the four of us together as we set off, as a family, you know." Tilting his head towards Mikka, who was oblivious to what was happening.

"Oh yes, how rude of me, sorry Kai. Manchu, I will see you all on the road, no doubt." Narpa bowed.

Manchu reached out and pulled Mikka to his side. Kai stepped forward. "Narpa, I will walk with you. Father, I will not be long." Manchu watched the two walk away.

"Father, are you not well?" Mikka was trying to pry his hand off hers. "Father, you are squeezing my hand."

"Oh, forgive me, my sweet." He let her go, then he drew her in and hugged her tightly.

"Father, what is wrong?"

Manchu hugged her for a long time, not caring that all tents had now been struck down, and he had many onlookers. Many had lost loved ones in the flood. They all understood, some smiled, some cried, some did both and holding Orton, Jong was amongst them.

When Manchu and Mikka returned to their camp, they found that everything was already packed and on the cart. Manchu looked at the laden cart. "How did you get all this on, my dear woman?"

"I would like to take all the credit, but Kito played a large part in the work."

Mikka was clearly excited. "He can see again, Mother?"

Jin sighed. "No, my daughter, but once I walked him to the cart, he just seemed to know what to do."

Manchu looked vexed with Jin. "How can you let an invalid do our duties?"

She looked him in the eye. "It would not please him to be called an invalid, Manchu."

Manchu closed his eyes in regret. "I am tired and am wrong to speak with you this way."

She peered long into his dark eyes. "What is it that troubles you so, Manchu?"

"Where is Kito now?"

"Mikka, can you take this headcloth down to Kito – he is resting under a tree by the river. Show him how to wear it like the men do in the summer. Be sure to tell him he must keep it on for a few days."

Mikka took the cloth and went off, humming one of Kito's songs on the way. Jin looked back at Manchu. "So, what is it that troubles you, my love? These should be happy times for us."

"Yes, of course, Jin. I just have not been at rest of late."

"But *what* is it that troubles you, Manchu?"

"Yesterday, when Kito talked with the Emperor, he was about to ask why we were not told about the coming water."

"Manchu, please … we must never talk of this again, never."

"Yes, but …"

"Never, Manchu. Please promise me. Never." Her fearful voice trailed off.

"I promise never to bring this up with you again, my love."

Satisfied, she patted down her dusty clothes.

"Jin, do you think Kito is a Master?"

Jin looked about. Nobody was within ears' reach. "I don't know how he emerged from the cage, I don't know how he came back from the muddy water, I don't know how he caught the whip or even walked himself back to the river just now."

"He walked himself to the river? How do you know he did not fall in?" Manchu turned towards the river, hoping to see Kito sitting beneath a tree.

Jin put a hand on his chest, drawing his attention. "All I know is we should look out for him until we are back at our home. Then we should take him to Sankun."

"What? Are you sure, Jin? I mean … you think Sankun would see Kito?"

"Yes, Manchu, I have given it a great deal of thought. I feel strongly that it is the exact right thing to do."

"Then so be it, Jin. If it is your wish, then it must be so."

37 The Staghorn

Kito, Kai and Narpa had followed the river's edge downstream for several days, being careful to stay under the cover of trees until it seemed unlikely that the Imperial Guard would pursue them this far.

Narpa pointed. "There is the track, Kai; I knew we were close."

The track would reunite them with the caravan, then it would take them one full moon to get to Kadra Village, just in time to start harvesting the crops.

Kito could feel the change in the air as they turned away from the river. As they entered the dense jungle on a narrow track, he almost felt at home. He kept his hand on Kai's shoulder for guidance. He and Kai had taken a liking to each other, but for some reason, Narpa stayed distant.

They travelled for some time before Kito spoke. "We should make camp soon; we will need more food and it will rain tonight."

The two men looked to one another, then Kai asked, "It didn't look like rain when we entered the jungle, Kito. What makes you think we will need shelter?"

Kito moved his head about like he could actually see. "Yes, I think it will rain tonight. We should find shelter, and I could help with the hunt if you wish."

Narpa raised his brows. "Yes, Kito, it would be good to have some fresh meat, but just how do *you* intend to help us with that?"

"I grew up in a jungle not unlike this one, Narpa. I learned much about surviving in it."

"And how can you possibly know it was jungle like this one, Kito?"

"Well, that's easy, Narpa. I can smell the rotting faeces of the orangutan. I know it was the orang's because I stood in it a little way back and it had the leaves of the prickly ash tree in it. They eat the leaves last because the berries give them indigestion and the leaves help clear it. I can also tell you that deer are around because I can smell the urine with which the male marks his territory. Not far from here are some wild boars. There is a staghorn up in that tree just over there. I can hear the bees working it and it is that staghorn that will bring the wild boar to us."

Kai and Narpa stood dumbfounded. "That was amazing, Kito, only one thing though."

Frowning, Kito asked, "And what is that, Kai?"

"How did you know about the pigs?"

"From the moment the two of you saw your first bit of turned ground, you could not stop talking about them."

"Ha." Kai grinned. "Very well, but how is the staghorn going to get us the wild boar?"

"One of you is going to cut a piece out of it." Silence fell. Quietly, Kito added, "Or I will, if you wish."

Kai held up his hands. "No, no, I will climb up and cut out a piece." He drew out a long knife as he looked up at the staghorn. "Just what piece should I be aiming for, Kito?"

"You need to be looking for a rotten, smelly part. I always find it in the middle of the curve. Make sure you cut a wedge down deep, you want the water and fermenting leaves to fall to the ground. It is the richest piece, a real delicacy that is normally only given to the boar when a tree has fallen."

Narpa leaned in close to Kai and whispered. "This is a load of nonsense, you know. There is nothing my grandfather does not know about this jungle, and this is not part of it."

Kai looked briefly at Narpa, then back to the staghorn. "Kito, I am ready. You just want me to climb up there and cut out a wedge, letting it fall right to the ground, yes?"

"Yes, Kai, that is what I have explained – is it not, Narpa?" Narpa gave Kito a look of contempt, then saw Kai who, taken in by this ridiculous plan, had started to climb the tree.

"Kai, you seem to be close now. There will be a big branch above it, but is there a good branch to stand on?"

"Yes, Kito, there is. I will be safe to cut a good wedge out of it."

"Good, but do not cut too much out or the staghorn will die."

The staghorn wrapped around the massive tree, its tail hanging down some twenty feet. Kai called down. "How much is enough, Kito?"

"Maybe one quarter. Cut hard, it is very firm inside and white, like the inside of a coconut."

Kai swung his long knife, it cut deep and jammed. He levered and pulled the knife out, then swung hard again. Bees began to swarm angrily.

"Don't mind the bees on your face, Kai; they are feeding, not stinging. When you think you are down to the trunk, slide your knife down between it and the tree. Lever it out, but don't be too impatient, you can break a knife doing this."

Kai kept cutting, making sure he had cut all the way down both sides, then he reached up to slide in his knife, slightly unnerved as the bees swarmed under his arms. Steadying himself with his left arm up on the tree, he gently pulled on his knife. To his delight, the wedge popped out. Narpa stepped back as it hit the ground with a squelch. Thick fluid ran down the side of the tree trunk and the bees quickly swarmed on it.

Looking pleased, Kai walked along the branch, lowering his sweating arms as he did, then screamed. Kito immediately called out. "Oh, and be sure the bees have left you before lowering your arms."

"Agh, now you tell me, Kito. Thanks for that one."

As Kito let out a small, deep laugh, Narpa gave him a sharp look. "Kai, are you all right, my friend?

"Well, of course I am not all right, Narpa. I just suffered several stings and under my arm at that!"

"Well, it is not my fault, is it? I am not the one who failed to tell you, am I!" He sneered at Kito, who was still smiling.

Kai climbed down the tree as Narpa made a wide berth around the fallen staghorn covered with a frenzied swarm of bees. "I'm sure no pigs will want to come for that! Hold your arms up, Kai, I will scrape the stings." Kai was quick to oblige as Narpa pulled his hunting knife and got to work. Gently but quickly, Narpa scraped away the stings.

Once done, the two men found Kito sitting with his back to the trunk of a huge tree, cross-legged with his eyes closed. Narpa scoffed, but Kai held a finger up to silence him. They went back to their packs.

Kai pointed to a fallen tree over to one side. "Narpa, do you want to hide behind the log?"

"No, Kai, I would not like to cower down behind a log like a rabbit hiding from the ferret."

"Suit yourself. You can sit with Kito; he has the other flank covered." Without waiting for an answer, Kai picked up his bow and quiver, leaving Narpa to begrudgingly head for the tree and its occupant.

Kito had not moved a muscle. He did not even seem to be breathing, just sat with his eyes shut. Narpa stared at him. *Where has this man come from?* His knife was now free of its holster. He balanced it in his hand. All he would have to do is lean forward and drive it up into that obstinate, thick skull.

Staring blankly at Kito, he heard a sound he knew well. It was the unmistakeable noise of wild boar on the move. Narpa looked towards the sound as he sank down behind the tree's roots. He looked across to Kai, who lifted his hands as if to ask, 'Are you ready?'

Narpa quickly set about getting his first arrow ready, standing the rest up within reach against the tree root. More than one arrow would be needed to kill a boar with its protective thick, tough skin and stiff bristles.

Narpa checked Kai; he was watching intently upwind. Their positions were perfect. Everything was right and yet, *Something is very wrong.* He looked at the bait, which produced an obnoxious stench, like rotting meat. Narpa shook off the ill feeling, moving his attention to the noise as it came closer. Kai had sunk down low.

The noise grew louder, not just a few wild boars were coming, it sounded like a herd. Then the pigs broke cover. Three sows and their brood of varying ages and more boars than Narpa cared to count. Both were ready but knew not to shoot too soon. Neither man would shoot a sow with young, but the oldest piglets would be good eating and there were several good-sized boars.
Narpa waited for Kai, it was the way they had always done it. Kai just seemed to know when the right time was. *But what is he waiting for?*

Then Narpa understood: Kai wanted to know if the bait was of any use. Then their answer came. The pigs attacked the staghorn, pulling it up and trying to run off with it, only to be bowled over by a rival as the herd fought over the one piece, sometimes getting it in powerful jaws and with leaves trailing overhead they ran about blindly, only to run into another pig or, on one occasion, into the very tree from where it had come. Piglets squealed as they were tumbled in the mayhem.

Kai shot the boar carrying the staghorn. Before the boar hit the ground, a sow picked up the prize. Kai let fly a second arrow into the first boar, a death shot in the now vulnerable throat. Narpa was quick to follow Kai's lead, shooting a good-sized boar, but it turned away so he could not finish the kill. Without hesitating, Narpa turned to a young sow, sending it tumbling with a second arrow. The pig bucked several times, then stopped dead. The herd returned to the narrow gully from which they had emerged.

As quickly as it had all started, it was over, with most of the staghorn gone. Narpa walked over to his first shot, the second arrow deep in its chest. Kai had covered his shot. Relaxing now, the two men celebrated their good fortune. They would need an extra day to dress and smoke the bounty, ready for when they caught up with the caravan.

Kai peered over Narpa's shoulder. "Where is Kito?"

Narpa turned back toward the tree where he had been left. "I don't know. I expected that he would follow me."

"How was he to do that?" Kai glared at Narpa as he walked to Kito. Grudgingly, Narpa followed, but when they got there, they stopped still in their tracks. Kito was still asleep.

Narpa scoffed. "That figures."

Kai ignored him and bent down close to Kito. He was breathing regularly, sound asleep, slumped over, though still sitting. Kai stood and headed back to their bounty. He did not notice Narpa caress the hilt of his knife as he stood over Kito.

****

Narpa couldn't take his eyes off Kito until something to his left caught his eye. He turned to see that the movement was made by some heavy, rotting leaves. At first, they slid around in a small circle, though the rest of the jungle was quite still. He stepped back as the leaves, almost without sound, turned faster, rising in a tight whirl, drawing in more leaves and gathering height. Narpa's muscles tensed as he was frozen to the spot. The leaves now towered high over his head, spinning fast. He wanted to call out to Kai, but couldn't speak.

Kai was busy collecting and cleaning arrows. "Hey, Narpa, what do you think?"

Narpa tried to call back, but still couldn't. Then, without warning, the leaves blew right into his face. Narpa fell backwards, sprawling onto the ground.

"We could hang them all over that branch right there and smoke them. What do you reckon, Narpa?"

At first, Narpa was unable to get off the ground. Finally, he staggered back up, though shaking, and he made his way over to Kai. "Yeah," was all he could manage to say.

Kai turned to see his friend, covered from head to toe in rotting leaves.

"What in the name of the Gods have you done now, Narpa?"

All Narpa could do was point at Kito.

Kai turned square on and placed his fists firmly on his hips. "Now listen to me, Narpa … yes, we have been friends for all our memories, but that poor, underprivileged slave dived into what should have been his muddy grave, miraculously came back with my sister, only to end up blind himself. He has just shown us a skill that not even your grandfather knew … now we have no less than three prime pigs to smoke for the caravan. Kito is over there asleep, and still you wish to accuse him? I don't know what your problem is, but you need to know, my family is in huge debt to him, and right now, he is in *my* care." Kai peered past Narpa at Kito, lowering his voice. "I have no idea but I would think if I lost my eyesight, it would be very tiring just trying to do mundane day to day things, let alone set out on a journey lik this." He held up a hand before Narpa could respond then turned and started clearing leaves at his chosen place for a fire.

Without further word, the two men went about making a fire, hanging the boar with long green ferns hung over them to capture the smoke. They made a simple lean-to against that. Narpa protested that it was a waste of time, but helped finish it anyway.

"So, are we still friends, Narpa?"

Narpa stirred the fire and did not look up. Kai went over and stood beside him. Narpa ignored him. Kai elbowed him. Narpa pushed his arm away. Kai shoved him. Narpa shoved him back harder.

Kai grabbed Narpa in a full bear hug. "Tell me we are still friends, Narpa. I would not want to live even one day without you as my friend!"

"Get off me, you fool. Someone may see the two of us and get the wrong idea." The two young men broke, laughing together.

After they had set the pork to smoke, they sat down for a well-deserved rest, sharing a water bottle and watching the thick smoke billowing out.

"Kai, have you heard the story about the Crystal Skull?"

"Well, of course I've heard the legend of the Crystal Skull, dimwit."

Narpa chose to ignore the insult. "Yes, we all know the legend, but do you think there is truth in it?"

Kai rubbed his hand over his face, tired after their busy day. Narpa did so love this sort of conversation. "I really would not like to say. It is like asking what sort of growing season we are to have the summer after next. We all know they come in cycles, but knowing just where we are in the cycle is anyone's guess."

"Yes, though we can just ask Sankun about the cycle and summers. She will know and tell us. But the Skulls are legend, even she cannot say if they are real."

Kai thought for a moment. "Mother asked her once, and she told her the Skulls are real and that they will be found soon."

"That does not mean anything. Herb doctors and spirit people have been saying that since the legend was born. No, it does not mean a thing."

Kai lay back, watching the smoke billowing up through the lower canopy. "No, Narpa, Sankun said to Mother, *The one who floats by the torch will see the Crystals and he will get the seven together for the better,*' and she said it will happen in her time. That's Mother's lifetime, Narpa."

Narpa faced Kai. "She never said that. You're just making it up."

"If you say so, Narpa, then it must be so," Kai responded flatly.

"Really, Kai? Sankun really said that? How long have you known this?"

Ill at ease, Kai rolled his eyes. "Please do not say anything to anyone, Narpa, no one. Mother trusted me with this and swore me to secrecy, but you are my best friend and, well, now you know."

Narpa spoke quietly. "Yes, I can see that, Kai, and it is safe with me. I swear I will not disrespect our friendship."

Lying down, Kai pulled over his pack and slipped it under his head to keep it dry from the rising damp of the jungle floor. He watched the thick smoke still billowing out, hypnotic almost and making his eyelids heavy. He smiled. "The pork will be good."

"Kai. Those pigs came up from the little valley to the north."

"Yes, Narpa."

"But the wind was coming from the southeast."

Kai opened his eyes. Narpa had a valid point. "Are you sure, Narpa? I hadn't noticed."

"I knew something wasn't right, but I just couldn't put my finger on it. Now it popped into my head, watching the smoke."

Kai knew where the pigs had re-entered the small valley. He checked their location. Narpa was right. Now he had a problem, in a world where black is black and the sun rises in the east, the pigs cannot come from upwind tracking a scent. "Unless the gully sweeps around to the south-east, then they may have just come up under cover."

"No, Kai, when in search of food, they would have followed the scent, not the valley. You know this."

"Well, we could take a short walk and see which way the valley goes, Narpa."

"Good suggestion, Kai. And would we like to put a small wager on it?"

***

"Really? And just what are we to use for a wager, Narpa? Neither one of us is worth anything at all."

Narpa smiled: Kai was nibbling at his bait. "Well, I was thinking it may be time to settle who is to carry the two pigs for the first day. I am saying, the valley does not go anywhere near the southeast, Kai."

Kai frowned. It was a narrow window of chance for him to win, but before he could answer, a deep voice replied. "There are three of us, Narpa. Why can we not carry one each? Would this not be fair in your village?"

Narpa saw Kito walking to the fire, unassisted. "Kito, your eyes are good?"

Kai watched Kito, with the burning question about the wind direction and the wild boar on his mind. He would only talk to his father on such a strange, impossible matter.

"No, Narpa, but half the jungle could find their way to your fire with all the talking." Neither man laughed. Kito sat down near Kai but turned to Narpa. "Is the track very hilly from here?"

Narpa searched his memory. "No, it is reasonably easy from here, and the track should be good. It is used by hunters on horseback in all seasons."

"When the two of you say it is time to leave, I would like to try a different method of tagging, so not to slow us down any more than I have already."

Kai shook his head. "Please do not concern yourself with that, Kito. The trip will take as long as it will take." He looked at the meat smoking over the fire. "And I do not think we are to starve out here, do you?"

Kito chuckled. "Not if the smell of smoking pork is anything to go by, Kai. I'm famished."

They settled around the fire in readiness of their bounty. Then they all heard it. The gentle pitter-patter of rain on the lean-to.

38 Revelation

The middle-aged man dispatched another two guards. Never had a man been seen to move so fast or gracefully. He heard the whip being drawn back in readiness for its launch. The whip was sent sailing forward like a snake to strike, and in one graceful move, the man sidestepped the whip, letting it wrap itself around his spear, then snatched the handle from the hand of the attacker. The brass butt whistled past him, hitting a guard in the back of his head, dropping him like a stone, with the whip coiling on his back.

The man turned to the Emperor. "Have you no more?"

The Emperor rolled his eyes as the man bent over and picked up the whip. After defeating all attackers, his breath was still steady. He walked to the young man sitting boldly on his meticulously groomed horse. "I believe this is yours, Chenghou."

"How dare you call me by my name! Have you no teachings at all, pilgrim?"

The man stopped just short of handing the whip back. "But of course. I had the very same teachings as your Emperor, you may call me Hannu Hasuca. Congratulations on making Commander, Chenghou. Your father would be pleased. I knew him well."

Hasuca gave a curt bow, handed the whip to the confused Commander and turned to the Emperor, smiling. "Hannu Koe. Greetings, my brother."

***

There was a call from behind the deerskin hanging on the wall. Hasuca woke with a start, rose to his feet and pulled the deerskin aside. It was Trina.

"Ah, my good friend and life companion, come in, please sit down for some hot tea."

"You will not have to offer twice."

The two bowed deeply to each other, then hugged like the old friends they were. As she stepped in, Hasuca took her coat.

"It's cool in the caves, Hasuca."

Hasuca put the water back on the boil. "I believe you just need to harden up, old girl."

A smile graced the dark woman's face. "If I were any harder, old boy, you would be too afraid just to be in the same room as I."

Hasuca's laugh filled the room, and Trina could not help laughing with him. He turned back to her. "The truth of it is, I don't know. Does winter feel so cold now because summer in the jungle was so hot, or am I just getting on in years, Trina?"

"Now who is being soft? You have many a good year in you yet, old boy."

Hasuca did not comment. As the water boiled, he filled her mug, sprinkling in some herbs.

"If you would like to open the door, my dear lady Trina, I feel like a hot soak. I know you will not turn down the opportunity to limber up your old bones." He grinned mischievously as she opened the door, letting him lead her out, she gave him a firm slap on the bottom.

"Oy!" was all he could manage as he scurried passed the lean-to with the two hot mugs.

They undressed in silence. Queen Trina wanted to continue the topic that had arisen in the cabin, and Hasuca wondered how to avoid it. The water was not hot, just pleasantly warm. He averted his eyes to let her in.

"The Gods were looking out for you when they put this in, Hasuca."

"Yes, I am indeed spoilt." He paused a moment. "Trina, I have news I wish to share with you."

Trina peered into his eyes, sparkling with excitement. "Go on then, out with it."

"I have a daughter."

Her face dropped. "What?"

"I found out just recently that Yaan has a twin sister."

Shocked, Trina stammered. "Yaan has a twin, and you never knew?"

"It is no wonder Sha'Doe, bless her memory, died on the table. She had triplets. Once I knew about it, I went back over those events to try and remember. It seems that Yaan and my daughter, Tanica, are twins in every way. Desora, though, was in a water carrier of his own."

"Hmm. You can say that again." Trina noted his grimace. She wanted to talk some more about this Tanica, as she had struck a nerve with her comment about Desora.

"Have you seen Kito lately?"

His face lit up. "Ah, yes! From what I have heard, I do believe he is quite the people's hero. The Emperor flooded the canal before the people had moved out, and Kito dived in and pulled out the only survivor. Can you believe it?"

Trina frowned. "Why did the Emperor flood the canal before his people were out, Hasuca?" She was careful not to refer to the Emperor by name. It was not her place to speak badly of him.

"I think he wanted to see what would happen, I guess."

Again, Trina found herself wondering why the Gods had allowed Hannu Koe to seize power, and why Hasuca had let him. *For the life of me, I can see no good in it.* She made an effort to move on her train of thought. "So, our boy is a bit of a hero then. Well, I never."

The joy returned to Hasuca's face. "You should have seen it, Trina, it was chaos, but he dived right in, no hesitation. He was just in time, too. By the Gods, that boy is fast on the foot."

Trina smiled at Hasuca's obvious pride. "Faster than you when you were in your prime, old boy?"

Hasuca laughed at Trina's cheeky grin. "On foot, maybe. As for the rest of it, well, we will see."

"Hasuca, did you hear that the Emperor has ordered an oversized vessel from the best yard in town? That's why I made the trip, or at least one of my reasons. It seems the rumours are true. The Emperor has made a maritime commission, though no one is saying why, how big or how many."

When Trina finished relating all that she had gathered, she sat silent. Hasuca stroked his lengthening beard as he put the pieces together. For a long time, he stared across the grassy clearing into the jungle. Trina could read his face well enough to know how troubled he was about what was happening. He sighed and looked down at his hands, lifting them out of the water and turning them to see back and front.

Queen Trina reached out and took his hand. "My dear friend, if it did not feel right at the time, then it was not right. You can trust that it was the correct decision based on the information you had."

Hasuca put a hand over hers. "But I knew he had plans that were wrong for our nation; I walked away. I came here. Am I but a coward? Did I outsmart the man, or have I just run and hidden, like the weasel?"

She shook his arm. "No. When you left the Palace, what was it that you wanted to achieve here?"

Hasuca remembered his dreams from the Palace. "I knew it was my duty to intercept the gifted one."

"Yes. And you did. And he is coming back to you, soon, Hasuca. There is a bigger plan, and we are merely small parts in the total of that plan."

"If I had just taken out Koe in the first place, none of those people would have perished!" He turned to Trina, "And the worst is yet to come, Trina. Much worse."

"What exactly is the gifted one meant to do, Hasuca?"

Hasuca's troubled face smoothed. "Ah, now, Kito really is a diamond." Hasuca tried to read her face, but he could not see past her cheeky smile. "What is it, Trina? What makes you doubt that he is part of the Gods' plans?"

Trina shook both his hands. "Oh, Hasuca, in the scheme of things, it is nothing really, but have you searched the meaning of the name, Kito?"

"No, I saw no reason to. Please, do tell."

"In my native tongue, it means a jewel."

Hasuca sat momentarily. "So, he comes on a vessel not knowing his family, village or land. An old woman he has never seen before, gives him a name in her own tongue and in your language, it means jewel? Did I miss anything?"

"No, that pretty much covers it, Hasuca." Trina had one burning question left. No matter how many times she rehearsed it, she thought it sounded self-indulgent, although it was only natural that she would want to know if she was to return to her homelands. She knew Mabutu had remarried. It still hurt, but the Pharaoh's offer had been very generous, and it was a good joining for both nations. She felt a pull on her hands.

"My dear Trina, I understand this of you. You have been taken away from your own lands, your own people and shunted into this life, a life that is not yours. You have spent years in fear, both for your son and for your own land. So, now that it is all about to come to a head, you do not feel you can burden your friend with that one question."

The two studied one another. In a low tone, Hasuca continued. "When you smell smoke like you smell the baker's bread, you must do what is right, and then you must go to the town basin. There, a friend will offer you the help you need. You will befriend your worst enemy – for you will need him. You will see peace, and you will walk the Valley of the Stone Temple. You will see your old and dearest friend, and you will see your homelands once more. However, you must leave me here. You must not look back or return after this time. This time will be our last."

Queen Trina tilted her head. He had fathomed out all these answers. Even though he doubted his own answers, he had searched out hers for her. She responded softly. "Oh, I am going to miss you. And I am never going to forget you. You must know, wherever I go, I will have your memory with me as a beacon. I will always carry your memory."

In silence, they gazed out at the jungle for the longest time. Trina pondered everything Hasuca had foretold. However, there was something else. Something had been said, and an insight was at the edge of her awareness. Then, it hit her so hard she was physically moved. She turned to Hasuca. He saw the colour draining from her face and pulled her in close, not letting her slip under the warm water.

"Trina! Queen Trina! What is it you have seen?"

She was shaking now. "In the name of the Gods, Hasuca, how could I have been so blind? It is so obvious, I looked right past it."

"What … what have we missed?"

"Hasuca, I know who Kito is!"

39 Sails

Admasin was rubbing down some new oars that were made for stock. They had already been meticulously oiled when completed, but after being on the shelf for some time, he liked to give them another going over. It helped keep the good reputation that his old friend, Bua, had earned for the business. Linseed oil rubbed in hard, then a coating of beeswax gave them long-term endurance on the harsh sea. His concentration was broken by some heavy footsteps as he finished applying the beeswax.

The gentleman spoke with a pompous tone. "Excuse me, I am here on very important business, of the Palace, no less."

Admasin put the lid on his beeswax and leaned on the counter. "Well, well, you would be the Asset La Chun, owned by our Emperor."

Chun's face reddened in anger. It had never occurred to him that he was *owned* by the Emperor. "I beg your pardon, old man. *No one* owns La Chun! Is this quite clear?"

Admasin fell into a deep, if not somewhat over-emphasised, bow. "I do beg your pardon, Asset Chun, I was unaware that you were being paid by the Palace." He bowed again, but not before he saw the startled look on Chun's face. *No wonder they are called Assets,* he thought, *Ass for short.* When he rose again, the plump Asset was standing quite still, with a clenched jaw and eyes glaring.

As Admasin led the way to the stairs, he continued, "Please, Asset La Chun, it will be an honour to attend to you for your very important business. My Master, Patch, has been expecting you."

At the top of the stairs, Admasin gave the large oak door a loud rap. There was a pause, and the sound of some scurrying from behind the doors. Admasin rolled his eyes.

"Enter," came the eventual reply.

Admasin opened the door and turned to the side, announcing, "Asset La Chun is here to see you now, if you would, sir."

Patch had never seen such a grand spectacle of etiquette from Admasin before. "Er, very well, Admasin, that will be all, I guess."

Admasin let Chun walk through before turning to back out. He could see the plump Asset boldly standing before Patch in an attitude of command. Looking to the back of the Asset's balding head, he mumbled, "Bet I could get some quality wax out of that." The door closed with a thump.

Chun spun on his heels. "What did he say?"

Patch slapped Chun on the shoulder, nudging him towards the balcony. "I believe he said, 'I bet there is some quality wisdom in that,' but do not pay him any attention, he worked solidly for my father and when he passed away some time ago I felt, well, that I should keep him on, you see."

Chun wasn't so sure. "Yes, yes, quite so, indeed, Patch. Could I ask you your name, young man? I do so disagree with the nicknames of the younger generation, don't you?"

Patch showed Chun his seat on the balcony. After Chun was seated and seemed comfortable, he sat down himself. "Yes, Chun, though my name *is* Patch."

Chun stared blankly. "Well, right then … Patch."

Alexa arrived with a decanter and two goblets. She poured some lemon juice, bending over as Chun looked down her top. She placed the decanter on the table and smiled at him, walking away with a suggestive hip movement. When Chun finally turned back to see Patch's raised eyebrows, he coloured with his blunder of etiquette. He mopped his brow with a small cloth and greedily drank his lemon juice. It was tart, very tart.

Patch let Chun squirm in his embarrassment for some time, then cleared his throat. "So, has the Emperor mentioned that he and I made a deal, and am I correct in suggesting you are here to deliver my papers to affirm the commission, Asset Chun?"

Chun glared at Patch coldly. It was plain that he had seen himself playing a bigger role in this, his first real assignment on behalf of the Palace after the demise of Asset Kain. "Yes, Patch, I do indeed have the formal papers to commission the deal." Adjusting his chair to fit his bulging belly between it and the table, he lifted his satchel then pulled out a leather-bound file, rolled it out and handed several papers to Patch.

Patch took the papers to read. The description was simple. It stipulated that the vessels must be no less than two hundred feet in length and twice the width of anything that ever set out on the ocean before. It also detailed the two top-deck cabins for the Emperor and his personnel.

Patch sighed. It seemed an impossible task, though not one he cared to discuss with Chun. The papers further specified that timber would be supplied to the yard according to requirements. Finally, if the price was reasonable, no fewer than fifty more vessels would be commissioned. It was a deal with an open price, already signed by the Emperor.

Alexa came to top up Chun's empty glass. She took the papers from Patch and returned to his desk without a word.

Patch looked out over his yard, which was a hive of activity. He could feel Chun's anticipation, and knew that Chun wanted something out of the deal himself. Patch remembered the sudden disappearance of Kain. The Asset's powerful black belt should by rights have been offered to Tark first, and certainly it should never have left the City. Yet here sat Chun, wearing Kain's black belt. Patch had to hold Chun in favour.

He waved to Alexa, who came over with paper. He took it from her, wrote upon it and handed it back to her. "Asset Chun, I will be needing some help with this deal. I think you may be the right man to do it. Shall we?" He motioned to the door.

The two men descended the stairs and went into the undercover workshop. There were three vessels at different stages of construction. Impressed with the busy scene, Chun slowed, absorbing it.

"My father set this up some years ago." Chun caught up with Patch as they walked through the building. "He said building a vessel should be done under cover, so the timber does not begin to warp before completion. As we know now, he was right."

Chun almost tripped on some timber, doing his best to keep up. "Ahead of his time?"

Patch turned his head without taking his eyes off his working men. "What?"

"Your father ... would you say he was ahead of his time, Patch?"

"Yes, bless his soul, I would."

They came to another door, Patch opened it and led Chun through. In another large, undercover area, neatly stacked to the ceiling were great quantities of sawn timber.

"This is where the timber is stored for seasoning. See the stakes separating the boards so the air can circulate? By the time it is taken to the factory floor or out into the yard, it is lighter but more importantly, it has cured so it does not warp as it is shaped into the ship's contours by our experienced craftsmen. I am lucky to have the best in the land."

Patch led Chun through another door into the fresh air.

"Yes, Patch, I have heard."

Patch watched the plump man drawing out his cloth to mop his bald head that was shiny with sweat, and smiled at the effect of the brisk pace he had set through the factory. "What is it that you have heard, Chun?"

Still mopping his head, Chun looked back at the way they had come. "I have heard you have the best location on the river and the biggest yard. And you do. Plus, you employ the best craftsmen in the business. It is not surprising that the Emperor wants your yard – and the local vessel builders want a piece of you."

"And what do you want from me, Chun? What piece do you have your eye on?"

Chun stopped mopping his brow. He gazed up at the tall, handsome man, and a quiver of a smile came over his face, fear and greedy hope in his voice as he replied, "You said I may be able to help you with a problem you have, Patch. What would that problem be, may I ask?"

"To your right is jungle …"

Chun blinked. "Yes."

Patch pointed down towards the river. "Over there, you can see the broad, heart-shaped leaf of the empress tree – over there, the king cypress and just over there is the ginkgo biloba. I know the people who own this land. Asset Chun, you could buy it – for a price."

Chun looked at the trees, then back at Patch. He had not understood.

"Chun, if you were to purchase this land, you could fell the timber and build a mill." Patch waited as Chun pondered.

"I would supply the timber to you … at inflated prices?"

"No, Asset Chun, you will cut the timber and use the power of the river to mill it right here, then have it stacked to dry. You will then supply it to the Emperor, at reasonable prices. In time, you float more logs down the river to continue milling here. Soon, you will be buying other property all around town just to use up all the notes the Emperor will give for your millings. You will be very busy, if the Emperor orders more vessels."

Patch began to wonder whether Chun was capable of grasping the opportunity. It was a sound business prospect. It would also give Patch access to the best timber, which, on occasion, had been a problem. To have an Asset as a neighbour, an Asset with access to the best timber, would be a sound business move.

***

Alexa wandered through the city's back streets, which she knew as if she'd been born to them. She strolled, feeling the sun on her back and the gentle sea breeze on her face.

Inexplicably, she felt a chill. She slowed down, and it washed over her again. She spun about but could see no one. She searched around some more. Nothing and nobody. Continuing, she picked up the pace as she made her way to the silk factory. She was relieved after passing the salt well and rounding the building to Tark's office, where she knocked. She heard Tark swear then call, "Come!"

She took a deep breath. Tark was detestable, but she had a duty to perform for Patch and she would deal with him. She straightened herself, swung open the door and walked in towards Tark, who was seated at his desk.

"Well, look who we have here, if it isn't my favourite vessel builder. Please have a seat, make my place your own." He eyed her cotton blouse following her feminine curves, her tight leather pants and high boots. Her skin crawled, but she managed to smile. Getting to his desk, she leant over. Tark moved forward, not looking at her eyes.

She reached out and lifted his chin gently. "Now, Tark, you know I am spoken for by a man with power in this town."

Tark straightened himself up. "You know my family carries a lot of power in this town, too. You could raise your own standing just by being in my presence, Alexa."

"Though you lost that power with the loss of the black belt. This you also know."

The confident smile slid away from Tark's gaunt face. "That's not fair, Alexa, not fair at all. You know what happened, and that was also not right."

"No, Tark, I don't know. There were a lot of rumours, but you can tell me, Tark. What really happened to Kain?"

Tark could not hold her stare. "Actually, I don't know Alexa. He departed for the palace but never arrived, never came back. Just gone."

Alexa almost felt sorry for him, but looking beyond to the salt well outside, she remembered what this man really was. "Well, maybe you can help me with another problem."

The lust in his eyes was gone now. "What is it then, Alexa?"

Alexa turned Tark's desk notepaper around and got busy writing. "We believe you have a talented seamstress. Patch and I would like you to have her make a white garment to these dimensions. It is intended to be a present, so discretion would be appreciated."

Tark raised his eyebrows inquisitively. "In silk? It must be for someone very special." He took up Alexa's notes and handed them back to her. "You can give these to a woman called Janing. She is outside hanging some newly dyed silk. She will make it to your instructions, but it won't be cheap, not even for you, Alexa."

She smiled and headed for the door. "Yes, but the price will not be a problem, not in my social circle, Tark." She left Tark, laughing.

Alexa made her way through the factory, saddened by what she saw. Most of the labourers were women, and the few men were all old. None of them looked up as she moved through the factory. Finally, she came to a door leading outside and, stepping through, she saw a woman battling the sea breeze which was trying to blow over a hanging rack. Quickly, Alexa grabbed some rocks and dropped them on the feet of the racks. The woman wiped away tears of frustration.

"I am called Alexa. You are Janing, I assume?" They both bowed, Janing waited for Alexa to stand first. Alexa handed her the measurements. "I am told you are the best around. I have spoken to Tark, and he said you could make this for me."

"You are most kind, Alexa." She read the note. A look of fright came over her face, putting a hand over her mouth.

"Janing, what is it? Have I written something wrong?"

"No, Alexa, but these measurements, are for the Asset," she whispered, "Asset Chun, are they not?"

Alexa was stunned. "How could you know this from a set of numbers?"

"I can't usually, but you do not see many people this oversized in this land, do you?"

"No, I suppose not, but you do see them."

Janing pursed her lips. "And white will go well with that black belt he now wears."

Alexa surveyed Janing; there was more to her than met the eye. Her explanation was insightful. Janing could see more, but was not about to tell a stranger. Alexa changed the subject. "Janing, do you often have these problems with the drying racks?"

Janing was pleased Alexa had not laboured the point. "Yes, I normally put the rocks down on a breezy day like this, but today I forgot." She rubbed her forehead, her face betraying how bone tired she was.

"How many days do you work before a free day, Janing?"

"A free day?" she laughed. "What is this you speak of? Tark owns us. How could we have a free day?" Not actually wanting an answer, Janing moved the conversation on. "Some days, when the wind is a little stronger, the racks just seem to want to sail away. There is so much energy in the wind."

Alexa felt it was her cue to leave. "How long would it take for this garment, Janing, just so I have an idea as to when to revisit Tark?"

Janing smiled. "I will have it ready in a handful of days, and it will be right for you, Alexa."

"I know it will, Janing. I thank you."

Alexa walked away around the side of the factory. Getting back to the salt well, she stopped. She decided to take a different route to go home, even though it was a longer way.

***

Back at the office, Alexa poured some cool water for them both. Patch explained the deal he had struck with Asset Chun and the parcel of land. His mother and sisters would be very pleased with the sale. They had talked of letting it go, but it would make a prime block to build a boat yard, and a competitor would pay a premium price for the chance to challenge Patch. A mill was of no harm to Patch. It was, in fact, a stroke of genius to have the mill right next door, on the last parcel of buildable land left on this side of the river.

Patch sat back in his armchair, and Alexa, as always, sat on his desk. As he finished his report, he looked at her dazzling smile. He thanked the Gods again for his good fortune in life and, mostly, for Alexa. He rolled his chair forward and reached up to kiss her. Patch then refilled his glass and leant back in his chair. "I see you also have a story. Please tell me how your day went, my love. Did Tark make another pass at you?"

Alexa sighed, rolling her eyes. "Yes, as always. Must you send me there?"

"Well, of course. You get both the best result *and* the best price."

Alexa leant forward and pinched his cheeks. "Oh, you are incorrigible!"

40 Kadra Village

With a smoked pig strapped to his back, Kito followed Kai. Although still blind, he no longer had a hand on Kai's shoulder as the route was now much clearer. Occasionally, Kai would call 'dip' or 'root' and Kito would know to adjust his step. He had learnt to listen to Kai's footfall and think his way along. Setting a taxing pace for the trio, Narpa was well out in front.

After several days, they caught up with the caravan. The young men were greeted warmly. Some had become concerned about the time they had taken, but others felt the young men had done well not to regroup too early, alerting the Imperial Guard that Kito still walked the earth. For the caravan travellers, the bounty of smoked pig was a welcome treat. Kito was a little overwhelmed with the number of people coming to greet him and ask after his well-being.

The caravan resumed its long and arduous journey to their village. The rear of the line, where Kito had chosen to walk, was also the dustiest. Some of the elders decided to walk with him. He argued that they should be in the lead, but they persisted in their resolve to keep him company. Because of the multitude of footsteps in front of him, Kito found he could not hear properly and asked to be led. The elders took turns at leading him using a rope, deeming it a privilege.

***

When Kito awoke on the last morning of the journey, the smell of salt air wafted up his nostrils. The elders talked about the sea tributary that was near the village. They had to walk right around to the far side, and this would take a full day. In an air of growing excitement, they set out early.

Kito reflected on the plight of these people, having been forced from their homes to labour on the Colonial Dig and being away from their village for a very long time. He asked the Gods that they could again be the proud people he knew they once were.

The caravan was most of the way around the tributary when Kito heard talk about three strangers approaching on horseback. As they reached them, he heard one of the riders.

"What beastly thing is that?"

Kito stopped and turned to face them. "That *beastly thing* can talk and *its name* is Kito."

There was an awkward silence, then one of the riders dismounted and came to stand before Kito. "Well, now I know that you are called Kito, let me introduce myself. I am Hao." He turned to his companions and continued, "The man on the left is Bolli, and the other is called Yaan."

Kito turned and bowed, as did the elders who stood waiting for Kito. "Yaan, may I ask you, what brings you down out of the jungle?"

"I am not of the jungle, Kito. I have travelled from up at the snowline, but Hao and Bolli have come even further."

Kito turned to the other horseman. "Is this so, Bolli? You have travelled from even further afield?"

Hao tried to signal Bolli to be silent, but it was too late. "Yes, Kito, this is true. Hao and I have ventured far to see the coast."

Kito smiled. "Ah, and where do you come from, Bolli? You have many streams?"

"Yes, Kito."

"And you have big forest?"

"Yes."

"And you hunt some of the biggest game, Bolli?"

"Yes."

"Big game like elk, red bear and snow leopard?"

"Yes, the north is a very dangerous place to be hunting."

"So, how is it, Bolli, that you feel you can come south and insult any stranger that comes along, just for not looking like yourself?"

The elders, together with Yaan and Hao, burst into laughter at the blunt question.

Bolli's face turned red. He kicked his horse, drawing his short sword in one smooth action. His horse reared then sprang into full gallop. It was all Hao could do to dive out of the way, his own sword in hand as he sprang to his feet. As the dust settled, he gazed in amazement. Startled, Bolli's horse was getting back to its feet but Bolli, by contrast, was lying on his stomach. Kito had one knee in his back and was pulling Bolli's head back by his long hair.

Kito pointed Bolli's short sword directly at Hao. "Hao, we do not wish for any bloodshed. So Bolli, you spoke of a *beastly thing*, did you not?" Bolli tried his best to nod. "Then you would have no problem apologising to myself and the elders here, for your offensiveness, would you, Bolli?"

Bolli moved his head in consent. Kito eased off a little pressure and turned to address Yaan. "And you, frozen to your saddle, why have you come down here to the lowlands? Are you looking for trouble also?"

Yaan shook his head, leaning forward in his saddle. "No, Kito, we are not looking for bloodshed. We have come a long way just to avoid it. I have been down here before, and I wanted to come back to the people of the coast, to revisit old friends. This was an unfortunate start to our visit. Now, Kito, would you be kind enough to release my good friend Bolli?"

Kito stood and stepped back from Bolli, who rolled to his feet, glaring at him. Kito flicked up the short sword; it spun in the air several times, then Kito caught it and handed it to Bolli, holding it by the blade. Bolli reached out for his sword, but Kito withdrew it a little and the two froze. Then Kito asked, "Would you mind walking with me, Bolli? I would like to get to know you, if I may?"

Bolli turned to Hao, who shrugged. Not taking his eyes off Kito, her said, "Well, I guess so, Kito, whatever works for you."

"Splendid, Bolli. I sure would like to hear some of your hunting stories. Maybe you could let one of the elders ride your horse if you are to walk with me. What do you say, Bolli? Maybe two of these elders could ride your horse."

Bolli looked about, Yaan slid from his horse and approached an elder. In no time at all, four elders were on horseback as Bolli helped two more riders onto his own. Kito was up front, making friends with it. As it set off, Kito gently grabbed it by the tail and fell in behind. He turned and waved his other hand to Bolli. "Well, tell me about hunting one of those big bears. I could not imagine such a thing."

A little bewildered, Bolli hurried to catch up with Kito, doing his best to ignore Hao and Yaan's sniggering.

As Yaan and Hao left Bolli to his boasting of hunting wild bears, they admired the land. To their left was the tributary, the turquoise waters as flat as a tabletop. To their right, rolling hills were covered with crops of intense green.

As it neared dark, they walked out along a narrow ridge towards two huge, wooden gates. Stone walls on either side said no one without invitation could possibly enter.

The gates were open and so they went inside. Bolli stopped talking, studying the impressive scene. The entire area was paved. In the centre was a well; directly ahead, a blacksmith's working area. The fire burned red hot and the smoke disappeared up a chimney that went through this remarkable structure of stone. Some areas were obviously used for food storage, others housed livestock. Up above, four ascending rings of balconies wrapped right around the inner circle. It was quite the spectacle.

Yaan slapped Hao on the back. "Boys, welcome to Kadra Village. Come, we will tend to our horses first." Bolli retrieved his mount, and they headed for the stables.

Kito had entered the gates as if he had been through many times before, but then hesitated. A man came up and spoke to him. Kito bowed, put his hand on the man's shoulder and the two left.

Hao looked over at Bolli coming towards him. "Bolli, what was it like to spend the afternoon with the man who thrashed you in front of the elders?"

"Here you two go again." Yaan drew an exasperated breath. "Would you both quit it, at least while we are here. I have brought you here as guests. Now show some respect."

"I'm sorry, Yaan, you are quite right." Hao turned back to Bolli. "Really, what was he like?"

Bolli stood square on to Hao with a defensive stance. "I will have you know he has a good understanding of hunting. I would put up my hunting knife on him giving you a run for your mouth."

Hao straightened his posture, and Yaan stepped forward. "Hey, if I could trust you both to be quiet for a moment, I will find out where we can stay … if they will have us inside after this afternoon." There followed the quiet Yaan had hoped for.

Yaan handed Hao his reins and turned to go and find someone he knew. He hadn't gone far when, "Yaan! Is that you, Yaan?"

Yaan saw the older man coming his way. He was not tall but fit-looking despite his long grey hair. "Kale, my old friend?" The two bowed deeply then slapped each other on the shoulders.

"Well, haven't you grown into quite the young man. You look proud, and so you should be." Kale saw the two men standing with the horses. "Is Maki with you?"

"No. Father said it was time for me to go forth without them. I believe he wanted his time with Mother."

Kale headed towards the two men left conspicuously on their own. "Yaan, you came with some friends, I see. Shall we?"

Yaan hoped they had stopped their childish squabbling. Hao was still looking at the amazing structure, pointedly ignoring Bolli, who was doing much the same. Yaan broke the silence. "Hey, fellows, I want to introduce an old friend. Hao and Bolli, meet Kale; he is the elder of Kadra Village."

The three greeted one another, then Kale turned, indicating the stables. "Please, my new friends, come. We can stable and feed your horses then go upstairs and see that you are bedded comfortably. Yaan, you will please stay with my family?"

"That would indeed be my pleasure, Kale, most kind. You have made some impressive changes. Is it working for you?"

Kale changed the subject so Yaan did not pursue it. "So, tell me about San and Maki. Do the two of them still fight?"

"They are as cantankerous with each other as ever, Kale, though never in malice."

Kale laughed. "Indeed, they are people of good heart, alright."

After tending the horses, the four men headed up. The stairs were on the inside of the building so that people moving around were not at the mercy of the weather. They reached the first level and turned back towards the arch, which cut away into the boardwalk. There was still plenty of passage room to walk around.

Kale made his way to a set of doors. Inside, the men were surprised to see a large cooking stove in the centre of a hall. Two long, curved tables wrapped around the stove, with many people busily filling their plates from the abundance of food. Everyone served themselves then went to sit on cushions at low tables throughout the hall.

Kale watched Hao studying the way the chimney went up through the floor of the next level. Bolli was looking at one table in particular, which had no fewer than four young ladies sitting at it. They were giggling and looking back at him and his broad smile.

A young man entered the room. Yaan turned to Kale. "Is that …?"

"Yes, and he would be happy to speak with you, Yaan. I will look after your friends for now if you wish."

Yaan bowed. "Many thanks," and he left.

Hao was surprised at the number of people who seemed to know Yaan. One by one, more came in and welcomed him. He was clearly highly respected. Hao looked to Bolli, still preoccupied with the young ladies. It did not go unnoticed by Kale either.

"Bolli, if you would like to get yourself some food, it is traditional for our guests to sit over here, at the window seat."

"I thank you, Kale, some food and a seat after such a long journey is most welcome, though I feel I would like to mingle with some company for a change."

"Yes, I am sure you would, but you will be more comfortable following our etiquette whilst in our company. You would not want to insult us, would you, Bolli?"

"Insult your customs? Kale, no, you are quite right. I would be honoured to sit at your table." Taking Hao by surprise, he bowed deeply to Kale, not once looking back to his favourite table.

After fetching their food, they followed Kale to his window seat, where they sat on cushions and looked out of the low window. The building was set on the top of high cliffs then the land sloped steeply away until the terraces started. Hao had heard about growing rice on a hillside. He counted seven more terraces before the bottom of the hill, then some clear land and the jungle, which went right to the sand. A rising, full moon lit up the water. He turned to Kale. "Your location is like nothing I have ever seen before. It is quite beautiful."

Kale dipped his head. "You see the important things in life, Hao."

"I like to, yes, Kale. The Gods must get frustrated when we do not admire their works."

"Do you like the work of our Gods, Bolli?"

Bolli looked surprised at the question. "Well, yes, Kale. On our way here, we stayed with Yaan's family for the winter. That hot water is extraordinary. Have you seen it, Kale?"

"Yes, but it was some time ago, I'm afraid." Trying to hide his doubt and sorrow, he added, "I must make the effort to get back to see them all, maybe after the planting next spring."

Hao looked around at the marvellous building. *Why have they gone to all this trouble? Would these people not have been quite as happy in a humble village?* He spotted Kito sat at Yaan's table with his back to him. Even from this angle, he was huge. He'd heard about some of the black people on vessels that came into port, but had mostly dismissed them as exaggeration.

Kale had been watching Hao for some time, and Hao could sense his stare. "What is it that concerns you so, Kale?"

"Do you not see, Hao? It is what concerns *you* that concerns me."

Hao considered this for a moment. "You need not concern yourself about me. I am young and have much I wish to learn. That is all."

"I would like to meet your mother and father one day. They must be remarkable, proud people."

Hao stiffened slightly. "Yes, they were proud people." They looked at one another for a moment.

Kale lowered his head. "Sadly, I feel we have much in common." Kale moved his attention. "Bolli?"

Bolli looked up from his second serving. "Huh?"

"How long have you known Hao?"

Bolli chewed quickly and swallowed. "About five seasons now, I think. We were serving on the Magnar Wall together, but we didn't meet until we were leaving. We put together a plan to go in behind Barbarian lines to set free their horses after the last and most fierce battle of the autumn."

Kale looked to Hao, who just nodded.

Bolli continued. "We ran the horses down into the rift, right over scores of the Barbarians and rode on into the night. At about daybreak, we came back to our own gates where we crossed over, back onto our side once more. It went better than we had hoped. We had not just set the horses free, they followed us right back. It will take the Barbarian clan many seasons to recover."

"Is this so, Hao? The two of you went alone into Barbarian lands and took their horses and returned them into the Emperor's lands?"

Hao simply replied, "Yes."

A little less modestly, Bolli added, "And, killed countless Barbarians in the rift on the way through."

Kale put his hands on the table, intrigued. "Whose plan was this?"

Bolli motioned toward Hao. "It was his, but it was done fully by us both."

The conversation faltered as Bolli's attention turned to the young ladies clearing the tables. Some of the young men seemed eager to help them with the task. One of them came to take their dishes. Her face was perfect, neither a blemish nor a freckle, tanned, yet soft. Her bending over the table was just enough to tease Bolli, her breasts bouncing under her cotton wrap. "Kale, are you going to introduce these fine young men?"

All three men stood. "My apologies, Luhou." Kale indicated Bolli first. "This is Bolli, and this man is Hao. Both men have served the Palace."

"This is a lovely homestead you have here. The rooms seem endless," Bolli replied, flashing his winning smile.

"Yes, it must seem so when you first arrive. Has Father shown you around?" Bolli's face dropped as he looked to Kale, who responded with a curt bow of the head. Luhou continued. "It would be my pleasure to show you about, if it pleases you?"

Bolli remembered Kale's earlier comment. "Um, er, no thank you, most kind but after such a long journey I had better have an early night."

Luhou shot her father a dark look, then, bowing to all, she excused herself. Her father smiled nervously, the awkward silence interrupted only by Yaan arriving at the table, holding an object in a cloth wrapping. "Kale, if I may, I need your insight on a matter."

"Of course, if I can help. Do you wish to see me alone?"

Yaan shook his head. "Not at all." Gently, he rolled out the cloth.

Kale sat forward, captivated as the small, ornately decorated knife sparkled in the candlelight. "Where did you find this beauty?"

"We found it in a dried-up riverbed. You probably know the one, where all the crocodiles used to live."

"Used to live?"

"They are all dead now."

Kale sat back, studying Yaan's expression. "You say the river is dried up now?"

"Yes, not a trickle."

"So, the knife was just there, on the riverbed?"

"No, it was with a small human skeleton. Hao and I buried her."

Kale looked to Hao, who confirmed the story. Bolli sat motionless, clutching his hat on his knees. Kale gave a heavy sigh. "The river you speak of is the longest in the region. I am afraid we are responsible for it not flowing anymore."

"What? How are you responsible?

"Our people started the Colonial Dig at the Great Western Divide, then once the eastern end was finished, it was released to flow through to the Yellow River. The river you speak of cannot flow past the Colonial Dig. I am sorry."

The three men sat in silence for a moment, absorbing what had been revealed. Kale turned the knife about. "Well, I have to say it is quite a find, Yaan. I have never seen the likes of it. It appears to have belonged to someone with great power. Was there nothing else with the body? Seems strange, only to have this beautiful knife."

Bolli shot to his feet. "Sorry to interrupt, but I really think it is time for me to retire now, please."

Kale rose quietly. "Well, fair enough, Bolli. You have come a long way. I will show you to your rooms."

Hao was intrigued by Bolli's sudden interruption. Gently, Yaan rolled up his knife and moved back to his table, though not without glaring back over his shoulder at Bolli and his strange outburst.

Kale showed the two men up one level to a room of their own. It had two beds and a wide, low window. Bolli sat on the bed, trying it for bounce. "Oh, this is the life. Imagine sleeping in this bed, in this place, for the rest of your days. It is a long way from Magnar Wall, that's for sure, Hao."

Hao placed his things neatly at the foot of his bed. "You have the gift with the women, Bolli. Do this right and you may just get what you wish for."

Bolli rolled over onto his elbow. "She is beautiful, though, isn't she, Hao? I mean, really beautiful."

"Yes, she is truly something, Bolli." He looked up at his travel companion. "But I thought you liked Tammirie?"

Bolli flopped back down on his back. "Well, yes, Tammirie is someone special, but what was it about her daughter, Jeng? Something just not right there, don't you think?"

Hao looked at Bolli, who was staring at the ceiling. "I am going to tend my horse." Taking his things, he opened the door.

Bolli snickered. "Something not right with you and that horse either."

Hao did not return to his bed that night.

41 Beyond this League

Back at the office, Alexa was pleased her bad feeling seemed to have subsided. Now that she had the new garment for Asset La Chun, she would not have reason to go to that part of town.

As always, the thought of getting back to Patch put a smile on her face, even in the darkest of days. Before she'd seen Patch for the first time, she had already heard so much about him, and when she did finally meet him, she knew she could not leave. Never had she felt like this about a man. She stopped at the top of the stairs and knocked on the big oak door.

"Come."

She walked in and closed it.

"Woman, how many times do I have to tell you, *you* don't have to knock!"

Alexa went around to sit on Patch's desk, giving him a coy look. "Have I been a naughty girl again, boss?"

Patch's eyes narrowed, and ever so slightly, the sides of his mouth turned up. "Oh yes, I think you have been a very naughty girl."

Propping herself on his desk, she slipped off her shoes, letting them drop to the floor with a bump and placed her bare feet on either side of his chair. "Well, I would not like to lose my position here. Is there any other position I could take to please you so as not to lose my job? I would do anything for you, sir."

The sides of Patch's mouth curled a little more. "Anything, girl?"

She slipped forward, not looking at him. "Anything, just to save my job, sir."

Patch put his hands on the top of her legs and began massaging the inside of her thighs with his thumbs, passion burning in him.

A crash sounded from down on the factory floor, bringing both of them back to reality. Patch leapt to his feet and called through the open the window that looked down into the workshop floor. "Is everything alright down there?"

Several of the men were running to an overturned bowl of glue that had apparently blown off a stand. One man looked up. "Sorry, Patch, we may have lost some of it; we will save most though."

"See that you do and be sure to clean the floor thoroughly. That stuff is gum-based and will take months to wear off."

"Yes, sir, it will be cleaned thoroughly as you say."

Patch closed the window, Alexa beside him, looking down at the workshop floor. He saw something in her gaze. "Alexa, what is it?"

She did not take her eyes off the men working feverishly with scrapers and rags around the spilt glue. "When I went to the silk factory to put in the order for you, it was really sad to see the people there. They were not a proud people, more like withered shells of their former selves. I was talking to this woman, Janing, I think her name was. She said that the wind was blowing the drying racks away."

Returning to his seat, Patch watched the curtains gently wafting on the breeze. "Really?"

"Yes. She said that sometimes they just 'sail away.' You know, she also said that they never have a day off. Can you believe that? Not one day, ever." Patch glanced at the door. She looked over and back to Patch. "What?"

Just then, there was a knock, and at the same time, Patch answered. "Come!"

Alexa shook her head. "That is spooky the way you do that."

The door opened and in walked Admasin. He did not look at either of them but turned side on to the door, proclaiming, "I would like to announce, Asset La Chun to you, sir."

Patch shuffled some papers on his desk. "Come in, please, Asset Chun."

Chun strode in, carrying a small bag in one hand and his cane in the other. He dipped his head in a cursory greeting.

"Could I interest you in some hot tea, Chun?"

Chun fingered his cane. "No, thank you, it is quite warm out there, with a nice day and that sea breeze." He eased himself into a chair uninvited.

With a knowing smile, Patch asked, "Well, may I interest you in some house port then?"

Chun's face lit up as he looked towards the cabinet holding a near-full decanter and some glasses, trying to appear surprised. "Well, if it is not inconvenient, that would be divine, I feel."

"Chun, I am relatively pleased with our agreement so far. We have prepared a small token of our appreciation for the goodwill you have shown the business. Alexa, if you would."

Alexa placed a drink before Chun and handed him the package. With a boyish manner, Chun took the carefully wrapped gift from Alexa. "Oh well, thank you, Patch."

As the pure white silk was revealed, he slowly rose to his feet, pulling the garment from the packaging. "Oh yes, quite so, quite so." Holding it gently, he gazed over it. The fine sewing was impeccable, double-stitched with a fold-back all the way.

Patch spoke quietly as Chun turned the garment back and forth. "It has three belt loops to carry all your belts separately, so one does not block another. There will be no mistaking your power as an Asset to the Palace."

Chun's chin rose, and his neck wobbled as he nodded his head in agreement. He carefully folded the garment and placed it on the desk then reached down to the floor, picking up his own bag and placing it on the desk. "We have an agreement regarding the neighbouring land, as you will remember, Patch. You said you could arrange the sale on my behalf."

"Indeed, I did, and I can, Chun."

Chun opened the bag and pulled from it another, smaller purse. "This should suffice, I do feel." He reached over the desk and placed it before Patch, then sat back looking rather pleased with himself. Eyeing Chun, Patch didn't move. He had expected a note of price, or even an offer of purchase. He looked at the purse and what could possibly be in it. He had not even discussed the land proposition with his mother.

Patch picked it up; it was weighty and rattled as he placed it back down. He pulled the drawstring to reveal the contents. There were more jewels than he had ever seen before – not just at one time, but in total, and these were in one place – his place. He kept a straight face, though he was pleased that Chun couldn't see Alexa standing behind him, practically drooling. He didn't touch the contents, sitting back in his chair.

Chun mopped his brow and threw back his drink. "Is there a problem, Patch? I feel it is adequate for the land." Blankly, Patch looked at La Chun. Sure enough, Chun felt compelled to continue. "And there will be more to come. Not for the land, no, no. I understand you have quite the creative mind. I, by contrast, have a mind for strategy and leadership, so I would be seeking for you to develop the mill, as you say, using the timber on the property to build it."

Patch clasped his hands together. "I can see where you are going with this, but I will need a written instruction as to how much round wood you would be storing, how many cubes per day milled and how many stored to dry. How many vessel yards are you intending to supply with your mill, Chun?"

Chun sat forward in his seat, leaning over his cane. "By the Gods, no! Let us not forget who we are serving, Mr Patch. The Emperor would not take kindly to my supplying your competition."

Patch held up one hand. "It is just, Patch, La Chun. Very well, first I must work out how we are to power this new vessel. Once I have committed to a plan, I will be able to work out how many cubes and of what timber I will need. Until then, the timber on the land can stay exactly as it is."

Chun's face slumped. He sat back in his chair, somewhat disappointed. "Really? I had thought of the timber being felled and cut to season as the other preparations are made."

"I am still working on the design, Chun. This will be a vessel like no other. In its design, I will have to develop many new things, not just for its ability to cross the ocean in one piece but to construct the biggest vessel ever made. Do you understand, La Chun?"

Chun nodded emphatically, his neck wobbled like ripples on a pond.

Patch reminded himself that this man didn't live in the biggest city of Samos, yet was the Emperor's choice to rule it for him. *Somehow, the Emperor will have good reason for that.* He leant forward and lifted the drawstring, the weight in the purse pulled it closed. He opened a drawer in his desk and dropped it in. "We have much work to do together, Asset La Chun. I feel we have made great gains to date and this can be a profitable union for the two of us."

He paused thoughtfully for a moment, watching the curtains billowing in the breeze. "There is no one on this stretch of water, or in the world for that matter, who can match what I have already done, let alone achieve what the Emperor has asked of this yard. You have the land next door. I will design and build your mill. Then, if you wish for me to run it in your absence, you will pay by the purse full. You will profit, as will I, but you will pay me for my effort." There was a pause. "Do we have a clear understanding, Asset La Chun?" In a lower voice, Patch repeated, "Asset La Chun, we do have an understanding, don't we?"

Chun agreed.

Patch smiled. "Good. I think this is going to be a very profitable union for you and me."

Patch stood and bowed, holding it as he waited for Chun to stand. Realising it was his cue to leave, Chun fumbled out of his chair. He grabbed his refilled goblet and drank its contents then dipped his head to Patch and gathered his gift.

"Alexa, would you be so kind as to open the door for our new esteemed business neighbour."

Alexa opened the door with a flourish and stood aside to let Chun make his way out, which he did without another word, puffing over his cane as he went.

With Chun halfway down the stairs, Alexa closed the door, whispering urgently, "What in the name of the Gods was that, Patch?"

Patch, by contrast, had his boots up on his desk and was looking out of the front doors again. He waved a dismissive hand. "Agh, he is a pompous fool."

"That pompous fool carries the black belt of the Palace."

"Yes, but when it came time to make a deal about the vessels of the Palace, the Emperor came all this way to see that his wishes were fulfilled correctly. Chun may have the black belt, but the Emperor has his leash."

Alexa was taken aback by Patch's comments, though she knew he was right. She gently asked, "Patch, show me the jewels."

He opened the drawer and, without looking, pulled the purse out and dropped it on his desk. Tentatively, Alexa reached out to it, biting her bottom lip as she pulled open the top. She didn't notice Patch watching her adoringly. She gasped. "Gods in their heavens above, Patch, they are stunning."

"Yes." His attention was again drawn to the open doors. "Alexa, what was it you said about the silk factory?"

She didn't take her eyes off the jewels. "What?"

"The factory, we were talking about it when Asset Chun arrived unannounced."

Alexa looked up, puzzled. "Um, was it the bit about them never having a day off?" She looked back into the purse and picked up a large green emerald. Her smile returned.

"No, I mean the other bit, about the drying racks."

Alexa dragged her gaze from the purse, looking at the ceiling, searching her memory. "Oh yes, I think she said something like, the wind just blows the rack away, or over." She looked back into the purse and pulled out another jewel, holding it up to the light to admire the colours.

Patch shook his head. "No, I mean the other thing she said."

Alexa held a large blue topaz up to the light. "How can something so clear give off so much colour? They are like magic, but good magic of the Gods, they must be their gift. Something as beautiful as this. They must be." She put it back carefully and took another. "Oh, the Gods, this one is a bone carving with a gem." She held it up. It was meant to be on a cord because it had a hole through the top of the bone. Three sides came down in a spiral, getting wider as they did, and at the bottom was a gem. She could only wonder how the carver got the gem in without breaking the bone carving. Then it dawned on her. "Oh, I know what she said. *'Sometimes they just about sail away.'*"

Patch leant forward, elbows on his knees, watching the billowing curtains that had preoccupied his attention. Slowly, Alexa became aware of his movement. She watched confused as he rose and walked over to the open doors. Reluctantly, she returned the ivory into the purse, slipped off the desk and followed him. He was on one knee, just short of the doorway onto the porch.

"Alexa."

"Yes, Patch?"

"Can you go out onto the porch and face me, then take hold of each corner of one curtain?"

She did as he asked and took hold of the bottom two corners. He shook his head. "No, not like that. Put one corner in each hand." She obliged. "Now lower them down to the floor gently."

Alexa went down on one knee, leaning forward to put the two corners on the floor. She'd only got halfway down when the breeze picked up slightly, pulling both corners free of her hands.

Patch jumped up and spun around, then stopped. Facing her, his hands covering half his shocked face. "Oh, the Gods in our heavens above. Do you know what we have just done?"

Alexa was bewildered. "Well, no, Patch. What have we done?"

"Take the corners again, hold them tight and draw them down."

Alexa did as he bid, holding tighter. Now, she drew it down slowly, more aware of the breeze. Patch's eyes were bright as he watched with bated breath. "That's it! Can you feel the tension in your hands?"

She gazed up at him, her face full of surprise. "Are we to pull a vessel, with this?" His eyes lit up watching the tight fabric. She could feel the corners pulling on her arms, she could now even feel the subtle change in the breeze. She smiled some more. "How are we to pull a vessel with this, Patch?"

"I'm not sure, but I do know the ocean always has a breeze. If we can harness just a bit of its power in this, *'sail,'* then we can build the Emperor's vessel."

The curtains slipped out of Alexa's hands. She rose to her feet and threw herself at Patch. "You have solved it! You are the one to take us into the next league."

"Next league, Alexa?"

Alexa realised she had just broken one of her own life rules, never to talk about the past, but it was done, she could not back out now. "My father always said, *'Until they learn to get past those oars, we cannot progress beyond here, but one day a man beyond this league, will come along and take us there with him.'* I had no idea what he was on about then but if you can make this work, and you *will,* then you are that man!"

42 The Pipe

Kito ran his index fingers over his eyelashes just to check his eyes were open. They were. It took a moment to remember why he was in a bed. Rolling over, he put his feet on the floor. He had learnt to lay his clothes so he knew just how to dress the next day.

With only his pants on, he went to the window to feel the morning sun. It was remarkable how refined his senses had become. He could tell just how far the sun had risen by the heat it radiated. Right now, it was barely breaking the horizon. He was alone, so began his stretches. He needed no eyes for that.

Luhou ascended the stairs and stopped at the door. It was silent inside. She knocked twice. She heard a light thump and opened the door to the strange, hulking man. The person she had been asked to call on to bring to the breakfast table was simply known as Kito. Before her, stripped to the waist, was this man, tall and broad, his shoulders rounded and lean, his stomach muscled all the way back to his sides. All quite disconcerting for Luhou. She immediately averted her eyes. "I'm sorry, Kito; I thought you were still in bed."

Kito was just warming up, his breathing was even and he could no longer feel the bite of the morning air. "It's quite alright, Luhou. I take it you have been sent to fetch me for breakfast?"

"Yes, Kito, this is so. Shall I wait for you outside?" He didn't answer. Bowing, Luhou backed out and waited patiently. Not long after, the door opened, and Kito ducked under the doorway. "Bumped your head often enough already, Kito?"

"I believe so, Luhou." Smiling, he held out his large right hand. Hesitantly, she put her left hand under it. In silence, she led him towards the cooking room, her discomfort evident in her tentative hand.

"The cooking fires this morning have made my mouth water; the food last night was divine."

Luhou was so preoccupied trying to smell the cooking that she almost forgot to answer. "Thank you, Kito, most kind."

"Not at all, Luhou, just stating the obvious." They walked in silence. "I am hopeful of a full recovery of my eyesight, so I am once again able to earn my keep."

Luhou frowned. Her father had made no comment of improvement in Kito's eyesight, now or in the future. She was careful with her reply. "Have you had any change as yet, Kito?" The uncomfortable silence was her answer. "Careful, please, Kito, we will have to ascend a flight of stairs."

Kito did not hesitate. "Yes, Luhou, then we go around to the right, to the cooking room."

"After just one night, your memory is extraordinary."

"What makes you think it is by memory that I know these things?"

She looked up to him as she led him up the stairs. He was looking out around the courtyard as if he could see.

Opening the door into the cooking room, Luhou was relieved to see her father already seated with Narpa, Kai, Bolli and Manchu. There were two empty seats, one beside Manchu and the other opposite Kale, who, seeing their approach, stood up and bowed. As the rest of the table's occupants greeted them, Kale held out a hand for Kito to sit opposite him. Kito dipped his head to Kale's gesture and sat down at the low table. Kale raised his eyebrows and looked at his daughter, who simply shrugged her shoulders. Kito sat in silence as they all resumed their seats.

Kale pondered him for a moment. "Kito, I trust you slept well. Was your room up to standard?"

Kito looked blankly at Kale. "No, Kale, it was not."

Kale spoke gently. "Were you cold? Was the bed not comfortable, Kito?"

"No, I was not cold, the bed was warm and comfortable, the room was quiet, neither mosquito nor fly annoyed me. I do believe the room is at a comfort level I am just not accustomed to, Kale. I barely slept!" Laughter and conversations ensued about their own rooms and how great the village was.

After breakfast, the group broke up and the women took away the leftovers. Kale motioned for Manchu to accompany him, and the two men made their way outside and up to the level above. They stepped out onto the balcony to rest on the railings in the morning sun. Kale pulled his pipe out and lit it. Manchu looked as he drew in the smoke and wondered how old he would be before he could take up this habit of the elders.

They watched Kito, who was finding a spot near the well, where he stood still for a moment, then moved to the sunny side and sat.

Manchu leant over to Kale. "What do you make of him, Senior?"

Kale removed his pipe. "You have known him for more time than I, Manchu, but tell me, how is Mikka coming along? So far, I have had little time to talk with most of you."

Manchu could not help but smile, like a boy just kissed for the first time. "Oh, she is just fine," then with a more serious look, "but it is a wonder that she has not suffered, you know, with how long she was without breath."

Kale puffed on his pipe, considering Manchu's comments. "But wasn't Kito under for just as long? Other than being blind, I see nothing wrong with him."

"Oh, there is nothing wrong with that young man, Kale. Kai said that when they were out on the hunting track, Kito could *hear* his own way. Can you believe that? He has only just turned blind and he can hear his way. No, there is nothing wrong with Kito." He paused. "Mikka will be fine, we just worry for her."

"I would think less of you if you did not, Manchu. I heard about how Kito pulled down Bolli. How does a blind man pull down a horse in full gallop, without moving from his place?"

Manchu looked towards Kito down by the well. "I have no idea, but I know who could show you." He turned to Kale with a look of disbelief. "The time he was in that mud, Senior, was long – inhumanely long."

"Yet, there he is … as is Mikka."

Manchu smiled. "Yes, she is."

Kale pointed with his pipe. "No, no. I mean, *there* she is, Manchu."

Manchu caught sight of Mikka walking towards Kito with a doting smile. "Oh, if I may be excused, Senior, I have had little chance to talk with my own daughter since our return." Kale only just had time to dip his head.

By the time Manchu had hurried down the three flights of stairs, Kito was standing up at the well, talking quietly with Mikka. Before Manchu could announce his presence, Kito bowed. Lost for words for a moment, he scrutinised Mikka gazing up at Kito. The silence was palpable.

"It is a beautiful morning, Manchu," offered Kito.

Manchu did not answer. Mikka looked at her father, confusion on her face. "Father, are you alright? Did you not rest well last night?"

Manchu coughed. "What? Um, yes, Mikka, I slept very well, back in our own beds. I am sorry, Kito, did you ask a question of me?"

"It is a beautiful day, yes?"

Manchu turned about, looking to the sky as if he had not yet seen it. "Oh yes, it is indeed a beautiful day, Kito. I think every day we work for one another from our own village, is a good day."

"Indeed, you are as wise as they say you are, Manchu. When do we begin the harvest?"

Manchu stepped back in surprise. "*We*, Kito? We will indeed begin harvest shortly, but you will not be able to help in the fields, I'm afraid."

Dejected, Kito implored. "I am a good worker, Manchu. I must be able to help in order to at least earn my keep. Manchu, please understand, if I cannot earn my keep, I must leave, though I have no way of going. I have nowhere to go."

Manchu felt compelled to put his hand up on the young man's chest. "You should understand, until we built these walls, all our daughters went missing to the slave trade. This makes the few we have living with us, so much more precious. Then you saved one of ours. You understand, Kito? You saved one of ours."

"Who took your daughters, Manchu?"

Manchu lowered his hand. "Armed riders came with wagons every year or so and took the ones old enough to work."

"They never came back?"

"No, never."

"How long has this been happening?"

"For the longest time."

"Does your Emperor know?"

"We sent messages into the city of Samos, but the messengers never came back either. So, we sent a messenger directly to the Palace. The previous Emperor promised he would immediately send a legion of guards to investigate, but then he suddenly died. We sent a further messenger to the new Emperor, Hannu Koe. He responded that he was busy on the northern wall and that we should be grateful for his protection from the Barbarians. That is what gave us the idea to build our own walls." Manchu watched Kito contemplating his comments.

"Kito, would you like Mikka to show you around this level? We are very proud of our heated tubs. If you never got the chance last night, I would be happy to see you get to enjoy its comfort tonight."

Kito dipped his head. "Yes, I do feel a walk would be nice, and I would be grateful for a hot tub tonight, to loosen some muscles."

"I certainly would understand if you have been a little tight, with the change in your life you are adjusting to, Kito."

"I had the pleasure of living with a Master for some time. He taught me the art of meditation, but yes, Manchu, I'm afraid I have struggled with the loss of sight. I do not think my Master would be pleased."

Again, Manchu placed a reassuring hand on Kito. "Kito, if your friend is a true Master, then he would be proud of your accomplishments to date. Is there something we can do to assist you in your meditation?"

"I think a long walk this afternoon, then your hot tub, would put me back in control of my thoughts. May I ask of you a favour, Manchu?"

"Just ask, Kito"

"You spoke of Sankun … if there is just the smallest chance she can help."

Manchu looked directly at Mikka, who shook her head emphatically. "Jin and I have spoken of taking you to her. We will make the necessary arrangements, though it is her choice whether to see you. Can you understand this, Kito? Sankun does not see anyone, unless by her own choice. Of course, we will try."

Manchu saw the disappointment, possibly the first expression he had read on the young man's face. Kito himself found it hard to contain. "It is all I request of you, just to ask. For this, I am grateful, Manchu."

"Mikka will show you around now."

Kito dipped his head, then held out his arm towards Mikka. She giggled as she took it. "It would be my pleasure, Kito."

Manchu's worries eased. Smiling, he turned and made his way towards the stairs until Kito's words stopped him in his tracks.

"Don't be in a hurry for your pipe, Manchu. It is yours when the time is right."

43 The Model

Patch held the door to the backyard open for Alexa, who was objecting.

"I just don't see why you have to use my good sheets for this, some old rag would surely do."

Patch latched the door behind her. "Oh, stop your huffing, woman. It's not like they're made of silk now, are they."

They wandered through the myriads of projects and timber strewn around the yard, heading for their smaller jetty upriver.

"Would that make a difference to your wanting to do this tonight?"

"No, probably not."

"Well, there you go then."

Patch eyed the clinker as they neared the water's edge. It was ready, as Admasin had said it would be. He smiled at the prospect of this maiden voyage. "Well, there you go then. What?"

"See, this is what I mean; you don't even know what I am talking about."

On the small jetty, Alexa stood with her hands on her hips. Patch sighed. "You think that, regardless of whether the sheet was cotton or silk, I would be taking it on this crazy ride in a clinker anyway."

"Why are we taking a clinker when we have smaller, lighter dinghies for the two of us?"

Patch untied the ropes. "I was right, wasn't I? I want the heavier clinker for this task."

As he took the oars, Alexa cast off, taking the rudder. "Why is it so important it gets done tonight, and for that matter, why does it have to be done at night at all?"

"It's because, since the Emperor paid us a visit, the yard has been under regular watch. Upstream, remember I said we are going upstream first."

Alexa pulled the rudder around. "Sorry, yes. Why are we going upstream?"

"Because there are no eyes upstream, that's why. I do not think our fat Asset can keep his mouth shut either, so be careful what you tell him, won't you?" He leaned into the oars now. The timber squeaked in the brass rowlocks, water slapping the hull.

"I know how much you hate being on the water, Patch. Tell me again, why do we have to do this now?"

Patch grunted with the effort on the oars; he had the momentum now and was not about to let his work fade. "We have a rare opportunity of the tide coming in on a full moon with a steady easterly. An excellent combination for this task."

"Oh." Alexa looked at the pole stuck up in the middle of the clinker, tied off front, rear and both sides. It had a pulley at the top with a rope through it, both ends tied off at the bottom. "How is this going to work again?"

Patch just admired Alexa with a smile.

Upriver was a large building, well known as the 'Happy House,' where lonely men would frequent at night. The hair on Alexa's arms bristled, and her ill feeling returned. On the balcony, the silhouette of a large man laughing with several women caught her eye. Her skin crawled. Turning away, she lowered her head. The laugh brought back shocking memories she had repressed for so long. Busy on the oars, Patch hadn't noticed.

They turned the bend to face due west, Patch knew this river like the back of his hand. "Alexa, can you steer us up onto the sand bank? It will take a little time to set this up."

Once aground, Patch pulled up a pole and placed it across the clinker, tying it off at either end. He then tied the two corners of the sheet to opposing ends, pulled out a second pole and repeated the process.

Alexa shook her head. "You should see your face right now. You look like a little kid."

"I feel like a little kid." He stared intensely at Alexa. "My father built a big business hoping that one day the Emperor would walk in and give him a contract. It never happened, so now we have one chance, and it all hinges on this working, right here, right now."

With that, Patch pushed on the oars, and the clinker slid off the sand bank. He rowed hard a few times, building momentum, then decisively, he placed the oars inside and pulled the rope through the top pulley, causing the cross-pole to rise. The wind caught the sheet, snapping it out tight. The clinker surged forward, catching him unawares. He tried to step back but caught his foot, falling backwards over his seat into the hull of the clinker.

"Patch! Are you alright?"

Patch glared at her with a pained expression. "Stupid question."

"Don't get all thingy with me just because you can't stand up in your own clinker."

The clinker stopped abruptly back on the sandbank. Patch got himself to his feet, holding his side. "Blessed vessels, they're all just man's failed imagination."

Alexa smirked. He was clearly in a lot of pain, blaming everything but his own clumsy feet. "All vessels, Patch? Even the *Shiraz?*"

He scoffed. "Especially the *Shiraz*. That is why no one has built another."

"No one has done another because no one believes they can match your design."

"But no one has copied it either. Now, let's get this thing off the bank and try again."

He made changes to the ropes. Alexa found it confusing, though she trusted his judgment. Once done, she took the rudder. Patch winced as he pulled on the oars, heading back upriver. Once there, he put down the oars and pulled up the rope, this time bracing himself firmly. The steady breeze snapped the sheet out tight, and the clinker surged ahead.

Patch began to laugh: they were making far better pace than the best of oarsmen.

Alexa began to realise just what the sheet was truly worth. With the trailing winds, they surged upstream, such was the power of her sheet. So preoccupied, she almost missed the subtle turn in the river as Patch tried to pull the rope tighter. She turned the rudder and the clinker tilted abruptly to the side. Patch, still standing, put out his foot to steady himself. It tilted some more and water poured into the small vessel. The sudden extra drag tore the sheet right up the middle and the clinker rolled over. Alexa swore as she gracefully dived into the river. Patch, a little less confident, hit the water with a splash. The pair grabbed hold of the hull as it turned slowly in the current, bobbing back downstream.

Brushing her soaking hair away from her face, Alexa frowned. "So now what?"

Patch laughed as he wiped his face, clinging to the clinker. "Did you see it go? We did it. We have it!"

***

Just after sunrise, Patch headed out to the jetty. It was no surprise to see Admasin already there checking over the clinker.

"Good morning, Admasin. The mornings are getting a little cooler, don't you think?"

Admasin grinned cheekily. "A little too cool to be taking late-night swims, I'd have thought, Patch."

"Hmm, my company is still a little cool about it this morning, too. Would you like to come up for a brew? Kalgan can open the workshop."

As they walked through the yard Patch noticed no one was working on the vessel in the dry dock. "How is it no one is on that job yet, Admasin?"

"They are cleaning up yesterday's tools, for today."

"Why weren't they cleaned at the day's end?"

"Because I used those men to set up your crazy clinker. Do you know how many times I had to explain it to them?"

In the office, they settled into their seats. Admasin smiled to Alexa as she walked in. "No leathers today, Alexa?" Patch scowled at him.

Alexa huffed. "No, strangely enough, when I got up this morning, they were wet! Weren't they, Patch *dear?*"

Patch remained blank-faced as Admasin chuckled before asking, "Patch, this idea of yours, how did it really go?"

Patch's scowl turned into a silly grin. "We sank."

"And you are happy about this?"

Alexa placed a decanter on the desk and poured two goblets, placing one in front of Admasin. "It is too early to be drinking," she mumbled before she downed the other and slammed the empty goblet in front of Patch and left the room.

"It is going to work, you know, Admasin. This sail thing. It was the sail that tipped us over." Patch missed the concerned look on Admasin's face.

Admasin threw back his own drink and reached over for a refill. "It tipped over ... but was a success? Explain this to me, would you."

"Well, the first time I pulled up the sail, the wind ripped it right from my hands. Look!" Patch's hands were red-raw. "Can you believe that? I have used my hands all my life, and I get rope burn. Fantastic!"

Admasin winced at Patch's hands. "Fantastic?"

"Fantastic! The second time, I changed the rigging then eased up the sail. It was amazing! There is no way a man could row that fast."

Admasin leaned in. "So why did it tip?"

"Two things happened at the same time. Firstly, Alexa turned the clinker for the river bend, so over it went."

Admasin flung his hands up in the air. "But that's no good, Patch. You can't always go in the direction of the wind!"

Patch nodded. "Yes, yes, we just have to make some minor

adjustments, but I felt the power of the wind, Admasin, a *lot* of power. We must work out some details, that's all." He slapped his thigh. "Every problem has an answer. We just need to search them out and implement them into my next design."

Admasin leaned forward, refilling both goblets. "It is too big a project to build and find it will not work, Patch. It is not my place to tell you your business, but ..."

"You think it will send us broke, Admasin?"

"I think it is not for me to know if you could carry such a failure or not, but it may be foolhardy." His face showed concern as he lowered his voice, "And what do you think the Emperor would do to us if his vessel tipped over in a side wind. By the Gods, it doesn't bear thinking about. I won't be waiting around to see that, let me tell you!"

Patch liked the old man's straight talk, listening to his every word. He turned to the curtains, almost hypnotised by them wafting in the breeze.

"What was the second thing that happened, Patch?"

"What? Oh yes, Alexa's sheet tore right up the middle.

Admasin almost spurted out his drink. "It is a wonder you came back at all."

Patch lowered his voice, checking for Alexa. "If I have a good day today, I am hoping to make it back into my own bed tonight."

"Was it a good sheet?"

"Yes."

"Did she mind you taking it?"

"Yes."

"Don't like your chances."

At that moment Alexa returned. "Those boys are playing on the jetty again, Patch."

"Do they have their models with them?"

"Yes. Why?"

"Because that's what they're doing – they're waiting for the outgoing tide to launch from our jetty and whoever gets to the last jetty first, wins.”

“What a great game. Are there any rules?”

“Yes, they must make their own vessels, and it must be upright at the finish line. Was that right, Admasin?”

“Yes, that was it. If my memory serves me right, they stopped playing for some years when you were a boy, didn’t they, Patch? Why was that?”

Patch shrugged. “Because they said I was cheating.”

Alexa looked at him. “Were you … were you cheating?”

“You need ask, Alexa? Well, that just hurts.”

“You’ll get over it. What made them think you were cheating?”

Admasin laughed. “Because he always won!”

Alexa questioned again. “No one always wins. What were you doing?”

“I wasn’t cheating!” He opened his arms in emphasis. “I mean, how could I? We all put in our vessels together, no one touched them, and we all pulled them out at the end.”

Admasin added, “But you came first, every time.”

Alexa stood at the end of his desk. “Patch, look at me.”

“Good Gods in heaven, woman, is this going all the way to the Emperor? Am I to be thrown to the wolves?”

“You have a flushing toilet upstairs; you designed the biggest vessel in the world, and last night you showed me how to pull a vessel with my sheet, which may be the most amazing thing I have ever seen.”

Patch held up a finger. “And it ripped as we fell into the river. I hate the water.”

Alexa stared intently at him. “How did you always win?”

Admasin had questioned his son, Kalgan, on the very matter. He waited for Patch to answer.

“Well, I would stand on the balcony, that one right there,” he pointed, “and if there was a breeze upriver, I would take a vessel that sat low in the water. If there was a breeze downriver, I took one that sat high in the water. If there was no wind at all, I would take my biggest one that had a deep hull so it rode the current.”

"The one that sat high in the water to catch the wind, why didn't it fall over?" queried Alexa.

Patch blinked and rose from his seat. Without further word, he walked out of his office, leaving the large oak door open in his absence. Admasin looked at Alexa. "Don't worry. I have never seen him hold a grudge."

Finally, Patch returned and placed three models on the table.

"My Gods, you still have them!" Admasin picked one up. "Is this the one for the downriver breeze, Patch?"

"Yes, that's it. I remembered once I found it, I went to the old mine up in the hills and got some lead for the bottom. It was the only way I could make it stay upright with the breeze."

Admasin stopped turning the model about. "How did you know about the old mine?"

Patch didn't meet the old man's gaze. "Oh, all the boys know about the mine."

"And what of my boy, Patch? Did Kalgan know of the old mine?"

Patch picked up another of his models. "Oh, maybe, I really don't remember."

***

Frowning, Admasin held up the model with the lead bottom. "So, *this* is it? I hold the future of the vessels of our world in the palm of my hand?" Alexa and Patch stopped still. Admasin was talking quietly, like he didn't even realise he was speaking. "Life is a subtle and precarious thing ..." Putting the model down, he looked to the balcony doors. "... but it will be a huge risk to you both. Can we minimise this somehow?"

Patch frowned. "What, like taking in a partner?"

"What about Asset Chun?" Alexa suggested.

Patch waved a dismissive hand. "No, not Chun."

"You said he was ideal because of his link to the throne."

"Yes, but that's not to say I want to partner with him in this, Alexa. For that matter, I don't want any partner. Asset Chun is

444

ideal for the mill because he can afford to develop it, but has no idea what he is doing, so I will do it for him. I am in control of both, without the risk. However, if he gets his nose in here, his ego will take over. He already has too much money – he wants the glory."

Alexa put her model down and went to the cabinet for another decanter. She turned back to him. "Patch?"

"Yes, Alexa?"

"What if we made a small-scale model, just as the Emperor wants, though only a portion of the size, just enough to carry a few men? How much risk would it carry then?"

44 Impossible Dive

Kito and Yaan sat in a small clinker on the estuary, each with a handline over the side.

"Kito, why is it that you insist on helping with the harvest? You know we are grateful to have you with us. We do not expect you to work the fields. The entire village is grateful for what you did for them, saving one of their own."

Kito sighed. He had been over this many times now. "That was then; now I must earn my keep. No one can rest on their laurels, we must all earn our keep. The young keep the old, and the parents keep the children."

Yaan smiled at Kito's calm, matter-of-fact manner, one of many traits he had come to respect in him. "And what of the elderly, Kito, do they have any role in a village?"

"Well, yes, they are our guides in life. They have a lifetime of wisdom to offer; we just need to listen; all is there for our benefit."

Yaan thought about his home in the caves and how the people worked together. His attention was brought to his line by a strong bite. He waited a moment, nothing. "A good fish is down there playing us, my friend."

"Yes but I think he is too hungry for his own good. His greed will deliver him to us. My second father once said, one of the reasons for the failed generation was that they grew so fast that the young ones had no one to turn to for guidance."

Yaan pondered this. "What do you mean, they grew so fast?"

Kito, too, had trouble with this. "Well, by the time the elderly were old, things had changed so much they didn't know what was happening either. There was no one to advise the young, and so they strayed from their values. This was compounded by each generation running astray with lesser values."

Yaan's line tightened with two strong bites. "How can you have an entire society moving at such a pace that even the old cannot keep up?"

"I don't know, but they did fail."

"Maki always said it was ironic that the earth removed almost all mankind, so returning to its own rhythm."

Kito stared at Yaan – he couldn't see him, but Yaan stared back all the same.

"Really, Yaan? My second father used to say the same thing. In fact, he used to say that it was a natural cycle of the Earth that it would do such a thing. In some ways, the failed generation got so far ahead of itself, they simply overlooked the obvious."

Kito got two bites on his line. "You know, Yaan, I think there is a very smart fish down there just toying with the two of us. He plays my line, then yours. If he keeps this up, I may go down there and get him myself."

Yaan laughed out loud. "You are the last one I would ever expect to make false threats."

Kito smirked. "How do you know it's a false threat, Yaan?"

"Because I have let my line down here with you many times this summer, we both know how deep it is and that, my friend, is enough on its own. I do not need to bring up the other obvious difficulties you would have down there." Yaan held his line as he got two more bites in quick succession.

Kito shrugged his broad shoulders. "Well, Yaan, if I can make the depth, the rest might be in my favour."

Yaan paused, a deep furrow on his forehead. "You're serious about this? You actually want me to challenge you to this, don't you?" As Kito slipped his tunic over his head, Yaan added, "Though you have already made up your mind that you are going to try."

Kito pulled a long spear from under the seats. He ran his thumb over the tip as he drew a long breath. "Someone has cared for this very nicely."

"Kito, you do not have to prove a thing to me. If I have heard the story once, I've heard it a thousand times, and every time it is no less impressive than the last. You do not have to do this."

Fossicking in the bait bowl, Kito found a large piece and slid it over the end of his spear. "What story?"

Exasperated, Yaan let out a sigh. "You know … *the* story."

Kito climbed over his seat, moving to the front of the clinker. Breathing deeply, the young man's impressive chest heaved. "The thing you need to understand here, Yaan, is that one person in that village had the kindness of heart and boldness of personality to take me in when others would not even speak to me. It was her I was diving in for, it was her, I failed." After one more deep breath and barely a splash, he was gone.

Time passed.

Yaan sat still, his line limp in the water, pondering Kito's words. Despite Kito doing such a brave thing, he still carried this burden of apparent failure. He looked over the side. Nothing.

He thought about the dreams he'd had about the failed generation and his conversations with Kito. He checked the water. Kito had been down an impossibly long time now. Again, nothing.

Finally, Kito broke through the surface, drawing air.

Taken by surprise, Yaan slipped off his seat, landing with a bump. Kito reached over the side and dropped in the spear. Red-faced, Yaan quickly returned to his seat.

Kito made his way around to the front. "Are you all right there, my friend?" He pulled himself up and swung one leg in, twisting his torso to land sitting on his seat. "Did I hear you having a little accident there, Yaan? Sorry, I didn't mean to startle you."

"I am sorry … I do not see a fish on the end of your spear, Kito. That was a long time, though. Did you actually make the bottom?"

Kito was busy untying his line from the seat. "Yes."

"How far was it?"

He pulled in his line. "As long down, as your line is out, Yaan."

Yaan closed his eyes at his own stupidity. "Okay, Kito, it's a long way. There's no way that I could do such a thing."

Kito gently wound up the line around his small wooden drum. "The man who says he cannot do something will inevitably prove himself right." The silence grew as Yaan wound his own line. "It was cold down there, Yaan. I do not think eyes would have been of any help either. I know it sounds silly, but it even *felt* dark."

Yaan looked at this man, who was not just different, but something special. Kito stood up. His arms bulged as he lifted a huge, pink snapper over the side.

"Gods above, Kito! Look at the size of that fellow!" He stepped over the seat to stand near Kito, looking at the massive fish lying on the bottom of the vessel. It had a hole behind the eye, the line was tied to its tail. "You ... you got this with the spear, didn't you?"

"Yes."

"Yes? That's it? That's all you are going to say, Kito, just yes? You dived an impossible dive, stayed down an impossible time, caught the biggest fish, and this is your big comeback?"

"I would like to say one thing, though, my friend."

"Knock yourself out."

Kito leaned over, pointing past Yaan. "Your line is running."

Yaan spun around. "Darn!" He fumbled over to his line, tripping over everything on his way.

Kito pointed. "Hey, be careful not to ..."

Yaan grabbed the line, which immediately burned his hand. "Agh, darn!" He dropped the line, reacting quickly by standing on it with his left foot. He grabbed at the drum as it bounced about in the bottom of the clinker. Finally, he got it and wrapped it in both arms with one foot up on the side of the clinker. The line pulled tighter as it came higher in the water. Soon, it was cutting a big arc around the front of the clinker.

"Kito! What is it?"

Kito was quick to respond to the concern in Yaan's voice. He knelt in front of Yaan, getting the line. "Yaan, I think you have the catch of the summer."

The clinker started to move through the water. "Darn!" Yaan repeated through gritted teeth. "Darn!"

Kito held tight, eyes closed, feeling the fish pulsing as it powered through the water. As the strange fish surfaced, Yaan saw it. Long and sleek, pure muscle, dark blue over the top and silver underneath, with a long, top bill and a huge fan along its back. It did not seem to be tiring, and was heading towards the estuary opening.

Kito had to do something, or let the line go. It would be a story for the lifetime of this humble cave-dwelling man. Kito did what he thought he must.

Exclaiming profanities and with cramping arms, Yaan held the drum as tightly as he could. He couldn't see the line as Kito's broad back blocked the view, but judging by the way his back was muscled up, it was evident Kito also had a firm grip on it. Time and again, he wanted to let the line go, but he could not … *would* not.

The fish was heading out through the estuary, taking them out to the inland sea.

"Oh no, Kito, confound it!"

In silence, Kito leant back, not letting the line slip through his hands. Yaan's arms screamed to him to release the drum. "Darn it, Kito, darn it!"

Yaan was almost at breaking point when suddenly, the fish ran up onto a sandbar. A voice sounded in his head. *The spear, Yaan, fetch the spear.* Yaan dropped the drum and grabbed at the spear as the clinker rode up onto the sandbar, almost riding over the massive fish. He leapt out, narrowly missing the thrashing tail and moved to the front of the fish. Without hesitation, he lunged in, kicking the fish onto its side and driving the spear in behind its eye. The fish trembled for a moment, Kito cried out, and the fish relaxed, dead.

Yaan turned to the sound of the villagers running towards them. He looked back at the clinker. "Hey, Kito, look who's coming!" The proud smile slid off Yaan's face. He couldn't see Kito. "Kito, come on! What game is this you are playing on me?"

Nothing.

Yaan's stomach knotted. "Come on, my friend, we've had such a good morning, don't ruin it. Kito?" As Yaan reached the side of the clinker, he found Kito slumped in the bottom, his stomach contents down the side of his face and over the clinker's hull.

***

The room was bright. Kito lay on a bed almost directly under the open window, the summer breeze gently blowing over him. A small group of concerned onlookers gathered at his bedside.

Yaan paced back and forth at the end of the room. "Kale, I have been over this so many times! I do not understand what could have gone wrong. We were both holding the line until the fish ran aground."

Kale tried to appease the young man. "Easy, Yaan, you're not at fault. We don't know what has happened here, but it is nothing you have done. I have seen this before when people have had too much sun."

Yaan stopped pacing. "What, too much sun ... in the morning?"

Kale grimaced. "Well, not exactly, but it does happen."

Yaan resumed his pacing. Manchu cleared his throat. "I once knew a man who was out fishing with stale bait. He just wiped his mouth and fell ill. He spent the first day vomiting but was fine after a few days."

Yaan turned to look at Manchu. "Was he unconscious too?"

"No, not as such. No, Yaan."

"What about this Sankun you spoke of. Is it time to call her?"

Kale shot a glance to Manchu. "Well, I do not think it is time to be bringing in the likes of Sankun, Yaan."

"What! Has she no time for anyone unless they are on the brink of death? He is unconscious! How close is close enough for you people?" pleaded Yaan.

A small man stepped forward from the back of the crowd. It was the old man, Jong. "Yaan, I have known your mother and your father for many years now, and you also. You have only known this boy for one summer. Why is it you feel so responsible for him?"

Yaan pondered Kito lying motionless on the bed. "Kito believes he is a failure because he did not get your dear Quinn, Jong. He takes little pride in the fact that he did save Mikka. He doesn't even like to talk about it. And Jong, he is *not* a boy."

Pain and anger etched across the old man's face. "You lost no one in the floods. You were not even present to see the sacrifice we all endured!"

Yaan lifted his chin, defiant to his elder. "No, I was not, but I have watched this man suffer every day. You have not given him the one thing he has asked of any of you. Forgiveness. Why is this? Has he not given enough? His eyes are not enough for you. He is so young. For his effort to get your Quinn, he lost his eyesight, yet all he asks of you is your forgiveness for his failure. Why, Jong, why will you not give it to him?"

They locked eyes, surrounded by a crowd of silent witnesses to their raw emotions.

Narpa stepped forward. "Jong …" Narpa knelt beside him. "Jong, I, too, must ask your forgiveness."

Jong peered down at the young man, then to Manchu. "What is this he speaks of, Manchu?"

Manchu seemed as lost as Jong. "Well, Jong, ask him, he is before you after all."

Jong peered down. "Narpa, stand before me, you do not need my forgiveness."

"Oh, but I do, Jong. Not for what I have done, but for what I haven't."

Blank faces looked back, awaiting Jong's answer. Impatiently, Jong demanded, "Well, out with it then. What could it be that you have not done?"

The young man made no effort to hide his shame. "I have not told my story of that day, Jong. The story of how Kito went for the one you miss so. It was not for the lack of trying, we all saw that, but what most did not see was that at the final moment, Quinn, the brave, selfless woman she was, pulled Mikka in front of herself. Kito got his target right, but Quinn changed the target."

Jong stepped back. "What? No!"

Narpa steadied the old gentleman by his arm. "I am sorry, Jong. I am sorry I did not say anything earlier, but I cannot be sorry for her final act of selflessness. I cannot be sorry that she saved Mikka. It was, for me, as brave a thing she did as was what Kito himself did. Yaan is right, he is a man, a brave man."

Jong backed up against the wall, tears welling up in his eyes. "How could she choose to leave us, to leave me? No. This cannot be true!"

Narpa continued. "I was on the bank. I tried so hard to reach out for Mikka, but I just couldn't get to her, then I saw Kito dive in. I saw the moment that Quinn made that decision."

Jong slumped to the floor. "What are you saying? Wat are you doing to me?"

Manchu and Kale held Jong gently as Narpa knelt before him. "You could not see because the island slid down to the Yellow River, but I did. I saw Quinn make the decision to sacrifice herself to save a younger soul, Jong. She glowed as she did it, she was content, she was at peace."

Narpa stood up. "I am so sorry, Jong. The village loved you both. We still do."

Mikka was at Kito's side, holding his hand, tears trickling down her cheeks. Narpa looked at them both for a moment, then made for the door and left. Mikka stood staring at her father with questioning eyes. He gave his permission with a small nod and she, too, was gone.

45 Uniter of the Seven

Some days later, as the morning sun was just breaking the horizon, Manchu and Kale sat in the window of the cooking room, enjoying their morning tea together.

"Another fine one, I see, Manchu. It has been a good harvest this year. We are almost finished."

"Yes, the elders have done a grand job in our absence with the Colonial Dig."

"Indeed, they have; we must acknowledge this at the harvest celebrations." There was a pause, and Kale took on a more serious tone. "Remember how Kito spoke to the Emperor? What of his comments about how the water was not to come from ..."

Manchu held up a hand, looking about furtively. "I promised my wife to never bring this up again."

"You haven't, I have. But why did you bring it up with your wife, Manchu?"

"For the same reason you have now, Kale. It was my understanding we were to break through into the Yellow River to let the canal flood upstream, then release the top, and it would begin its natural flow back down. No risk, no loss of life."

Kale's answer came in a whisper. "Yes, this was my understanding also. Jong told me that Kito had seen the Emperor on the nearby mound the day before. If this is so, he had ample time to inform us of the coming water. It flowed from the far western ranges, this would have taken days."

"Indeed, it would, Kale. You are quite right, suggesting he chose not to. What was that talk about the coach? I'm afraid I did not follow this."

Kale refilled Manchu's cup. "Yes, I do have to admit, I also knew nothing until I heard the story. I feel Kito may have the key to that one. I sent a messenger to the city of Samos as soon as you arrived back. It would seem that our Asset, Kain, has vanished. He was said to have left for the Palace, though never arrived."

Manchu frowned. "Are you saying that the chain man, Tark, now runs the city? Heavens, what will come of us?"

Kale shook his head with a weary smile. "No, my good friend. It is stranger yet."

"How could it be stranger than that?"

"Tark does not wear the black belt."

"Then who does?"

"La Chun."

Perplexed, Manchu took a moment. "Chun? Chun, from the little village north-west of the city?"

"Yes, precisely."

"I thought the belt had to stay in the city. Doesn't the next of kin carry it to the Palace meeting, to seek his worthiness of the honour?"

"Yes, this was the tradition for more generations than I can know, but it would seem that this Emperor feels he is destined to change all tradition."

"What else did you hear from the city, Kale?"

Kale took a sip of his tea and was about to answer when the door opened. Mikka entered and with a hand on her shoulder, Kito bent as he walked through the doorway. She giggled childlike, waving to her father. Kale beckoned them over as Manchu glowed with pride.

Carefully, Mikka led Kito over to their table. Once settled, Kale placed a mug before Kito and opened the conversation. "You had everyone worried for some time, young man. What do you think happened?"

"I had done a deep dive some time earlier and had handled the bait. Some of it was quite rank, but I could not say for sure."

Kale nodded as he poured tea for everyone. "This dive you did, just how deep was it?"

Kito took a sip of tea. "I don't know, except to say I couldn't have gone much further."

Manchu intervened. "Please do not be offended by my asking, Kito, but how does a blind man spear a fish, on the bottom of the sea?"

Kito took the question in good humour. "It is good of you to ask. I have heard a great number of people talking about it, but you are the first to ask. Firstly, I had tied a bigger weight to my line the last time I had it in. This I followed to the bottom after tying the top to my own seat. Once down, I put the weight on my lap and sat with the bait between my heels. I just hoped the fish was game enough to come right in. I could feel where he was with my toes. The rest was easy."

Manchu slapped the table. "You had the weight in your lap so you could know the way back up? Well done, young man, well done. Your ability to adapt is remarkable, Kito."

The four drank their tea. The door opened and Narpa entered. He smiled upon seeing Mikka. He dipped his head, and she, in return, giggled.

Kito looked up towards Mikka. "Could you ask Narpa to come over, please?"

The three at the table looked blankly at Kito. Mikka waved Narpa over.

Kito faced Kale. "Yaan, Bolli and Hao came in some time ago. Would you think it rude of me if I was to join them? I have not yet had time to speak my gratitude to Yaan."

Manchu responded. "Do you really think it is necessary, Kito?"

"Yes."

Kale could see the eagerness in the young man. "Well, I see no reason why not, Kito. Please do not leave without stopping back here. I would like to talk further with you."

Kito dipped his head, smiling at Narpa. "I would be happy to give you my seat, if in return you could deliver me to Yaan's table without me knocking over everyone's breakfast."

A chuckle went about the table as Kito stood. No one noticed Narpa's uneasiness. He had spent so much time resenting Mikka's obvious friendly nature towards Kito that he'd neglected to realise he had, in fact, failed Kito when he needed a friend. He put Kito's large hand on his shoulder and led the way to the table where the others were.

When Narpa returned, he sat in Kito's spot, eyeing Mikka. The pair was oblivious to the rest of the room.

Manchu gave Kale a knowing smile. "I think he will be alright, Kale."

"Indeed, Manchu. He may have heard Yaan and the others talking, but how did he know when Narpa entered?"

Manchu placed the porcelain bowl on the hot stone. "I have no idea. Do you wish for him to return for talks on the carriage matter?"

"Yes, that too. Also, I was wondering if you could join me and Kito upstairs this morning?"

Awkwardly, Manchu responded, "I was going to help in the fields once more."

Kale smiled at the man's correctness. "They have nearly finished. I feel it is time for you to begin your next level, if you wish it to be so."

Kito's words resonated in Manchu's mind. *Don't be in a hurry for your pipe, Manchu. It is yours when the time is right.*

"Manchu, why do you frown when I have made such an offer?"

"If you think I am ready, then I would be honoured to be a part of this. It is also a pleasure for me to be of help to Kito."

"You think you owe this to Kito, Manchu?"

"Well, yes. You do not?"

Kale was pouring tea. "Maybe you do. Or maybe he owes you, Manchu."

"How could that be, Kale? I don't understand."

"Do you think it has been a coincidence that of all the people that went into the deluge, it was your daughter who was pulled back out?" He put down the bowl, then shrugged. "I, too, cannot know."

The thought had never occurred to Manchu. "Maybe I am too close to see where you are going with this, Kale. Please explain it for me."

"I do not understand fully myself; there is something about how Kito is adjusting to his loss of sight."

"You think this is all about him?"

"As I say, I cannot know, though I feel that our visit upstairs this morning will help us both."

Manchu thought about how Kai had explained how Kito had brought them the wild boar, upwind, then carried one, running unassisted to meet up with the caravan.

Yaan, Bolli and Hao led Kito back over to Kale's table. Yaan, having known Kale for some time, was chosen as the speaker. "Kale, may I speak with you?"

"Well, of course, my friend, how may I help?"

Yaan never usually spoke with his hands, but somehow this morning, they were talking more than his tongue. "Well, we were all wondering if Kito could come up and work in the fields with us this morning. He assures us that he is fine to work now."

Kale did his best to hide the smirk. "Kito, have you misplaced your tongue since you left our table?"

Kito did not change his calm stance. "Not at all, Kale, but I did feel that Yaan had the best hope for winning you over, though I feel you have clearly seen through it."

Kale now laughed openly. "Kito, you are a man of great depth. I would like to meet the people of your village one day."

There was the slightest shift in Kito's demeanour. "Maybe one day you will, but for now, it is time I earned my keep. The harvest is all but over."

The elder took on a more serious tone. "Whilst you live in our community, you are in our care and care for you we will. However, you must also belong with us. If we say it is not right, then you must respect this, or we may find it discourteous and untrusting. Can you understand this, Kito?"

Yaan and Hao gazed at the floor; Bolli and Narpa waited for Kito's reaction. He was unmoving, unreadable. "Yes, I do understand this, and I do respect it. Please understand, it may be a cultural difference. I wish to earn my keep, nothing more, nothing less."

Manchu intervened. "You have nothing to earn with us, Kito. I don't just mean because of Mikka. It is not in our culture to do what you did with the Emperor."

With his closed eyes, Kito turned to Manchu. "But that was then, Manchu, and this is now."

"Remember I asked you to return, Kito. I have good reason for this, so I am sorry but you must stay here, at least for this morning."

Kito turned to his companions, dipping his head. There was nothing more to be said on the matter. They paid their respects to the elders and hastily left, leaving Kito to do as he was bid.

He took a seat and spoke calmly. "Is this the day you take me to the Sankun you have both spoken of?"

"Would you like some tea, Kito?"

"Thank you, no, Kale. Is it this morning then?"

"Yes, Kito. Sankun has said she would like to meet with you this morning."

"She is a powerful and highly regarded person. I am most grateful for the invitation."

Kale studied him closely. "Kito, why is it you can show such respect to Kadra village and its people, yet in the presence of the Emperor, you showed none whatsoever. Please explain this to me."

"Firstly, he is your Emperor, not mine, and secondly, he lied to me. I believe no one here would do such a weak, short-sighted thing. Most of all, I hold no respect for the way he treats his own people. I believe he has forgotten that he was born to *lead* you all, not *own* you all."

The three sat in silence for a time.

The door opened, and Luhou entered, giving her father a signal. Kale downed his tea. "Well, if the two of you are ready."

Standing, Kito turned to Luhou. "Good morning to you, Luhou. I trust you have had your morning walk?"

Manchu could not resist. "This time I have to ask, Kito, how did you know it was Luhou?"

"I know that Luhou is most trusted with many of the errands around here. When the door opened, Kale downed his tea and did not refill it. Also, Luhou bathes in aniseed and eucalyptus oils …" He faced the young woman. "It is most compelling."

Luhou caught her breath but quickly recovered. "I think it is time to take you to your very special appointment, Kito." Smiling, she put Kito's large hand on her shoulder, and the four made their way to the top floor.

The procession stopped, and Luhou reached to knock on the door. Gently, Kito drew her away. "Kito, is everything alright?" He pulled at his tunic, trying to straighten it a little. Luhou reached up, doing her best to smooth over the ruined garment. "You look fine, Kito. She will see much more than your clothing, so do not concern yourself with that." She peered up into his blind face then at her father, who closed his eyes and nodded. She patted Kito on his chest and whispered, "She will see you for the man you are. Relax, Kito, be yourself, and you will be fine."

Luhou knocked twice. There was a long pause.

"Please enter."

As the door opened, Kito ducked whilst Luhou led him by the hand. His senses worked hard. He could locate a small fire in the centre of the room, feeling both the heat and hearing the gentle crackle of the coals.

Manchu looked about, his first time in the room also. The entire room was completely white, the ceiling high, somewhat higher than in the other rooms; the numerous broad but short windows were near impossible to get an arrow through. Somehow, it was larger than he had thought. He saw her, the woman he had only known about for all these years. He had seen her once as a child – she had seemed old then - now here she was, with her long, grey hair down over her shoulders, a simple but beautiful white garment that hung almost to the floor with a red cloth belt tied off on her right hip. A buxom woman, only shoulder high to him, gave her a dumpy appearance, which was probably not fair since her old bones had bent her into almost a hunch.

Everyone's eyes were now on Kito.

As Luhou let herself out, Kale and Manchu sat themselves by the fire, leaving Kito and the old woman, Sankun, facing each other.

Kito broke the silence. "Sankun, what is it you wish for me?"

Sankun smiled. "I have had many people before me, but never has anyone asked such a question. Let me ask you, Kito, what is it you want from *me*?"

Kito remained impassive. "You awaited my arrival even before you were told of my presence here. I knew this at the Colonial Dig, more than once. What is it you wish for me, Sankun?"

"It does not matter what I want, Kito. What matters is what you have in your destiny. I can see this for you, but I have no control over it, so the question is not what anyone *wants* for you but, what is *destined* for you."

"Will I make it to my home soon?"

Kale and Manchu looked to each other with surprise. Sankun's eyesight had faded somewhat over the years, her beautiful brown eyes gone milky grey, but when she looked at Kito, they sparkled. "Yes, Kito, you will make it home."

"Soon?"

"Soon enough."

"But I am not to stay home?"

Sankun saw beyond Kito as if watching a distant story unfold.

She shook her head. "Other people will need you more than your own, Kito."

Kito breathed deeply and sighed. "You have looked at my destiny. Is it pleasing to you?"

"Does it matter what I think of it, Kito?"

"Yes."

"Please, be seated." Sankun turned and hobbled over to the high windows. She hefted herself up onto a stool that looked down over the rice fields below. She placed her hands behind her back, closed her eyes and enjoyed the morning sun on her old face.

"I saw a young boy, staring down the one of the chain. I saw him swimming and training with an older man. I knew the man, he had greeted me in our dreams; we dream together many times. He never gave a name, though I know it. I knew it because I know where he had come from and why he left. I watched as the city of Samos burned, the innocent and guilty burning with it."

She paused, hands gently directing her dreaming. "I have seen the Chosen One fight for strangers in a faraway land. I watched him fight for the freedom of the many, always out in front, leading the way, prepared to die in that moment, on that day." Her voice quivered as she took a breath. "I watched him float into the dark with only a torch, to find the Sacred Crystal. In my visions, I could not see the man, only what he did."

Manchu looked at Kale. He had his head down, letting the dream come to him if it chose to. Kito, too, was sitting with his head down. Manchu knew about the legends, especially of the Crystal Skulls. They had only been whispers of the elderly, now he was not sure what Sankun was saying or meaning. He wondered if he belonged there.

Sankun eased herself down from the stool. Eyes glazed over, she saw Kito. "Are you with us?" she whispered.

Kito lifted his head. "It would be rude of me to go far at this time."

"Please, my friend, be comfortable. We will be some time."

"Yes, I spend so much time sitting these days. Sadly, I am not allowed to work the fields."

"I have heard your protests, Kito."

"I can care for myself. A man must earn his keep."

"Some believe you already have, Kito."

"If you have heard of my protests, you will also know that I believe that a man cannot live on yesterday's work, but should go back out every day to earn tomorrow's keep. Would you not agree, Sankun?"

"Kito, how old are you?"

Kito brushed down his worn, tattered tunic. "I don't actually know, Sankun."

She sat opposite Kito, shuffling pillows to make herself comfortable. "The older man you grew up with, what is his name?"

"Cusaha. He is kind, brave and gracious, a true Master."

Sankun picked up a poker and busied herself with the coals. "How did you meet him?"

"I was being taken to the Palace to be thrown to the wolves for the entertainment of your Emperor. He intervened and persuaded Chain Man to release me into his care. I would say he saved my life, would you not agree?"

"I'm sorry, Kito. I missed your point."

"Under your rules, he should not have to work anymore. But under our rule, that was yesterday; today there are still chores to be done to have food for tomorrow."

Sankun tilted her head inquisitively. "So, you are living here with us but, living under the rule of a man who is not here, Kito."

"I respect yours, but I also live under my own beliefs. I follow my own heart, in my own life. If I may ask you, when your children of this village grow up and move out to start their own lives, do you think they follow the values of this village?"

Sankun scoffed. "Well, I would hope so, or I think we would have failed in our duty to our culture, our land and our Gods."

"This is my point, Sankun."

Kale and Manchu laughed openly. The fire suddenly flared up, letting out a hiss, and sparks flew towards the ceiling. Sankun glared, silencing them both, then continued to stoke the crackling coals, settling the fire. "Kito, tell me about the day you went fishing and fell ill." Carefully, Sankun watched the young man.

"Of course. It was a nice, though cool, start to the day. Yaan and I had been fishing for some time with moderate success. A large fish was stealing our bait, and I was quite sure he was laughing at our expense, so I thought I would try a different tactic. I dived down and speared him. He was a good fish, well worth the effort."

"So, isn't that earning your keep then? Fish are an important part of our diet."

"There will be time for that when the harvest is done. I was wasting time in a clinker when I could be working in the field."

"Still, Kito, you earned your keep in the clinker. I understand you also caught a sailfish."

Kito shook his head. "No, Yaan caught that one. Now that was a real catch. I believe everyone had a taste, and there was more left to go around."

The three sat remembering Yaan's catch when Kito quietly spoke again. "I think I turned seventeen last spring."

They all stared at Kito. Even as he sat on his cushion, he looked so big. Sankun was no longer in any doubt of the young man sitting before her.

He was indeed the *Uniter of the Seven*.

46 Under the Sail

Alexa stirred; it was late, and Patch had not come to bed. Slipping out, she dragged off the top sheet and wrapped it around herself. The stairway was dark, but she had walked this way often of late. Getting down to the next level, she saw candlelight glowing under the heavy oak door. She didn't knock but gently opened the door and softly stepped in.

Patch was standing at his desk with papers strewn everywhere. He mumbled as he worked, picking up a paper, reading it under two candles and making notes on another paper. Alexa wondered, *How did it come to be that Boa, who was the best vessel builder in the industry, got handed a baby boy found on the wharf, who then became the best vessel builder in the world?* When everyone else saw a stone wall of a problem and stopped, accepting this as the limit, Patch would see it as a platform to climb upon to see ahead. She smirked as she let the sheet drop away. Now naked, she slowly walked towards his desk.

He worked on.

She reached his desk and stopped. Still, he worked on. Slowly, she picked up a candle. Nothing. She picked up the other candle. He leant in, looking at his work now in the dimming light. Eventually, he looked up. Alexa stood with her elbows at her side and her forearms out straight with a candle in each hand, wearing nothing but her glowing smile. With her hourglass figure, full breasts and plump lips, the vision of the model vessel quickly evaporated in his mind. He stepped back from his desk, the animal waking in his trousers. He gulped the full goblet, wiped his mouth with the back of his hand, smacked the goblet back on his desk and drank in her image. Alexa was focused on the back wall, unmoving.

He moved around the desk, removing his tunic. She remained still as he stepped in behind her, slipping an arm around her small waist. She could hear his breathing now, deep and raspy on the side of her neck. She tried not to squeal as he bit her on the shoulder. She tried not to tremble with excitement as he breathed in her ear. She could feel him pulling at his belt, his trousers falling away. He slid his rough left hand up her silky, smooth stomach, up between her breasts to her neck. His right hand moved up her back, and he slid his fingers up, gripping her hair.

Excitement raced up her spine as she clenched the candles. He tilted her head ever so gently and leant in, his hot breath on her. He nibbled her neck, sucking the skin into his mouth, making his way up to her earlobe. Her lips trembled. She could feel him firmly on her back, whispering his desire in her ear.

***

Patch woke first. He was in his large chair with Alexa's naked body curled up on his lap, with the sheet over them.

The two went upstairs to freshen up and have breakfast. Patch returned downstairs to work, feeling truly alive. He spread out his notes and began to pour over them to get back to the train of thought from before he was so pleasantly disturbed.

There was a knock at the door.

"Come."

Admasin stepped inside. "How is the design progressing, Patch?"

Mumbling, Patch started shuffling over his papers. "The thing is, Admasin, with the size of the vessel, I can't see any grown man holding the rudder to turn her. The length would be too great to shift on its axis."

Admasin studied the drawings. The problem would never have occurred to him. "Well, the model is ready to go, with a rudder. Do you think we can manage that?"

Patch's eyes lit up; he had been so busy with the figures of the overall design he'd not so much as looked out of his window. "Really, how close is ready?"

"When have I ever told you, or your father for that matter, that a vessel is ready when it has not been *completely* ready, son?"

Patch leapt from his chair. After months of planning and doing the sums, there it was, just as he had seen it in his mind.

He had made the front higher than normal. This was a vessel that was going to plough through the oceans rather than ride over them. There was a big open deck for cargo, but it also had large opening hatches for cargo to be lowered into its hull. The biggest change of all, almost right in the middle, was a tall, hardwood pole. It towered over the vessel. Behind it were two separate cabins, separate so the rudder man could see down the middle at his cargo and the other vessels when coming in to dock. The raised, rudder deck was nothing special on this scaled-down model, but the real thing was going to be well out of the ordinary.

"Patch, when do you wish for us to take it out?"

Patch did not take his eyes off the model. "Well, tonight, of course, Admasin. There is no time to waste. It would be naive to think it will be right from first sail, now wouldn't it? There will be adjustments to make, and I won't be starting the first, real vessel until this model is true and right. Have you spoken to Kalgan? Does he have the right people ready?"

Admasin smiled at Patch's respectful tone. "Yes, I have, Patch. He has gathered the friends he can trust. If you wish, we can be ready for tonight."

Patch clapped his hands. "Perfect! There is no moon tonight, and we will have to go downstream."

"You know we will be seen going through the city, don't you? Everyone is watching you, and I don't just mean a few spies, Patch, I mean *everyone*."

"Very well. See that the appropriate flags are ready and the oars are in place for us to leave at first light tomorrow."

Admasin flinched with the change. "But Patch, they will …"

"Yes, Admasin, they will anyway."

***

It was still dark the next morning when Patch and Alexa walked into the warehouse to look over the new model.

"Good morning, Admasin, I trust you slept well?"

"About as well as you have, Patch."

Patch rubbed his puffy eyes. "Yes, and Boa would have been just as nervous and excited."

Admasin chuckled. "Yes, I believe he would."

Walking around to the bow, Patch and Alexa knelt to look along the length of the vessel. On the underside was a deeper than usual spine, to each side of it were riveted a multitude of lead bars.

"You damn fool man!"

Hearing Patch, Admasin came back, waving his hands. "What the blazing fires is the commotion? I will be the only one getting around here using language like that. Now what's wrong?" He knelt beside Patch and peered under the vessel.

Patch pointed at the spine. "I only used that much timber so I could fasten the lead to it. I could have just put the lead inside the hull; that would give better water slip."

"And there I was thinking we were going to have to abort the maiden voyage …" Admasin waved his hand at the spine. "… but, this is why we built a model, Patch. So, we can learn from it. Heavens forbid we make a mistake like this when we do it for the Emperor." He slapped Patch on the shoulder several times as he got up and went back to his work.

Alexa pulled Patch to his feet, and they went on around the vessel. There was a difference between the planking on the upper and the lower vessel.

"Patch, this new flush timbering on the lower level looks amazing."

Looking just a little bit proud, he replied, "I've decided to try it on the model. I think we can now have all the planking like this.

468

The vessel is stronger and, because it is smoother, it should also cut through the water better."

"I see that, but why not do the whole vessel?"

Patch had worked it all out to the last detail. "Ah, but then the whole town would see it, wouldn't they? No, this will be our secret until we launch the Emperor's *Ocean Conqueror.*"

Admasin's men worked feverishly. Talk was limited, without anger or raised voices. The two massive doors were open, and the light of a new day was breaking on the horizon. Using large torches, the men began to pull the ropes to draw the model out into the cool morning. If Patch's calculations were correct, they would have no more than a hand span clearance for the top of the pole and a small cutting had to be removed from the west wall to get her out. In the dim light, Admasin stopped the vessel twice before a young man offered to be hoisted up the pole to check. With an affirmative hand, he waved them on.

Outside, the vessel was rolled down to the water by ropes passing over pullies. As she floated off the carriage, Patch took a deep breath. The men were quick onto the wharf and, with a gentle bump, she was tied secure.

Patch noticed how light the sky was already. The men were in place, oars at the ready, silently waiting for him. He was ill-prepared but leapt from the wharf and climbed the stern.

Facing the men, he spoke in a clear, confident voice. "You all know I cannot take this first sailing with you, but I send my best to guide you on your path. You will, as always, listen to Admasin's every command, and if it is not carried out to the letter, you will be answering to me on your return. To the bow, you will have noticed almost a dozen empty barrels tied together. If she goes to the bottom, then the barrels are there to keep you all at the top." The men were happy with the backup plan. "Should it be stuck on a shallow bank, I have instructed Admasin to use the tinder and flint to burn her through immediately. I will walk you through town to draw most of the heckling. There will be plenty of it. Be safe." With that, he walked down onto the deck and jumped back onto the wharf.

Admasin climbed on board, and Alexa stepped forward to follow.

"Alexa, what are you doing? You cannot go on this voyage."

Alexa propped her fists on her hips. Admasin grimaced. The men gathered around for the show, knowing Patch and Alexa could be fiery.

"Oh, is that so, Patch?"

"Yes, it is. Not even I know how watertight it is."

"Well, you were pretty quick to take me on the clinker!"

"And look how that ended! Besides, legend has it you can take neither bananas nor women on a maiden voyage."

Alexa was about to give him his dues when Patch heard an 'Ouch,' from behind. He turned to see Admasin standing with eyebrows raised. Patch rolled his eyes. "Yes, Admasin, your opinion on the matter."

Admasin clasped his hands behind his back. "Well, since you asked, Patch, Alexa has worked every bit as hard on this vessel as anyone."

There were murmurs from all the men. Patch pursed in silence then laughed aloud. Stepping forward to the edge of the wharf, he held out a hand. "My dear Alexa, after all of your dedicated work on this prestigious project, may I help you aboard?"

She stepped forward, taking his hand. "What, a woman and a banana too?"

Patch frowned. "There are no bananas here, Alexa."

She leaned in close. "Oh, so you *are* pleased to see me this morning."

Admasin choked back a laugh as he stepped aboard. With a red face, Patch threw off the ropes and watched the men work the vessel out into the channel.

He followed the vessel through town as he had said. Many noticed the vessel that appeared so different, then saw Patch coming on foot. Some negative observations were launched at him. Patch had been different all his life, so people's observations just bounced off him. Most could not appreciate what they were looking at. They laughed at the strange flagpole in the centre and the weird bow and the oarsmen on the top of the deck, baking in the sun.

Alexa sighed at the badgering being given to him. They didn't even understand what they were criticising. She resisted yelling back how foolish they sounded. Patch just followed the model downriver until the end of town, where he stopped and watched them row out of sight.

***

A gentle westerly blew as they broke out of the river Sollya and onto the inland sea. Perfect. They turned east, making their way well clear of the river mouth.

Admasin gave the signal and Kalgan had the men put away their oars. As a team, they lifted the two long poles that had been laid hidden during the passage through the city. Patch had been adamant that no one was to see the cloth already fixed to them.

Admasin saw the crew were ready. "Very well, men, take up the ropes and wait for my calls."

He called the order, and the crew began to pull the ropes, lifting the top pole. Little by little, the cloth ascended the tall, centre post. About two-thirds up, the wind caught the cloth, pulling it tight with a loud thump.

"Men, hold."

At the rudder, Kalgan and five other men followed Admasin's signal. The vessel surged ahead, turning downwind. They almost let go of the ropes as they tried to look over the side at the water rushing by. With gleaming eyes, Alexa looked at Admasin, who was busy caring for the men.

"Eyes on your job, men. Hold steady."

Unable to resist, Alexa watched the water rushing effortlessly past the smooth boards. She wiped away tears. "Admasin, Patch

471

should be here for this. It is the most amazing event of our time!"

In his excitement, he put an arm around her. "Indeed, it is, Alexa. It seems strange to me that a man so afraid of water can create this!" He waved at the sail with an excited fist.

***

Patch paced back and forth, occasionally peering downriver into the dark. *Has she sunk or been burnt?* He imagined a hundred things that could have gone wrong. He had even thought they might have lost control and been blown out to Devil's Pass, only to be sunk by Balzac's magic iron ball, or worse, on the jagged reef.

Just as he was imagining the very worst, they came around the bend towards the city. He saw Alexa and Admasin, safely at the bow pointing the way for Kalgan.

Alexa saw Patch walking along the wharf with his torch. "What are you doing out here?"

"I could ask you the same question. You took your time."

Admasin stepped in beside Alexa, recognising more than one set of prying eyes. "Patch, it has been a poor day on the water, and we are feeling parched. May I suggest you go ahead and light the torches?"

Hiding in the darkness were the silhouettes of some of Patch's biggest competitors, the same men who had been there that morning, laughing and making scathing remarks. Lowering his lantern, Patch went on ahead.

He made his way around the waterfront to light the wharf for his crew. To his astonishment, it was already done. A glow of lanterns lit the workshop, and entering, he saw all his tradesmen huddled around in a tight circle, chattering and shouting. There was a flurry of paper notes making the rounds.

As the noise simmered down, Patch gave a cough. The group burst open and several footsteps could be heard running off into the darkness. The rest were frozen to the spot, wide-eyed.

Patch walked over to one and snatched the wooden paddle out of his hand. "This is a 'two-up' paddle, is it not, Tonkin?"

"Yes, I believe it is, sir."

Patch waved the paddle in front of Tonkin. "You have always called me Patch, everyone here does, don't change it now."

Tonkin lowered his eyes.

Patch stepped back, looking at everyone. "So, you were all playing two-up, an illegal game as set by the Emperor himself. Is that what I am to believe?"

The younger men looked down at their feet. A few of the older crew stood with their hands in their pockets. "Why," said Patch as he pulled two round discs from his pocket, "have you never invited *me*?"

The men burst into laughter and quickly huddled back in.

***

With the wharf lit up, the job of docking was quick. Admasin turned to Kalgan. "Before anyone leaves for home, this vessel is to be inside that workshop. Any questions?"

The exhausted men groaned, and Kalgan stepped forward. "Sir, if I may?"

Admasin stepped onto the wharf. "Yes, Kalgan?"

"Well, sir, we missed the tide coming back in and so the men and I … well, sir, we are all very tired, sir."

Admasin raised his eyebrows. "You think I do not know the tide right outside my own workplace, young man? This vessel is not staying out here for the night, and I do not think I need explain the reasons to you. Now, if you wish to press your questioning of my authority, I will be right over there sorting out that unruly lot. Do you wish to join that lot, Kalgan?"

"No, sir. The vessel will be ready to recover on your return."

Admasin marched along the wharf, making a beeline for the tight group huddled in the workshop. No one noticed him approaching. "What in the ocean's fury is going on here?"

The group scattered, revealing Patch, down on one knee, holding the paddle.

"What? Oh, what? Patch?"

Patch stood up coyly. "Ah, yes, um well, me and the boys were just passing the time awaiting your arrival, Admasin."

Admasin pursed his lips. "Right then. Okay, men, you can now go and arm the ropes to return this fine vessel into the workshop." They scurried off, pleased to have escaped the wrath of the old man.

"Fine vessel, Admasin?" enquired Patch.

Admasin, now joined by Alexa, grinned broadly. "Yes, son. This sail thing worked. Boy, did it work!"

Alexa put her hands on his chest. "You are the one, Patch. You are the one."

Patch beamed, childlike. "What about the rudder? Was it true?"

"The vessel has some problems we need to work on, but the principle worked, almost too well. We missed the returning tide because we went so far under sail, so it was a long way to row back."

Patch strode over to stand on some stacked timber and whistled to his men. "I thank the men who worked so hard on the vessel today. It was a brave act with such an unknown design. I thank the men who put out the lanterns tonight and waited to help upon its return. It shows initiative and loyalty to those around you. All of you, except those who made a run for it earlier ..." A chuckle went around the workshop. "... you can all come in at mid-morning tomorrow!" A cheer went up as the men dispersed, heading back to retrieve the vessel. Patch returned to Admasin.

"Patch, do you really think that was necessary?"

Patch did not take his eyes off the crew aligning the vessel with its carriage. "If no one had been waiting here tonight, I would only just have all the lanterns out, and we would have less than half the team to pull her back into the workshop. We would be here most of the night. So yes, Admasin, I think the men more than deserve it, and what's more, the workshop will be much better for it tomorrow. They have a win, as do I. Now, would you be so kind as to make sure they have that vessel aligned correctly on the carriage."

"Yes, indeed, Patch."

Admasin strode out of the workshop with his hands clasped behind his back, a small smile on his face and a glow of pride in his heart.

475

47 Master of the Guard

As always, Desora, the would-be Master of the Guard, had to train to fight in all manner of battles. Well outnumbered by enthusiastic young players, the most enduring – the Sword Masters – came last. It was tradition to use hardwood swords, and towards the end game, one of the young men dealt what would have been a deathblow to the prince. Everyone saw it. The prince had failed. It meant that he had to train for a further four seasons before he could re-test.

Many of the young men had crowded around the winner to congratulate him. The prince had dressed and stood alone, watching. His anger built. Raging internally, he fingered his sword with his left hand, his mind toward a move taught to him by Xiang. His blood ran hot in his veins, and in a heartbeat, he drew out his sword. Flicking it high in the air, he leapt forward, turning as he did, his eyes on the sword as the blade sang in the air. Aware of his target, he snatched the falling sword with his right hand, spun round and drove it into the young man's back. The young man cried out as he recognised the blood-stained blade protruding from his chest.

Desora moved in close behind him and whispered, *"The Prince always wins,"* and withdrew his sword.

How great it felt to push the sword into the young man's body, rasping against bones as it drove through, the feeling of joy as the young man cried out, and the sweet taste of success as his lifeless body fell away.

***

Stood in his office bay window, the Emperor's mind was busy going over the plans for taking the City of Samos. At last, the time of reckoning was here. He went over the plans, as he had a thousand times before. Everything was accounted for, and if it wasn't, someone would pay with their life. He admired the trees, changing colour with autumn. Small groups of soft, snow-carrying clouds hovered ominously above.

A slamming door drew his thoughts. *Desora walking down the stairs.*

"How many times have I told you? You must knock before you enter my office."

Undeterred by his father's scolding, Desora pulled the cork from the decanter and poured the contents into two silver goblets. He strode over and handed one to the Emperor.

"So, Desora, who is it that we're going to take? Have you made a decision?" The Emperor eyed his son closely. "You really should have let someone check that cut to your forehead, Desora. It has been some time and never faded."

Desora turned to the desk, trying to ignore his father's irksome reference to his humiliation at the hands of an old man.

The Emperor gloated further. "Master Xiang really did do a job on you."

Desora spun back, pointing his finger. "That, Father, was many seasons ago, and you should know better than to mention *his* name in my presence! *I* am the Master of this place now and you know it! What's more, I do not think we need anyone, other than *myself,* to take the city of Samos!" Desora seethed, his anger as evident as it was instant.

Slowly, the Emperor turned his back on Desora to gaze back out of the window. "Very well, my Prince, that is settled, but be aware, if you lead the men directly, you will have no one to blame if it goes wrong. Also, my Prince, you will have to lead in person, in *every* battle."

"I have no problem with that and nor should you. Anyway, I do not expect there will be very much resistance in the city, do you?"

Distracted by his thoughts, the Emperor's reply was barely audible. "No, I suppose not, Desora."

Desora sat, feeling pleased with himself, vindicated. "When do you think we need to leave? Winter is upon us once more."

"It is up here in the mountains, Desora, but down at sea level, they are still enjoying the last of summer."

"I really do not care what season they are enjoying in Samos, I just wish to take it."

"Ah, you do have my blood running through your veins after all. You wish to feel the power of leadership. You can taste the winning, the success, can you not?"

Desora rose smoothly to his feet, the goblet in his right hand, his left resting on the hilt of his sword. "I do not need to crush a small city of peasants to get the taste of success. I am already a Master."

The Emperor did not turn from the window. "Are you? I mean, really?"

Desora's mind spun back to the day he was awarded Master. He eyed his father's back as he strode forward, then paused. He breathed deeply, calming himself and stepped in beside the Emperor. He peered down at the forest floor then to the sky, all with little interest. "I might go and see what is happening at the Den, Father."

"You know exactly what is happening in the Den, Desora. No, you need to stay here to go over preparations with me."

"I have been over the preparations more times than I have rehearsed my moves. Enough is enough, Father. At a certain point, it becomes obsessive, not to mention boring." Desora turned to leave but only got as far as the bottom step.

"Desora?"

"Yes, Father?"

"Try not to get too high tonight. We're leaving at first light. Understood?"

"Yes, Father."

"Oh, and Desora?"

"Father?"

"Do you remember the time I warned you about how you did not flow from one of your moves to another, and the black fellow was going to step in and break your nose with his elbow? How did that work out for you?"

Desora slowly turned, eyeing his father's back as he continued to look outside. His temper bubbled under the surface. He could feel the power of it. His mind raced over the possibilities as his fingers massaged the hilt of his sword. Dropping his empty goblet, Desora walked out.

The Emperor watched Desora's reflection in the bay window. Seeing the empty goblet roll back and forth, he released the throw-knife inside his long coat.

***

The following morning, the sun had barely crested the horizon as the Emperor and Desora trotted their horses through the palace gates.

The Emperor inhaled the crisp morning air. "Ah, it is agreeable to be free of the Palace, don't you think, my Prince?" He grinned at the prince's pained face. He well remembered staying in the Den for too long when he was a young man. At first with the best intentions, reassuring himself, *One wench, one red wine and off to bed,* but it never worked like that because one couldn't really have a red wine, without a pipe. That was the trap, one red and a pipe, and no more thoughts of the morning.

The Emperor nudged the prince. "For someone with so much to say in my office yesterday, you have little to say today."

The prince winced. "I still do not understand why we could not have taken the Royal coach."

Derisively, the Emperor responded. "Well, the reason is all in my notes. If you had stayed to go over them, you would know exactly why. Trust me, my Prince, there is very good reason indeed."

The prince straightened in the saddle, taking a long drink from his water bladder. He touched his lips with his pocket cloth.

"Emperor, I think it is time for you to begin calling me Master. We are, after all, on official Palace business, and I feel protocol is essential to lead the Guard." He gazed over the land with the proud manner of ownership.

"Well, look who is up and on his job this morning. Yes, Master Desora, I could not agree more. Do you wish to share how you intend to conquer and hold the city for me?"

Master Desora glanced at his father with a smirk of satisfaction. "Yes, but first, could you tell me about what you intend to do once I have overthrown the city?"

"Again, the notes, Master. Though lucky for you, I am in a talkative mood. We will take one of our new vessels, with many hundreds of guardsmen, to meet up with Mensa. He will, of course, give me the third Crystal Skull and the location of the Stone Temple. That's when I will go to the Sacred Crystal and fulfil my destiny!" He shook a vigorous fist, spitting his passion and greed.

"You already have two Skulls, why is the third so important?"

The Emperor nodded enthusiastically. "As explained to me by your mother, Princess Sha'Doe, with the gold she brought here, three is enough for me to gain Godly power to retrieve the rest. You will become the son of a God-King!"

Desora struggled with his temper. "And what's in *that*, for *me*, Emperor?"

The Emperor smiled at Desora's drive to prosper. "Ah, until now I have kept this to myself but, since we are on the verge of domination, you should know. Once we have our leadership over all known lands, you will take our new fleet of Imperial ships to your mother's birthplace, Palusa, where you are also a prince. Therefore, you will rule. It is a land said to be wealthy in gold beyond belief. That gold belongs here, in the palace where your mother died. It was not by chance she was sent to me. It was not by chance that I got her pregnant with you. It's interesting that the very downfall of the Gods was something of their own design."

The Emperor laughed with abandonment.

Desora reached for his water bladder.

When the Emperor had finally calmed himself, he turned to Desora. "We do digress, Master. Your plan for the city?"

Hanging his water bladder on his Imperial saddle, the Master damped off his lips. "Indeed, Emperor. Because of the shape of the city, I have divided it into three sectors. Jundi will take one, Kung will take another and Chenghou will care for the last. I will be located on Yuson Ridge. From this elevated point, I can watch over the entire project."

The Emperor made no effort to hide his surprise. "Well, I am pleased to hear it, Master. That seems a sound plan. You intend to separate and therefore, weaken any would-be resistance."

The Master interrupted. "Yes. Of course, I will also have three messengers to keep the groups informed of my needs."

"Are you sure three are enough? If you send one message to three …"

"Yes, ample, I would say, and I really do not have the head for your prodding this morning. This other land you say I am a prince to, tell me more about it."

The Emperor was about to put the young Master in his place when a rider appeared from the direction of the city of Samos. He was riding hard.

Holding the reins, the rider leapt down from his saddle as the Master held up his hand to signal the group of following horsemen to stop. He eyed the man. "Well, out with it then. What is your message?"

The man was in as bad a condition as his horse. "Sire, it is said several vessels are leaving the city of Samos with rice and grain."

The Master pointed at the man's horse with its head down, breathing ragged and sweating profusely. "You ran an Imperial horse into the ground for a message like that!"

The Emperor spoke before the man could defend himself. "How long before another shipment comes in from the farmland?"

The man ignored the Master, responding to the Emperor. "It is hard to say, sire. The farmers come and go as they please, but it seems that, if you could be there in a few days, sire, after the last vessel leaves, the stocks would be almost exhausted."

The Emperor smiled. "What is your name, Messenger?"

"My name is Xi, Emperor."

"Xi, can you tell me the name of the last vessel?"

"Yes, sire, the biggest on the ocean, the *Shiraz*. She has just arrived and will be there for a few more days."

The Master scrunched his face to his father. "What a bizarre name for a vessel."

The Emperor was still looking at Xi. "Yes, Master, it is the grape they make red wine from. I believe the captain has a bit of a drinking problem. Xi, you have given us valuable information at an important time. You are to go to the palace and tend your horse. You may both rest up for one day before making your way back to Samos. You will find Master Desora up on Yuson Ridge; there you will take your service."

***

The Master's face bore a sly grin. Xi bowed. "You are most kind, sire."

The Emperor straightened in his saddle. "Perfect. We will have this like a fine wine. Master, double-time it for the city."

Almost knocking Xi over, the Master kicked his horse, galloping off for the city of Samos.

48 The Serpent

The cool air flowed out onto the fields, and with it came the scents of some of Kito's favourite jungle inhabitants. He listened to the bird songs, as colourful as their feathers. Around him, the people sang the songs he'd taught them at the Colonial Dig. Sometimes it made him think of his good friend, Baako, but mostly, he simply enjoyed the songs and sang along with them, his deep voice adding depth and harmony.

They were in the final field; the season was finished. The harvest had been good and some of the workers had been kept back at the village to start threshing to make room for the rest of the harvest. Kito had been offered work there, but he wanted to work out in the fields. They finally relented and agreed that a sickle was best for him. Once he had been led to a starting position, cutting back and forth along the edge of the field was no obstacle for him.

Behind him came the women, bunching and tying the cut rice. Luhou, Jong and little Orton were amongst them. Most of the elders worked, claiming it gave them a reason to get up in the morning. One woman, Sinta, said it kept them young, and Kito believed this to be true and right; when he first arrived at the Colonial Dig, he could not put an age to them. It had resonated with him; they had their multitude of wrinkles on leathery faces, though they were also agile and fit.

The women dropped the bundles at the rear of a cart where, using a pitchfork, Yaan threw them up. When a cart was stacked high enough, it was pulled away by a mule.

Waiting for the next cart to arrive, Yaan wiped the sweat from his brow. With concern, he saw Jong approaching Kito, who was standing in the shade, waiting for a guide. Kito heard the footsteps coming his way. Jong stood before Kito, who stepped back and bowed deeply.

Jong spoke softly. "Please do not bow before me, Kito."

Kito straightened, slowly. "I bow to all my elders, Jong, you know this."

"Yes, though I also know it should be a sign of respect. I have not given you reason to have respect of me, young man. I apologise for it." Kito began to object but Jong spoke over him. "Do you know what Narpa said he saw on that day, Kito? At first, I could not believe it. I *refused* to believe it, but just a few nights ago, I had a dream. My Quinn came to me in my dream and said, '*Please my love, do not feel bad for our loss but instead remember our love. My time was not far anyway. I await your arrival, take your time and enjoy the young ones.*' Can you believe that, Kito? 'Enjoy the young ones,' that is what she said to me."

Jong knelt before Kito and took hold of his hands. "I know you did your best. No one here could have done what you did that day. No one. I lost, but others won. It is the way in life sometimes." He kissed Kito on both hands. "My friend, will you forgive an old fool?"

Kito drew the old man to his feet. "A fool is a fool and he is not to be forgiven; you are the man who saw me when others would not look at me. The two of you opened your home and your hearts. Jong, I welcome your grace back into my life." He stepped back and bowed again. Pleased to be free of the tension, the two relaxed and chatted together.

Yaan had observed quietly. The issue between them was at last resolved. He called over. "Kito, my friend, have you finished harvesting over there yet?"

"You know I have. The last of it is being bunched as we speak. It has been a dusty day. I may require a swim this afternoon."

"We'll get the last of the bunches on the next cart then a swim is a fine idea. Of course, I would like to help with the threshing, but I don't know if there's enough room in the threshing shed for my handsome shoulders."

A few of the elders listened in the shade of the jungle, enjoying the young men's banter.

"It is true you have fine shoulders my friend," countered Kito, "But I fear it is your ego that would have the problem fitting into the shed."

A terrified shriek pierced the air.

Yaan saw Sinta being lifted off the ground by a giant serpent. The serpent had wrapped itself around a large branch before coiling around the old woman with its tail. As it tightened its hold, her life was being squeezed from her. Yaan charged forward with his pitchfork raised like a spear.

The serpent struggled to lift its prey up into the tree, it had an unexpected passenger. Kito had leapt on it and was trying to unroll its tail. With the tip of the serpent's tail over his shoulder, he pushed his feet against the serpent, trying to unroll it. The serpent struggled and twisted.

Yaan yelled, repeatedly spearing the serpent with his pitchfork. It hissed and swung down, snapping at Yaan, who leapt about, trying to inflict more damage. The serpent broke the pitchfork handle with a single bite, leaving the sharp prongs lodged in its side. It reared up and hissed wildly.

Through gritted teeth, Kito called, "My sickle, Yaan! My sickle!"

Yaan dropped the remainder of the useless pitchfork and grabbed the sickle. He slashed at the serpent squeezing the old lady. It hissed and lashed down at him. Yaan slashed back, both missing their target. The scaly skin was tough, the sickle barely scratched it.

The tunic on Kito's back tore as he strained to hold the serpent's tail from closing any further on the old woman. His arms burned and his eyes watered from the strain, grunting at Sinta to stay with him. Tears streamed down Sinta's face as blood vessels burst beneath her skin.

There was only one way to finish this. Yaan screamed as he leapt up onto Kito's back, enticing the serpent. It hissed, bearing its fangs and eyeing Yaan, now well within striking range. It drew back and lunged down at him.

Suddenly, the serpent went flaccid, dropping the three, who sprawled out into the undergrowth. Yaan jumped to his feet and began leaping about, yelling and punching the air. Slowly, Kito rolled onto his hands and knees.

"Yaan! Yaan, how is Sinta?"

Her limp body lay silent, then incredibly, Sinta drew breath. The group looked on with disbelieving eyes as she rolled onto her side, coughing. Next to her sat Kito, leaning back on his hands, still breathing hard. He held up a hand as the group came to offer help. "Please do not move her. She will be all right on her side."

Kito lay flat on his back as Yaan approached. "Kito, are you all right, my friend?"

Kito responded between gasps. "Give me a moment to recover. I once tangled with a king cobra, but this serpent was something else."

"You tangled with a king cobra?"

Kito sat up onto one elbow, took another deep breath, then stood. "Yes, but it was a long time ago."

"You were a boy and tangled with a king cobra? How close did you and this king cobra get, Kito?"

Kito went to the serpent. Its tail was laid out on the ground, the body had wrapped around a large branch some thirty feet high, the head hanging back down.

"Oh, we were entangled for a time, but we both made our escapes."

Kito examined the death strike. Yaan had driven the sickle in through its mouth and up into its brain. Instant death. The broken pitchfork was firmly stuck in the serpent's side. He turned to Yaan, pointing at the pitchfork. "You brought a fork to a battle with a serpent?"

Yaan paused, then his face lit up. "Kito? You can see!"

Kito waved his hand at the fork. "You came to this fight, with a fork?"

Yaan feigned a slap on Kito's chest with the back of his hand, Kito gently parried it. "Kito! You can see!" Yaan yelled enthusiastically. "Everyone! Kito can *see!*"

Kito drew a breath as he stared into Yaan's eyes. He was mesmerised.

"Yaan, my friend, your eyes …"

Yaan laughed as he reached up to hold Kito by his shoulders. "Kito, you have *your* eyes back and you comment about *my* eyes?"

Kito didn't notice the group gathering around them. He stared into Yaan's eyes, his mind reeling back. "What did you say your father's name is?"

"What is it you see in my eyes, Kito?"

"Before today, nothing, but now they are the most revealing thing I have seen."

***

That evening, elation and celebration filled the cooking room. Although the threshing would go on for more days yet, all the rice had been harvested and was inside under cover.

Kale stood and bowed his head; it was the signal for the room to fall silent. He looked about the glowing faces. "It is with great sadness that I take this time to remember those who should have returned from the Colonial Dig but did not."

The silence was only broken with a few sniffs.

Kale tapped a porcelain cup to the hot stone. "Firstly, I must thank the elders who did not make the arduous journey to the Colonial Dig. We have a bumper harvest. We are in your debt for the work you did in our absence. However, you would all have heard – I think even the Spirit World has heard by now – of what occurred today." A warm laugh went about the room. "Kito, Yaan and Sinta, would you come and join me in this story, please."

Slowly, the three made their way to the front. Kito stooped under trusses and beams, standing next to Yaan as Kale resumed.

"After the report of almost losing Sinta came to me, I left to inspect the scene. I received firsthand reports about how it all happened and what a story it made! Let me tell you, the serpent was a fully grown anaconda!" A *'Whoo'* echoed. "These two men took it down …" The crowd began to clap as Kale stood beside Sinta. "… and saved this wonderful woman from an unfortunate ending!" Again, the room clapped fervently. "But! …" He waved a finger at the ceiling. "… they left behind my sickle so I had some of our enthusiastic young men retrieve it for me." He motioned towards the door. "Could I have the sickle returned now, please?"

In strode four young men carrying a table. Upon it was the anaconda's massive head, the sickle still protruding out of the crest. People gasped, mingling forward to see.

Kale held up his hands. "The table will be left for everyone to see. Please be seated, I haven't finished. We've had another miracle today."

Reluctantly, everyone took their seats.

"We have known them both for some time now, but over this last summer, we've all become very fond of Kito and Yaan. Today, they did something I would ask of none of you. They risked their own lives for one of our own." He pointed to the serpent's head now on display, "And against all odds, they succeeded!"

The room thundered with applause until Kale bowed his head to quieten them down. He walked over and stood beside Kito. "This, rather large young man, ran in and stopped the serpent from crushing our Sinta to certain death." The villagers talked animatedly as Kale stepped in beside Yaan, putting a hand on his shoulder. "And I am told that this young man did not back off one hand span throughout the battle. Using Kito's sickle, he gave the deathblow! What's more, he ran up the serpent's own tail to do it. Have you ever heard the likes of it?"

The villagers stood and cheered. Calling out over the clapping, Kale continued. "This is one of the most amazing stories I have ever heard. I give you, the three that made it, Yaan, Kito, and Sinta!"

As the crowd congratulated them, the three began to make their way back to their seats. Kito had only taken two steps when he felt a tug on his tunic. He turned to see Kale give him a wink and a gentle motion to stay.

Kale bowed his head and the room fell quiet again. They'd all heard the rumours and had seen Kito walking proudly without a guide. "As most of you know already …" Kale put a hand up on Kito's arm, "… another miracle happened today. Kito, would you like to tell us what that miracle was?"

Kito's smile warmed the room. "Today, I got to see all your beautiful faces." The room let out a gentle *'Oooh'*. "To those of you, like Luhou, Jong and others who have taken your time to help me, I am forever in your debt. If ever you need anything, all you need to do is call my name, and I will be there to serve you." Kito bowed deeply. One by one, everyone stood in silence and bowed back.

Unnoticed, in a corner of the room, sat Sankun. She did not stand but she did bow, as well as her old bones let her. Kito stood straight and waited for the room to sit. "I'm also sorry to say, it is time now for me to leave you all."

Kale flinched. "What? Kito, what's this about?"

"I know this comes as a shock to you. I have made many friends, and you are like family, but please understand, somewhere out there, I also have my own family. It is them that my heart seeks. My journey can only be finished when I am accepted back into my homeland, my village and my family."

Kale glanced to the darkest corner where Sankun gave a hand signal. His attention returned to Kito. "Where will you go first, my friend?"

"I must go and seek out my second father. I owe him my life. I left on a hunting trip and never returned. I must make my apologies before going to Samos."

Kale watched as, silently from the shadows, Sankun nodded her approval.

***

Before dawn the next morning, Kito made his way through the kitchen and helped himself to last night's leftovers from the cooler. The roasted goat was mouth-watering. Kito smirked. At least those blessed 'goat' things were good for something. Removing his shoulder pack, he loaded it with cheese, fruit and vegetables that didn't need cooking.

He had been told Samos was only a few days northwest. Now his own man again, he intended to move fast.

Silently, Kito headed down the stairs. A horse neighed. He didn't look but headed straight for the gate. Walking out along the narrow ridge, he paused with the feeling of eyes, watching him. He turned and saw on the top level, Sankun and Kale.

Kale turned to Sankun. "How does one get one's eyesight back from fighting a serpent?"

She leant her old bones on the balcony rails. "I do not believe he got his eyesight back from fighting the serpent. He got it back from the apology."

"But he lost his sight in the river, not from failing to save Quinn."

"Yes, the muddy water took his sight but swimming in salt water would've healed it. Though he did not know it, what he really needed was Jong's forgiveness." They bowed to Kito and held it. When they stood up, he was gone.

***

Kito only ran for a short time before he felt unprepared, constricted. Under a shaded tree, he stopped and did some of his stretches, surprised at how tight he had become. He pulled on his backpack and headed off again. His strides were easier, but his

490

lungs ached; he didn't push himself too hard, or he wouldn't have been able to keep going. All his senses had become finer, sharper, he was more aware of his surroundings than he had ever been before.

The next few days were happy ones, free and on the trail. His lungs began to open and he could push himself up hills and cruise comfortably on the level. Life was good.

Nearing the city, the track became wider and he passed more and more people. Full carts headed in the same direction, with empty ones returning to various homes and farms. He stopped to inquire as to how far it was to the city of Samos. The farmer frowned and walked around, giving him a wide berth.

Kito loped on until he approached a wide stream with a stone bridge over it. A smooth pond lay to his right, where willows hung their weeping branches into the water like fingers feeling the gentle current. Along the heavily wooded banks to his left were wide, shallow rapids as the stream flowed off around a bend. He smiled at the beauty of it all.

It was growing dark. Kale had spoken of the stone bridge just before the city so, after crossing, Kito turned right and headed out onto the grassy plain, moving away from the road. He decided to set camp under a willow tree near the water's edge. He would make a fire tonight. Plenty of fires had been lit here before, and the last few nights had been cool. He chided himself for not having allowed one more day for preparations, and to mend his near-ruined tunic. All he could think about was finding Hasuca, the *Shiraz* and his way home.

After a long swim in the fresh water, he gave his clothes a good wash, then set about making a fire under the willow. After eating, he leant back against the tree. He could hear people coming and going over the stone bridge in the distance though he took little notice, staring mostly into the fire. It was calming, hypnotic.

His reveries were disturbed by the sound of approaching horsemen. Strangely, he felt at ease but chancing nothing, he rose smoothly and made his way out of the hanging branches, skirting around the outside. As he did, one of the horsemen called.

"Knock, knock."

Kito chuckled as he stepped out from behind the willow.

"Bolli, Hao, Yaan! In the name of the Gods, why are you here?"

49 Samos

It was first light when the Emperor and Master Desora walked along Yuson Ridge. Gazing down over the city of Samos, torches glowed everywhere. Apparently the city never slept.

To the Emperor's satisfaction, Master Desora had gone over the plans with his men the night before. Chun, too, had sat in on the discussions, though it had seemed to the Emperor that the chubby little man was doing a lot of nodding and very little thinking.

It was a simple plan, and the Master had been thorough. It was to start when the Emperor gave the signal, a burning building. A scare tactic, to show the people of Samos that they were serious and not to be messed with. The smoke would be seen from all over the city.

Taking with them a legion of soldiers, the Master and the Emperor rode down the hill into the city.

"Emperor, just how are you going to find a silhouette, at dawn?"

The Emperor turned to the Master. "Well, it will be a game of observation. I do have one firm lead, though. It may be nothing, or it may be just what I have been looking for."

Intrigued and somewhat put out that he had not been appraised of this lead, Desora raised his eyebrows. "Oh, and what lead is that, Emperor?"

The Emperor seemed distracted. "A dark woman has been seen coming and going from the city via the same route, though I do fear we may be too late, as she has not been here for some time. However, if nothing else, I will get to hear from her what she has been doing."

"You know where she lives?"

"Yes, but first I want to see how my new vessels are coming along. I spoke to Asset Chun last night. To say he was vague would be an understatement."

The Master was keen to make a start. "Is it really necessary to check on such matters now? Could we not meet the builder when we have the city under our control, Emperor?"

The Emperor waved an index finger as he led the way through the streets. "Patience, young man, business must be taken as the opportunity brings it along."

"So, you have informants that gave you the address and name for this dark woman?"

"Well, of course I do. She works for a baker and her name would be Trina. Why do you think Xi almost ran his poor horse into the ground bringing critical information about the city stocks?"

"Because your source sent him to you."

"Precisely, Master. Xi is one my informant's messengers."

"So why did your source not just follow this Trina?"

"They did, several times. However, she would go up into the jungle and simply disappear. I personally cut the throats of two of my best trackers and the third begged for his miserable life as I took his young wife. Alas, they just could not track her. Disappointing, to say the least."

"So, they quit looking? Hardly worthy of the Palace, I would have thought."

The Emperor shook his head. "No, they did not 'just quit.' I hounded them. They tracked her to where she spent her first night out of the city. Apparently, it is a strange place called the Cove of Lost Souls. The men watched her make a fire in the cove then, when it had burnt down the next morning, she was gone. With no fire, the cove continued smoking and then, some time later, the fire slowly rebuilt itself, and she could be seen sitting behind it once more. The superstitious fools called her the Guardian of the Lost Souls. Then one day, she just stopped going."

The Master frowned as they turned another street corner. "Do you think she got wind of them tracking her?"

"No, I think not, Master; rather she changed all her patterns at the same time. Something else caused her to change them. Observations, Master, it is about watching human behaviour. This is why I fear I am too late."

"Too late?"

The Emperor rolled his eyes. "Yes, Master. I fear something else has killed Hasuca before I can get to him to do it with my own bare hands."

"So, you are chasing up the lead just to be sure?"

The Emperor's eyes lit up as he waved his finger. "Exactly, Master, you must always follow every lead to its end, or you are simply running on assumptions. You cannot run a Palace or the greatest nation on Earth on assumptions. Besides, I wish to show these damn superstitious peasants who it is that they must fear and it will not be her when I have finished, let me tell you!"

A man stepped out of the shadows. The Master's hand dropped to his sword.

"Steady, Master, this would be the man I am expecting." The Emperor stopped his horse just short of the man. "I take it you are ready to take me to Trina then, tracker man?"

The little man did not speak but merely bowed.

"Good. First, we will go to the salt well, then on to Patch's yard." The Emperor eyed the little man. "You understand who I mean?" The man nodded, then turned and trotted off down the street. They followed as he made several turns until he stopped at the end of an alley. He bowed, then pointed. They looked across the open courtyard led to it by many alleyways. Right in the centre was the salt well.

The Emperor glared at the tracker man. "Well, lead the way, fool!"

The tracker man sprinted to the well, then stopped with eyes to the ground.

The Master scoffed. "A man of few words."

The Emperor threw his reins at the tracker. "That would be because when I got tired of his begging; I took his tongue."

Blankly, the Master looked at the little man. "Was his wife any good then?"

"I don't remember. Are you coming?"

The Master slipped from his saddle, walked over and peered down the well. "So, what is this about then?"

"This seems like any other well, but I have heard stories of its purpose."

The Master could see nothing unusual. "Emperor?"

The Emperor pulled the rope to retrieve the bucket, plonking it down on the stone side. Rocking back and forth in the water was a human skull, full of fat maggots. They crawled over the bucket as the Emperor seethed. "Murder! Murder in my city without my consent. Blood will flow for this!"

"It would appear so, Emperor, but by whom?"

The Emperor studied the numerous shops and factories leading into the open area. "Observations, Master."

Across the courtyard was the silk factory; standing inside the window, smiling back at him, was Tark Fly. He was using the morning sun to flash a gold piece from the Palace archives. Not just any gold piece but a one-of-a-kind piece that had gone missing on the night of the fire. The very night that Hasuca had also gone missing.

Without a word, the Emperor marched across the courtyard, his long strides reverberating on the cobbles. The Master did his best to catch up whilst retaining his dignity.

The Emperor rounded the large factory as Tark opened the door with a small bow. "Good morning to you, and the Prince."

The Master hastened up beside the Emperor, snarling, "To you, I am Master." He was stopped by his father raising a gloved hand. Arrogantly, Tark eyed the Master. The two locked eyes as the Emperor continued. "Are you to invite your prestigious guests in, or should we arrange for an appointment?"

"No invitation is necessary for yourself, or the Master, for that matter."

The Master coloured red with anger at the pompous tone. The Emperor stepped in, searching the office and there on the wall, hung three tapestries. One hanging depicted a beautiful woman in a vibrant orange dress. The next, a long bridge that disappeared up into a spiral of fog. The third tapestry was, to the Emperor, further proof of the Crystals. There was no mistaking where they had come from. The blood surged through his veins so hot and hard he had trouble hearing Tark.

"So, you like my wall hangings, Emperor?"

The Emperor controlled his temper. "Yes Tark, very impressive. You remember how you acquired them?"

"Well, of course, Your Excellency. You had them sent for the protection of myself, my factory and its people."

The comment visibly struck the Emperor. "Yes, of course, and that was in exchange for?"

Tark was clearly confused. "Well, for the little brown boy, Chan Kito."

This time, there was no hiding the rage that coursed within the Emperor. Tark turned a ghostly pale. The Emperor could smell his fear as he stepped in close. "How old was this boy, Chan Kito?"

"I could not be sure – a handful, a handful and a half ..."

"You lie!"

"No, I could never lie to the Palace, never." Tark began to panic. "It ... it was not m-my idea, Emperor."

The Emperor's eyes narrowed. "Then whose was it?"

"It ... it was one of my staff." His nervous finger of accusation pointed to his workshop.

"Oh, and which one of your staff would that be, my good friend?"

Tark's mind raced. He remembered the old hag, but for the life of him could not recall her name.

"Very well, Tark. Let us come at this from another angle. Who was it that took Chan Kito to the Palace?" The Emperor walked back around Tark's desk, giving him some space as he watched Tark struggling.

Relieved, Tark smiled. "Well, that is easy, Emperor. It was me!"

The Emperor closed his eyes. "Very good, Tark. And who did you hand him over to?" Tark dropped his head, nervously stepping back. "Tark, it is a wonder you can remember to get up in the morning. Who was it that gave you the wall hangings?"

Tark's eyes lit up. "Oh, that is also easy. His name was Cusaha!" Standing just before the window, Tark folded his arms, pleased with himself.

The Master stood back, loath to interfere with his father's rising rage and with good reason. Without warning, the Emperor lifted the solid oak chair on his side of the desk, over his head. Amid the sound of shattering glass and timber, both the chair and Tark ended sprawled out over the stone cobbles outside.

"Master, fetch those wall hangings, would you. The capsules in which they travelled will be in the desk. They belong to the Palace."

The Master watched as the Emperor gathered some chains off the office wall and threw them outside, smashing more windows. As the Master followed the instructions, the Emperor barked his orders to the legion. "I want all the chains hanging in the office brought out here. Seal all the doors and windows. No one is to enter or leave, death to any who try! Then set it alight. GO!"

***

Kito rose with the three other men. He put a small log on the fire to heat some tea. As the fire rekindled, he walked upstream, finding a place to undress and wash. He dived into the cool water, twisted and turned before surfacing. He swam against the gentle current for some time then returned to the shallows where he could stand waist deep to wash his face and rub down his body. Invigorated, he wiped off the excess water and dressed. The sun was up; he realised they had all overslept.

"It's the willow tree, you know."

Kito turned to see Yaan coming his way. "The willow tree is responsible for what, my friend?"

"Well, sleeping in late, Kito. We did it in the caves, too. The darkness seems to fool the senses."

"Can you always see what people are thinking, Yaan?"

"No, not at all, though this was an obvious one," chuckled Yaan.

"I was not wearing my poker face." He slapped Yaan on the back. "I was heading back for some hot tea. Join me?"

"Yes, but if you want to stay and talk, I'd like to follow your lead and wash first."

Kito sat down on the grassy bank, crossing his legs. Yaan waded out into the water before diving under. He cried out as he surfaced. "Oh, that is fresh." Before Kito could answer, he dived again and came up scratching his scalp and running his fingers through his long hair. He repeated the same process as Kito had, waist deep in water. Kito sat with his eyes shut, the sun now shining on him.

"Kito?"

He opened his eyes. "Yes, Yaan."

"What's a poker face?

"It's when a person does not give away his thoughts with facial expression."

"Does it not strike you as a strange term? I mean, we know what a fire poker is, but a poker face?"

"Yes, I, too, ponder such things. I guess some of it is like saying why is the sky blue and why is it blue in more than one language? How does that work?"

Yaan stared blankly at Kito. "You know more than one language?"

Kito stood as Yaan dressed. "Apparently, yes."

They pulled aside the weeping branches of the willow tree. Immediately, sharpened sticks were pushed towards their faces.

Yaan took the cooked meat from the end of Hao's stick though Bolli did not miss the instant change in Kito's face as he pushed aside the stick. However, at Yaan's laugh, Kito accepted his own piece of cooked meat. They talked, ate and drank their tea before preparing to leave.

Kito departed first with his customary, easy run. After the three men had doused the fire and loaded their horses, they too made their way back onto the track. At first, they just walked their horses, until Yaan suggested, "Come on, let's see how long it takes to catch Kito."

Hao was about to set off when Bolli answered. "Let's see who can run the boy down first," as he set off in a gallop.

The three made good time, largely because Bolli seemed to be in such a rush. It was not until they came to the crest of a hill that they saw Kito waiting. The three came to a stop beside him.

Kito looked up at them. "It has been my pleasure to have known the three of you. Now it is my own journey I must follow. It does not lead via the city of Samos."

Hao and Yaan dismounted to make their appropriate goodbyes.

"Is there no chance that you will accompany us into the city?"

"The city holds nothing for me, but what comes on its tide, Hao. As soon as the right one comes, I shall leave this land for my own. I hope you can understand this."

Looking somewhat disappointed, Yaan spoke quietly. "So where are you going first from here? I see no track for you."

"There is no track, but from here I know where I am and will find the man I owe so much to, my second father. You could come with me if you wish. I could go another way to accommodate your horse." Kito was hopeful of getting Yaan to Hasuca.

Bolli's horse nudged past Hao's. "I do not wish to break up your little party, boys, but there is smoke billowing from the city. Black smoke."

Thick, heavy smoke billowed from the city below them. Hao was first into his saddle. Yaan quickly embraced Kito, then abruptly released and mounted his horse.

"I hope you find what you are looking for, and that it is as you wish it to be. I will miss our conversations and your company. May our Gods watch over you."

Before Kito could answer, Yaan prompted his horse, galloping off in pursuit of his companions, leaving Kito alone in the summer dust wafting about his feet.

The three horsemen rode hard, heading for the source of the smoke, which was visible far and wide. For all the commotion going on, everyone was running away from the fire, not in to help.

They came to a roadblock manned by the Imperial Guard. Hao and Bolli were wearing their uniforms, but to say they were in poor condition was an understatement. Also, and more to the point, they had not been given a discharge from their unit, though that was a long time ago and many districts away.

Bolli and Hao rode up to the blockade, where a guard armed with a long mace stepped out. "Stop! No one is to enter or leave."

Hao sat forward, indicating Yaan. "This man has important information for the Emperor, and we have ridden all night to get it to him."

The guard checked the horses. They were sweating heavily but he held his mace firm.

Yaan spoke from behind. "I have been on this horse for too long." He thumbed back at some cottages. "Is there somewhere back here I can get a hot meal and a bed? If you are happy to take responsibility for the message not getting through, then that is fine with me."

With a nod of approval from the captain, the guard moved his mace, and the three men galloped over the bridge and down the street.

Bolli raced over the cobblestones like a man possessed, Hao and Yaan straining to keep up. Eventually, they came out onto a courtyard where throngs of people were yelling abuse at the Imperial Guard who surrounded the burning building.

Bolli and Hao wasted no time in pushing through the crowd into a standoff area between the people and the Imperial Guard.

Wearing uniforms and being on the wrong side, they didn't dismount.

Bolli saw a large, dark woman staring at him. "What is happening?"

The woman shook her head. "You don't know? The slave workers are still inside!"

Bolli looked at the burning factory building and back to the dark woman. Despair etched into her face as he warned, "Nothing of any good will come of this. Leave! Get away from this place!"

All the factory doors were boarded up. The building was burning from the outside in. Bolli looked at Hao and Yaan, acknowledging their anger, despair and disgust.

They had two obvious advantages, the element of surprise and all the guards were on foot. Hao had heard a little of what the dark woman had been yelling. He couldn't watch a burning building collapse, knowing it to be full of workers. He turned about to consult Yaan, when Bolli leaped into action.

Without fear or delay, Bolli let out a cry, a cry Hao had heard a number of times on the Wall. Bolli knew only one way. War! As his horse dropped its rump and reared forward, the decision had been made and, without hesitation, Hao followed suit. Bolli galloped straight towards the guards in front of one of the wide side doors. They cried out as the horse ploughed into them. Bolli's sword flashed and blood quickly stained the cobbles and walls of the burning factory.

Hao took on the second wave, charging through the guards and sending more of them to the cobbles as they tried to pull the rider from his seat. Yaan positioned himself at the corner of the factory, attempting to prevent more guards from joining the fight. He was just one man on a horse, wielding a long knife. Bolli and Hao tried clearing the guards from the doors, their horses slipping on the blood-soaked cobbles.

Bolli called out. "The doors, Hao! Get the doors!"

He drove back the last of the guards as Hao leapt from his horse and ran through the smoke to the doors. He attempted to lift the locking beam but the guards had nailed it. He fell back, choking on the smoke. He saw a new wave of guards coming from around the rear of the factory, swarming around Bolli's horse. Through the heat and smoke, Bolli laughed as he fought the fight of a warrior, but there was too much blood on the cobbles, his mount faltered and went down. He sprang from the horse as it did, rolling once and surging forward, wielding his sword as Hao rushed to his side.

Shoulder to shoulder, the two men fought against impossible odds. Slowly but surely, they were beaten back, with the fire growing stronger and hotter behind them. Their eyes burned and it took all they had to tackle the next sword thrust towards them. The next slash, the next jab.

Suddenly, and without apparent reason, the tables turned, and the guards that fought them fell away.

There before Bolli and Hao, stood Kito, covered from head to foot in blood, a guard's sword in each hand. Through the smoke, he strode towards them, stone-faced. He walked past the two men, dropped his swords and, taking up one end of the timber beam, he hunkered down to lift it. Through the haze, Kito's hulking body swelled from the strain. The timbers groaned but did not shift.

Yaan and his horse broke through the guards. "Out of the way Kito! Go!" His horse pranced about, pig-hopping. The horse wheeled about and kicked the doors, the noise reverberating throughout the factory. As Yaan and his horse repeated the process, the crowd pushed forward in earnest. Finally, there was a crack and the timbers gave way.

The doors were breached.

While the men held the faltering guards at bay, those inside needed no ushering to come out. Covered in black soot, coughing and choking, they came in their droves. Kito threw the guards' disused swords at the peasants' feet; the angry peasants now outnumbered the Guard.

It was a standoff.

The little tracker man ran steadily down a narrow alley with the two horsemen following. The Master complained to the Emperor. "This is not the way to the shipping yard. Where are we going now?"

The veins in the Emperor's temple visible, he grunted, "We are going to find the dark woman, Trina!"

"If I may, Father, what was it that finished it for you back there? I listened to you and the way you extracted information, but at the end?"

The Emperor gritted his teeth. "Cusaha is not even a name. It is the man that everyone told me was dead! It is that man mocking me, but I always knew. I knew he was alive!" He clenched his fist with his raging temper.

"I do not follow, Father."

"The name is forbidden in the Palace. Just this once, I will forgive your oversight. Rearrange the letters. Cusaha, C-U-S-A-H-A, is Hasuca!"

The young Master's eyes widened. "Are you telling me, your brother Hasuca came close to the Palace and intercepted the bastard boy Chan Kito?"

The Emperor closed his eyes with the pain of it. "It would appear so, yes. Do not forget your title. You asked for it, so now use it with appropriate decorum."

"So how did Hasuca know about the boy? And what was Kito to him, Emperor?"

"I have wondered the very same. I expect this dark woman may be able to tell us."

The prince's eyes lit up. "Oh yes indeed. I feel this will be fun, Emperor."

***

They turned many corners before the tracker stopped and motioned to a small door.

The Emperor smiled as he slid from his horse. He entered a small, dark room. Removing his riding gloves, he smelt the air. "Ah yes, the smell of freshly baked bread. Nothing quite like it, I think."

A small, old man emerged from behind a counter and bowed.

"Well, yes, fine. You are decidedly happy to have our company in your humble shop, and so you should be. You can stand now."

With a voice old and trembling, the man asked, "Sire, how can I serve you and the Prince, Your Excellency?"

The old man moved to the side of his counter as the Emperor helped himself to the warm bread. The Master strode past the Emperor and drove his fist into the old man's stomach. With a groan, the little man exhaled and fell to the floor holding his abdomen, terror and confusion showing in his weathered face.

The Emperor continued to eat the loaf he had broken open. "You know," he said to no one in particular, "this is really quite good."

The Master leaned over and grabbed a handful of hair, twisting the old man's head so they were face to face. "I am The Master! Got it?" The Emperor stood over the old man as the Master threw the old man onto the stone floor.

"Now that we have corrected our titles, I have a few questions for you. As civilised gentlemen of the new world, we can converse, yes?"

The old man pulled himself up against the counter, nodding weakly.

"Good then. As I'm a busy man, I will keep it simple for you. You understand, don't you?" He looked at the old man, struggling to breathe. "Good right fist there, Master."

The Master rubbed his leather-bound knuckles. "Plenty more where that came from, Emperor."

The Emperor knelt beside the old man. "You have a dark woman working for you. Where is Trina now?"

The old man stared into the Emperor's dark eyes. "No, sire, I work the business myself."

Trina pondered over what the man wearing the strange hat had said. 'Nothing good will come of this.' She knew he was right. She remembered Hasuca talking about the city 'Smoking with fire.' She needed to get back to the bakery and carry out Hasuca's instructions quickly.

Pressing back against the crowd was not easy, but Trina, a foreigner in this country, had a small advantage – height. It was her height that had enabled her to look back when she heard the horsemen call out, the sound of hooves on cobbles, the crying out of the Guard. She was confused. The crowds hadn't been able to do anything until those three men on horses had come. Oddly, two were in uniform and had attacked a legion wearing the same uniform. The Imperial uniform. 'A strange day, a day of change,' as Hasuca had foretold.

Tears welled up as she remembered her best friend. He had been adamant. 'After today, you must never return.' She had promised. Hasuca knew best, and as he had said, nations were at risk.

She was well clear of the courtyard now, never looking back. As she trotted through streets and alleys, the urgency to move faster grew. She was making good time until she came out to a bridge crossing. There the Imperial Guards blocked all movement across. Boldly, she walked up to the guardsman. "Good morning to you."

The guard studied her, scorn in his face. "Nobody passes, least of all you."

Undaunted, she replied, "I only want to return to my place of work. Do you wish to stop me from my work?"

"And where might you be working then, woman?"

Trina pointed down the street behind the man. "At the Rising Bread bakery. If I were to be allowed to pass, I could bring back a hot loaf for you all to share."

The man holding the mace checked his captain, who shook his head. Trina considered making a run for it. She could run down the silly man with the mace, and one blow to the face would dispatch the captain. The other two had their back to her, but she did not fancy the distance with no cover. The men had crossbows. Although they were not cocked, she wasn't too fast these days. She backed away and went down a side alley.

She didn't like the city. She had made the best of a bad situation, and working in the bakery had made her many friends in this area. She made several turns before emerging beside a stream. There was no bridge, but enough turns so that the Guard upstream couldn't see her. Trina knocked on a door.

An older man answered. "Trina! What a wonderful surprise. We have just boiled some tea. Please, come inside."

"Wengan, I need to return to my workplace immediately. Please, could you boat me across?" She was dishevelled and flustered.

"What is wrong, my dear? What has happened?"

Her eyes misting, Trina pointed to the sky behind his small cottage. "I don't know, but the Imperial Guard has stopped all access to the city. They have blocked all the bridges and set the silk factory alight."

In disbelief Wengan's eyes widened as he marched out and turned in beside her. Heavy, black smoke billowed skywards. He made two fists as if preparing to fight. "What in the name of the Gods?"

Trina held Wengan by the shoulder. "Could you cross me over the stream?"

Wengan leaned in through the doorway. "Etti, I am going to run Trina over the stream, all right?"

"My dear, of course, but I have some tea on, bring her in."

Wengan had already begun to walk away, but went back to the door, calling, "Yes, I have already offered her some hot tea, but she is in a hurry." He turned to leave, seeing the look of anticipation on Trina's face, but Etti called back. "Why is she in such a hurry?"

"The City is under siege, come and see!"

Quickly, Etti was at the door, wiping her hands on her apron. "What is this nonsense you speak of?"

Trina and Wengan were pushing a small fishing vessel into the stream. Wengan barely stopped to point to the black smoke mushrooming over the city. Etti covered her mouth as she gasped. "Who is responsible for this?"

Wengan grabbed the oars as Trina answered. "I believe it is our own Emperor."

Etti spun back to her husband. "What nonsense. Why would our Emperor burn his own city? We all know this is his city." She frowned. "Why can't you use the bridges like we do every day?"

Wengan leaned a little to the side of Trina so he could explain without yelling. "Because the Imperial Guard has blocked them all."

Etti wrung her hands. "Gods, what is going on?"

Once crossed, Trina hugged her old companion farewell. He promised to stay near the front door so if she, or anyone else, needed to cross the stream, they just had to wave. Telling him to be careful, Trina walked up the embankment and into another alley. After several turns, she finally arrived in the narrow alleyway to the bread shop.

The alley was long and curved, and as she slowed and stopped to wipe the sweat from her brow, she hesitated. Smelling the air, it had a heavy pungent odour she didn't recognise. Then she heard men's voices and froze.

There was a clatter of horse hooves on the cobbles. If they came her way, there wouldn't be enough room. She turned to a wooden door beside her, it opened outwards. She pushed it, and it bounced open only a little. She shoved it a little harder, but it didn't open much further. She couldn't get her fingers in enough to open it. The horses were coming closer. As she looked down the alley, a small man walked into view, a fit man, maybe a messenger for the Guard. He subtly motioned for her to get out of the way, shaking his head slightly. Trina looked on, questioning, as the sound of clattering hooves drew closer. He seemed to be leading them. She bashed at the door with all her might. It opened enough for her to manage to pull it open. As she did so, she heard a call from one of the horsemen.

"Hurry up, tongueless fool! I have waited too many years for this day to be waiting for you, here and now!"

Trina pulled the door closed behind her as the messenger man ran by. He seemed to mouth a word of apology as he went. She held the door closed. After the horses had passed, she eased the door open and walked slowly around the corner to the bakery. The smell became stronger as the knot in her belly grew tighter. She pushed open the door into the bakery. The smell was nauseating, and the sight before her made her rush back outside.

She vomited.

Trina wiped her mouth and went back in. It was worse than she had first seen. Strapped to the front counter was Arif, covered in blisters, some still bubbling. The men had taken every baking skewer in the shop, heated them to red hot and touched them on him in varying places, then pushed them into his arms and legs.

She held his head with her hands. "Arif, oh the Gods, Arif. Who did this to you?" Arif rolled his eyes and grunted something. Trina let go and scurried into the kitchen, where she found a knife and a bowl of water.

Cutting him free, she gently laid the old man down on the floor. She damped off his forehead, pulled his arms to his side and began removing the skewers. It would not save Arif, but she could not allow him to be left like this. The skewers were still hot to the touch. Gently, she washed his face.

"Oh, Trina, what have I done?" he groaned.

Trina held a finger to his mouth. "Shh, save your energy, my friend."

He shook his head ever so slightly. "No, I have no regrets." He gave a feeble smile. "Oh, how I wanted to tell you of my love for you, but alas, I knew it was not the way you looked at me."

Trina had known the way the gentle man had noticed her, but she had never been able to forget that she was a Queen to her King. She softly stroked Arif's cheek. "In another life, I would have chased you, and you would not have stood a chance."

Arif's eyes closed, and his body shook. She knew that, in there somewhere, Arif was laughing. Then, he grabbed her hand. "I am sorry for Hasuca. I have failed you both today."

Trina stopped wiping his face. "What?"

Arif took a laboured breath. "The Emperor and his Prince were here."

"It was they who have just left?"

"Yes. Please understand, I am just a baker. I could take no more of what they had given me. Now they are headed for Hasuca's place. I'm so sorry, Trina. I know how much he means to you."

Trina was confused. *How did Arif even know about Hasuca, let alone where Hasuca resided?* None of that mattered now.

"Do not concern yourself with Hasuca, Arif. For it is I who has brought the Emperor to you today."

With a feeble hand, Arif motioned. "I have saved enough notes to buy your son back from that Tarrant. It is stored upstairs in an old flour sack behind my desk. It will be enough to get you both a pass to your rightful place."

Trina began to shake her head.

"Listen, woman! You are, at this point, still in my ownership and this is my last, dying, command that you will fulfil as your duty to me, your owner, Arif. Understood?"

Trina nodded. She had never heard Arif bark commands at anyone before.

"There is no point in you waiting here, now go."

"No, Arif, I will stay here for your time."

"Trina, it will be chaotic out there. You must do as I have instructed and get to the wharf before everyone else who is escaping this mess does. My dying wish is to hear you getting your belongings and leaving. Then I can rest happy. Now Trina, go!"

He smiled, trying to be brave.

She knew he was right. She put the cloth back into the bucket and stood. "Listen for your name, Arif, for I will say it in the most complimentary manner for the rest of my time. Gods speed, my brave hero."

Resolutely, she headed for the stairs. She made much noise getting her belongings together and collecting Arif's saved notes; she knew him to be listening. When she came back down, she passed back through the front room and went into him. He was smiling.

Trina opened her mouth to say goodbye, then realised he was already gone.

***

The Emperor and the Master pulled up at one of the bridges. The guards stepped aside and bowed. The Emperor addressed the Master. "I will go to the camp and take another legion on horseback. I am heading into the jungle. By sunset, I will have vanquished the throne's only threat."

With a snide look, the Master responded. "I hear he was quite a formidable arts Master, with or without weapons."

"I am the greatest! I could take my own brother in the blink of an eye. Many know this, why else would the spineless fool flee the Palace as he did? Do not forget this, Master!"

The Emperor's horse began stamping and rearing, feeding off the Emperor's anger. He spurred it and headed for Yuson Ridge, dust wafting in his wake.

The guards stood to attention, staring at the Master.

"What! Do you wish to take on this Master?" Eyes averted and the guards shuffled back to their duties.

The smoke was seemingly spreading south. From an alleyway, a guard came running towards the Master. Almost breathless, he gave a quick bow. "Master, there has been a travesty."

"Yes, so out with it!"

"Three men on horses, two of them in uniform, came from nowhere and set free the factory workers, Your Excellency."

The guards on the bridge shuffled nervously at the news. The messenger sank onto one knee.

"To your feet, guard!"

As the guard sprang up, the Master rode over, leaning down with his right hand, the guard swung up behind the Master, who kicked his horse into a gallop.

From the rear, the guard directed the Master back to the salt well. The factory was well ablaze, and the fire had spread. The Master stopped his horse and searched for the three riders who had thwarted the Emperor's plans. He couldn't get close as people were running about with buckets, oblivious to his presence.

Then a pointing arm went up beside him. The guard yelled. "There! The one with the silly hat!"

The Master saw the man with a strange hat turning around in his saddle, waving his sword over his head.

"Hand me your crossbow," sneered Desora.

In seconds the bow came forward, cocked and loaded. The man on the horse was wheeling about. It was going to be a long shot for a crossbow.

50 Demise

The timber exterior of the silk factory was now well ablaze. Under lapping flames, Kito was first to the smashed door. Leaning in, he saw nothing but heavy, red glowing smoke. "Come towards my voice, you are safe to come this way."

The factory workers scrambled to the exit, covered in soot and coughing badly. Kito was shocked at the heat that was expelled through the door with them. It was incredulous that anyone in there was still able to breathe, let alone get up and walk. He searched for those he knew, but with their soot-covered faces, it was hard to make out even males from females.

He grabbed the last one by the arm. "Are there any left in there?"

"Only those who have already perished. There is no point in risking life for them. I am the last."

Several large pieces of burning roof slid down and smashed on the cobbles. Someone shouted. "Get back! It's getting in the roof! The fire is getting in the roof!" It was Bolli outside the entrance, struggling to contain his horse in the mayhem and waving his sword over his head. "Get back! Everyone, move back, it's not safe! Move back!"

Whilst Bolli wheeled his horse, trying to create more space from the crowd, the three other men helped the choking people to move away. "Careful, we will not leave anyone."

Yaan, with a soot-covered peasant under each arm, was almost knocked from his feet. He looked down to see Bolli had fallen from his horse. He lay on his back, spitting blood onto his chest. Yaan handed the coughing peasants to bystanders, yelling at Hao, who quickly arrived together with Kito. Protruding from Bolli's chest was an arrow point. Only the Palace had such arrowheads.

Hao stood, pulling his bow from his shoulder, looking about for the assailant. Seeing nothing but terrified peasants, he mounted Bolli's horse, searching further for his would-be target. On the far side of the courtyard were two men on a single horse. The man to the fore was in black clothes, behind him was a guard pointing. The front man lifted a crossbow.

Hao froze. For a fraction of time, he saw the bolt released, speeding directly at him. He didn't hear the roar of the fire, the screaming of the crowd. The horse beneath him was no longer stamping its hooves and turning about. All movement had stopped. All but the deadly projectile, coming towards him, ever so slowly. Hao clearly saw its deadly head as it neared then, from nowhere, a slate, cast high in the air, collided with it. The sparks flared with the impact and the bolt was projected away.

Hao looked for the source of origin of the slate. He saw Kito, pointing towards the two horsemen and yelling at him, "Shoot! Shoot back!"

Hao saw the figure in black lowering his crossbow. He rose in his saddle, took aim and released. His longer arrow carried more power and traced true. The rider swayed to the side, letting the arrow strike the guard behind him. The rider turned and looked at the arrow protruding from the man's chest and pushed the guard away. Turning his horse, he broke into a gallop, disappearing up a nearby alley.

Hao urgently slid from his horse. "Bolli! Can you hear me, man?"

It took Bolli a while to focus. "Hao? Hey, you remember that night?"

Hao looked up to Yaan, who was as perplexed as he was. "What night, my friend?"

"That night on Magnar Wall. I know what you did, man. You made the perfect plan. Only you could have pulled it off."

Hao shook his head. "You would have done the same thing."

Bolli laughed. More blood ran down his chin. "I don't know, Hao. I hate those Barbarians. They are not right, you know, just not right."

"Come on, my friend. We will get you out of here and sorted." He went to slide his arm under Bolli who screamed through gritted teeth.

"I can't feel … Hao, I can't feel my legs. Please, my friend, just cut me. Just shove me in through that door and cut me. Do not leave me here, Hao. Don't leave me on the street." Slowly, he flicked his hand towards the burning factory, staring Hao in the eyes. "When you get out of this mess, I want you to go with Yaan. Go back to Tarim Caves, back to Tammirie. I so wanted her, but she wouldn't do it. We shared the furs in the cold, but she would not … you know? She just would not."

With an unsteady hand, he picked up his hat and slapped it on Hao's head. "Take it, Hao. Wear my hat. It will be worth it." He laughed, blood dribbling from his mouth. He grabbed onto Hao's shirt and held up his knife. "Take my knife, Hao. Kiss my knife."

Hao kissed it and took it. He stood up and grabbed Bolli by his shirt collar. Bolli looked back at everyone, laughing through bloodied teeth. With a heave, Hao resolutely dragged him through the smoke and fire into the burning factory.

For some time, Yaan and Kito stood numb to the tragic event. At last, Hao emerged from the burning building, wearing Bolli's smouldering hat, despair on his face.

Kito, soaked in blood, stood stone-faced and unfocused.

Yaan nudged him. "Hey, Kito, what is it, my friend?"

"I must go. Something is wrong with Father. I have to go. Now!"

"You have come out of your way to see us right. We now have a spare horse. It is your call, Kito, but we would be proud to be in your company."

Kito stared at Yaan. "This is something *you* must do. Come on." He mounted Bolli's horse, and the three made haste from the city.

A man was sitting at his table. Only of middle age, yet time had aged him beyond his years, his hair was long and greying, as was his moustache and beard. A rap at the door brought him smoothly to his feet. He had been waiting for this day. He took a breath to calm himself, then opened the door. Two spears were thrust at him. He grabbed them in his left hand, pulled the would-be attackers off balance and smashed their heads into the door with his right hand. Both men instantly collapsed, and lay still. Thrusting the butts of the two spears into the belly of a third attacker, the man bellowed as he fell onto the upcoming foot. He, too, would see no more of this battle.

The man swerved and parried his attackers, kicking and knocking them to the ground without spilling a drop of blood.

On the edge of the jungle was a group of men on horseback. Unbelieving, they watched this battle unfolding. The one in the centre was dressed in black suede. It was the Emperor, Hannu Koe. Beside him, a young Commander grew restless.

"Emperor?"

The Emperor held his hand up. More of the Emperor's Guard fell. The Commander's horse now grew skittish. One after the other, the Emperor's Guard fell. The smooth, rhythmic moves of the man showed speed and grace.

"Emperor now!?"

Still the Emperor was unmoving. The Commander could see the Guard falling, while the man was untouched. Soon, there were only a few guards left. The Commander could wait no more. Standing in his saddle, he drew his horse whip back and drove it with all his might.

The man dispatched another two guards. Hearing the whip, he sidestepped, letting it wrap around his spear then yanked it from the hand of the Commander. The brass butt hit one of the Imperial Guard in the back of his head. He dropped like a stone as the horse whip coiled across his back. Everyone stopped, staring at it. Only one person had such a whip – Commander Chenghou.

The man turned to the Emperor. "Have you no more?"

The Emperor rolled his eyes. The aging man bent over steadily and picked up the whip. After defeating all the attackers, his breath was still steady. Taking the whip, he walked to the young Commander sitting boldly on his meticulously groomed horse.

"I believe this is yours, Chenghou."

"How dare you call me by my name! Have you no teachings, pilgrim?"

The man stopped just short of handing the whip back. "But of course. I had the very same teachings as your Emperor, and you may call me Hannu Hasuca. Congratulations on making Commander, Chenghou. Your father would be pleased. I knew him well."

Hasuca gave a curt bow, handed the whip to the confused Commander and turned to the Emperor, smiling. "Hannu Koe. Greetings, my brother."

The seething Emperor leant forward in his saddle. "Well, aren't you full of surprises." He gazed at the cabin. To him, it appeared a ruin, being held up by the cliff. "I must say, Hasuca, I really expected better of you."

Hasuca looked to his cabin. The remaining guards had regrouped and were approaching slowly with spears thrust out in front. They all stepped back a pace and shuffled nervously when Hasuca turned. He smiled at his brother. "I have plenty to eat. I stay dry in the wet, warm in the winter. What more does one need?"

***

The remainder of the sooted peasants stood watching the factory burn, at a loss about what to do or where to go. The day had started like any other morning, working under lanterns. Then there had been yelling from Tark's office, smashing glass, followed by the building being set alight. Tark had not been seen. Gossip had started between the factory workers. Janing, Len and Ringcha all agreed that the big man covered in blood was the boy, Kito.

Janing broke away from the rest. "Kito?" Her voice was weak and there was plenty of other noise; she kept walking, certain it was him. "Kito!" She tried to make her way over to the big man. "Kito!"

The man with the silly hat heard her this time. Out of breath, she fell to one knee, reaching out for Kito with one arm as Hao leant over. "I will tell him of your gratitude, I promise."

Before Janing could explain, Kito had galloped away, Hao quickly following in pursuit. Janing looked back at Ringcha, who shrugged her shoulders.

Inside the factory, lay several bodies of the elders. With them lay the body of a great warrior. Bolli. Leader and saviour of their friends. With red-hot embers raining down, together, they began to cremate.

The heated silks and timber frames now glowed with heat. When the fire finally penetrated the roof, everything exploded with a fury. The explosion blew the doors off their hinges, the fire drawing oxygen without mercy, turning the entire space into a fireball. Burning shingles exploded high into the sky, descending over the greater city. The courtyard emptied quickly as peasants fled for their lives. Some ran to check that their own cottages were not ablaze. Countless glowing red silk fibres were thrust high into the air. Carried on the southerly breeze, they rained down onto cottages, shops and, the Riverside Happy House.

***

At the back of this establishment, in an alley, was a large man — the owner and operator. "Well, well, well, look who is in town. If it isn't the elusive Lucia."

The woman backed up to a wall, fear and hatred on her face. "I am not that little girl anymore. Come any closer and I swear I will gut you like the pig you are."

The man stepped forward. "Is that any way to greet me after all these years? You know your mamma and pappy would be very happy to see you back where you belong."

She spat at his feet. "Never! I will never set foot on that island ever again."

The big man waved a finger at her. "Now, did your mamma not teach you that you should never say never?" He stepped forward once more. Lucia spat on his leading foot. The smile faded off his face.

The thick pall of smoke overhead had blotted out most of the sun in the alley, though she saw the glint of the knife he had drawn. The building behind her jutted out, like always. Uncle Devrez had her in a corner, but this time she was not a little girl. One way or another, it was here that things were going to be different.

She spat on his other foot and looked him in the eye. "Neither man nor beast gets away with anything in the eyes of the Gods. Somehow, somewhere, we all pay our debts of right and wrong. It is the justice of the Gods."

Devrez threw his head back and roared with laughter. "Oh my, you are still the innocent one, aren't you? You went to your mamma, and what happened, hmm? She did not want to believe you, silly girl. You should have gone to your father. He would surely have gutted me, or had someone else do it; heaven forbid if he got his hands dirty." He wiggled his fingers sarcastically, and Lucia could see the knife loosely tucked under his thumb. "But no, you went to mamma, and she told you not to cause trouble. It took me some time to talk her around, but what a treat."

Lucia shook with hatred; her mother's voice again echoed through her head. The voice that had been silent for so long was once more unleashed. It was an involuntary reaction; she spat on Uncle Devrez's shirt. Again, his smile slid as he looked down. Slowly, he scraped up her spit with his knife and turned it in a stabbing fashion. "So be it, bitch, you are a bit old for me now anyway."

He lunged forward, wielding his knife. Lucia dived down and rolled into his feet. He tripped over her and fell hard. She sprang up, ready to give him a kick as he tried to get up, but it was all he could do to roll onto his back.

"Look what you have done now, you silly bitch! You stupid bitch!"

Lucia came in close enough to see the handle of the knife protruding from his chest. "It was not me, you fat pig. I told you, it is the Gods' justice."

Devrez reached down for the knife but couldn't bring himself to touch it. "Please, my beautiful little girl, help poor old Uncle Devrez."

For the first time, her uncle was helpless. She looked to the Riverside Happy House. There, the sparsely dressed women were running around with buckets. Clearly, it was hopeless. They didn't even know she and Uncle Devrez were in the darkened alley.

His voice was soft, alluring. "There's a good girl, Lucia, good old Uncle Devrez needs your help."

She peered down at Devrez and his painful wound then stepped forward and leant down. "Uncle. Uncle Devrez."

"Yes, my little angel?"

Lucia held her hair to one side as he gazed up at her. "The fire is coming now, uncle …" She spat in his face. "… and *that* should help keep good old Uncle Devrez from burning. Gods speed."

Lucia straightened up and ran for her life, not in fear of Uncle Devrez, but for concern for the workshop. She had not realised how much the fire had taken hold. Cottages and buildings all around her were well ablaze. Holding her shirt over her nose, she ran on. She tried checking for any smoke in the direction of the workshop, but it was useless. The smoke was too thick.

Out of breath, she turned the corner to the workshop, slowed to a walk, then fell to her knees. The vessel yard, with its entire building, was well ablaze. The heat was too much. She could go no closer than she already was. If there was anyone in there, they had surely perished.

Then out of the smoke came a familiar figure. It was Admasin. Lucia leapt up and ran to his aid; he was clearly struggling. Neither spoke. With Admasin's arm over her shoulder, she walked him well clear and directed him down onto the riverbank where she sat him down to catch his breath. She ripped the bottom off her shirt and dunked it in the river. Returning to his side, she began to dampen his forehead.

"Admasin, why did you stay so long? You were lucky to make it out at all!" She dropped to her knees, her eyes begging. "Please, tell me Patch is not …"

"That damn vessel … he was hell bent I tell you."

She put her hand over her mouth as the tears began to stream down her cheeks.

"I tried, Alexa. I tried to tell him we could build another, but the fire got into his office, and once he saw his plans were gone, that was it. He was bent on saving that damn vessel."

It was all she could do to put a hand onto Admasin's chest as she cried silently into her other. There was a loud splash, and the river hissed angrily. They both looked to see the Vessel of Sails, well ablaze to the waterline, now without its mast, floating by.

Shaking her fists in anger, Alexa screamed. "Nooo!"

Admasin, with tears streaming down his sooted face, pulled her in close. The burning vessel slowly passing by symbolised so much. The yard he'd worked in all his life, firstly with Bua, then Patch and Alexa. Then this cutting-edge vessel of sails, now burning to its waterline as it floated by.

It was gone. It was all gone, and with it, Patch.

***

Trina stayed off the main roads now that the Emperor knew of her. With the smoke hanging heavy over the city, the alleys were dark, leaving her pleased to arrive at the wharf. Through the haze, she could see Imperial Guards everywhere.

A woman whispered behind her. "I dropped in to see you were all right, and well, poor old Arif."

"Etti, what are you doing down here?"

Etti shrugged as she peered about the wharf. "Well, I thought about what I might do if I had nowhere to work or stay, had the

Guard looking for me and standing out different from the rest of the people. Wengan is minding the river. He has had a few visitors, let me tell you. So, I thought I might take a stroll down here, to walk my dear old mother over to the vessels."

Trina wondered if Etti still had a mother, then she noticed the clothes and the stick that Etti was carrying for her disguise.

A captain walked along the wharf. Cung Seo was proud of his newly acquired rank, even his father had complimented him on his promotion. He saw two women standing on the edge of the wharf, one clearly middle-aged, the other heavy set, bent over with a walking stick and a shawl covering her head and shoulders.

Captain Seo strode to them. "What is your purpose here, women?"

The younger of the two, spoke. "I am trying to get my dear mother onto that vessel over there."

The captain was objecting before Etti could finish. "No, my instructions are clear. No vessel to dock, no vessel to leave port."

Etti dipped her head. "Yes, we understand and would never seek to disobey the commands of our esteemed Emperor. My mother has bad lungs, and this smoke is dangerous for her. So, may I ask, if I paid you to send us over in a clinker to that vessel docked on the other side of the river. Of course, the clinker and I would return immediately, would that be breaking the commands of our Emperor?"

The captain quickly checked around. "Pay me?" he inquired.

The old woman under the shawl began coughing with a rasp so loud the captain squirmed, taking a small step back. As she finished coughing, a note popped out from under the shawl.

The captain checked the clinker, then snatched up the note and quickly stuffed it into his top pocket. He turned to a nearby guard, waving him over through the thickening smoke. "Guard, you will row these two women over to that vessel."

The guard saw the vessel. "But, sir, I thought that …"

The captain slapped him. "Are you refusing to obey an order, young man?"

The guard staggered back. "No, sir, never, sir. Two women to that vessel. Yes, sir!"

The woman under the shawl shook and once again began hacking. The captain stared at the crippled old woman and growled. "Guard."

"Yes, sir?"

"You had better be snappy about it."

"Yes, sir."

In no time at all, Etti had delivered her mother to the vessel. Then, as quickly as she could, she returned on the clinker back on the wharf. She bowed and thanked the captain once more before scurrying down the alley from where she'd come.

The captain was pleased with himself, the note would go a long way to supporting his family. He continued to see over his men guarding the wharf when a strange vessel came floating down on the current. It was burning to the water level. A messenger came up to him and bowed.

"Yes? What do you want?" the captain snapped.

The boy handed Captain Seo a message. As he did so, he noticed what the captain had been watching. It was an odd sight, the strangest-shaped vessel he had ever seen, burning fiercely, drifting along on the current, getting quite close to their jetty.

The captain read the note:

'Captain Cung Seo: There is to be no person or persons leaving or arriving from the port of Samos. Furthermore, you and your Guard are to be on the lookout for a black woman of heavy build. She is to be taken, dead or alive and kept for either of the Royals to inspect. Signed: Your Emperor and God-King, Hannu Koe.'

Captain Seo looked over to the vessel across the river. *Could she have been dark?* The vessel was now invisible for the burning vessel passing by. Almost knocking the messenger into the water, he stormed back along the wharf. "Guard! Man that clinker again!"

Janing's mother, Ringcha, nudged her and beckoned her to follow. "Come, we have found him. We have found Chain Man," she explained. She took Janing by the hand and led her to the salt well. There, hanging over the well, was Tark, bound with his own chains, cocooned like a spider's victim. It wound around the hardwood roller several times then a long length led all the way inside the burning factory. The chain was beginning to glow; dirt and dust on it crackled and popped as it fell away.

Every survivor of the factory was watching Tark. For a moment, Janing too, was captivated, then calmly, she walked over to Tark. "Good morning to you, Tark sir."

Tark raised his head. "Ha, it's about time one of you came to do the right thing. Now unbind me this instant, Janing!"

She sat down before him, crossed her legs and pulled her sooted hair away from her blackened face. "Who did this to you, Tark? Who was it that yelled at you this morning?"

Tark grimaced. "No one! No one would dare come into my factory and yell at Tark Fly. I come from a long line of Flys, and no one would dare to interfere with us here."

Janing merely let him see her gaze at his burning factory. "So, Tark, what really happened to your father?"

Tark scrunched his face. "How dare you bring that up now, I will whip you raw for that!"

"Where is the silk garment that you had Ringcha make?"

Tark's face went blank for a moment. "You mean, the garment I had made for Alexa?"

"Yes, Tark, that would be it. Only Alexa and Patch gave it to Chun. The chubby little Asset is now wearing that garment, with your father's belts."

Tark was still blank-faced.

"Yes, Tark, I think you have it now. Patch and Chun have quite the business deal going. That would be why Patch gifted Chun with the garment. You didn't notice the dimensions, Tark?" Janing paused as Tark took it all in. "What did happen to your father? He was summoned to the palace, is that right?"

Tark barely nodded.

"But he never arrived."

Tark shook his head.

"I heard, only gossip really, but I heard that two trees had been cut down and made to fall right across the road, both on blind corners. Two trees, different corners. He never stood a chance, did he? That would be up in the mountains, Tark. Not in Kain's territory, but in Chun's territory, is that right, Tark?" Tark hung from his chain, immobilised. "Tark, did Kito come to see you?"

Tark slowly looked up to Janing. "Who?"

A woman handed Janing a bucket with a ladle. She stood and served Tark first, he slurped greedily as Janing continued. "Kito. You know, the little boy that you took to the Emperor … as a 'Gift of Goodwill,' I think Kain called it. I think you agreed to call him, Chan Kito."

Tark's left eye began to twitch. His voice was small for the size of the man. "Kito? Chan Kito was here? When?"

"So, Kito didn't do this to you, but yes, it was definitely Kito who let us out of your factory. He has just left."

Tark shook his chains, screaming. Some stones shook free, splashing into the water below.

Janing resumed. "Well, let us not waste any more of your time, a man of your stature, Tark sir. We did wonder whether Chan Kito could have trussed you up like this, but there would not have been an argument in your office first. No, this was the work of someone you answer to. Who could that be, Tark? Would it perhaps be the Prince who did this to you?"

Tark's eyes were glazed red, full of anger. "Never! I would never succumb to that little swine. A *prince* indeed. You know that spoilt little swine has the audacity to call himself a *Master!* Hah! Can you believe that? That swine, a Master? He does not know the meaning of it!"

Janing smiled. "Your father was killed by Chun, who now wears your handmade garment, together with your father's belts. Chan

Kito somehow eluded certain death at the Palace, only to return here to free all your workers from their certain death. But what I would like to know is, how did the Emperor know to enter your office this morning, Tark? What was it that brought him to you this morning, when he clearly has no use of you?"

Tark's face went blank, deep in thought.

***

Kito led the way. Bolli's horse was as eager as Kito to leave the burning city. Hao and Yaan followed close behind and before long, they were up in the hills moving along a well-used jungle track.

Kito slowed down. The jungle echoed of stampeding horses. Abruptly, he motioned his horse to the left, up a steep slope and along a cliff top. Below them they could see the Emperor leading a Commander and his legion towards the city.

With increased pace, Kito led the way deeper into the jungle.

They rode well into the night. The full moon shone over them as they cantered along a narrow track. Ahead, the jungle flickered with a fire. Around the bend, they came out onto a clearing. Kito jumped from his horse as Hao and Yaan pulled up behind him.

To their left was a small shack, on fire, the flames reaching well up the cliff face. Despairingly, Kito began pacing about. Then Hao saw what Kito was searching for. In the trees on the far side of the clearing, was the figure of a slender man strung out between two saplings, his head slung low.

Hao drew his sword as he cantered across the clearing. Slashing at the back of the sapling, it bent down under its load. Kito ran to gather up Hasuca as he was lowered to the ground, whilst Hao cut the rope to the other sapling, setting him free.

Gently, they laid him down on the manicured grass.

"Master, can you hear me? It is I, Kito."

Yaan was at his side with water. Kito gently held up Hasuca's head and tipped a little water over his face, trickling a few drops into his mouth. He coughed slightly, then took another drink. Kito trickled more water through his hair. "Can you hear me, my Master?"

Hasuca brought up one hand and placed it on Kito's face. "Oh, it's my favourite young man. Kito, how are you, my friend?"

Kito smiled softly. "It is not how I am, but how you are, Hasuca?" The two chuckled together.

Hasuca patted Kito's hand. "Ah, you have a sense of humour, not so serious now. This is good, this is good. I grew up a prince, became a Master and was just for a time, Emperor. But you, *you* … my friend, are my best and most important achievement."

Forlorn, Kito cradled Hasuca's head. "Shh, hold your energy, Master. We can talk all we wish when you are better."

"Only yesterday a friend of mine said, '*No, my time is here and now,*' and now, it is my time, Kito. You must realise this."

Kito had seen the whipping cuts his old Master had taken, and as he had been strung up naked, he could not miss the fact that his manhood was lost. "Hasuca, why did they cut you? Why?"

Hasuca scoffed, his hand in Kito's. "Ah. As I told my brother, where I'm going I will have no use for it anyway." The aging man laughed quietly. He smiled at Kito's expectant face.

"Many years ago, there was a woman, and what a woman she was. She was the only woman that my brother ever respected. She fell pregnant. It was much talked about. The Emperor had finally got one of his concubines pregnant. But she did not have one child. She gave birth to three. And one boy showed a difference, he had different eyes."

"Eyes like yours, Master?"

Hasuca broke into a coughing fit, at last replying, "Oh yes indeed. I had to leave immediately."

Kito spoke softly. "So where did this boy go then?"

Hasuca looked content as he spoke. "A man called Maki took him. Took him far away from the palace to the sandstone caves. There, I have watched him grow into a fine man." Hasuca grabbed Kito's tunic. "Would you go to Maki and my son. I wish you to tell him about me. You know me as I am. Can you tell him about me?"

Kito shook his head. "No, Master, I will do better than that."

Hasuca looked confused. Kito waved to Yaan to move around to the other side. Yaan came and knelt beside Hasuca, taking up his other hand in his own. They gazed into each other's eyes, and the reflection of their own.

Hasuca was spellbound. "So the Gods *do* keep some things to themselves."

"Hello, Father, it is my privilege to be in your presence."

Hasuca shook Yaan's hand with all his might. "Nonsense, my son, it is all mine."

"Before your time here today, you need to know, we, the family I grew up with and all in the caves, know the sacrifice you have made for the survival of the greater good. We understand."

Hasuca sighed. "Yes, Yaan, but the rest of the people do not. They still think I have forsaken them to the Emperor who burns his own city."

Yaan looked up to Kito; he was as hurt and lost for Hasuca as Kito was.

Hasuca continued. "There is something more important, son. Both of you, listen. There is a girl at the palace … she is different from the others. She is different because her mother was of another land. Her mother's name was Sha'Doe. I am her father. Yaan, your full twin sister's name is Tanica."

Kito looked at Yaan's white face.

Hasuca whispered again. "Kito, I know you wish to go home, but you must not. Not yet."

Kito looked down at the only father figure he knew, shaking his head. "Master?"

"It was not by chance that I found you. I waited for you. Remember when you were on the *Shiraz*, you brought the fish for everyone to eat."

"No, they just happened. The Gods made that happen for the love of their people."

"Like the Gods made the king cobra at Turtle Pool happen, Kito? No. You gave the *Shiraz* fish, you controlled the king cobra, and you saved Mikka without thought for yourself. I saw you do it again at the factory. That is unconditional love for your fellow person. The Gods have given their people a warrior of peace. You are the one, Kito."

"The one *what*, Master?"

Hasuca struggled to draw breath. "The *One*, Kito. You have done things no man should be able to do, yet you can. You are born with ties to many nations. If you can see into the Crystals, you can absorb their knowledge."

"The Crystal Skulls?"

"The Crystal Skulls. There is much unrest … and it is going to get worse, much worse and not just … for this nation, but *you* are key. You are the Chosen One of the Gods … and now, you have brought my son here with you. Kito. Do you really think this is all by chance?"

"But Master, all I have wanted is to go home."

Hasuca's hands had stopped trembling. "You must provide no limit for your abilities, Kito. Instead, you must push them out as far as you can to achieve your destiny. But remember the fish Yaan caught? When he killed it, he nearly killed you. If the one you blend with dies, Kito, you die with it. Remember this."

He took a ragged breath and smiled. "It was not by chance that I found you. It was no choice of my own that I left the Palace. I am merely the groundwork for you to drive to your potential, neither for me nor you, but for the people that wish to live in peace. They are the many."

Then came a whisper. "I love you, son."

And he was gone.

Yaan had only just met the man who was undeniably his father. He knew of the love and respect Kito had spoken of for his

Master. He watched Kito as he lay Hasuca's hand down on his chest, and what he saw unnerved him – hatred, spite and revenge washing back and forth over the huge man as he stood.

Kito took a deep breath and roared but one word to the heavens.

"*FATHER!!!*"

About the Author

Gregory Thomas grew up on a dairy farm in the north of New Zealand, where his early desire to write grew despite the challenges of dyslexia. In the early 2000s, Gregory moved to Australia, and several years ago, he decided to channel his creative imagination into writing, resulting in his first fantasy novel series, *The Sacred Skulls*

Gregory now resides in Perth with his wife. He balances his time between working in the mines of northern Western Australia and writing in his free time, continuously crafting ideas for new worlds and stories for his readers.